SORCERY IN ALPARA

JUDITH STARKSTON

BRONZE AGE BOOKS

Map of Hitolian Empire and Egarya

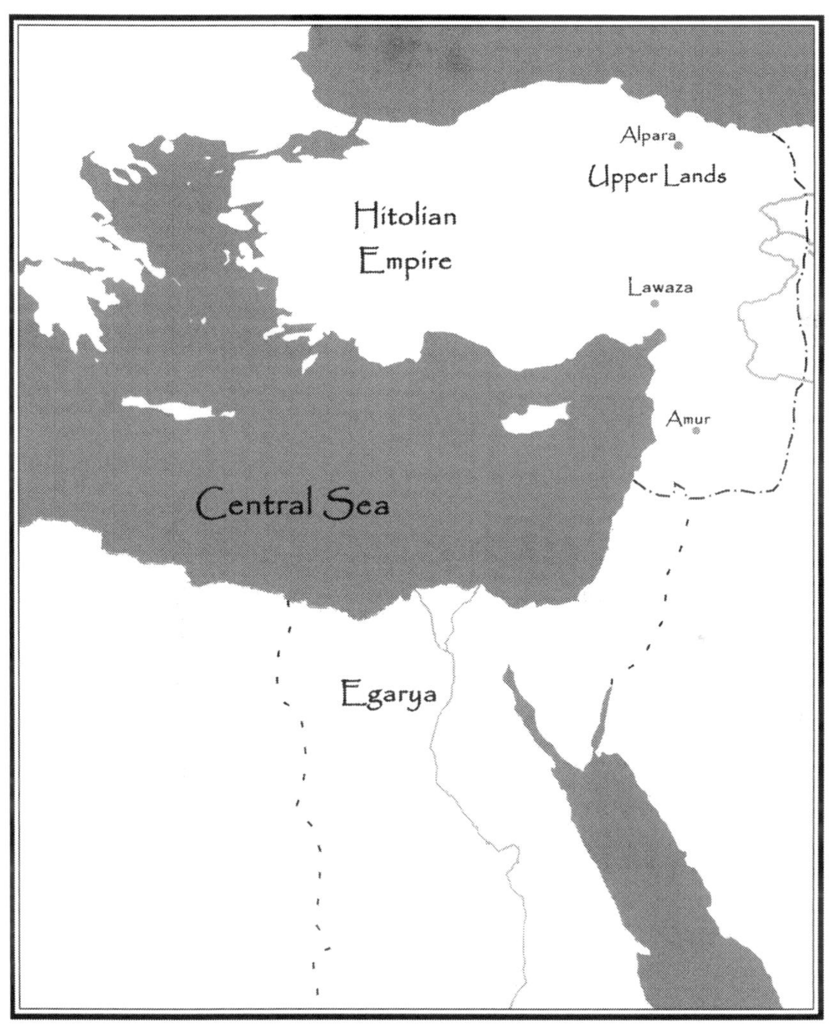

Alpara and the Upper Lands

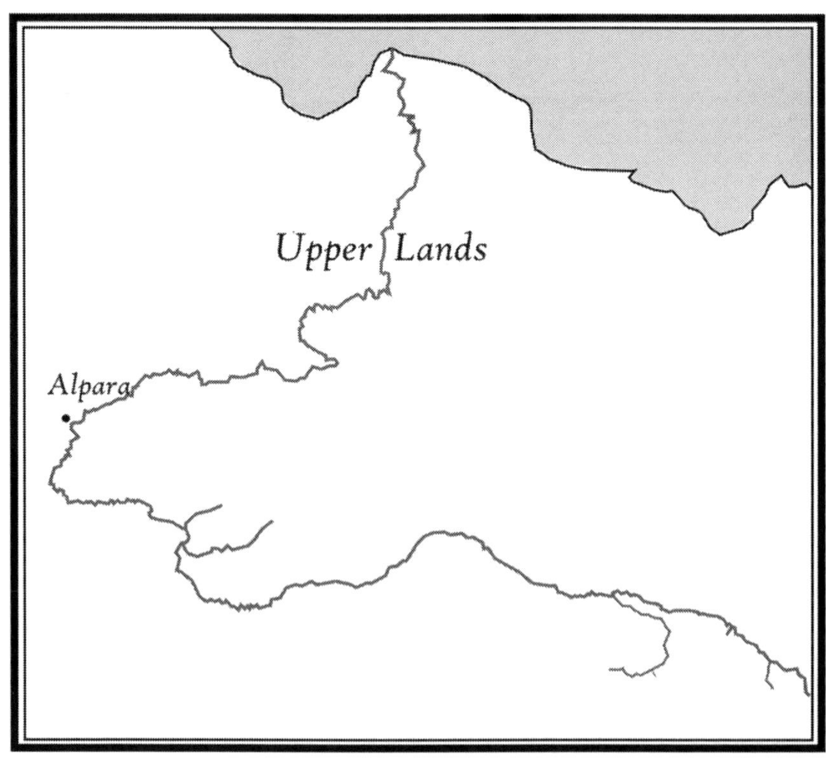

1

———————

It was happening again.

The tortured gasps of her husband's breath worried Tesha more than usual. With her handkerchief, she wiped away the beads of sweat that ran down Hattu's face despite the cool evening. His gaze swept the twisted trees and briar thickets that surrounded the royal encampment. Only the gods knew what threats he imagined lurking there—not the actual dangers that distressed her. A familiar dread tightened low in her belly. His alarm would escalate if she couldn't calm him.

Their weeks' long journey from Lawaza to King Hattu's capital, Alpara, was almost over. They had retired for the night in dense woods apart from Hattu's troops. The campfire generated more smoke than brightness, weighting the air so that it stuck in the back of Tesha's throat. These close surroundings and the fading light only added to Hattu's growing uneasiness. Too much like that cell he'd been locked in.

Tesha shifted her stool closer to Hattu's and put her arm around his shoulders. Hattu's gaze ricocheted around the forest. Under her fingers, his shoulders seized as hard as stone. He jumped to his feet with a hoarse scream, knocking her to the ground.

"Get back," he shouted, staring at empty space.

She pushed onto her scraped palms and scrambled up.

He thrust his hand into the fire and snatched a burning branch. Ignoring the flames at his fingers, he waved it in front of him. "I will not be crushed."

Burning embers fell on Hattu's arm. Fire licked his flesh. Tesha yelped and knocked the branch from his grip. She clasped her arms around him to use her body as comfort, but he shuddered and drew away.

Several days had passed since his last nightmarish vision, and this time was by far the worst. The grim campsite had set him off. His outcry showed he still relived being crushed by those walls of the cell her father had once locked him in, a terror that returned over and over. Haunted by an unnatural fear, he'd grab any inferno to drive back the abyss of darkness.

A good wife should be able to pull him out.

She faced Hattu and pulled him close, her cheek pressed against his chest. His constricted breathing wheezed in her ear. She squeezed away the memory of another burning torch, a shepherd's wound, and a vulnerability that had awakened a demonic curse. *Ishana, my goddess of love and war, give me strength. Stand by me now as you did then. Keep us safe from such evil forces.*

"There are no walls to crush us here." Tesha soothed as she clung to him. "Your army camps around us. Your soldiers will fight to the death to protect you."

"I'm their king. I should protect *them.*"

"You always have. You will. This one weakness will pass when you recover from your imprisonment."

Perhaps this concern for his nearby soldiers would quiet him. He couldn't afford for his panic to be overheard again. She'd already noticed his men looking at him with uncertainty.

The forest hid from view even the closest tents of Hattu's soldiers and muffled the sounds of the army cooking and settling for the night. The privacy the trees gave would have been welcome to them as newlyweds, but not in the presence of these shadows that tormented Hattu.

Hattu's loud cry had sent a different terror through Tesha, a well-founded one—it might alert Paskan raiders and draw them near. Ever since they'd entered this mountain range the Paskans claimed as their own, she'd feared an attack. The tribes hated her husband and the Hitolian Empire that had driven them from their pasturelands. Even with an army almost a thousand men strong, traveling through disputed territory meant vulnerability to ambushes.

She and Hattu turned at the sound of footfalls crashing in the forest. Hattu's hand leapt to the dagger at his belt, ready to confront the intruder.

A soldier clad in the saffron-yellow tunic of the royal army burst into the small encampment. He scanned the campsite in confusion, his curved sword held at the ready.

"Sir?" The soldier turned to his king.

Tesha stepped forward, straightening her veil and smoothing her skirts. "Thank you for your attentive watch, but all is well here."

"But I . . . I heard—"

Hattu shook himself as if tossing off a blanket. "Return to your duties. It's been a long day and you've earned your rest." He ducked inside the tent in a clear dismissal, but the soldier hesitated.

"All is well," Tesha repeated more firmly. "Return to your comrades."

The man shook his head, but he sheathed his sword.

Tesha knew what the soldier thought. Hattu's men had witnessed other displays of their king's lingering trouble. His army's confidence in his leadership had to be unquestioned in a kingdom fractured by enemies. If only Hattu's second-in-command had come running instead, trustworthy Marak who understood his friend's turmoil and what caused it. Marak had been with her when she had brought Hattu from that windowless cell; he knew it was enough to give any man uncontrollable terrors.

"I foolishly came too close when I added wood and almost caught my skirts on fire," Tesha said. "King Hattu shouted a warning and pulled me safe."

The soldier's brow puckered. He didn't believe her, and it was vital that he did, that he imagine only the reaction of a concerned husband and nothing more sinister.

She didn't like it, but she had to convince him with her magic. There was no choice but to hide the damage her father had done to Hattu with that long, lonely confinement. One more day of travel and they'd arrive at his palace, where Hattu could surely recover. He'd led his men through so many successful battles that their confidence in him held despite the recent trials, but more gossip now would harden their suspicions. She had to prevent an irreparable blow to her husband's authority.

Tesha pulled the gray binding thread from the pouch she wore on her belt and began to work the spell. She had concealed this forbidden magic from her husband as well as the power it gave her to influence moods. Now her fingers moved to bend the soldier's will, but sometimes she had to use it on Hattu. This secret made her feel disloyal both as a wife and as a priestess of Ishana, but undoing the harm of her father's actions was her responsibility now.

Between the folds of her full skirt, she tied the first three knots. "It was my mistake," she said to the guard, who focused his attention on her. "The king protected me. He kept me safe, just as he guides and protects the army through these dangerous lands." The knots would combine with the words to give them validity in the soldier's mind. Hattu *was* an excellent general and a fierce warrior. What should matter to the soldier rang with truth. She hoped it was enough to wipe away this latest damning blot of Hattu's fears. Tesha's fingers ached with the increasing labor each knot required as the thread turned unmalleable and resisted her. It felt like bending bronze. The greater the chasm of belief she had to bridge, the harder the knot tying became. The last knot sent bolts of agony through her arms and into her chest. "Fortunately, the king was alert and saved me."

The wrinkles of worry between the soldier's eyebrows relaxed. He nodded. "I'll build up the fire for you. Priestess, you should not do work like that."

Priestess. Tesha felt a tinge of regret that soon she wouldn't be called by that familiar form of address. To be crowned Queen of Alpara and the Upper Lands excited her, but at the same time she felt uneasy at the thought of the undetermined duties and untested power that implied. As Priestess of Ishana she knew what to do. As queen she stepped into the unknown.

The soldier placed several logs on the fire, adding some light to the dim campsite. She should have insisted on that earlier.

"Does my sister need me?" Tesha asked the soldier. It bothered her that she couldn't see Daniti's tent in this dreadful place. Daniti wasn't alone, at least. Hattu had insisted Tesha's two maidservants reside with her blind sister in the large tent intended for the king, putting Daniti's needs over his and Tesha's. And Kurala always stayed at Daniti's side. Her sister found great comfort in snuggling their little flying pet with his soft cat fur and smooth feathered head. But it was still Tesha's job to take care of Daniti, and she couldn't even see her tent from here. "Did Daniti ask for me?"

"I don't think so. Lady Daniti and your serving women retired into their tent."

Tesha nodded, although she doubted Daniti would have asked for help even if she needed it. Her sister would never admit to a limit to her independence, especially now that Tesha's marriage created a separation between them. It'd be better when they reached the palace. Everything would be better.

Hattu came out from the tent, his face still flushed.

The soldier bowed to him. "If there's nothing else?"

Hattu waved a dismissal, then touched Tesha's shoulder.

The soldier pushed through the shrubbery and disappeared.

Tesha pressed close to Hattu and his arms locked around her. She tilted her head and followed his gaze to where it was fixed on the fire.

Thank the goddess Ishana that the soldier had interrupted Hattu's imagined return to the pitch-black cell. Redirecting the soldier's thoughts had been easier than drawing Hattu back. If Hattu was too agitated and didn't listen to her words, the thread of the binding invocation didn't work, and sometimes the spiral of terror caught her up also. Worse, each use of the invocation repeated the lie at the core of their marriage. They were newlyweds of only three months, and she wondered how much strain their bond could sustain. This solution had to be temporary.

They held onto each other until his ragged breath eased.

His eyes still held the haunted look that overcame him when these dark visions possessed him.

"I feel that darkness crushing me. I'm suffocating. A king cannot have such fears."

"They will pass. They are no more real than nightmares—only haunting memories. Don't think of them. Remember the sign of love Ishana gave to us at our wedding. If the goddess believed you bore an unforgivable flaw, she would not have blessed us so."

Hattu's expression softened. Tesha pictured the scene and felt again the melting warmth that had filled her then.

She and Hattu had stood before the towering statue of Ishana on its pedestal of green nephrite. The goddess's sacred ornaments of jewels and gold glittered in the morning sunlight entering through the high windows of the temple sanctuary. They exchanged rings and had their foreheads consecrated with oil. The priest said the prayers and declared her Hattu's wife in front of her family and the other nobles of Lawaza. The priest considered the ceremony complete.

But the moment that meant the most came next, unplanned. They stood face-to-face beside their goddess, ready for the procession out of the sanctuary. But instead, Hattu pressed her hand against his heart, his hand laid gently over it. At that moment, light burst from the scepter Ishana held and cascaded around them. No wedding had ever received such a clear blessing from the goddess of love and war.

Tesha lifted Hattu's hand now, surrounded as they were by grim forest, and pressed it to her heart. "Before you took my hand and sealed our love, I was full of fear—for the wedding night, the role I must step into as queen, and a life far from my childhood home. But your gesture and the goddess's sanctification remind me each time I think of them that I can overcome my fear. You gave me that strength."

She tipped up her face and Hattu kissed her.

"It has been a long journey," Tesha said. "You are overwhelmed by exhaustion that lets these worries grow greater than they ought to. We should lie down and rest until dinner is brought." She ran her hands across his muscled back.

He held her close. "I am tired."

They went into their tent. Hattu stretched out on the pallet. Tesha slipped off her sandals and unpinned her veil so her long black hair fell free. She cradled herself against Hattu, her arm across his broad chest.

Hattu rubbed a strand of her hair. "In all the world, there is nothing as soft as your hair." His eyelids already fell heavily.

It was often like this once a fit had passed. A peaceful rest in his own palace in Alpara would mend him. Tesha let her own eyelids fall closed.

Sounds in the forest around them edged Tesha awake. At first she thought it was the servants bringing their meal. From a distance came the sound of pounding hooves and voices raised in alarm.

Hattu raised his head.

"What is . . .?" Before she could finish her thought, Hattu had jumped up.

He grabbed his sword belt, which was slung over Tesha's dowry trunk. "That's fighting. Paskans. Stay hidden."

"Paskans? But . . ."

The shouts came louder. "I'll send guards here."

Tesha nodded and got to her feet.

Hattu ducked through the tent flap.

Tesha tried to tie and pin her veil, but her fingers faltered and she tossed it onto the pallet. Terror flooded into her. She had heard ugly stories about what the Paskans did to captive women. Barefoot, she raced from her tent toward her sister.

Sharp stones pierced her feet, and briars snagged her skirt as she shoved through the forest. Ahead, she saw the large tent where Daniti was attended by Tesha's two serving women.

Kety, Hattu's Egaryan slave-groom who had grown attached to Tesha and Daniti, crouched next to the tent. He stuck close, their self-appointed protector despite his scrawny size.

The tent flap fell back and Daniti appeared in the opening with the maidservants.

"Go inside," Tesha called, running toward her. "We're under attack."

Kety's small figure bolted from beside the tent like an angry cat, teeth bared and hissing.

Emerging from the forest, two men with swords drawn vaulted forward. Hattu's guards? Their brown clothing registered. Not Hattu's men. Tesha shrieked and dodged. Kety jumped between her and the raiders, pointing the wooden amulet hanging from his neck at the men. A bright light flashed from the carved figure toward the foremost raider's sword, and the weapon flew from his hand.

The raider cried out, grasping his wrist in pain. "Grab the queen!"

The second man raced toward the tent. "Servants also?"

"Leave them."

Tesha pointed and screamed to Kety, "Daniti!"

Kety snapped his head around and scooped up the fallen sword as he and Tesha darted toward her sister. The injured man scrambled after them.

The terrified maidservants clung to Daniti and yelped like wounded dogs, but the raider slammed into them with the hilt of his sword, knocking them backward as he grabbed Daniti.

Tesha and Kety reached Daniti at that same moment, Kety holding the sword with both hands. The disarmed raider snatched Kety's shoulder and twisted him away. Kety swung the curved blade at the man's middle, bringing both the man and himself down with the force of his movement.

The Paskan bellowed in pain, but he signaled the other Paskan onward. "Take her. Go." He fell back, blood soaking his tunic.

The raider seized Daniti and swung her over his shoulder. She shrieked and pounded her fists against the man.

"No, let her go!" Tesha screamed.

Tesha pulled at Daniti, trying to drag her off the man, but the raider held her sister tight. He swung at Tesha with his sword. She swerved back, the blade ripping her tunic and grazing her skin. Her legs tangled in her skirt and she crashed to the ground.

With Daniti over his shoulder like a sack of grain, the Paskan headed toward the forest. He called out a command, and a previously unseen Paskan cantered from the foliage with two horses.

Tesha pushed herself up.

Marak's war cry reverberated over the clearing. Hattu's second-in-command was coming.

Kety darted after the Paskan, ducking when the raider threw a dagger at him. It bounced off the flash of light from his amulet, but this delay gave the Paskan the moment he needed. He flung Daniti up, spreading her legs astride a horse, then mounted behind her. They plunged through the trees, and the horse without a rider went with them at a fast pace.

Accompanied by several soldiers, Marak broke through the undergrowth and stopped short in the clearing. Tesha called to him and pointed to where the mounted Paskans had disappeared. "They took Daniti."

Kety whinnied again and again. Tesha guessed this was some command Kety used to speak to horses. He had a mystical way with animals. With a clatter of hooves, the riderless beast cantered back.

Kety grabbed the reins and tossed them to Marak. "They go. They go." He waved into the forest.

2

———————

Daniti heard Marak's war cry. She screamed a long, piercing sound that would guide him to her, even as her captor rode off with her. A voice inside that she usually ignored whispered that for *her,* Marak would dare a rash rescue.

Her captor's hand clamped over her mouth. "Shut up or I'll slice off your nose."

His threat shot through her as if she'd plunged through brittle ice in winter.

The horse seemed to fly. Soon she'd be too far from Marak.

She'd never been on a horse. The distance from the ground seemed unfathomable, but she pitched herself sideways to break free of the Paskan's hold, wrenching her bodyweight with as much force as she could. He locked his arm around her waist like a bronze bar.

The Paskan yanked her tightly against his strange body and breathed hard on her neck, the fetid staleness suffocating her. Her skirts were hiked above her knees, and the unaccustomed air was cold on her bare legs.

The harsh up and down disoriented her. The enforced closeness to her captor's body, his vicious cruelty, the blank, unknowable space surrounding her overwhelmed her senses. Ordinarily, she could judge her distance from objects around her with a low, humming click of her tongue and the layering of sounds that came to her, or by the touch and smell of her world. She judged moods and reactions with precision, but now fear paralyzed her.

The two horses pounded through the forest. Branches thwacked against her as the Paskan sped on. Warm stickiness dribbled down her right arm from a scratch that burned near her shoulder. She curled inward and clung to a wisp of horse's mane she found under her fingers. The pain of jolting against the horse seized her legs and cramped her insides.

"What was the light shooting out of that man?" the other Paskan asked from his horse.

The Paskan holding her grunted in disgust. "And how did Pahhur lose his sword? There were no soldiers. One skinny slave."

"I don't like leaving him."

"No. But we got the queen. On with the plan."

So these men *had* mistaken her for Tesha. She'd thought as much and would keep it that way for as long as she could. Soon they'd be too far away to consider going back for the true queen. Tesha had everything to live for. Daniti let her curls shield her face, hiding the telltale white-filmed eyes that everyone noticed when they looked at her. People thought she couldn't sense their staring. People were ignorant and rude.

Through her disorientation she heard the rhythm of a horse's hooves behind them. Her captor kicked his horse and they surged ahead.

Two men against one. Not such terrible odds for a fighter like Marak. A morsel of hope.

The trailing horse drew nearer.

Her captor released his hold on her and pushed her forward. She heard the hiss of a sword sliding from its scabbard. The flat of the blade bumped against her back as he swung it out, and she cowered lower over the horse.

A whoosh of something moving fast through the air cracked, and her captor jolted backward. For a brief, terrifying moment he dragged her with him, but she twisted hard and jabbed with her elbow. Her tunic came free and she stayed astride, clutching the mane while the Paskan crashed to the ground.

Her horse stampeded in distress, and she clung to stay on.

"I've come for you, Daniti." It was Marak's voice. Hope opened like a blossom in her chest.

Daniti scrambled for the loose reins and pulled back on them, calling to her horse as if it were a frightened child. Her horse slowed as Marak's approached and she imagined he'd swing up behind her and race them both away.

But the other Paskan charged toward Marak's horse. Hers veered away in fright. She heard bronze strike bronze. Horses backed away from each other, then one of them plunged toward the other. A horse must have reared as it shrieked, and she heard a startled cry—not Marak's, she was almost certain. Swords clashed and whistled as they sliced through the air.

She listened for the man who'd been knocked off her horse. She didn't hear him rise. Marak had only to take down the man he fought. Should she flee back the way Marak had come? Into a forest of dense trees she couldn't see and in a direction she couldn't be sure of?

Pounding hooves, lots of them, crashed toward Daniti and Marak. In confusion, she spun back and forth. Had she gotten turned around? These reinforcements didn't come from the direction Marak had, from the direction she thought Hattu's army lay.

Whoops of war cries broke out around her, strange, harsh ones that no Hitolian soldier had ever made.

Someone yanked the reins from her hands and led her horse away from where Marak fought. The sounds of sword fighting continued, the time between blows growing shorter and shorter. She heard a man scream in pain. Was it Marak? Maybe.

Marak whooped his distinctive war cry—almost as if he understood that was the only way to reassure her. But there were so many horses around them, so many Paskan warriors.

Men bellowed. Horses whinnied in distress. How could one man hold off so many? She followed each grunt, yell, crash, and clang.

And then Marak cried out. Not a war cry. Not gathering his strength for another blow. Pain, frustration, despair.

"Bind him. Throw him over one of your horses."

"He's wounded."

"If he dies, so what? That jackal Hattu won't know as long as we keep the body. Don't you recognize him? He's Hattu's second-in-command. The king will come after us for sure—his queen and his best commander. Double the bait."

Another Paskan swung up behind Daniti, replacing the one Marak had struck off. She cringed when his arm bound her tightly against his chest.

As the Paskans rode away with her, she pieced together bits of their conversation about a Paskan Marak had sliced open with his sword. They brought the dying man with them even though the horse ride would hasten his death. Even dying, they said he could still be useful. Something about getting his revenge if he could hold on long enough.

The big group of horses rode off at an even faster pace than before, rattling Daniti as she bounced against the horse's back. She listened for Marak, for some sign of how he was, but there were too many horses to pick out a single thread of the noise. Soon most of the Paskans stopped and dismounted, but not her captor.

"This is the place," a Paskan called out. "Set the trap. You four, take the prisoners."

Her captor took her onward. Now she counted only three horses around her. One of them held Marak and a Paskan. She recognized Marak's breathing. The ragged rasping worried her. She had no idea how badly he'd been wounded.

The trap. What could that be? Hattu had talked about the danger of underestimating Paskans. She had to get away with Marak.

3

——————

Tesha stood in the middle of the army camp. Interspersed between the pines, the many canvas tents looked ghostly. Abandoned cooking fires smoldered as bright sparks in the growing dusk. The wind caught Daniti's empty tent flap, flicking it in reproof at Tesha.

Next to Daniti's tent, Tesha watched the forest where Marak had disappeared in pursuit of her sister. Hattu raced toward her. He'd driven a group of Paskan raiders from the livestock before learning where the real crisis lay. Stealing horses had been a decoy.

While the soldiers rounded up enough scattered horses to pursue the Paskans—this delay was the other thing the raid had accomplished—she and Hattu formed a plan. He would take fifty of his best men to search for Daniti and Marak. He had to rescue them before the Paskans disappeared into their mountain hideouts. But they also decided what she would do.

"It's more than a kidnapping, isn't it?" Tesha asked.

He nodded. "Stalling the army—"

"An ambush here while you're distracted—"

"Or an attack on the capital."

"Either way, we should not stall here," she said.

"I agree. Get the army moving. Lead a night march. I've got men who've guided night maneuvers before. Outsmart the Paskans. They may have your sister and Marak for now, but don't let them get my army or my capital. Think of this mountain pass as a large game of Sphinx and Griffin."

They had first connected over the checkered board of Sphinx and Griffin, pushing each other's strategic skills to the limit. She glanced at the surrounding forest, the road cutting through, and the mountain slopes crowding that escape route. Daniti and Marak's lives and the safety of the kingdom rested on her and Hattu.

"They'll never catch you," Hattu said. "Not a chance." A ghost of a smile flickered on her beloved's face, then he kissed her hard and long. She hoped the darkness hid *that* from the soldiers racing around them.

"Bring them back," she whispered in his ear.

As they brought up his horse, he turned to the lieutenant, the same one who had come to the rescue when he'd heard Hattu cry out. "Priestess Tesha is in command. Get started while there's still some light."

Hattu clasped Tesha's arm. "We'll catch these rats, get Marak and Daniti back, and I'll join you on the road." He swung onto his horse and raced off.

Tesha watched the line his pursuit took through the forest. It started off in a similar direction as the road to Alpara she'd take with the army. *Please, Ishana, let him rescue Daniti and Marak quickly and rejoin me on this night march.*

Tesha's mouth felt dry, but a spark at her core came alive. Lead his army by herself, at night? She caught the lieutenant's dubious look and straightened her back. She looked upward for Ishana's twin red stars. They weren't up yet, but her goddess wouldn't fail her. And she wouldn't fail Hattu.

"You heard your king," Tesha said, hoping her voice held the same authority as Hattu's. "Pack up the camp and ready the men for a night march. Bring the men King Hattu mentioned, so I can discuss his plan with them." She fingered the thread in her pouch in case she needed it.

The lieutenant straightened and lifted his head. "As you command, Priestess."

SHE WAITED for the lieutenant to bring the men who could guide the army through the dark. A bitter realization came to her. Daniti's way of using her thrumming to sense obstacles would have made *her* the best guide on a night march.

Next to Daniti's tent, Kety crouched over the Paskan he'd wounded. When Tesha came over, he shook his head. "Dead. I not stop other one." A tear ran down Kety's cheek. "Sorry. Fail." Despite Kety's newness to the Hitolian language, he always managed to express himself clearly.

"There were three of them and only one of you. You did your best. Don't blame yourself." She'd failed Daniti also, and it hurt.

"I go help round up horses and animals. Paskans slow soldiers well." Kety waved his hands up at the sky where the stars were beginng to show as dusk fell. "Yellow stars go wrong."

The first time Kety had used that expression, Tesha had been baffled. Now she knew its meaning. When the yellow stars go wrong, the world goes wrong. Some Egaryan saying must be hiding behind those Hitolian words. The yellow stars represented the majority of gods who did not lay claim to the more distinctive blue and red stars, so he must have meant the gods had let things go awry. *Ishana, put them right again.*

Tesha gathered her disheveled serving women close for propriety's sake as the soldiers and lieutenant approached. He brought six men to her, all claiming to be skilled at moving through the night. She discussed Hattu's plan.

The men stood in front of her with stiff postures. They were not accustomed to a woman's leadership.

She asked them to explain what the chief difficulties were of such a night march and how best to overcome them. They seemed knowledgeable. Their stances relaxed as her willingness to listen calmed their initial resistance. The guides showed the necessary knowledge, and her panic died down. She was going to lead an army, an entire army.

She set them to organizing the army's packing and deployment on the road. The order to break camp had already gone out, and around her, soldiers took down and folded tents. She needed to pack Daniti's things.

In the privacy of her sister's tent, Tesha sank onto a stool. She pressed her tongue to the top of her mouth to hold back tears. No time for that. Henti, the older of her maids, patted her shoulder. Henti was a trustworthy woman Tesha had known all her life as her mother's maidservant. Her father had purchased the other one, Ashu, as a wedding gift for Tesha. He'd given her both as part of her dowry.

Tesha wanted to slouch against Henti for comfort as she had done as a child. Instead, she said, "Pack up quickly."

Henti lit two oil lamps. The tent, soaked in resin to hold out water, smelled like fermented pine trees.

Tesha opened Daniti's travel chest and folded a sleeping tunic to put inside. Thank Ishana her sister hadn't changed into it yet when they seized her.

Daniti's jewelry box lay open on the floor of the tent, not that it held much. Their father viewed his daughter's blindness as a sign of Ishana's shameful rejection, and he never provided her with jewels like he'd given Tesha. Instead, Daniti had filled her box with treasures she had found or Tesha had given her. A small glass vial glinted among the smooth pebbles, ribbons, and tiny ceramic figurines.

Tesha picked up the vial, pulled out its stopper, and sniffed. Daniti's perfume. She closed her eyes and imagined her sister next to her.

"Ishana, you already struck Daniti with blindness, and she did nothing to deserve that," she whispered to the goddess. "My prayers were at fault, I know. I never forget. Daniti did nothing to deserve being taken captive, either. She does not always trust that your hand directs all our actions, but do not retaliate against her because of her doubts. You afflicted her with darkness. Did you think that would bring her understanding of your presence? Do not let her captors harm her. Bring her safely home to me."

Tesha waved the vial through the air and inhaled the scent that had always meant her sister was near.

Daniti mixed her own perfume. It didn't smell like any other scent; it was part earth and part clean spring breeze. Daniti said most perfumes blocked her ability to smell what lay around her, but not her own mixture. Her sister refused to say what she made it from. "Then you'll make it and start wearing the same scent as me. It's mine, and mine only."

Tesha hadn't quarreled. Fair enough. After filling her nose and memories with Daniti's scent, Tesha couldn't put it away.

The small birdlike head of the sisters' pet peeked out from underneath the jumbled covers on Daniti's pallet. "Come here, Kurala. I'd forgotten all about you. Poor thing."

Tesha quickly twisted two threads of wool together, bound them around the narrow neck of the vial, and slipped it over her head as a pendant. It would be her talisman that Daniti would come back unhurt.

She lifted Kurala into her arms. He pawed the air with one of his tiny hooves and groaned.

Tesha kissed his feathered head. "I know. Her scent makes us both sad. Marak should have come back with Daniti. He was right behind. I don't know what has happened, and now Hattu has gone after them both. Who knows when we'll see him again or if he'll find them."

A tear fell from Kurala's eye. He'd never cried before. Tesha wouldn't have guessed he could. He had always seemed more human than anything else, even with his peculiar body made up of a bird head, bat wings, deer feet, and a cat's body. She and Daniti had heard some preposterous travelers' tales that put his homeland in the realm of the magical creatures in the old stories, but the sisters didn't know where he'd come from. He adored Daniti, who claimed she and Kurala spoke through their thoughts.

Tesha put Kurala down and placed the rest of Daniti's things into the chest. Kurala took flight around the tent. He did that when he was nervous. His wings shifted from brown to purple to bright red, a sure sign he was distraught. Then he shot out the open flap.

Tesha ran to the doorway and called to him, but he didn't stop. She could barely see him against the trees as he disappeared between the branches. Tesha shook her head and shrugged. He'd fly his fear off and return or find them on the road.

Tesha sat on a pallet and wrapped strips of linen around the cuts she'd gotten from running barefoot. She slipped on a pair of Daniti's sandals and tied her hair into one of her sister's veils.

Ashu folded the blankets and piled them on one pallet.

Henti crouched next to Tesha and wrapped an arm around her shoulders. "Daniti is strong. You and your sister always made me proud. Worried your mother sick, of course. You'll both get through this somehow. The king is bound to find her."

Tesha rested her head on Henti's shoulder. "You come with me. Ashu can pack up my tent."

Through the tent flap, she watched the soldiers' organized bustle. They'd be on the march soon. She looped her arm through Henti's and walked through the whole camp, giving the men assurance that they had a leader, even if her insides quivered.

She glanced up at the pines along the horizon. The moon, nearly full, had begun to rise. They'd need that silver light.

She took Henti's hand as her trepidation mixed with a taste of thrill. "Come along, Henti. I have a night march to lead."

4

Hattu slid low over his horse's neck, searching for any sign of Daniti and Marak. At his flanks, his two best trackers alternately scanned the ground and glanced up to avoid obstacles. They followed the trail the Paskans left in the soft dirt and torn grass. The kidnappers sought speed over secrecy and the light held—barely.

The large force of soldiers followed. They had lost precious time gathering the horses the Paskans had so thoroughly scattered, but he had his most reliable fighters with him. He would deal later with the incompetent guards who had allowed the Paskan raid. That stank of spies and bought men.

Hattu grew desperate as twilight gave way to darkness and Marak didn't speed back toward them with Daniti.

The smell of wood loam and crushed pine needles thickened the air, choking his breath. He shrank against his horse's neck. The close-set underbrush thrust him back into that cell where the walls had closed in on him. Dusk drew dark circles around him, circles that threatened to swallow him.

A headache slammed through his skull with mounting pressure. He'd been plagued with them whenever his memories threw him back into that strangled feeling he'd had in the prison cell. Darkness pushed at the edges of his sight, and floating flecks of color blinded him. Knifing pain pulsed behind his eyes. Hattu wiped the sweat that ran down his face.

The tracker on his right called out, "Should we turn back?"

"Turn back?" Hattu righted himself and blinked to clear his sight. The Paskans couldn't be far ahead.

"It's getting dark. They're moving faster than we can track," the scout said.

"Track faster."

Hattu glared at the scout until the man lowered his head and kicked into a canter. Hattu knew it was almost impossible to see the Paskans' traces now, but that wasn't why the scout had spoken up. The man observed his king with too keen an eye. Hattu breathed in and out, concentrating on the coolness of the air filling his chest and letting the men on either side of him take the lead. Some king and general he was. Ishana curse this darkness that sucked him down. And curse Tesha's father as well.

The scout slowed. With a cry, he slid off his horse and crouched low. He moved along, hunched to observe the hoof prints.

"Sir, it's bad. More than thirty horses, I'd say. Shifting all directions, like in a battle. And Marak's trail disappears into the middle of it."

"Search for bodies," Hattu shouted to his soldiers.

His men quickly walked the area. Nothing.

The two scouts approached Hattu, pointing at one side of the glen. "The group rode out that way. They are cutting a wide swath, leaving a trail we can track even if we have to light torches. Do you want to follow?"

Hattu glanced around at his men in the process of remounting, his best fighters. The horses and men were accustomed to chariot fighting, not horseback. Both had held up well on this race. His men outnumbered the Paskans, but these woods were their realm, and the Paskans loved night ambushes.

If the Paskans escaped with Marak and Daniti, he would likely never see them alive again. Paskans did not observe any diplomatic niceties with their captives. The fiends blinded the able-bodied men they took. The women they took to their beds. They were nomadic herdsmen ruled by informal councils of warriors. The gods only knew what they'd ask for ransom. His brother, Great King Muwatti, would never grant the wild demands for territory that always lay at the heart of Paskan dreams.

"Let's find them. We leave no one in Paskan hands," Hattu said.

His soldiers cheered and moved out. Good men. Hattu hoped they'd live to see the sunrise.

He forced himself forward, fighting to quell his misgivings. He glanced up at the sky, darkened enough to show that Ishana's twin red stars were just now rising, surrounded by a sprinkling of the lesser gods' yellow stars. The Stormgod's blue had not yet wheeled into the heavens. He held his gaze on Ishana's gleaming crimson and prayed to her. *Please, Goddess, stand by me and deliver Marak and Daniti unharmed.*

Wild hunts were Marak's job, not Hattu's. A strangled laugh coughed from his chest at the cruel jest of that. The men on either side glanced at him. At least the gloom hid the worry on his men's faces. He didn't need to see it to know its depth.

The head scout called back to Hattu, "Sir, up here."

Ahead, a glade opened up, a glimmer of openness as evening descended. Among the tangled weeds lay a man. Hattu slid off his horse and hurried toward him. His guards formed up on either side. Scouts spread out to scour the area.

"Marak?" Hattu saw in fragments as blotches of color swam across his line of vision. He rubbed his eyes and peered down. Blood covered the man's tunic and face. A gash ripped through his torso. Not Marak. Hattu sucked in air. Thanks be to Ishana. Not Marak.

The Paskan was alive, but he wouldn't last long. One of Hattu's soldiers brought a torch.

Hattu stopped a couple arm lengths away. "Where are they taking the woman they kidnapped?"

The man's eyes told him he still lived enough to understand, but Hattu saw defiance in them and got only silence.

"Where'd they go?"

A slight turn up of the man's lips was the only answer.

Hattu's head throbbed and the lights danced before his eyes. He blinked to clear his vision. "Did my man attack you?"

A nod. "Won't again."

"Is he dead?"

Nothing.

Hattu huffed. "Why did they leave you behind but not him?"

"A message." The man struggled and his words came out faintly. The amount of blood made it hard to judge the extent of the wound, but it was surely fatal.

With a tip of his head, the man beckoned Hattu closer. The soldiers on either side put up warning hands, but Hattu ignored them. The man was nearly dead, and he was their best chance to find Marak and Daniti.

Hattu knelt by the wounded man. "Tell me where they've taken them."

"One of your Hitolians told us about your journey and your new wife. Told us to get her." Blood dribbled from the man's mouth. "Said you'd pay plenty for the sow. Said . . . tell you . . . pay or he'll make her pay."

"Where have they taken them?"

The Paskan moaned as he shifted his weight. From under his tunic he rolled an odd, fist-shaped ceramic jar sealed with a plug of lead. Hattu recoiled at the violence of the shape and the threat of the lead, that base metal sorcerers used to trap Underworld demons.

With a grimace, the Paskan lifted the jar. "For you." Blood spurted from his mouth as he smashed the vessel against the rocky ground.

Thousands of blood-red centipedes swarmed from the shards, secreting a black vapor. Swirling fingers leapt like leather whips aimed at Hattu. He tried to jump back, but they fastened to his limbs and slammed him against the ground. He flailed, unable to break free.

The centipedes poured over Hattu's body, myriad legs twitching over his skin with a clicking sound. Curved claws on either side of their heads pierced his skin like daggers, searing pain deep into his flesh. He shrieked and plucked at the creatures, but their venom deadened his limbs.

"Help," he gasped, struggling for breath in the murky vapor.

The wriggling masses coated his hands in a sticky mucous, gluing his fingers together. The vapor hissed from their bodies and clung to him, closing in tighter and tighter.

He gathered his strength to wail, but his soldiers stood frozen around him as if they were stone carvings. Curls of blackness wormed into their mouths and ears. Only their bulging eyes showed the terror they experienced.

That Paskan. He'd done this. Hattu could no longer see the man sprawled before him. He choked out, "Release me."

The dying man's laugh rasped. "Can't. Your weakness let curse in. I can't stop it now."

"Paskan sorcerers."

"Made this, but they can't release you. Your weakness. Yours." The Paskan's voice faded.

Hattu no longer saw his soldiers. No trees, no sky. He dragged up his enfeebled arms and swatted at his crawling skin with his useless, sticking fingers.

The black miasma clung to him ever more thickly, a wall closing in, molding itself against his body and squeezing until he heard the sound of breaking bones.

The squirming vermin slithered toward his mouth. He pressed his lips closed, but they passed through his skin. His mouth filled with vapor, and pricking legs moved down his throat. Each time he tried to cough them out, pincers of agony tore into his gullet, infusing more punishing venom. His muscles no longer pulled in breath. No air got through the seething mire. Suffocation turned to faintness. The blackness closed in.

5

The man's grip around her waist didn't loosen. His smell forced its way into Daniti's nose.

Her captor and the three other Paskans didn't speak to each other. They plunged on in silence disturbed only by the pounding of hooves and the wind in the trees.

Did she dare speak to Marak? What if he had passed into unawareness, that state so close to death? "Marak, are you all right?"

She gasped in pain as the Paskan holding her shoved a blade against her chest. She felt a trickle of blood.

"Silence, bitch." He tapped the blade against her skin in warning that the dagger would be ready for more.

But she heard three thumps from Marak's direction. He'd bumped a limb against the horse and spoken in a language she understood, but the Paskans didn't notice enough to retaliate. They didn't need to. What could either of them do?

Blood dribbled between her breasts from the slit the dagger made. First warm and wet, then as cold as the fear under her ribs.

The jarring up and down of the horse went on and on. She braced her hands against the animal, then a different sort of voice reached her, one she often heard inside her head.

"Where are you?" the voice asked.

Tesha always dismissed that voice, saying Kurala couldn't talk to Daniti. But he did. Strange mixed-up creature that he was, it hadn't surprised Daniti that her pet spoke in this clear but silent manner—and only to her. She gathered in sensations no one else did. It was a skill unique to her. She didn't think it was only her blindness, but that helped.

She held still and hid her joy so she did not alarm her captor. She sent an answering thought to Kurala, "On a horse in the forest, surrounded by three other horses. Bring soldiers to save me and Marak."

"Finally! I hear you, I hear you! I've flown all over. You must be close enough now, but I don't see you. Soldiers are coming. The king with others. Behind me, not too far. I'm flying toward your voice."

"Guide Hattu's soldiers. Don't let these evil men see you."

"I'll stay where I can hear you or I'll lose you again. I've been so—

Panic, wordless and all-consuming, filled the space where Kurala's message thoughts had been.

"What happened? Did the Paskans capture you?" Daniti sent her thought into the fear.

Through Kurala's frenzy, Daniti sensed a black cloud as it reached out like an arm and struck Kurala. She felt his terror as he tumbled downward toward hard ground, unable to make his wings hold him in the air.

Then she felt nothing. No thoughts or panic, her head an empty cavern.

She listened and listened, extended all her thoughts to Kurala. Nothing. Nothing. Nothing.

Tears overflowed her eyes. Her sweet friend who could bring all the rescuers she needed had been nearby. And now—she had never received such silence from him. Before, she had been able wake him even from a sound sleep. He'd wake up very grumpy, but . . .

She hiccupped up a sob at that thought. The Paskan flipped his dagger against her skin, reopening the slit that he'd carved into her. She stifled her tears.

6

———————

Fear sweat ran between Tesha's breasts and from under her arms. The dampness made her shiver under her cloak. She sat tall on the driving board of a wagon, behind the first group of soldiers who led the column. Beside her, a brawny soldier guided the mules. Kety and her maidservants squeezed in behind her on the floor of the wagon, surrounded by rolled tents. The soldier had a bow with full quiver, three spears, and a shield at his feet to defend her. Kety had his magic amulet.

The army set off on the road. She'd placed soldiers in front and back of each supply wagon and livestock group so they wouldn't present a weak spot for the Paskans to attack. Tesha hoped she hadn't stretched her resources too thin. Planning the formation of the marching column had changed her sense of the army's size. Marching near her each day, their numbers had seemed vast on the journey. Now deployed for each essential purpose, the thousand or so men in Hattu's army suddenly seemed far fewer.

She looked across the landscape. The road followed a pass between steep flanks. Hattu had started out going this same direction but aimed higher on the slope through the forest where the Paskans had disappeared. She couldn't know how long he and his men held to this direction, but her eyes kept stealing upward and ahead. Was she was getting closer or farther from him now? Had he caught up to Daniti?

The army's "eyes" guided the front, but the pace of these experienced soldiers slowed as full darkness fell. The long chain of men and animals needed that extra time as they stepped in the dimness, moving along the dirt road that showed as a faint track under the moonlight.

When Tesha had told Kety to sit behind her, he'd looked uncertain. He always stuck close when he could, but in this case he'd murmured that an armed soldier in the wagon would provide better protection. He always discounted that amulet. Its powers were exclusively defensive, and only for Kety. When he'd jumped in front of her as the Paskan charged toward them, he'd provided protection. Too bad the protection hadn't extended to Daniti.

Tesha glanced back at the wiry figure squatting on the floor of the wagon. His boney knees poked out around his torso and his stick-like arms rested on thighs no wider than her maidservants' calves. He reminded Tesha of a cricket.

"Trust king to bring sister home," Kety said.

Tesha leaned down and answered in a soft voice, "But what if he doesn't? I need a plan. Hattu thinks this Paskan activity is a diversion to keep his army from reaching the capital to counter an attack, but maybe it's something else."

"Ransom?"

"They think they have me. They took someone Hattu cares about. Either because he'd follow or because he'd pay."

"Hattu follow. Maybe good, maybe bad," Kety said. "Nothing you do."

"Nothing I'll be able to do about the ransom they'll demand, either. They'll want land. What they call *their* land."

"Make them think you give when you not."

"Hmm . . ." Tesha nodded and straightened up. How could one give land without giving land? She'd persuaded men to agree to various compromises while negotiating the temple's business as a priestess, but the stakes had never been life or death.

She focused on the forested slopes around them, watching for movement from oncoming Paskans as if she could see well enough for that in the gloom. Thinking of her sister's sensibilities, she tried to listen for horses from the woods, but she couldn't distinguish far sounds over the nearby crunching of wagon wheels, the creak of the mules' harnesses and clop of their hooves, and the solid undercurrent of a thousand men's booted footfalls. The soldiers marched without speaking. They passed through the mountains as quietly as an army could.

Kety tapped a finger against the driving board to draw Tesha's attention. She leaned down.

"This good place for trick," he said, nodding toward the slopes and mountain pass. "And Pharaoh know tricks. Maybe Gerose do this?" Kety's years with Pharaoh made him the best one to understand, but still . . .

"How could . . .? This is Paskan territory not Egarya."

Kety shrugged.

She remembered the "blind" seer's threat that he'd written Pharaoh and told him about Hattu's political vulnerabilities. Gerose could have taken advantage of that. Though the false seer had less cause, he hated Hattu even more than Runda did, the man who had started the conspiracy against her husband. The Great King had removed Runda from office, replacing him with Hattu as the leader of Alpara. Muwatti intended only to appoint a man who could control the Paskans, but he'd given his brother an implacable enemy. The arrests of Runda and the seer ended that problem, but not the continuing danger arising from Pharaoh's animosity. Hattu had beaten Gerose in battle, and Pharaoh couldn't forgive that.

Kety touched Tesha's arm. "I think," he said. "You think, too."

Tesha sat up. Could Gerose arrange a kidnapping from faraway Egarya by using Paskans? Tesha wondered if Kety thought of that possibility only because he felt bad about the assassin his old master,

Pharaoh, had sent to kill Hattu. Kety had done everything he could to stop that assassin, but only Marak had succeeded.

Tesha returned her vigilance to the surroundings. She grew accustomed to both the jolting of the wagon beneath her and the rhythmic noises of soldiers and livestock marching around her and found she could tune into the larger landscape. An owl's broad wings swished as it dove for its prey, followed by the screech of a field mouse as the bird's talons found their mark. A distant waterfall crashed against rocks. On the far horizon, she saw the outlines of mountains, and closer in, the towering spikes of trees, more intensely black against the night sky with its moon-infused glimmer.

The moonlight created blacker areas of shadow as well as relative brightness in open spots. On the nearby slopes, unlit patches were interspersed with silvery ones in a pattern. But farther off, a solid darkness caught her eye. It lay on a hillside at the end of a valley that cut perpendicular to the road. At first she guessed that the distance and placement made this dark expanse appear different, but then it undulated like a banner in a breeze. Tesha rubbed her eyes and studied it.

On most of the mountain slopes, she could make out the shadowy pines, but this patch blotted out what lay underneath like a dense cloud hovering over the forest. Its elongated shape wasn't like any cloud Tesha had seen, nor was its writhing movement.

She closed her eyes. Daniti had taught her that sight was the least reliable sense. Tesha opened herself to that moving darkness. She was accustomed to listening for a voice inside her. The goddess's presence lay as a golden glow underneath the beat of her heart, which she could summon when needed to reveal Ishana's will. She sent a plea to use Ishana's divine awareness in a new way. She breathed in and out, letting the goddess guide her.

A wail of pain and confusion filled her, but it hadn't come through her ears. She saw an impenetrable blackness, the familiarity of which made her quiver, but she hadn't opened her eyes. Voices and panic pushed against the muffling darkness, trying to break free. Her mouth filled with a sticky vapor. She gasped and clutched her throat, willing away the perception she'd brought into her, and air flowed in again. During Hattu's nightmarish visions, he cried out about darkness suffocating him, squeezing in around him, swallowing him. This seemed similar but more extreme.

Along with the thump of her own heart, she felt another faster, more volatile one. She recognized the power fighting through that beat. Her husband's heart echoed inside of her.

As if her arm could stretch out to that hillside and touch those inside the cloud, she reached out with the goddess's presence and spoke with that inner voice. *I'm coming. I understand.*

7

———————

"Your king is trapped under that cloud." Standing on her wagon, Tesha called out so that the soldiers could hear her. She pointed. The darkness at the end of the valley shuddered and rippled. *Can the soldiers see it?*

"Paskan treachery." She heard horrified murmurs. That much she only guessed at, but it would win the soldiers' cooperation.

"Draw together the wagons and livestock to defend them if necessary. I am going there." She pointed to that hostile blankness that seemed so visible in the distance. She wished she knew what she would do when she got there.

The lieutenant stepped forward. "It isn't safe. You must stay here. I'll take men to that—"

"To attack a cloud?" she asked. "I sense sorcerous treachery that no soldier can battle. I must go." The lieutenant's brows drew together, so she conceded. "I welcome a contingent of men to protect me."

The lieutenant nodded and called out orders.

On trembling legs, she climbed down from the wagon and set off through the valley with soldiers marching around her. She moved as near a run as she could manage in the moonlight. Her feet slipped over loose rocks, but she kept on—Hattu lay trapped ahead. She followed a faint track. Perhaps the goddess lit her way.

Her guards carried torches. She glanced back and saw a growing tail of men following her, fifty or more. Despite her command to protect the vulnerable wagons, a large number of the men chose to defend her and go after their king. They believed her. She was boosted by relief that they hadn't thought her mad. Even they sensed the evil.

The walk seemed never-ending. She thought of Hattu's command to get the army to Alpara as fast as possible. She couldn't abandon him, but was she sacrificing their capital by pursuing this long chase after an unknown darkness?

Her clammy sweat gave off a rank smell. She'd been taught about curses—if that blackness was a curse—and in her mind the range of ways to drive them off shuffled and dodged from her. Curse removals were the one kind of magic that priestesses had openly recognized permission to perform, but her lessons didn't describe anything as huge and pervasive as this. Tesha had always trusted her knowledge, her hard-earned bedrock. But she didn't know this.

As she neared the blank black hillside, the accompanying soldiers put arrows to their bows, unsheathed swords, and raised spears. Their tense necks and wide eyes showed they shared her fear.

She shuddered and turned to the soldier nearest her. "Do you hear the screams I hear?"

His eyes widened. "No, but I get a creeping feel of evil when I look at that curtain of blackness." He looked at the spear in his hand. "And I don't think this will kill it."

Another soldier at Tesha's shoulder spoke up. "What will you do?"

"Dispel the darkness," she said in as determined a voice as she could muster.

The soldiers nodded as if that were an answer.

With ordinary fog, the edge blurred. This cloud had an edge like a bubble. It was clearly defined, curved, and somehow wet, although she did not dare touch it, and its darkness gave off no glimmer.

Up close, the screaming came to her louder. Without words or even sounds, it resonated inside her chest, a jumble of sharp pains and spikes of terror. The goddess had granted her request for awareness; it had brought her here, but it didn't offer much help. The suffering she sensed stripped away her strength, her legs growing heavier with each step.

A soldier held out his torch for her to take. She almost laughed. A torch to dispel darkness was such an obvious choice. It might even work.

She prodded at the edge with the flames. The torch crossed the border between the world where she stood and the blackness before her. It disappeared. She gasped and pulled it back before her hand passed inside. The flames no longer burned. It was as if they had been dipped into water.

She had managed to bring the torch back out, but if she stepped inside, would she be able to return? Would her light be quenched?

Wisps of smoke curled from the torch, thickening and spreading. Tesha knocked the torch against the ground to extinguish the last of it. Instead of going out, the sinister outpour increased and billowed down the slope. A coil of it touched Tesha's cheek, clinging and sticky. She dropped the torch and swatted her cheek. Her hand came away covered with something like black spit that she couldn't shake off. It spread into her nostrils and over her lips. She tugged off her veil and used it to rub her face.

Around her, soldiers fought off the same invasions of black swirls that wrapped like cocoons around them, binding their arms and legs, covering their faces, and pulling them into the blackness. The soldiers' writhing motions spread across the slope below. The cloud dragged in all the men who had accompanied her.

Tesha stopped fighting. She closed the inner pathway the goddess had given her through which she shared her husband's agony and that of the soldiers consumed by this evil. She had used it to find them, but now she needed strength. She sought light.

But the cursed onslaught filled too much of her being to allow her to become the empty vessel, the floating nothingness that could receive the divine presence.

She clenched her fists in frustration, and the black swirls bound them shut.

When Hattu had first appeared in her life, she had held a burn curse in her arms and sent it into the sky. She'd contained that evil spell before it spread. Waves of murk swept past her now, beyond her control.

"Reach for it." A strong, loud voice gave the command.

Tesha did not know what she reached for, but she obeyed. She spread her arms wide, dragging against the webs that adhered to her. She set her legs firmly in a broad stance with her head tipped up. Her hair, free of the veil, lifted as if in a strong wind, although the air lay stagnant and cloying. She stretched outward with all her strength, her muscles straining, her limbs seeming to extend into the earth and sky as if guided along taut threads beyond her sight.

Each time she reached a point where she could no longer endure the wrenching sensation, flecks of golden light ignited inside and fueled her until finally, with a fiery jolt, she connected with a power even greater than those golden flecks. The goddess had sustained her until she could span out into the same source that Ishana herself drew upon.

Through her fingertips and feet rose the power that crackled in the stones of the earth, the light of the stars, the rampage of streams, the winding of vines, and the steady growth of mighty oaks. Her body expanded and served as a channel for absorbing the sacred potency. The small golden glow that had rested under her heart for most of her life now filled every part of her as a blinding light. Threads of it wove her together with all that lay around her, farther than any eye could see.

This light drove back the vaporous muck from her chest and belly. The sparking strength flowed down her limbs into a ball at her core, drawing from the promise of the world. This glowing sphere whispered without words and she followed its wisdom. She rounded her hands and brought together her spread fingertips, creating an empty ball of space. She closed her eyes and concentrated on the inner sphere until she no longer felt separate from its light. Drawing its power up, she blew it softly into the round enclosure of her hands.

A bubble of light shimmered between her fingers. She widened the space between her hands and the sphere grew. She experimented up and out, expanding it until it surrounded her. She stepped forward, pushing the bubble's edge outward beyond the actual reach of her limbs. With each step the sphere enclosed more territory of grass and bushes, pushing back the tendrils of unnatural darkness that it met.

She approached a soldier who thrashed against the entangling miasma. His body bumped against the outer edge of her light. His despair shot like lightning into her. She stumbled and threw her arms out to catch herself. With a crack of thunder, her protective orb snapped, and darkness closed around her.

The cloud fetters confined her again. She pinched in the muscles around her eyes and bore down on her inner focus, calling to the intense threads she'd found before. No spark responded.

She remembered that Daniti said she did not need to see colors to know them. Each color had its own feel arising from the smell, temperature, texture, and sounds of the object that held the color. Tesha had argued that many objects of the same color would not smell or feel the same, but Daniti had laughed without rancor and said Tesha didn't perceive color fully.

Tesha imagined the sacred golden sphere with all her senses, inner and outer. Her fingers glided over a polished shimmer. Honey sweetness rolled on her tongue. Penetrating warmth loosened the knots of muscle across her shoulders and back and filled in the openness with energy. Her nose embraced the smell of freshly baked bread. A bird call, fierce and courageous, reverberated in her chest.

With her eyes closed, she touched her fingertips together, remade the potent emptiness with her hands, and breathed her senses into it. She expanded it and met the soldier's torment with those combined sensations, shielding both of them from the overwhelming suffering. The bubble melded around the soldier without bursting.

Step by step, she grew her kingdom of light. She reached deep into the earth and far above to the stars, asking for the blessing of their power. She absorbed several struggling soldiers into her sphere, shaking with the outpouring from her that this required.

Again and again she stretched wide until she had liberated a battalion of men from the black cloud. They stood up and tried out their newly released arms and legs, gazing in awe at the light that shone around them in the middle of the night. She listened for the one heartbeat she most wanted to free, but Hattu lay beyond her reach, buried in the deepest shroud.

The vitality flowing in through her feet and fingers no longer required her will to draw it in. The disparate threads of light from earth and sky found joy in their united cascade, and they acted without her volition. For now, they gave her all the force she needed, but she no longer exerted control over them. If their flood built beyond her capacity to contain, she would perish, an inner immolation. But until she had freed Hattu, she didn't want to stop.

She clung to the twin heartbeats, hers and Hattu's, and expanded the bubble of light toward his cadence. The darkness fought her. The responding deluge of power through her limbs scorched her flesh, but the sticky blackness retreated. Hattu's piercing agony diminished. Her mind's eye caught hold of Hattu, and her hands peeled layer after layer away from his body, but inside his chest a separate darkness spun out more vapor. She formed a part of the golden light into a pointed spear and aimed at that source.

A vision of thousands of squirming dark flecks flashed through her mind. The multitudes burned to ash under the light's searing pressure. Hattu pulled in air, and the shock of that freedom ran through Tesha also. She tried to speak to him, but her message of love stayed within her, rebuffed by some force she couldn't identify. The spear of light rejoined the expansive glow of the sphere, and the gateway of her shared awareness with Hattu narrowed toward silence. As that vision was closing, she glimpsed a twitch of dark movement, and then she was alone.

She wavered under the strain of holding the sphere of brightness around her, the edge of her capacity stretched so far that it might collapse and pull her back into the stream of power she used to form her sphere. Would losing herself in those coursing threads be good or bad?

Suddenly she felt muscled arms around her, a solid chest supporting her, and a familiar warmth drawing her back into her body and away from the golden power she had drawn up from the world, the power that threatened to consume her. An endearment murmured into her ear returned her to the ground she stood on. The power crackled out of her limbs and she collapsed into Hattu's arms, limp and drained, but herself. *Thank you, dearest Ishana. Thank you, my beloved Hattu.*

She opened her eyes to the accustomed world around her. The sphere of divine light had vanished. The moon shone its gentle offering, casting the forest in a patchwork of silver brightness and shadow. Gone was the absorbing blackness. Hattu's soldiers gathered in close.

Perhaps the moonlight stripped the color from Hattu's face, but he had the pallor of a corpse. Hattu kissed her lips. "How . . . ?"

She shook her head and rested its heaviness against Hattu's shoulder.

"Are you . . . ?"

"Tired." Her legs didn't hold her.

Hattu swept his arm under her and lifted her body against his. She felt a shudder run through him until he found his accustomed strength. His body had returned. She saw questions she couldn't answer in the lines of his face and the depths of his eyes.

A soldier stepped forward. "You saved us. There was that dark cloud, and then I was lost in it. I don't understand, but thank you, Priestess. It was you, that much I sensed."

The soldier turned toward the others, and they burst into a loud cheer.

8

————

The ride went on and on. The only comfort Daniti found was the sound of Marak's breath, uneven but unceasing.

Her legs ached from the constant jolts of the horse's gait and the unaccustomed spread of her legs over its back. The press of the Paskan's body repulsed her, but he never loosened the clamp forcing her tight against him. An icy cord of terror bit ever deeper into her vitals. To survive, she dragged her attention outward.

Air brushed her face, the chill of night. Pine and the hard mineral smell of boulders and rock faces combined in her nose. Beyond the clomp of horses, the wind moved through trees, complaining of confinement in the close-packed forest.

Then the space around them opened so that the brisk air came as a slap to her cheeks, and the wind shifted to whistle of freedom in high expanses where trees dared not grow. Her captors had brought her a long way.

She drew her senses in, to the horses on either side of her and to Marak. His breathing had fallen too quiet, its rhythm full of sickening pauses.

She wanted to comfort him, but their captors wouldn't let her touch him or even speak. When she sent out clicks and thrumming noises, they came back to her as solid objects around her, their position and size. Could she send Marak her desire for him to live in some kindred way? She could talk to Kurala through thought, but only Kurala.

She sharpened her will to make him feel her yearning as tangibly as her soundings allowed her to sense the outer world. She sent Marak wave after wave of concentration, and her own strength spilled out with them like a stream in a spring flood. None of her efforts connected.

She slumped over the horse's neck, the Paskan's locked arm digging into her innards. She listened, but what came from Marak grew weaker. She'd been foolish to think she could help him.

Then she twisted her head back and forth. Her sense of Marak's flagging didn't pass through her ears. She *had* connected to him inside.

If she could sense his withering spirit, perhaps she could use that path to send him renewal. She would reach his heart without words.

Pressing her hands against the horse as a brace to counteract the draining sensation, she held to her purpose for a long stretch. The regular jolting from the horse's gait became the cadence of her efforts until warmth flowed into her chest, the measure of an inner place not her own. Marak's. His spirit lifted as she supported him. In turn, she received an answer of comforting calm to the terrifying tension that bound her vitals.

She and Marak were not communicating with the precision that she did with Kurala, but this went deeper.

Daniti held onto that warmth and the sureness that Marak survived until the horses stopped. Her captor dismounted. Another voice called out to them—some Paskan who was waiting for them wherever they were now.

Hands grabbed her hips, yanking her from the horse. Thrown into emptiness, she lost the ground's orientation and crashed onto her hands and knees. Stones sliced into her palms. A bolt of pain leapt through her right knee. The Paskan jerked her onto her feet.

Her legs wouldn't hold underneath her. He stood her up with her face toward him.

She locked her knees and dropped her head, trying to cover her face with her hair, but his fingers dug into her arms.

He called out, "Bring that torch here."

Someone thrust heat and light at her face. Her eyes could distinguish areas of light from total darkness. She drew back.

Someone pulled up her chin. "Hey! What is this?"

Some other Paskan came close, and bone-hard fingers twisted her face to and fro. "Her eyes. What's that white? She's a witch, not the queen." He thrust her away.

"But we . . . She's the queen."

"Look at her."

"That Hitolian sow tricked us. She switched this useless woman for herself."

"Switched? How could you be so stupid?" A Hitolian accent, startling among the Paskans. Daniti recognized the cruel twist of that voice.

"It doesn't matter," the Paskan answered. "Chance favored us. Our other prisoner must have been enough bait. Didn't you see the cloud?"

"Of course it matters," the Hitolian said.

Daniti feared the anger that boiled under those words. She recognized the voice of the henchman who did the dirty work in the conspiracy against Hattu. He'd almost killed Tesha, but he'd escaped, even after an attack on their mother. Something mysterious had happened that time, something Tesha did that Daniti couldn't pry out of her. It lay as a heavy secret between them. Something Daniti feared screamed for revenge.

And she and Marak were the only ones at hand for that revenge.

"The king's undone," the Paskan said. "We have no need for her. Let's kill this witch before she casts her evil on us."

"I have need of her," the traitor Riam said. That was his name, Daniti remembered, and the icy cord inside her strained tighter. "She may be a witch, but she's the sow's sister."

Daniti heard a groan that stole all her attention. They were dragging Marak off a horse.

"Should we leave him tied?"

"He's in bad enough shape," a Paskan said. "He's not going anywhere. He's the one with value, so let's try to keep him alive."

Marak took some steps and tripped, then someone caught him and propelled him forward. He came beside her, and she tried to match her steps to his, clicking her tongue against the top of her mouth for guidance.

"Silence. No spell-casting, witch."

Marak pressed lightly against her arm and shoulder, guiding her as much as he could. She kept up, ignoring the stones her feet stubbed against, the obstacles she had no way of avoiding. Twice Marak stumbled, and she reached to support him, feeling how his wound had depleted him. The Paskans surrounding them didn't object. They kept their distance while driving them on.

Even without her thrumming, Daniti sensed the narrowing of a doorway and the echoing of their footsteps against walls.

"Get in there," Riam said. He shoved her, and her footsteps brought her outstretched hands against a rough wall. Her fingers took in uncut rock, not the wall of a building. A cave?

She heard the retreating footsteps of Riam and the Paskans. Marak leaned against her, whether out of weakness or need for contact, she wasn't sure.

"Our prison," Marak said. "They've piled straw on the floor, presumably for our comfort. Can you help me lower to the ground without crashing? Being tied up like a sack of grain and bounced over mountains on a horse is not conducive to being able to use one's body when the ride is finished."

Daniti gasped in surprise that he could still ask with that joking tone. "And you're wounded. Where?"

"Only my calf."

She felt for his torso, braced him against herself, and brought him gradually to the ground.

He sighed in relief.

She sat next to him. They both rested against the wall. Its bumpy surface poked into her back, but the steady cold stone was far better to lean against than a Paskan captor.

"Fortunately, they bound my knees when they tied me up. I think they accidentally helped stop the bleeding, but it's opened again. I should do something about that." He kept his voice at a murmur that wouldn't carry.

"I'll help."

"Can you tear a piece from my tunic for a bandage? If I do it, the bending might finish me off." He laughed softly. He was doing everything he could to lighten the horror of their situation.

She took the lower edge of her own tunic between her teeth, unraveled it and ripped.

"I didn't mean your tunic."

"Women's clothes have more fabric to work with."

"Hard to argue with that."

He laid her hands around the outer edge of his wound so she knew what they worked on. Blood coated her hands, making her fingers slippery and awkward. First he tried to wrap the bandage while she held the wound closed, but that didn't work. The bandage slipped and the bleeding continued.

Daniti tore off more strips from her clothes. "Let me do the bandage."

He pressed the wound together, and she tied and wrapped, working around his hands with a sureness that surprised her. The fabric felt familiar under her touch, but not a man's hands, callused and powerful. They could protect or destroy. That alien intimacy brought her heart into her throat as well as a heat that had nothing to do with the blood she sought to slow.

His hands shifted and gradually lifted away as her progress moved up the cut with tight bindings. When she'd bandaged his calf, she wanted to run her fingers upward over the contours of his thigh, but there was no excuse for that, even for a blind woman abandoned by the gods.

When she finished, he pressed her hands against his tunic,

wiping his blood from them. Under the fabric's weave, his heart beat fast and hard. She clasped his hand in hers. It was wrong of her, but she didn't care. He let her rub his hand without withdrawing it.

His head came to rest on her shoulder. "On the way here, when I didn't think I could bear it anymore, I felt something. Strength. Warmth. I held onto that the rest of the way. It was you, wasn't it?"

"No more than the strength you sent me. I felt it too." Daniti cradled his hand against her belly.

The bandaging seemed to have taken everything out of Marak. They sat in silence. Marak breathed in and out, and Daniti listened until the rhythm smoothed and deepened. She knew he would stay with her.

After what seemed like a long time, she heard footsteps approach.

A gruff Paskan voice said, "Here's water and food."

There was a soft clunk on the dirt floor. The Paskan left.

Marak edged upright. He took her hand and placed it around a wooden cup. "Drink."

She took a couple of sips and returned it to him. "You also."

Marak gave her a strip of dried beef. She reached over and felt his hand to be sure he had one as well. Chewing the tough jerky made her teeth ache. With each chew, the taste of old meat opened up in her mouth, but her body called for nourishment. She ground it between her teeth until it grew moist enough to swallow, then forced it down. She could hear Marak's jaw working.

"Surprising what some food can do," Marak said, his voice barely a whisper.

"If you can call that food." Daniti matched his softness.

"That noise you make, you use it to guide you, don't you? On the journey from Lawaza, you impressed me with your skill."

"Tesha never trusts it. After I lost my sight, I discovered I could sense what lay around me if I made a clicking sound."

"I'd trust you to lead me."

An unfamiliar lightness grew inside Daniti. "How are you feeling?"

"I'm still alive. Your bandages are holding well."

Daniti squeezed his hand, and she didn't let go.

"This prison is high on a peak. By the moonlight I could just make that much out, even upside down with my face against the horse's haunch. They built this hideout into a cave. It's going to be hard for Hattu to find. He may have to negotiate us out, but he's the best negotiator. You hid your identity, didn't you? They thought they had Tesha, and you didn't try to get away by revealing who you were."

"They would have killed me and gone back for her."

"Possibly. We can hope they believe we have enough ransom value to keep us alive but not so much that they make impossible demands."

"Don't Paskans always make impossible demands?"

Marak grunted in agreement. "The Hitolian who recognized you, he's Riam. Why I didn't kill him when I had the chance, I'll never know. At the time, getting away seemed enough."

"And living. Tesha told me he had a knife in your neck."

"That too. But this isn't just the usual Paskan ambush."

"A trap. That's what they said."

"A trap? I didn't hear that part. I went in and out. What sort of trap?" Marak had dropped his voice even lower. His breath brushed her ear with each word.

"I have no idea." She hesitated, then leaned in even closer to Marak's ear and told him about Kurala and her communication with him.

"In your head?"

"Tesha doesn't believe me, either."

"I believe you, but I don't understand."

"It doesn't matter, anyway. Kurala must be dead. But I think the trap killed him, whatever the trap is. It might have gotten Hattu. Kurala said the king was right behind with soldiers."

"Then it's up to us to escape. We're at the back of the cave. There's a wooden divider between us and our guards, but we have to slip by them to get outside. I haven't heard any movement from them. Have you?"

She listened. The nearness of Marak had drawn all her attention.

Now she reached out. Beyond the cave, she heard night sounds, wind, an owl, and the echoing of wide spaces. Nearer, nothing. Then a rustling of a body moving a little. Then nothing again.

"They might be asleep," she said.

"It's pitch dark. They don't have a fire inside, and the last of the torches they brought with them have gone out. Seems like an advantage we have over them—your ability to move in darkness."

"But they'll hear me."

"There's that. How softly can you do it and still maneuver?"

"Right now, this building is all unknown emptiness to me. At home I know the space between each piece of furniture and doorway."

"There are two rooms. This tiny space we're in and another room, also closed in across the cave front with a wooden wall."

"I can try sounding it out. But what would we do if we escaped? In the woods?"

"I'll settle for getting away. The dangers of forests have been exaggerated."

Daniti rose. She clicked her tongue against the top of her mouth, aiming the vibration in a gradual sweep. About four paces ahead and to one side was an opening. The ceiling bulged down in some places. Marak would need to watch his head. She took a step forward. Marak stood and placed his hand on her shoulder.

She whispered into his ear, "They will notice me if I go to the opening and sound."

"Maybe they'll sleep. If they waken, we'll say we're stretching our legs. No harm done. Those who do not dare, do not fare."

"But to fare well . . ."

"Sometimes doing something is better than nothing."

Daniti led him to the opening and measured the next room. It was longer, widening at its front end. She tested that farthest wall and found what must be the door. It gave back a solid feel. Closed. They'd have to open it, with all the noise and disturbance that meant. Along that front wall on the ground, she found four stretched-out piles softer than the stone and wood. She listened. Breathing. Their guards.

She brought her lips against Marak's ear. "Four guards. There were five men, counting Riam."

He put his lips to her ear. "One must have gone to the other Paskans. Riam, perhaps? They don't have who they thought. They need to report this to the rest."

She vibrated her tongue, building a more detailed view. The men stretched out in front of the door. Blocking it.

She turned and whispered this to Marak.

"Weapons. I need a weapon, then. They'd be on the men." He gave her a little push, gentle but clear.

She checked the space in between for obstacles and stepped through the opening, Marak's hand on her shoulder. They edged across the small, irregular room toward the sound of four men sleeping. She clicked her tongue as softly as she could and still maneuver.

The sleeping rhythm broke, and she heard rustling against the floor. She froze.

More noise like a man standing. "Hey! What's that sound?"

The others awoke. She heard the distinctive slither of swords coming from sheaths.

"It's that witch. Get away from us."

Marak tugged on her shoulder. She guided him back the few steps they'd taken through the opening.

"Come into this room again and we'll run you through. Either of you."

Marak pressed close beside her, his arm around her shoulders and the cave wall against their backs.

"Good job. It might have worked. Now you know where you are and where the way out is. Something is better than nothing."

With Marak's warmth calming the pelting of her heart against her ribs, something *was* better than nothing.

9

Hattu coughed. Leaning over the side of his chariot, he spat out a black glob and shuddered at the memory of his mouth full of those things. He glanced at Tesha. Asleep in the bed of a wagon propped on pillows, she hadn't noticed. He guided his chariot close to the wagon, keeping watch over her.

Caught in sleep, her face, unlined and soft, was that of the sweet young woman who nestled against him each night. Who had she been when she broke through to him inside the curse? He hadn't seen her, only sensed her presence and the heartbeat that called to him and gave him hope.

Kety sat in the wagon near Tesha, his head bowed. Hattu assumed he dozed, as exhausted as everyone else. Kety served as a most unlikely protector, but his faithfulness to Tesha couldn't be questioned.

After he had sent his best scouts out in search of Marak and Daniti, Hattu had led his army as fast as he could to the capital—the plan he and Tesha had devised. He struggled to understand what had happened inside that cursed darkness, but one result from whatever spewed out of that jar seemed clear. It had slowed down their return to Alpara and debilitated many of his soldiers. The Paskans must have intended to take advantage of that weakness and focus on overtaking the capital. If he lost his impregnable fortress, his kingdom would unravel thread by thread.

After he'd lifted Tesha into his arms, she'd fallen into a deep sleep. He wanted to know how she had driven off the curse unleashed by the dying Paskan, but he could not rouse her. His soldiers spoke only of the black cloud. He hoped even Tesha did not know about those wriggling masses that had gone inside him. Her magic had driven them out. That horror was done. But how? He feared he'd harm her if he woke her. The Paskan had said no one could release him from the curse, but Tesha had. At what cost? Would she ever awaken?

He needed Daniti. She might be able to sense where her sister lingered and how deeply. Daniti had an uncanny ability to know what went on inside others, or so it seemed to Hattu. Occasionally he suffered twinges of jealousy about the connection between the sisters.

He'd ordered the slow ox-drawn wagons and herds to the rear of the column with a small force to defend them. They could catch up later. Better to lose them than his capital. The dark night kept their pace slow, but he pushed his soldiers forward as fast as possible. Such a demanding march might be the worst choice if it left them too exhausted to defend the city. The battle with that black cloud had taken a lot from so many of them already.

He watched his soldiers. No one else coughed up that sticky muck. As they marched, their breathing did not constrict as his did. Even riding in a chariot, he struggled to draw air.

It would pass. He couldn't tell anyone about it. That dying Paskan's words haunted him. *Your weakness let curse in.* This was his fault. These difficulties he now suffered were too similar to those that had struck him whenever he remembered that prison cell—the sense of being cut off from everyone around him, that soul-stripping isolation he'd experienced when Tesha's father had locked him up. The Paskan curse had wormed into him through that hole, *his* vulnerability. He should trust the soldiers who'd fought so many battles at his side, but as he peered through the darkness at them, he felt uneasy. Would his men see his weakness and turn against him?

Hattu looked at Tesha. He directed his horses on the edge of the road next to the wagon she lay in. He wished he could smooth back the silky strands of her hair from her brow. As overtaken by darkness as he had been, could she still love him? She had rescued him twice. Once from the entangling conspiracy of Hitolian enemies, now from the evil magic of the Paskans. Her actions shook him. She commanded power he did not understand.

But he loved Tesha. Ishana, the guidepost he'd always relied on, had sent dreams commanding them to marry and then blessed their bond during the ceremony. His need for Tesha ran through his body like his blood.

He nudged his horses and chariot as close to the wagon as he could and reached toward her. As soon as he imagined touching her cheek, pain shot down his arm, and he clutched it to his chest. Something stabbed him on either side of his neck from the inside. He tried to clear his throat and damp down his panic at these lingering signs.

Tesha had overcome the curse. This would pass. He'd work it out of himself. It would pass. *Please, Ishana, make this pass.*

The pincers tore into him again.

Please, Ishana, help me. He willed a stillness into his throat. He would not feel that pain. He prayed to his goddess and swayed with the rhythm of the chariot under his feet.

Ishana had brought Tesha into his life. He recognized the divine hand in that fateful meeting when the goddess had brought him to the temple in Lawaza to offer his thanks for his victory over Pharaoh Gerose. The moment he'd seen Tesha, she'd won his allegiance. He'd handed his war-won treasures to the goddess, but it had been Tesha he wanted to please. She'd captivated him with her cleverness.

Hattu whispered a prayer. "Ishana, my Goddess, do not take Tesha from me. Pour your strength into her so that she will awaken." He paused. "Don't let her mistrust me now." Twin spasms choked his throat. Gradually he regained control.

Kety sat upright, alert again.

"Take care of her while she slumbers, Kety," Hattu said. "I fear for her."

The skinny man nodded. "To protect herd, shepherd dog chases lion. Sometimes lion eat dog."

Hattu's horses shifted their gait, trying to avoid the close wagon. He needed to guide them to the front and lead his men as he did for every battle and march.

He was good at being a general. The old, strong habits flowed into him, despite his unease. He rolled his shoulders, releasing the worries and memories that distracted him, and turned his attention to his army and to where their progress had taken them. He'd traveled this poor excuse for a road often enough to recognize where they were, even without daylight. Ahead on the road, he could make out a narrowing and remembered the towering gorge walls the road passed between.

He beckoned the mounted scout he kept close for running messages.

"Sir?"

In a quiet voice, Hattu said, "Tell the guides at the front to halt the army. Then go ahead alone without your horse. You do not want to be seen or heard." He pointed to the right side of the road. "On this side, just before the rock wall of the gorge begins to go straight up, there's a rough trail that climbs to the top. It's hard to find in the daylight, so you'll have to be careful. There are two equally sized boulders, each taller than a man, close together with no other large rocks near. Go around the farthest boulder. Behind it is the beginning of the trail. Climb silently. If those thirty or so Paskans we were tracking earlier know we have escaped their curse, this is the best place to stop us from reaching the capital."

The scout shifted on his horse and looked at the dark landscape around them. "I agree."

"If I needed to set an ambush, I'd choose that gorge, and I'd station my men on the ridge above. Check for me." His voice rasped. The creatures clawed the back of his throat. Struggling to be heard, he leaned closer to the scout. "You understand?"

The scout nodded and spurred his horse toward the front of the army column. Hattu ran his fingers across his lips, half expecting to feel blood.

Hattu waited in tense alertness. Twice he thought he heard sounds from the gorge. They might have come from the top, but he couldn't be sure. A stream cut through the gorge, plunging in first as a waterfall, and that might account for the noises. That was another danger the gorge posed—a river filled with snow melt. Not good to be backed into.

He'd only sent a scout up one side of this trap. Was that a mistake? Getting up onto the other side of the gorge's cliffs from here would be slow and surely impossible at night. Could the Paskans have gotten into position there from some other direction?

The rock face on that other side loomed over the gorge road so much that it would provide some protection to those below. Not the location to launch an attack. Paskans always used the landscape against him in the most effective way possible. All thirty of them would be on the right side where nothing would stop their spears, arrows, and boulders from hitting his men below. Except he hadn't put his men inside the gorge.

Was he imagining dangers that didn't exist? The familiar sureness after a command decision would not settle in. If this delay gave the Paskans time to attack his capital, then his fearfulness would undo him.

By the time he judged his scout must have reached the area above the gorge, his impatience had made him jittery. He twisted the leather reins back and forth in his hands. He tried to judge how long until the scout returned. If the Paskans found and killed his scout, that would send an essential message through his absence, and Hattu was aware of the possibility. That would present a much tougher battle with the loss of secrecy, but it was still better than being trapped between two stone walls.

The leather strap of the reins beat a soft rhythm against his palm. The oval disk of the moon climbed higher.

At last the scout returned. "Paskans on the ridge over the gorge. I stayed away, so that's all I can report."

Hattu smiled to himself. He'd been right. The confidence that had directed him in the war against Pharaoh surged through him. The experiences of that past victory burned away the uncertainty that had slithered into him from the darkness.

He waved to the band of his fiercest fighters that he'd positioned around the wagon Tesha lay in. He told them where the enemy waited. "Ready for a counter ambush?"

The men nodded in silence, but he felt their eagerness.

"We must defeat these warriors, but as we do so, watch for Marak and Daniti. If I were the Paskans, I would not bring the captives here, but if they have, we want to free your commander and my wife's sister, not kill them."

On his orders, they dismounted, and other soldiers took their places as bodyguards. Five soldiers held shields over Tesha's limp body in the wagon. Kety squeezed in next to her at his command.

Word moved up and down the column.

A shield wall formed at the front and along the sides. They'd left the livestock and ox-pulled wagons far enough behind that defending the line was far easier now.

"It's a steep footpath. We'll be vulnerable on the way up, but we'll outnumber them once we get there," Hattu said to his huddled men as they pulled on armor and weapons. "They could well know the army is near the gorge by now, but hopefully not that we're heading up to challenge them on top. Weapons at the ready. The waterfall will mask the sound of our approach."

Hattu took the lead. At the trailhead, three of his men stepped in front of him and started the climb. He hesitated, but they were right. Better not to lose their king. Marak would have insisted he stay with the main force, so he'd respect this much caution from his men.

The lower portion of the trail posed the greatest danger because it allowed only single-file climbing. It would be too easy to pick them off where there was no room to form into blocks. The only safety here was secrecy.

The moon had climbed to the center of the sky, and together with the bright-colored stars, it gave almost too much light, but the scrubby oaks that clung to this rocky hill blocked from view his soldiers' stealthy movements. The stream below them rushed in spring fullness and masked their footfalls.

They made silent progress. His plan might work.

He could feel the men grow confident and they sped up, trying to reach the top before the Paskans noticed them.

Then one man slipped on the loose stones of the trail. A shower of rocks cascaded down the mountain. Everyone halted, motionless. Hattu expected an outcry from above, but only the stream's roar filled the night. He gave a hand signal, and they continued the climb.

He relished the chance to strike out at the men who'd tried to destroy him with dark magic. He both prayed that Marak and Daniti were up there and prayed that they were not. In this night battle and rough terrain, rescuing them rather than getting them killed would be dangerously difficult.

With each carefully placed footstep, blood thirst vibrated through his body, and he no longer struggled to breathe. The chill air brought vitality into his chest. Hiding above were warm bodies to cut down, not the strangling vapor and helpless feeling he dreaded.

It was possible that they climbed toward more sorcery, but creating a curse like the one Tesha overcame would take the rarest skill and strength. He would have said no one living could produce a curse like that. Someone could. But twice in one night must be beyond the power of this hidden sorcerer. On that limit, he was betting these men's lives—and his.

The steep part of the trail broadened into a passable slope, and his men formed up five across and ten rows deep. They had to part around trees and boulders, but they held together as a group. Hattu stood at the center of the second row. Now they could block with their united shields and go on the offense when they chose. It mattered much less if the Paskans discovered them, as surely they would.

Just before the crest of the hill, where Hattu remembered a flat area—perfect for setting up an ambush to send down weapons on those walking through the gorge—they were spotted. A Paskan cried out ahead of them.

Hattu called out, "Forward, attack!"

His men burst over the crown before the Paskans could rally. Hattu scanned the ridge. Men ran, but not in formation. Dark mounds by the edge of the cliff face must have been boulders to roll off as weapons, but now there was no one below to roll them onto.

Nowhere did he see a telltale cluster around someone with a woman's skirts. Even when his men came into striking range of the Paskans, he held off his command, peering across the ridge. No man with bound arms. Every figure he saw reached for weapons. Bitter disappointment washed over the relief.

Hattu scanned one more time and called out, "Archers, launch!"

Those moving targets would be hard to hit even with the starlight, but abrupt collapses showed some success.

He repeated the command. More arrows loosed.

He signaled the back half of the block to march forward and double their breadth across most of the ridge surface. Spears flew as Hattu's warriors mowed down Paskans like a scythe at harvest.

Paskan volleys clanked against the upheld shields around him. One of his men grunted with pain. It looked like an arrow to his shoulder, but the soldier kept up with the rest. They closed with the remaining Paskans and shifted to sword fighting. His two best guards held their places on either side of him.

A Paskan leapt toward the back of one of Hattu's soldiers while the soldier yanked his spear out of another Paskan's chest. Hattu raced in between and swung low at the Paskan's knees, knocking the man off his feet. Hattu's guard finished the man off with a sword slice across his neck.

Hattu's gaze darted across the confusion of the battlefield. The open ground glowed under the moonlight, but the trees and boulders threw black shadows that were difficult to distinguish from the murky figures of Paskan fighters. His soldiers held the advantage, but he had to keep them from falling into the lurking perils of this unconventional fight. They closed in on the Paskans with impeccable form. Along the edges, he looked for any trace of Marak and Daniti. Nothing.

The fighting thinned. Hattu turned his focus to any Paskans trying to retreat into the woods that fell steeply away from the gorge face. He pursued anyone he saw, and his men followed suit, but even so, a few Paskans escaped. News of the slaughter would get back to this tribe, putting the Paskans in a mood for vengeance. That wouldn't bode well for Marak and Daniti.

10

Tesha's leg jostled painfully against the corner of something hard. A wooden chest? She tried to shift her thigh, but it stayed jammed where it was. She tried to lift her head and see what blocked her. Her head would not lift. Her eyes stayed closed.

She told her eyes to open. She smelled horses and heard shuffling feet and voices that barely spoke above a whisper. She tried to lift her hand to feel her eyelids, but like her leg and head, it would not move. Her entire body had turned to stone.

Panic sizzled. The last thing she remembered was collapsing into Hattu's arms after the curse. She had driven it back by drawing up power from all around her, a power that was too much for her to control. When that golden, crackling force had drained away, she'd been unable to hold herself up.

Had she died?

If she couldn't move, would everyone assume she was dead?

But she could feel the air filling her chest, flowing through her nose.

Opening her eyes did not take strength. She had to be able to do that much.

She offered a prayer to the goddess and concentrated on lifting her eyelids. She recognized the rattling around her as a wagon's movement. So, she lay in a wagon, drawn by horses. She could hear their clomping rhythm. She pictured the wagons that the soldiers loaded every morning as they decamped on the journey. Their sides were built up of saplings trimmed straight and tied together. In her imagining, she saw the bristly brown cording woven around the wood, binding each stick to the next to form a panel. The picture was very distinct. And then she realized she actually saw it less than a hand's breadth from her nose. She had opened her eyes.

No other part of her body moved, no matter what she commanded.

The wagon passed between two mountain slopes. They towered over her, leaving only a narrow band of gray sky visible between. Dawn approached. She had started the army on a night march. They must still be at it, delayed by the curse.

"Priestess! Awake."

She recognized Kety's voice, but she couldn't turn her head toward the nearby sound.

"How are you? I tell king?"

She tried to speak. Nothing.

Kety's face swam over her, concern deepening lines around his eyes. "Soldiers say we not far from capital. You rest."

She couldn't rest. She had to save her sister. Where was Daniti? How could she be in such a helpless state when her sister needed her so much?

Tesha closed her eyes and pretended to sleep so no one would expect her to speak. She'd hide her weakness.

During the last few days she'd wondered if she might be with child. She hadn't wanted to eat in the mornings. Women always said that was a sign of it, although she didn't feel anything else. Even Daniti had said something about sensing a child. Now Tesha couldn't move. What would that mean for the infant, if she was right? But perhaps she'd only been tired from the journey. Surely there'd be some more distinct feeling if she held a baby in her body.

Hattu came near and talked to Kety. "Take care of her until I get her into the safety of Alpara."

She thought about what awaited her at the capital—yet another problem, less piercing to her heart than Daniti's kidnapping but still dire and one she'd long dreaded. She couldn't arrive appearing help-less. *Please Ishana, give me back my strength before we reach Alpara. I can't face Nerik like this.*

Hattu's son. He talked about Nerik often—when Hattu could bring himself to talk with her. His muteness . . . It wasn't that Hattu didn't love her. She knew he did. But it was as if that lonely cell had stripped him of his will to converse. She longed for another conversa-tion like the one they'd had that first day they'd met—before her father arrested him.

Now *she* couldn't speak. She concentrated on moving her mouth. Nothing. *Please make this pass.*

Nerik. Hattu acted as though his son were still a child, but Nerik was Tesha's age and the Crown Prince. Even if Hattu didn't see a prob-lem, Tesha had one.

She sifted through the last conversation she and Hattu had about Nerik. They'd been seated by their fire one night after the army made camp. She'd watched Hattu's face in the flickering light of the flames. He'd been calm all day, no hint of the troubles, and he talked cheer-fully, eager for the coming reunion with his son.

Tesha had surmised he felt guilty about the long separation. She weighed his outsized regret with the bits of his past he'd shared with her and thought she understood why the guilt had grown so overlarge.

When Hattu was six, his father had left him at Ishana's temple, separated from his family. The intent had been for the goddess to heal his illness, and Ishana had, but along with that blessing had come a strained relationship with his father and siblings. Hattu didn't say it quite like that, but he'd felt abandoned by them. And then, as a king, his duties had often separated him from Nerik, and so Hattu saw himself doing the same with his son.

It wasn't as though Hattu had any choice about being away, but that didn't seem to matter. As part of the royal family, Nerik should understand why his father had little time for him. From the sulky young man she'd heard behind Hattu's stories, she suspected Nerik truly believed his father neglected him and used Hattu's guilty feelings to get his way. She thought of her own father. She would have loved less of *his* attention.

That evening by the fire, Hattu had been full of little moments he remembered.

"Nerik used to play with a small wooden sword, giving commands with a baby lisp to the servants as if he were a general. He was so sweet. He still had the round belly that little children have and soft tufts of dark hair."

It had been a long, exhausting day of travel. Tesha's scalp itched from a layer of dust lodged in her hair. She longed for a proper bath and dinner somewhere other than a camp stool. But Hattu's face glowed with an inner joy. As long as he would feel that way about the children *she* would have with him. Nerik was his first, but Tesha didn't want him to stay Hattu's favorite.

Hattu's first wife had died giving birth to Nerik. Hattu didn't say much about her except he owed her so much for giving him a son. His dead wife didn't seem to hold a spot close to his heart anymore, but Nerik did. And he should, but Tesha would not be third in their kingdom. She needed to come to Alpara with her full-fledged power on clear display, her place beside Hattu unquestioned. Two equal thrones and perhaps a stool nearby for Nerik. That's how she pictured it, even if stepping into the role of queen also terrified her. One had to do the terrifying things—especially the terrifying things.

A regal entrance that set the pattern for all to come did not involve lying prone and speechless in a wagon. The rest of her life couldn't be that. She'd overcome the curse, freed Hattu and his army. That had to count for so much, but not if . . .

Hattu had been full of stories about Nerik that evening by the fire.

"I'd grab a stick and pretend to parry his sword thrusts," Hattu had said. "One day I guess he got frustrated being so little, and he climbed up on a bench and then onto the table so that he could challenge me at my height. I pretended to be vanquished and tumbled to the floor. He liked that and declared himself king."

That had struck Tesha as revealing.

"Then I jumped up and hugged him," Hattu continued. "He still smelled so sweet. Why is it that we lose that honey scent when we grow up?"

Tesha remembered laughing. "Have I lost my honey scent?"

Hattu took her hand and kissed it. "Never."

That wasn't true on this filthy trip, but she had returned his kiss.

"That was when my dear son was an easy child to play with. He lost that belly and some of his sweetness as he grew. Sometimes he wanted to do things he wasn't old enough for, and I was so often pulled away."

Hattu's face lightened again. "But Marak filled in for me. He's always good with Nerik when the boy wants some ill-considered thing. Doesn't cause Nerik's anger to flare. I remember one time when they went hunting. Nerik had thrown the killing spear. It was a huge boar, an ugly thing with tusks that made me blanch at the idea of Nerik facing him. But Marak had kept him safe."

She'd commented about what a good friend Marak was. Nerik had been grown enough for hunting, and she didn't see why a boar should concern Hattu so much. All she needed was a "son" with a bad temper. Maybe he'd view her as a sister. She was good at that.

Not anymore. Daniti. *Daniti.* Tesha felt a tear slip from her eye into her hair. At least she could still cry. Her hand clenched into a fist of frustration.

Her fingers. They moved. She wanted to whoop with joy, but gently wiggling her fingers was good enough. *Thank you, Goddess.*

There'd been such yearning for his son in Hattu's face. "He's got the same broad chest as mine. A strong arm and excellent aim. He'll make a good warrior."

"He sounds like he's already a good warrior. You didn't consider bringing him east with you when you battled Pharaoh?"

"Against the Egaryans? Ishana protect him! Those were bloody battles. No place for a child."

"He's fifteen?"

"Hmmm . . . almost sixteen now."

"Am I a child?"

He'd looked so surprised. Not a hint of understanding. He could out-strategize any general, but he was not prepared for this. "You're my wife."

And fifteen years old. Old enough that most of her friends in Lawaza had been married before her. No longer a child. Nerik would not like being called a child. Maybe she could use that to win him to her side.

Or maybe he would find more reasons to dislike her.

"Did Nerik ask to come with you?" She hadn't been able to resist the question.

"Leave that be, Tesha. He whines about a lot of things that aren't good for him. I can make up for the time we were apart."

She'd asked several times about Nerik's childhood, what trusted nursemaid had minded him. She could ally with that servant to win him over. But Hattu avoided answering. He'd only said Nerik had been mothered quite enough. Hattu had been about to say more, but he'd lapsed into one of his dark silences. That servant must be dead and another sad subject. She saw in his eyes that he wanted to speak but couldn't. That *couldn't* was her father's fault, so she held in her resentment.

She worked her fingers until she could move them more easily. The day brightened, and the sky glowed pink along a horizon framed by mountains, shading to a pale blue above her. Stunted pines struggled to grow between outcrops of granite. The army column had climbed high up.

Kety leaned over her again. His eyes widened in happiness. "You now awake. I tell king?"

She smiled. She *smiled*. Her lips stretched wide and then wider. She opened and closed her jaw a few times. "I'm awake."

11

———

Kety propped Tesha upright by stuffing some rolls of canvas underneath her pillows. She tried to conceal how useless her limbs were, but Kety's fussing and frown showed he wasn't fooled.

"Don't tell the king. It will pass."

Kety pressed his lips together in disapproval, but he nodded. "King Hattu wishes to ask you."

Tesha sighed. "Not yet."

The wagon rattled along, and the narrow passage between peaks broadened out. The army progressed into a valley with a broad river flowing through it. Fields of grain stretched out on either side of the river. Tesha hadn't seen so much farming anywhere else in the mountainous Upper Lands. They passed villages of farmers' huts made of mud brick and twigs.

The city of Alpara stood on a peak above the slow-moving river the locals called the Green River. Tesha studied the water. It did have a green tone, and the fields were lush with barley and vegetable crops.

From her makeshift pallet, she saw only natural rock covering the mountain until they made their way farther through the valley. Then she noticed the fortification walls. Fashioned of cut stone, they clung to the cliff faces, interrupted by stretches so steep no other protection was needed. Several rings of these walls wound around the mountain. At the top, more squared stone rose into battlements.

Somewhere must be a palace, a less forbidding spot to live. She hoped. This was life surrounded by enemies. And there'd be traitors inside—the unidentified nobles who'd participated in the conspiracy to overthrow Hattu. She'd be locked in with them too.

She would need to sprout wings to reach her new home. That would be some good magic. She couldn't even walk.

Hattu rode in his chariot close by. He called to several scouts. "Make a complete circuit. Let's make sure last night's battle was the Paskans' last try." She'd heard him earlier sending out riders on their flanks and front. So far, the battle she'd slept through seemed to have finished off the Paskan threat to the capital, but where was Daniti? Hattu had sent out more than fifty scouts to search, but none had returned.

She listened as Hattu called over one of his commanders and they made plans for an even more extensive deployment of scouts. The commander would organize from inside the city, but they'd send out the first wave of men now, a hundred strong.

"There's too much ground to cover, but we have to find them," Hattu said to his officer. "Put as many skilled men on it as you can."

The officer agreed and rode away to implement the plan. Tesha prayed they'd succeed. *Bring Daniti back to me, Ishana.*

The army, along with the caravan of baggage wagons, wound around to the back side of the mountain, where a less precipitous slope made possible a road up to the fortress city. She fought the limpness that permeated her limbs and tried to will power into them. That was the problem, though. They'd been too full of power, and her own strength had flowed out with that borrowed force. How would she explain it to Hattu? She'd been a vessel, but not a passive one. An understanding had opened up in her and the knowledge remained, but that would be a secret between Ishana and herself. Without words, Ishana had made it clear that this divine gift could not be shared with anyone else, not even to speak of it. Tesha carried a power she could call on again, but it might kill her. This time it nearly had.

Tall walls rose ahead, formed from massive cut stones. Her wagon passed through the first gate, thrown open to welcome its king and army.

The wooden wheels bumped over a cobbled street that turned sharply to the left to climb the first in a series of switchbacks. This lowest area of the city surrounded her in close-packed mud-brick buildings. Families and workshops crowded into rooms in these buildings that rose with stepped-back stories two or three high, accessed by ladders. Common areas with brick ovens and open cooking hearths filled the narrow spaces between them. People leaned out dark doorways to watch the army's procession.

After three turns in the road, Tesha saw another defensive wall with towers and a second gate. She had noted multiple rings of walls from a distance, but up close they impressed her far more.

Despite the crammed-in feel of the streets she'd just passed through, the builders had left a wide, empty space below this wall. She smiled because it reminded her of Lawaza, where the open space left in front of the citadel walls had been filled with Ishana's beautiful gardens, but the purpose of this bare area was the same. Near defense walls, it left no shelter or hiding place for a secret attack. It would provide the defenders up high a clear view to strike the enemy. She wasn't a warrior, but she knew how to organize a city's protection.

She looked on either side at this second ring of her new city. The wagon barely fit between the houses on both sides of the narrow road. People stepped back into their doorways to make room as she approached. This neighborhood held somewhat grander homes, but still, the buildings accommodated the steep slope. None of them had the big courtyards and scale of her childhood home.

When she passed through another bronze-reinforced gate in a third thick stone wall, and then, after a few turns, a fourth, she began to feel uneasy. It made perfect sense to have an outer wall around a lower city and a second, far stronger wall around a citadel, but how many rings of protection did this city need? Did Paskans attack so often and so fiercely?

Another gate loomed.

Too soon she'd greet the people she would rule as queen and meet her new son, Nerik.

The road widened as they entered a marketplace square. Prosperous-looking shops edged the area with goods that tumbled out their doorways. This part felt more welcoming.

"Kety, call Hattu near." She breathed slowly to calm the trepidation that tangled her insides.

Hattu signaled the driver of her wagon to stop and brought his chariot as close beside her as he could in the square. "We're almost there. I thought I'd lost you. How are you? Both Kety and I worried."

"I'm improving, but . . . I wanted to show the capital their soon-to-be queen."

"You will. And the savior of their king and his soldiers."

"I can't walk. Or even lift my arms."

Shock passed over her husband's face. "What? How can . . ." Hattu's horses jostled, eager to continue with the other chariots and wagons. Hattu reined them in. "I have an excellent physician in the palace. You'll get better. Ishana gives you strength."

"Your capital has so many walls. It's intimidating."

"Alpara has many foes," Hattu said.

"No one could get through these defenses."

"You'd be surprised. They rarely do, but watch as we climb through the next ring. Then tell me what you see." A smile flickered on Hattu's face, breaking through the lines of exhaustion that cut deep around his eyes and brow.

Hattu let his horses carry on. Her wagon lurched back into motion.

The shadow of the towers on either side of the gate fell across her. Through open doorways on either side, she noticed the beginnings of stairways disappearing into the upper darkness. Once she passed through the gate, she glimpsed soldiers' heads behind the battlements along the wall above her. Dark slits slashed into the inner face of the wall created even more places for soldiers to send down arrows and spears upon anyone caught below.

Unlike the other levels, the bareness of this one stretched from one wall to the other with only the switchbacks of the road interrupting it. There were no buildings in this ring. She saw straw targets for archery practice, benches, racks to hold weapons, and other signs that the area served as a military practice field as well as a defense structured into the city.

Hattu pulled his chariot near again. "Well?"

"I would not like to be an enemy caught between these walls. This is more than the open space any city puts before its walls. If I could clap my hands together, I'd show what would happen to any foe stopped here. They would be smashed between the soldiers on either side."

Hattu laughed. "You noticed. I had this ring cleared, and we added access inside the walls. You saw the staircases inside the towers?"

She nodded.

"It's more than that, though. You'll like this part. I designed hidden passageways. It takes a local soldier who knows the tricks to navigate through the inner access, so even if the enemy kills the tower guards and makes their way inside the wall, they won't get far. The rest of the defending soldiers remain safe."

"Really? Like a giant puzzle?"

Hattu nodded. "When you are better, you can explore it. This field is useful for training my soldiers, and given how essential a standing army has been since I became king, I don't regret keeping this bare. My brother gave me the most unstable part of his empire to rule, and so I've adapted. The soldiers refer to it as the field of death. They don't mean theirs."

Tesha shuddered as she imagined the kind of slaughter that could happen here. If the Paskans knew of this "field," that alone would discourage attacks. But Hattu would keep this strategic trap secret.

"The palace and citadel are just above, through that final gate," Hattu said. They climbed the last turns of switchback.

Her palms were damp when her wagon reached the final gate. The guards peering down at the long procession of Hattu's army cheered the return of their king. They must also be inspecting the woman he brought back as queen. What a compelling sight she made, flopped on her back and in filthy traveling clothes.

Her wagon drew to a halt inside the final level of walls. Much of the army had already dispersed into barracks at earlier levels. Tesha scanned the crowd of citizens that had poured out of houses as the news of their arrival moved through the town. She'd have to make the best of this. Her arms and legs felt slack and far too heavy to lift.

One group stood out from the rest because of the richness of their clothes and the space the crowd allowed around them in the packed area. Two older men in fine robes stood at one side. Counsellors to Hattu? She wished he'd told her more about his inner circle here. Three women in the center wore elegant gowns and jewels. Tesha glanced at herself. The stickiness of the curse vapor had drawn a thick coat of dust to her practical but plain travel skirt and tunic. Tesha scanned for Hattu's son.

One of the older men hurried forward. Hattu jumped down from his chariot. Instead of greeting the nobleman rushing toward him, Hattu came and stood by her wagon to include her, even though she could not move. They understood each other.

The well-dressed courtier bowed to both of them. His face looked pinched with worry despite an extra chin and rolls of flesh. "King Hattu. A Paskan envoy arrived just before you did. He demands an audience, the arrogant wretch."

"They didn't waste any time," Hattu said in a voice that sounded more animal growl than human.

The courtier looked confused.

"They have kidnapped Marak and Priestess Tesha's sister," Hattu said. "They used sorcery to prevent the rescue."

"What? Sorcery? Marak's a captive?"

"I'll speak to this Paskan. I've got no choice. None of my scouts have returned with news." He turned to the wagon. "Tesha, this is Shatim, one of my most helpful advisors."

Shatim bowed.

"I am honored to meet you," she said. To Hattu, she added, "If we sent this Paskan envoy back to his people, would a scout be able to track him to Daniti and Marak?"

Hattu shook his head. "They won't be keeping them prisoner at any of the villages or where they gather for assembly. And that's where the envoy will go. The Paskans have always had secret places for their warriors to take cover after raids. I already sent the scouts to the hideouts we've found in the past, but . . ." He shrugged. "I've got scouts searching everywhere."

Over Hattu's shoulder, Tesha saw a young man break from the others—he had the same imposing chest as Hattu, and there was a clear resemblance in their faces. Nerik. Some strong emotion shadowed across the young man's face, and not a happy one. He squared his shoulders and walked toward Hattu.

"Father."

Hattu turned and drew the youth into an embrace. Nerik did not return the warmth of Hattu's clasp. Tesha's heart ached for her husband, although part of her quietly exulted. Nerik would lose his primary place if he acted surly in response to his father's love.

Nerik's eyes were as dark and almond shaped as Hattu's, and they were equally expressive as they darted between his father and Tesha. Interesting. So, he felt as apprehensive about this meeting as she did.

Hattu rested one hand on Nerik's shoulder and the other on Tesha's hand. "Nerik, this is Priestess Tesha, my wife and soon-to-be Queen of the Upper Lands."

Nerik's eyes ran over her body in a way she did not like. He bowed his head slightly. "We have talked about you a great deal, ever since word of Father's marriage came by messenger." He bowed his head slightly. "Your arrival has been much anticipated."

"Tesha, this is my son, the Crown Prince."

"May Ishana bless us all with happiness," Tesha said. That seemed a safe greeting.

Hattu briefly told Nerik and Shatim of their long night, Tesha's role, and the reason for her exhaustion. "It will be interesting to see if this Paskan is aware of the battle we fought against his fellow warriors last night. He may have set out before it. Frankly, that slaughter has weakened my ability to succeed with any ransom discussion. They'll be thirsty for revenge, and in no position to exact it except by killing the captives."

Tesha cried out, and Hattu murmured an apology.

"I thought my arrest in Lawaza was the worst I'd ever endure," Hattu said. "But I was wrong." Tesha squeezed his hand. He added, "For both of us." He lifted her out of the wagon. "I will be your legs and strength. You were mine inside that cursed cloud." He didn't look at her when he spoke. His voice came out scratchy. His throat must have been damaged by that dark vapor. She blinked to clear the gray haze her tired eyes saw edged around Hattu.

Tesha glanced at Nerik. Power came in many forms. This beginning with Hattu's son felt good enough. For now, she'd concentrate on freeing Daniti and Marak.

Farther away, next to the three women in elegant clothes, a younger boy jiggled from one leg to another while one of the women tried to restrain him. He shot out from under her grip.

"Uncle! Uncle!"

Hattu smiled as the boy barreled at him.

Nerik tried to block the child's approach. He caught the boy and shoved him back toward the women. "You weren't summoned."

Nerik certainly didn't want to share his father's arrival. Rude of him. Tesha couldn't guess who the boy was—or who those women were. Too fine to be servants, they seemed to expect to be greeted by the king, but they weren't free to come forward. Too much lurked unknown here, and Daniti's loss burned too painfully to face these other fears and confusions.

"Samsi, come here," Hattu said, ignoring Nerik's roughness. "Let me introduce you to my wife, Priestess Tesha."

Samsi leaned against Hattu while looking up at her.

"Careful, child, my arms are full. Tesha, this is my brother's younger son, Samsi. Muwatti placed him in my care a couple of years ago."

Tesha wondered at that, but now wasn't the time for an explanation. Surely a royal son would have a brighter future if raised in the center of power at the Great King's court, not removed to one of the less important corners of the empire.

The family group headed toward a stone and mud-brick structure at the top of the street. It must be the palace. Tiny slits of windows ran high up across the forbidding front. A wave of homesickness washed through Tesha. Daniti should be here to make this home.

Hattu tossed his chin to one side to point out an imposing building standing behind a gated courtyard. "That is the temple of the Stormgod, Alpara's main temple. Not as grand as Ishana's in Lawaza, but we keep altars for each of the gods there while we give preeminence to the lord of the sky." He smiled down at her. "I did make a special place for our goddess inside the palace."

They carried on toward a broad double door. "I hope you will like your new home."

The twists of tension binding Tesha didn't loosen.

12

As he climbed the stairs to his palace with Tesha in his arms, Hattu registered the deep exhaustion in his own body. Not the time for that. He ran through what ransom demands the Paskans were likely to make, what he could give, and how he could trick this envoy into revealing where they held Marak.

His palace, cramped and built into the mountainside, lacked the grandeur of the temple where Tesha had served. He feared she might be disappointed with her new home. They entered the main reception hall where he held court. The most impressive of the palace's rooms, it was spacious and high-ceilinged, with mosaic floors and frescoes. She'd like this part.

The familiar sight brought him joy. The darkness that had taken hold of him in that prison cell edged back when he saw the frescoes of his hall. Ishana dominated one wall, riding a battle chariot at the front of his soldiers. Opposite her, the winged sun disk that his family used as their royal insignia indicated how beloved they were to the Sungod, the All-Seeing one who loved justice. Below the royal seal, two priests were depicted making sacred offerings beside a tree of life. On both sides of his throne, he'd chosen to have painted two griffins as a sign of his power. They lifted their massive wings over crouched lion bodies and fierce eagle heads. Divine protection, justice, devotion to the gods, and kingly power. These symbols reassured him in warm reds and yellows, refreshing greens and blues. He gazed at the groups gathered to welcome them and smiled at his court.

Then he noticed the three women at the back of the hall. They must have hurried ahead. He'd ignored them outside. His heartbeat pummeled his ribs. *Not now.* Not while Tesha was ill. Not before he had a chance to explain their presence to her. He'd kept postponing that. He couldn't make the words come out. He'd tried several times. A huge mistake. The courage he found in battle failed him when it came to explaining those three, who, as though sensing his displeasure, slipped through the door that led to the women's quarters. He pressed Tesha close to his chest, although her body tucked against his jarred him for the first time in their marriage. Painful jabs registered down from his neck.

Hattu turned to Shatim, who had followed close behind. "Have the Paskan brought in." He said softly to Tesha, "Do you want to stay for these negotiations, or would it be better to bring you to your bed and send for the physician?"

She stopped gazing at her surroundings and locked on his face. He saw the determination that had won his heart in Lawaza. Even limp in his arms, she could muster strength.

"The goddess will restore me, not a physician. I'll stay. A chair with arms will do."

"We'll outsmart the Paskan envoy together," he whispered to her. Hattu directed a servant to bring a chair.

Tesha's face tipped up toward his, so close and intimate. He coughed as wriggling and scratching disturbed his throat. A smell like sour milk wafted up and he wrinkled his nose, shifting his gaze away from Tesha.

His reception room was designed for the assembly of large groups, with little furniture besides his throne. There was only one throne, and it was stone and without arms. Imposing and uncomfortable. Besides, he couldn't give it to Tesha and have no throne for himself.

He surveyed his court, *his* kingdom. The irritation in his throat cleared. The constriction in his chest loosened.

Hattu looked at Shatim. "I don't suppose the Paskan demands will be limited to treasure."

Shatim's frown sagged. "For Marak you'd empty your whole treasury if you had to, but they will not make it that simple."

Tesha said, "I'd empty the treasury for Daniti."

Shatim jumped a little at her comment, but then he bowed his head to her.

Hattu placed Tesha in the cedar chair a servant brought. Another servant tucked cushions around her with gentle care. She'd already won his household over to her side. It was her beauty. Even as disheveled as she was by all they'd gone through last night, she was irresistible. He stayed close to her, and she leaned her head against his side. He rested his hand on her shoulder, then coughed away another pricking sensation from his throat.

"They'll want territory, lots of it," Hattu said to Shatim. "And you know how my brother will react to that."

"Isn't the Great King ill?"

"Unfortunately, yes. We'll hold off asking his opinion."

"Cautiously, though," Shatim said. "Your brother isn't known for granting forgiveness after the fact."

One of Hattu's courtiers entered with a towering giant of a man. The Paskan envoy. Hattu felt Tesha quiver at the sight of him. She must think her sister had been captured by monsters.

Hattu leaned close and whispered in Tesha's ear. "They always send the biggest man they can. To intimidate us."

Tesha pulled back her shoulders.

The giant stood before them. His black beard and hooded eyes added to his fierceness.

The Paskan did not make obeisance. Hattu knew better than to stand on formalities. He wanted cooperation from this brute. He studied the man's face. Maybe not a brute. Cunning hid there. He glanced at Tesha. Did she see it also?

Hattu thrust out his chest, crossed his arms and stepped forward. "Your people have wrongly taken captive one of my men and a woman. You do not wish to bring the wrath of my army down on your villages and herds. Return them without doing any harm. Immediately. I would not like to be forced to seek revenge against your people."

Tesha's eyes widened in surprise at this gambit. She wouldn't know you had to threaten first with these Paskans. You couldn't look weak—like she did right now, despite her determination. She sagged into the chair. Worse, almost hidden by the arm of the chair and the folds of her skirt in her lap, she fidgeted limply with a dirty bit of thread. That wasn't like her. He should have sent her to rest.

In contrast, the Paskan, looked amused, damn him. "Go to war and you know both of the hostages will be killed—and we won't make it an easy death. But go ahead if you must. It would hardly be something new from you Hitolians. Stealing land and slaughtering innocents entertains you."

Silence fell over the group. Hattu knew he'd have to wear the man down just to get started. He scanned his courtiers and checked to see if Shatim would assist him. Shatim signaled with a small shrug—no help there. But he noticed his physician enter the reception hall, the only Hitolian in the room with a beard and that distinctive wide-eyed gaze—fixed on Tesha. Perhaps a different sort of help from him— Tesha's restored health.

The Paskan filled the silence first. "The woman we took is blind and not what we expected. But that man—I've faced him in battle at the head of your army. He's worth a lot to you. More than a bit of flesh like that one, if we'd gotten her." The Paskan tossed his head in Tesha's direction.

A ripple of anger started in Hattu's belly, but Tesha's face calmed him.

Perhaps it was just her exhaustion, but she showed remarkable restraint at the insult. The man could have asked about the weather.

Her blank expression made her look dull—definitely an illusion, maybe a trick to snare the brute. Even the odd fussing of her fingers, unable to hold onto that thread, added to the effect.

But still, Hattu wasn't sure what to say next.

The Paskan shifted his weight comfortably to one side and adopted a bored expression as if to show Hattu how meaningless his threats of attacks were. Not meaningless, since they reminded this ogre of the greater military might of the Hitolians. But if burning villages worked, the Paskans would have been finished off generations ago. Still, he couldn't hand over his lands to get Marak back.

"The blind woman you took," Tesha said. "She's mine."

What was Tesha up to? Her voice came out strong, but that twitching of her fingers—her debilitation showed. That must be what drew his physician to step so close. Tesha's hands held him transfixed.

"As you say, she's worthless," Tesha said to the Paskan. "Send her back to us. It's surprising your men couldn't tell a blind slave from a queen. Call it an act of good faith to get these negotiations going. You'll gain more than she's worth."

Free Daniti and leave Marak to die? *That's* her plan? It hurt Hattu's eyes to look at her. Did treachery make her glow? He pressed his eyes shut. Tesha must have a clever reason to propose this. She must. Why did this flush of anger at her feel right? Had he missed something? He barely heard the Paskan's reply.

"She's not a slave," the giant said. "If she were, that commander wouldn't have bothered to rescue her. Rode right into our hands, of course. You'll pay for the witch, whoever she is."

"He assumed your men had taken me, and that's who he went after. Not the blind woman."

The Paskan shook his head. "Not how I heard it. So, we have two valuable captives. Now for the ransom. Pull your garrisons out of our lands in the north between the Marashanda and Green rivers. Relocate the intruders who are farming on our territory. Give us back our homeland."

The Paskan demands were as bad as Hattu had anticipated. "If we are going to make progress with these terms, I'll need to send my advisers to discuss them with your tribe—with my commander present."

The giant laughed. "I'm not a fool. Discuss with me, here. I'll take word back." The man rubbed his beard. "You won't find where we're holding them. These are our mountains, after all, not yours. Despite this rock pile." He twirled his finger to indicate the palace.

"Your demands are absurd. You know that. So go onto something more realistic. I will give thirty measures of gold for the man and twenty measures of silver for the woman."

The Paskan chuckled. It wasn't a pleasant sound. "We'll take your gold and silver, but not without regaining our homeland also."

"Two minor human beings for all that territory you love to pretend is your homeland? In my past experience with Paskans, you never placed such a high value on any person's life."

The insults and offers continued back and forth. Tesha didn't speak again. She left it to him. Hattu began to force the Paskan to define the boundaries of the lands they wanted in more specific terms. If you draw a line, you can move that line.

Hattu gradually drove the line farther north within the Paskan's demands, a smaller slice off his brother's empire and a more forgivable one. He was aiming to push the territory he'd concede above one particularly holy city. He didn't control that city now, but he'd sworn an oath to Ishana to bring it back into the Hitolian realm. He would make no agreement that jeopardized that goal.

But the Paskan refused to budge far enough.

It was obvious the Paskan knew too well that Hattu pushed for lands he held only tenuously. A few scattered garrisons and farms that could be driven out if the Paskans committed enough raiders to it.

That didn't matter to Hattu. If he put a Paskan "homeland" into a treaty on lands so far south, weakly held or not, he would be giving their ridiculous claims a legitimacy he could never agree to.

They were stuck—closer to an agreement than when they started but still too far apart. Hattu's frustration mounted. He needed Marak free now.

The Paskan made a dismissive pucker of his lips. "I'll return to my tribe with your unreasonable demands. The assembly will no doubt laugh."

Hattu couldn't let him go yet. They needed more areas of agreement, some way to speed things along when this man consulted the assembly of his peers. The Paskan didn't care how long he held Marak and Daniti prisoner.

Tesha cleared her throat. Hattu turned to her in surprise. The Paskan looked even more taken aback.

"What precisely makes you want these lands? I mean, what will you do with them if you control them?"

The Paskan looked puzzled. "Do with them? We would put our herds to graze, plant some fields, build villages. Live on them. Why ask this?"

The Paskan's expression implied that Tesha was a simpleton and Hattu should keep his womenfolk silent. But Hattu thought he saw where Tesha was going this time around, and he had no intention of quieting her. She was finally contributing. A sneaky idea, but why not if it was against Paskans?

"The range of mountains you mentioned, the ones that lie north of whatever that city is that my husband spoke of . . ."

Hattu held in his smile. Tesha knew all about the loss of such a holy place, any priestess would. But she wasn't letting on that that particular city mattered. She understood the lands in dispute after she'd questioned him on the journey about the layout of his kingdom. The fight over the Paskan homeland, she'd insisted, was less about land and more about stubbornness.

"So," Tesha continued, "the lands north of that mountain range, near the Dark Sea, those could perhaps be held as Paskan lands both in name and control. The lands south of there, while staying under Hitolian control, well, ask your people if they would like to put their herds to graze there, plant fields, and build villages there nonetheless. All while living near villages of other peoples with whom they might trade their produce and wool. They also can enjoy the protection of our garrisons. I have gathered that the different tribes of

Paskans often war with each other. They steal and raid from each other. Perhaps your tribe would like the use of expanded territory where other Paskans will hesitate to cause such troubles. I don't know, perhaps herding your flocks and growing your food in safety is not what the men and women of your tribe really want. But as you said . . ."

The Paskan could not find words. Tesha's offer made sense, so it was hard for the man to refuse, and yet it gave him none of what he and the other Paskan warriors wanted: to once again put the Paskan name on their homeland—the whole territory of the Upper Lands with no exception. She offered the use but not the name. Tesha had laid a trap.

The majority of this envoy's tribesmen might see the advantage of it, and that was how Paskans ruled. No kings among them. This consensus system usually worked against negotiations, but with this idea of Tesha's, twisting what the Paskans partially had already but expanding a little more generously so they could thrive, might sound entirely satisfactory in exchange for two insignificant people. Especially if the women had a say, and they would, unofficially.

Hattu saw an advantage to looking at things through Tesha's eyes. She stripped the Paskan warriors of their pride, which wouldn't necessarily work in the long run, but the strategy might free Marak.

The Paskan's face darkened.

Hattu jumped in. "Now you have some ideas to discuss with your assembly. See what they think. Surely it is your obligation to represent this offer to them. We can see what they suggest in return. You will come back and we will continue."

The Paskan gave a curt nod. Paskan custom bound him as envoy to report fully. There were ways to let the whole tribe know if their envoy played untrue, and this man knew it. He might not like where they'd ended up, but he'd go forward honorably.

Hattu turned to study Tesha, his beloved. She gave him a weak smile. She'd gained them some progress. He felt pride in her.

He held onto that, pushing away the choking movement still inside him. That would pass. If he ignored it, it would pass.

13

Hattu pressed Tesha's hand between his. "Let me show you the women's quarters. You must be exhausted. We'll stay together in your quarters tonight."

She *was* more exhausted than she'd ever been.

Nerik and Samsi came forward. They'd waited at the side of the great hall during the negotiations with the Paskan. Nerik stepped in front of Samsi. "Father, how could Marak have been taken captive?"

"The Paskans took Tesha's sister. Marak pursued them alone before my men could follow."

"Her blind sister? He went alone? Why?"

Outrage burned in Tesha. Even her slack limbs felt scorched with it. "Because he values my sister. You don't think we should let Paskans kidnap our women, do you?"

Nerik's face flushed. "But—"

Hattu interrupted, "Marak assumed more soldiers would follow quickly. He only chased two men. If a much larger group hadn't caught up to them, he'd have freed her."

"So, it was your fault, Father? You didn't send help fast enough?"

"That's unfair," Tesha said. "The Paskans had scattered all our horses. This is a foolish argument. We must get Marak and Daniti back—that's what matters."

"Don't call me foolish."

Tesha was too exhausted to navigate this boy's bristles. "Excuse me, but I need to rest."

She looked up at Hattu and then blinked a couple of times. Sometimes her vision was blurred by a gray haze. The continuing effects of the curse, she supposed, but she did not want to see a dark cloud around Hattu after what they'd been through.

Hattu turned to Nerik and Samsi. "Tomorrow we'll spend time together." He lifted Tesha into his arms. "Let me show you where I sacrifice to Ishana."

"Oh, yes. Let's go there." She needed her goddess in this new home.

Hattu carried her through a hallway and up a staircase. They came onto a broad, open air terrace, and she gave a wordless cry of delight. Hattu smiled down at her. This sanctuary was nothing like Ishana's temple back home.

"Not the imposing temple of Lawaza, but it has its own grandeur," Hattu said.

Tesha pressed her head against his chest and admired Ishana's view of a towering peak. Lush pines packed the lower flanks. The upper summit of gray boulders looked as if giants had laid them there to hold up the heavens.

"It's stunning. The holiest of places—a mountaintop. It's as if you gathered it inside the palace to be Ishana's home."

Hattu kissed her forehead. "I knew you'd understand."

A rectangular basin took up a large portion of the terrace. Ashes and bone fragments indicated its role as the place for burnt sacrifices. An altar in a protective niche had been carved from the bedrock. On it stood the goddess, carved from a creamy white stone. She held a bundle of arrows in one hand. She held out the other hand, open and palm up, offering her worshippers something they could not see but surely felt—love. Her ripe breasts lay bare above a layered skirt falling in delicately chiseled pleats. Gold leaf adorned the tips of the arrows and her rosebud nipples. Tesha sighed with the beauty of her goddess.

"I felt Ishana in this place when it was only a narrow ledge," Hattu said. "She showed me in my dreams how to expand it into a proper home. Even when the wind howls and snow banks against the walls, I can hear her speak to me in this sanctuary."

Hattu pressed a kiss on her lips. His eyes were full of tenderness. His arms pressed her close. It had been a long journey, but now in her new home, gratitude for their love replenished her soul.

"Blessings on Ishana that she brought you into my heart," Hattu said. He gave her a wry tweak of his eyebrows. "She gave me exactly the wife I needed—strong and beautiful."

She savored the joy of this moment. He would get better now that he was in his home. The fits would settle away.

Tesha closed her eyes and waited for the goddess's presence to fill her. Then she prayed for Daniti's safety and for the understanding to be a good queen.

Hattu carried her down the stairs, and they entered a warren of narrow hallways with cramped rooms jutting off at odd angles. She hadn't expected a palace to be so dark and winding.

The palace had been built into the rocky contours of the mountain itself. As they climbed a series of stone steps, Hattu pointed out the storage rooms that housed his treasury, and the hall that led to the wing containing workshops of metalworkers, weavers, and other essential laborers for the palace.

Tesha couldn't help a shudder of dismay at the feel of this new home.

Hattu carried her down a hall to the women's quarters.

The women's reception hall had a high ceiling and a round, central hearth. She liked the pretty carved chairs and side tables but not the dust that covered them. The frescoed walls were dark from hearth smoke.

"No one has cleaned this room."

Hattu glanced around. "I guess not. You'll see to all that."

Tesha was still taking in her surroundings when she felt Hattu stiffen. She followed his gaze. The three women in showy clothes she'd seen earlier had entered the hall. They bowed to Hattu.

The one who appeared to be the oldest, about Hattu's age, said, "Welcome home, husband."

Husband? What did this woman mean?

Quickly Hattu placed Tesha in one of the chairs. His face had gone dark with anger. "My *wife* is here, Priestess Tesha, soon to be Queen of the Upper Lands. It is not your place to come forward to greet me or her until you are called for."

Tesha's relief at Hattu's response did not remove her horror. These women had some claim to her beloved, whatever he said. Why were they part of his life?

"These women will attend you," Hattu said.

Tesha frowned. "Attend me? Why are—"

"You know that the Great King and the other men of the royal family must have . . ." Hattu stopped.

"Have?"

"The need for children of royal blood is too great—generals, vassal rulers, wives to foreign kings. One woman can't . . ."

"So these women *are* your wives?"

"No, I've never let them use that term." He glared at the woman who had greeted him. "I'll have no secondary wives."

"They're concubines?" Tesha had heard that term used of the Great King's many women. They didn't have much status, but they were usually referred to as secondary wives, regardless of what Hattu had said. The Great King, yes, but for Hattu? She had never heard this idea that *all* the men of the royal family had concubines. She had assumed only the Great King himself did. The noblewomen in her circle had whispered with horror about the many wives of the Great King. She was quite certain they'd never included the Great King's younger brother in their gossip. Why hadn't Hattu told her?

Hattu lifted her hand in both of his. "I know this is unfamiliar. Not like your father."

"Not like any family I grew up with. Why didn't you warn me?" *Before I married you.* The words seared through her mind. Her sister gone, her body barely alive, and now this? How could Hattu have done this to her?

Hattu backed up a step. He started to cross his arms over his chest, then dropped them. "I tried. I wanted to."

She blinked again as the illusion of a dark mist around Hattu returned. Would she ever be allowed to sleep?

He turned toward the three women. "They will attend you. Like servants."

He pointed to the older one who had claimed him as her husband. Her face was heavily lined in downward furrows around thin lips and eyes narrowed by surrounding folds of skin. Her veil bound her hair out of sight and made a harsh frame that emphasized the hardness in her face.

"This is Agat. She took over the care of Nerik when my young wife died during his birth. She already had an infant and nursed both children. She has been loyal to my son ever since."

The woman's eyes narrowed even more. "I have cared for Nerik as my own son, and I have run your household—as a wife does. Even when you broke your promises to me."

Tesha would never gain this woman's help winning over Nerik. She wished Hattu would look at her, but he focused on these women. He needed to face *her*.

He pointed to the next woman, very young and with her gaze held to the ground. The flush on her face indicated her discomfort with this scene. Her thin frame seemed to pull in on itself as if wishing to disappear.

"This is Pasul."

Pasul dipped her head and chest low in a bow. "It is an honor to be introduced, Priestess."

Tesha murmured a greeting. At least this one was polite and respectful.

Her husband pointed to the last woman. "And this is Ija."

Ija looked directly into Tesha's face, and for a moment a flash of something in her expression made Tesha draw back into the chair, but the look passed so quickly that Tesha thought it must have been a trick of the dim light in this room. Only some of the shutters had been pulled open on the clerestory windows above them, and the afternoon was drawing to evening.

This woman was unusually pretty, even more so than Pasul. But Ija bowed respectfully.

Hattu patted Tesha's shoulder. "These women have provided my court with children, as I said. They do not always know their place, but I count on you to make that clear to them as my wife and queen, ruler with me of this kingdom."

The shock of these women didn't feel real to her. She'd noticed many awkward silences during the three months she'd been married to Hattu. It was her father's fault, Hattu's inability to talk freely as he had been so good at doing before imprisoned. But she'd never suspected this was one of the things he couldn't speak about. The intimacy of her life with Hattu could not fit in the same world as these women.

They had expectations of his attention, clearly. She shifted enough so that Hattu's hand fell from her shoulder.

Hattu waved dismissively at the three women. "It will serve you well to be gracious to the new Queen of the Upper Lands, who is now in charge of the women's quarters and your lives. Now go."

The one named Agat emitted a sharp gasp. She pinned Tesha under a scowl. "I warned Nerik that you'd be overbearing." As she turned on her heel, Agat muttered, "She's not the queen yet. A woman must first be chosen and then crowned. Who knows better than I?"

Tesha studied the other two. They had frozen at Agat's words. Bitterness bubbled up in everything this woman said. The others hadn't expected this stern reception from Hattu. Tesha thought they would have done well not to let Agat speak for them if they did not wish to be tossed out so unceremoniously.

No one was going to greet Hattu as husband but her. And no one was going to threaten her as Agat had.

"You are not Hattu's wife. I am."

Agat turned back toward Tesha. "I am clever. I run Hattu's household, but I also do far more. He comes to me for advice about the kingdom. You think you're different from me? What makes a wife not a wife? Do you think it's because he holds you close? Can't get enough of your body? Look at those two. Quite beautiful. So was I once. And yet, here you are. One more woman. A wife? Enjoy your husband."

Before Tesha could put this dreadful woman in her place, Agat pushed through the curtain that separated the concubines' side of the women's quarters, and the other two scurried after her.

"I'm sorry for Agat's rudeness," Hattu said. "She's not my wife. You are."

But what made Tesha different than Agat? Good question. Agat said she was clever, an advisor. She knew about needing another's body close to you. How did this woman understand Tesha so well?

14

Inside the hideout cave, Daniti awoke with a start. A man's rough hand pressed against her mouth to silence her and another grabbed her skirt, pulling it up to her waist. Her bareness jolted like a sword slicing her open from neck to groin. She thrashed away, but he tangled his fingers in her pubic hair and yanked her hips toward him. He threw his weight on top of her, his flesh coarse and hairy. Beast, monster. His stench choked her.

She kicked her leg that wasn't pinned under his body and bit the fingers digging into her lips. Sourness coated her tongue, then a gagging thickness of blood, but his hand gripped harder over her mouth and cut her lips against her teeth. He covered her nose. No air. No air.

Other movement. Someone else. The weight of the monster lifted from her. She pulled in air. The thud of a body hit the ground.

Marak rescued her. He and the man scuffled near her. She pulled down her skirt and rolled away from them, bringing her knees under her.

Marak moaned in pain. His leg wound, the strain. The fighting men flipped toward and away from her. Fists met flesh. A strangled sound, not Marak's. Marak choked her attacker.

Other Paskans came close and made noise in coming. They brought a blur of light that must be a torch. Bright enough she could discern a dim glow. The light plunged toward the men fighting on the ground. She heard Marak's cry.

"I've got him," a Paskan voice said. "Can I kill him now?"

"We have our orders. She's worthless, he's not."

"What were you thinking taking her so close to the Hitolian? You're an idiot. Drag her outside if you need to."

"Who would have thought the Hitolian would bother fighting over her? Cursed blind thing. I wouldn't touch her, would you?"

"That blank whiteness in her eyes. She's a witch. I want sons. I'm not uncovering my balls near her."

"He's not as incapacitated by his wound as I assumed, but it looks like he got the worst of this fight." Someone spat.

The men left her and Marak.

She heard someone stir the fire and prop open the door for the smoke. Unlike the first night, the Paskans who guarded them had now lit a fire inside the cave, although they'd let it die down and closed up before stretching themselves out in front of the door as they had before.

"You, keep watch. No one goes near them. Wake me for the second watch."

A new watchfulness. Even less chance for her and Marak to escape. And more reason to. She'd thought the long, terrified day of waiting to hear if Hattu's men would find this hideout had been bad enough.

Daniti crawled through the scattered straw until she felt Marak's leg. She pulled back her hand. "Did they wound you anew?"

"Not much. I wish I'd killed him."

"I do too."

"Did he . . . Was I quick enough?"

She couldn't speak.

"It wasn't Riam," Marak whispered. "I expected this from him."

"Tesha did something. He must hate her . . . and us." Daniti had never understood what Tesha had done to Riam that day she'd protected their mother from the villain.

"Are you all right? I saw blood on your face before they took the torch."

"I'll be fine." She heard the lie in her voice. Marak would too.

Daniti reached out until she could lay her hand on Marak's arm. She pressed and then withdrew her hand, hoping he understood.

Terror pulsed in her limbs and twisted her heart. The weight and the pelt of flesh shoved against her wouldn't leave her. Rescued and not rescued. Her bones crawled with revulsion.

Marak didn't say anything else. She heard the rhythm of his breath, soft and regular beside her. She let it in, and it gradually replaced the terror.

15

Tesha sobbed into her pillow. That morning, she'd gotten up and dressed, ready to do something, anything to help bring her sister back safely. But Hattu had raced off to an urgent council with his military commanders, the ones left to him since Marak's capture. He hadn't thought to bring her with him. She didn't really know what ruling as a queen involved. She would have liked to listen to this council and learn more. It had something to do with Paskans, so maybe she could have contributed to a plan to free Daniti.

Her legs were still shaky. She had to lean on someone's arm to walk. It wasn't easy for her to go anywhere. But Hattu running off without her and without saying anything had started the tears and they wouldn't stop.

Her new life was not—

She shuddered at complaining about anything while Daniti faced Paskan captivity, but the tears poured down anyway.

How could Hattu have said nothing about those women? How could he have thought she didn't need to know? People didn't talk openly about the royal concubines, the ones the Great King had—not her friends, anyway. They did gossip, just not about how apparently every man of the royal family partook of this "necessary" custom.

Hattu had betrayed her. He had no right not to tell her before she married him. He could not assume she somehow knew about the women who called themselves his wives. They did call themselves that. It didn't matter what he said. He had children by them. They lived in his home. What had he thought she would do? Politely ignore his cruel silence and pretend it was all just fine? Other women in his bed? Really?

And this place, this *palace*—would every moment of her life be etched with fear of Paskans? It was a dark, cramped fortress that Hattu called home. The palace didn't even have a bathing room. There weren't any springs on the part of the mountain where the palace had been built. She'd have to go somewhere else to get clean.

She was tired and her heart was broken. Her sister was in grave danger. At least that giant Paskan said Daniti was still alive and they wanted ransom for her. That meant they wouldn't kill her or hurt her, didn't it? They were Paskans, so they might do anything. In fairness, she'd met one Paskan that Hattu had negotiated with in Lawaza. That Paskan wouldn't have killed or hurt a captive. He'd hated Hattu because he thought Hattu had hurt his tribe's women and children. Maybe Daniti would be kept safe until they could negotiate her release.

Tesha pulled on the thread around her neck, slipped Daniti's vial of perfume out from under her gown, and rubbed its surface. She'd put it back on this morning. She had to.

"Lady Ishana, bring my sister back safely," Tesha whispered and kissed the vial.

A foolish fancy, her charm for Daniti's safety, but she couldn't let go of it. She hadn't shown the vial to Hattu. He felt bad enough about not saving Daniti and Marak. She'd kept it secret.

Her new life was full of strangers and hostility, and she had no one on her side. Even Hattu felt distant. For the first time since they married, she and Hattu had not made love last night. Her slow recovery, his exhausting battles. Excuses abounded. But a suspicion snaked in that she couldn't push out—before he had joined her in her rooms, had Hattu pacified those angry women? Perhaps one or more of those women had enjoyed the contact Tesha herself had craved and not received.

She didn't like sleeping in this chamber that hadn't been used since his young wife's death many years ago. To live where her predecessor had died in childbirth frightened her. Her hand rested on her belly. She might already be heading toward that same dangerous process. It worried her that Hattu had gone for so long without needing to fill this part of his palace, the part intended for a true wife.

Henti kept coming in and patting her back, trying to soothe her. She had deployed three serving women to clean Tesha's receiving hall and sleeping chamber. "Scrubbing away the ghosts" Henti called it.

Tesha did find it cheering to see all around her bed the newly glistening squares of polished stone in alternating colors of tan, red and green. It reminded her of the Sphinx and Griffin board. Banishing the stale, abandoned feel of these rooms helped, but the overwhelming sense of looming disjointedness still haunted her. The tears ran down her cheeks into the damp pillow.

Henti came in again and rubbed her back. "Now, now, things will get better. Dry those tears, child. I've got the servants washing down the walls to brighten up the reception hall."

Tesha raised her head. "The frescoes? Did you tell them to rub the walls with pieces of bread first to remove the worst of the smoke? I don't want them to ruin the images."

"I have them doing exactly that. Just as you had the servants do back home." Henti smiled encouragingly.

"Are they using very clean water afterward and soft wool? They make such a fuss about water in this place. Don't let them spread dirty water over the frescoes."

"I had to send for a boy to carry them fresh buckets of water, but they've got it right, Priestess. There are very pretty dancing women and flowers under all that soot. You'll be so pleased."

That was all very well. Henti was sweet and her familiarity was a balm this morning, but Tesha sank her face back into the pillow. Her marriage felt broken, and her sister—how would they ever rescue

Daniti? This strange place would never be home until her sister was here at her side.

The tears welled up again. Henti handed her a clean handkerchief and she blew her nose.

"All this crying is just wearing you out." Henti stayed at her side, one hand on her shoulder.

Waves of uncontrollable sobs rolled up inside her. She never felt this way. She never gave up, but she felt helpless and friendless.

"I'll send for that little Egaryan fellow, the groom Kety. You and he had a good talk in the wagon. He might cheer you up."

Henti rose. Tesha let her go.

16

"Kety's here to speak to you. He's brought something for you. You need to get up and dry those tears. I can't bring a groom into your sleeping chamber."

She wasn't sure what getting up would accomplish, but Henti had done her best. She sat up.

Henti straightened Tesha's veil and dabbed at her face with a handkerchief. "That's better." Henti wrapped a warm shawl around her. Even on a spring morning, her quarters in this northern land were chilly.

Tesha rose and let Henti support her to a chair in her reception hall. The color in the frescoes was startlingly bright now.

On the other side of the room, the midnight blue curtains that led into the concubines' part of the women's quarters twitched. The moving bands of yellow trim edging the dark curtains caught Tesha's eye. That was where that Agat and the other two had disappeared last night. Tesha wished they'd fallen into a bottomless pit, but instead they were spying on her through the curtain. The decoration carved into the wooden frame around that opening mocked her. Above the fluted pilasters on either side, lively dolphins played across the top of the lintel. The sea waves painted around the creatures looked suspiciously like bedding, and Tesha could imagine those women in a different romp, laughing at her.

Tesha beckoned to Henti and whispered into her ear, "Tell those women not to eavesdrop at that curtain. They must use whatever other entryway their quarters have and stay far away from my reception hall. I will not be spied on."

Henti nodded with a grim, thin-lipped expression.

Tesha looked around for Kety. The Egaryan groom lingered in the doorway, waiting for her to signal he should enter.

Tesha turned to the skinny, undersized man. Even with that funny linen head wrap, Kety had an entirely unimposing appearance. Perhaps that was what made him calming. She'd insisted he add a tunic over his loin wrap so he was properly covered and kept warm. He wasn't in hot Egarya anymore.

She motioned him into the room.

He bowed and held out his hand to give her something.

"What is this?" A gift from a slave? She took the small leather sack.

"Make to sleep. In Egarya for my children. For you, make difficulties in new home go."

Tesha thanked him. She opened the sack and sniffed the dried yellow flowers. Chamomile. "I'm sure this will help me."

Kety had never mentioned that he had children in Egarya. How his loss must ache. She shouldn't let her own troubles overwhelm her so. Kety's presence reminded her about something.

"Do you have Kurala with you somewhere? I forgot about him when we first got here with all that happened, but Henti hasn't seen him. I figured he must be with you, pouting about Daniti and eating all the food he can convince you to give him."

Lines bunched up around Kety's eyes and brow. "I not see bird-cat-deer-bat."

"You haven't?" Not Kurala lost also.

"Bird-cat-deer-bat flies. Loves Daniti. Maybe fly to Daniti?"

"Oh, do you think so?" The idea hadn't occurred to her. A tiny bit of hope.

"He not here."

"Maybe he's helping her. Maybe he can show us where she is."

"If he find you."

When Henti returned from the concubines' quarters with an even grimmer expression, Tesha told her to bring word about Kurala to the officer organizing the scouts' search. They should be on the lookout for him and bring him back.

"Is there anything else we should tell the soldiers about Kurala?" Tesha asked Kety.

"No. Soldier not talk with him like sister."

"She doesn't talk to Kurala. She just says that. She understands what he wants, so it seems like she can hear him."

Kety shrugged. Henti hurried out to take the message to the scouts.

Hattu's voice carried to them, a loud interaction with Nerik and Samsi. He sounded happy.

During her brief conversation with Hattu before sleep, she'd learned why Samsi lived in Alpara. Before leaving for his showdown with Egarya, Great King Muwatti sent Samsi to Alpara to protect him from their horrible stepmother. Neither Muwatti nor Hattu had ever liked the woman their father married late in life, but since their father's death, she'd become decidedly noxious. She had given birth to two sons before the old man died. Now she had designs on the throne for those sons, even though by law of succession Muwatti's own children would inherit. But Samsi and his older brother, the Crown Prince, were a concubine's offspring, not a first wife, so they were vulnerable to being passed over at the prodding of this ambitious woman. Muwatti had feared she might conspire against his sons if he was wounded or killed in the Egaryan war. He'd insured one son's safety by sending Samsi to Alpara, even while his Crown Prince stayed in the capital to inherit the throne if Muwatti died in the war.

Tesha clenched her jaw. Concubines and their consequences seemed to be everywhere in her new life. Worse, if Nerik based his view of stepmothers on this harmful woman, no wonder he behaved so cooly toward her.

As Hattu entered, Kety drew back against a wall as a good servant should.

Her husband's face clouded when he saw her. That strange darkness furled around him again before vanishing behind his usual smile.

"No good news," Hattu said.

"I just sent Henti off to tell the scouts to keep an eye out for Kurala," Tesha said. "He's missing. Maybe he found Daniti and is trying to get back to us. He could show us where she is."

"Your pet? How would he find her to begin with? And lead us back? You shouldn't bother the scouts with this."

That gray fog reappeared momentarily around Hattu. She shook her head. "Kurala is smart. He'll have a hard time traveling so far, but he might have found her."

"Well, Henti will have told them. Don't fuss about this more."

She wasn't fussing. Kurala could be very useful. He might get distracted by hunger, but he loved Daniti. She turned to Nerik and Samsi. "How are you today?"

Samsi smiled. He looked around the room and came to stand next to Tesha's chair. "You made it nice in here."

Tesha patted Samsi's arm. "Thank you. Everything was filthy. Rooms need proper care on a regular—"

Nerik interrupted, "Did Agat say you could do this to her reception hall?"

Tesha wanted to slap Nerik. "This is my hall."

Samsi backed toward the door.

Hattu grabbed Nerik's shoulder. "Be respectful to your new mother."

"She's not my mother."

Samsi turned and ran out.

Tesha was alarmed by the bitter look Nerik gave his father. "I will be mother to many of Hattu's sons and daughters if Ishana grants my wishes. But you and I are close in age, and you need only view me as a friend. I can be that much to you."

"No, you cannot." Nerik's face was red, his shoulders thrust back.

"You are a sorcerer. You should be put to death. At the barracks, I heard what you did. The soldiers say you used magical powers."

Tesha rose from her chair, her legs steady beneath her. "Priestesses are commanded to remove curses. I prayed to Ishana, and she sent her power into me to free your father and his men. Divine power, no magic of mine." Nerik could not be allowed to call her a sorcerer. She was a priestess. None of them needed to know that she could access the magic buried in the world.

She reached for Hattu. He stared at Nerik, turned away from her. She blinked several times.

It was as if she saw Hattu far in the distance with the setting sun behind him, blurring the edges of his form and casting him into shadow. But he stood right beside her. A trick of the eye. She'd learned from Daniti not to trust the quick impressions of sight. She squeezed her eyes tight and then opened them wide. The effect disappeared. Fortunately, Hattu no longer showed signs of that cough that'd lingered after the horror on the mountainside. They would come through this together. She wouldn't let Nerik say otherwise.

Hattu stood next to her, but the words of support she expected did not come.

"I saved you, Hattu," Tesha prompted. "Tell your son. You were suffocating."

"How did you know that?" Hattu asked. "I don't understand."

"Ishana showed me. The goddess always stands by you. In this trial as in your previous troubles."

Hattu nodded. "You drove away the curse and freed me." He sounded like he was persuading himself. A look of pain crossed his face, and he rubbed at the base of his neck, first one side and then the other.

Tesha stepped closer to him. He drew back and his nose wrinkled. She rested her hand on his arm. This, of all things, they had to agree about. "Ishana freed you. Not only you, but your soldiers—they all report the same." Tesha turned to Nerik. "You misunderstood what Hattu's men meant. They are grateful to me. To the goddess."

Hattu shook himself as if clearing an unwelcome thought. "As you should be," he said to Nerik. "You nearly lost your father. Be glad Ishana loves Priestess Tesha so much."

"If it's true," Nerik muttered.

Tesha leaned against Hattu, thankful he understood. The experience had been so disorienting. She hadn't told him what she had heard and felt. Too much of it seemed forbidden by the goddess to speak about.

Through a gap in the door curtain, she saw an eye peering. Not again. The hostility from Nerik and those women was Hattu's responsibility.

Nerik's stance hadn't relaxed. "Father, we need to hurry to the city gate. You have to send off your troops. You should do your job as king, not listen to this woman."

Hattu stiffened. "You should speak to me with more respect."

"Troops?" Tesha asked.

Hattu turned back to her. "An unusually large force of Paskans have invaded north of the city. They haven't raided this close to Alpara for years. I have to stop them decisively. I've ordered out most of my troops to drive them back."

"Are you going with your army?"

"No. They have a fine commander. Things are too unsettled here." He turned to Nerik. "You can see off the men."

Nerik's eyes narrowed. "They'll want you, not me. You've never given me command of the troops. You've made sure they don't feel any loyalty to me, but that will change."

"Of course it will. I'll make up for the time we've been apart. You'll hold command in time."

Tesha worried that Hattu missed part of Nerik's hurt, but Nerik's hostility toward his father puzzled her too.

"When you were my age, you were Chief of the Royal Bodyguard." Nerik's voice rose almost to a shout.

"And I made foolish errors because I was too young. Do you want to carry the burden of mistakes you cannot undo?"

"But you let Agat's son go with the troops. Why does Luwa get to fight Paskans? He's only two months older than I am. We're both your sons. You trust him but not me, never me. Shatim treats me like a real king, but you never do."

"Shatim? He's a fine advisor, of course. I'm glad he's respectful to you."

"He actually listens to me. He's not just some empty advisor to me the way he is to you. He's my friend. You can't even act like my father—"

"Of course I treat you like my son. That's why I didn't send you out today. I cannot risk your life. You are the heir to the throne of Alpara."

Nerik muttered something that sounded like "hardly." Tesha had seen dogs bristle up their neck fur so they'd look more threatening. If Nerik had fur, he'd be similarly puffed up.

"You'll never let me become a warrior. You like being the only one the soldiers look up to."

Hattu waved his hand dismissively and turned away.

This quarreling between father and son didn't serve either of them well. On the journey north, Hattu had spoken with such yearning of making up for lost time with his son.

"There must be many duties for those left defending the city." Tesha had no idea what those duties might be, but if Nerik grumbled less, he'd get more attention from his father. She turned to Hattu. "Couldn't Nerik take on those duties?"

Hattu murmured something about seeing to that, and Nerik actually smiled for a moment.

Her maidservant Henti slipped back into the hall and gave Tesha a nod. That much done, if the soldiers paid any attention to her suggestion about finding Kurala.

Tesha encouraged Hattu to take Nerik to see off the troops. "After that, perhaps you could practice sword fighting together. You talked of it on the journey here."

Nerik looked surprised at this encouragement, but not particularly pleased. An impossible young man. Tesha crossed her arms over her chest.

Hattu's eyes lit up. "Have you learned how to drive your sword under a shield?" He led Nerik out of Tesha's hall.

"You never taught me anything, and you took the best swordsmen with you."

"I'll teach you now."

17

A knock on the doorframe startled Tesha out of a daydream. She'd imagined the troops that Hattu had sent to counterattack the invading Paskans had returned with Daniti and Marak. Not, unfortunately, what they'd been sent out to do, but she'd nonetheless let the idea grow in a reverie. She'd hugged Daniti so tight, and for a moment it felt more real than this cold hall in the women's quarters.

Tesha turned to see who had knocked. Henti, always attentive to her duties, stepped up and greeted the visitor.

Tesha had seen this bearded man in Hattu's reception hall while they'd negotiated with the Paskan envoy. He'd caught her attention because he came so close and watched her with such intensity. Now she'd find out who he was.

She straightened in her chair and let Henti announce him. She was almost the queen, after all. Her coronation would come soon, surely. In her mind rang the spiteful words of that woman who claimed Hattu as her husband—Agat, that was her name. *She's not the queen yet. A woman must first be chosen and then crowned. Who knows better than I?*

Tesha would remind Hattu to arrange her coronation.

"The court's physician, Lord Utar," Henti announced.

A physician—that explained his interest the day before, since her impairment had been apparent when Hattu carried her into the court.

The tall gentleman bowed. His large brown eyes, surrounded by curly black hair and a beard, gazed intently at her. A physician should study a patient, but this look bored into her like a pig rooting for scraps.

"You suffered injury on the journey to Alpara," he said. "I've come to see if I can be of assistance."

"Thank you. I am recovered." Tesha rose and stepped toward him to demonstrate. "As you can see." She didn't want questions about the Paskan curse and her role in breaking it.

"I did not hear how you were injured."

No doubt he had heard enough.

"Ishana sometimes commands her priestesses to perform rites that challenge our strength. But all is well now."

"A rite?"

Tesha smiled politely and did not answer.

"The soldiers describe a curse that swallowed them up in darkness."

"Removing curses is an essential part of any priestess's training."

"I've never heard of a curse that struck so many men all at once. No ordinary rite would have removed it."

"Did your studies as a physician include curse removal? I thought only priestesses were entrusted with that knowledge."

"I do not have your training, of course. But the health of the soldiers is my concern in such unusual circumstances."

Silence clogged the air like the smell of rotten fish. She'd keep those unusual circumstances to herself. She had removed a curse—the proper duty of a priestess, as long as no one knew the depth of magic she had employed. No curse rite taught to the priestesses included what she had actually done.

"Thank you for checking on my health. I will let King Hattu know of your consideration. As you can see, I am well. Others in the city must be in need of your care."

"There is another matter," Utar said. He glanced at Henti as if to invite Tesha to dismiss her maid for privacy's sake.

Tesha ignored this signal. Henti would always be on her side, and her presence gave this disturbing visit propriety. As to those spying concubines, she glanced at the curtain but saw no sign of them. Henti kept watch.

"Your unusual power in removing the curse is not all that concerns me. This morning a group of soldiers told me stories of troubles with our king. A kind of madness that he began to suffer in your presence. These reports gave an even greater significance to what I observed yesterday."

So she and Hattu had not sufficiently concealed his prison-born terrors. His reputation had already suffered. She'd have to help repair that damage. She'd dreaded talking openly with Hattu about his fits, but that might now be necessary. The greater danger of the curse had almost driven that worry from her. Perhaps the physician could help Hattu.

"When you discussed terms with the Paskan envoy," Utar went on, "I noticed something you hid unsuccessfully. You held a gray thread and tied it in specific knots—or tried to. A weakness in your hands prevented the completion of your spell. The Great King's laws forbid such magic for good reason. You have been using magic on King Hattu—that is the source of his madness. I do not yet know why you are harming my king in this way, but it is my job to stop you."

Tesha's legs gave way, and her pelting heart seemed to drive her to the floor. Henti caught her and helped her into her chair.

This man spoke lies—she only helped Hattu—but he recognized that she used magic, and she'd hidden that magic from Hattu. It would be a problem if he learned of it from this hostile man. Overall, magic was forbidden on penalty of death, but her knot-tying was permissible for priestesses. The problem lay in the generations that had passed since the Great Kings had granted this dispensation. Now any hint of magic panicked the current Great King. If this situation reminded him of the priestesses' continuing use of magic, he would abolish it. And he might lash out at her, ignoring the traditional protections he certainly did not agree with.

If she did not persuade this physician that she posed no danger to Hattu—quite the reverse—his misunderstanding of what she did could be fatal to her. She pressed her hand against her heart to slow the frantic battering inside.

"You don't believe what you say. If you did believe such a terrible thing of me," Tesha said, "why say it only to me? You aren't protecting Hattu very well." This physician chose a private challenge as if they could settle this between them, and it appeared they shared the same goal of protecting Hattu. "You can't even convince yourself I've done Hattu harm. I love Hattu more than anyone."

"If the people believe he is under the control of a sorcerer, he will not be our ruler for long. Stopping your magic must be private."

Tesha rose and closed the distance between them to draw his trust and dispel any hint of weakness. "For that discretion, I thank you. It isn't magic that causes the king's fits. I do not control my husband, but the stories the soldiers brought you are true, and we must work together to quiet them. I have worried that such stories might undermine my husband. Hattu does suffer from a sort of madness, but not from sorcery."

"He acts as one possessed," Utar said. He crossed his arms over his chest and shook his head.

"How do I explain this to you without being disloyal to my husband? We do not speak of it even with each other." If she resented talking openly of Hattu's trouble, how much more would Hattu view it as a betrayal? This physician poked his nose where it did not belong.

"I am the one charged with preserving the king's well-being. For the good of everyone. All I want is for King Hattu to return to health. I looked for a cause of his trouble and saw you."

"I do bear responsibility for his troubles, but only indirectly. My father imprisoned him for weeks. He did it to protect his city from a man he believed was a sorcerer. Can you imagine being locked in a tiny stone cell in the dark? No one to speak to? No hope? Hattu still fears the walls will crush him. Would such a dark abyss leave a mark on you when you finally won your freedom?"

Utar's eyes widened. "A dark cell? For a king?"

Tesha nodded. "He relives this nightmare even in the daylight. Small things remind him, and he is lost. Only for a moment. He remains a good king and a brilliant general. You heard about the battle he won on the march here?"

"At the gorge?"

"He outmaneuvered a Paskan ambush and saved his army."

"What you say matches with the details from the soldier's stories. But it leaves out the crime you hid yesterday. You performed magic, for which the penalty is death. You are very young. Perhaps you have been enticed into such dangerous practices by someone else. I can teach you how to avoid this evil. I will not allow the insidious danger of magic into this realm. I, at least, am faithful to the Great King."

"I hold the same loyalty. Twice over. He is my ruler and also my husband's brother."

"And yet you committed a crime he will never forgive."

She considered claiming she just fidgeted with thread—no magic. He seemed willing to believe Hattu's fits had no magical source, a truth that could help her cover a lie. He held Hattu's best interests as his concern and seemed eager to let her cast aside her knot tying as a misguided mistake, but he was dangerous.

Then the physician's vulnerability dawned on her. She could silence this foolish willingness to confront his future queen. She held power here.

"You are mistaken. What I did is permissible. Magic? Yes, I did try magic to win the Paskan over for the king—that was my goal. I used an old invocation granted to priestesses but unknown to others, even physicians. The goddess's power is not present in your work. *I* broke no law, but *you*—your recognition of the magic reveals forbidden knowledge. For you, the penalty is death. The crime belongs to you."

She turned away and sat down to give her answer time to sink in. She mustn't look guilty. She rested her hands on the arms of the chair, open and relaxed. Her fingers fell in the grooves between each claw of the carved lion's paws.

Utar said, "Recognizing what you did is no crime. It is my job as a physician. How can I protect the kingdom from a danger I cannot discern?"

"When I uncovered the conspiracy in order to save King Hattu in Lawaza, I revealed a sorcerer at the heart of it. Not Hattu, as my father thought, but a man named Kudur. Commander Marak wished to question this sorcerer to learn whatever we could about his forbidden magic in order to protect against it. The same as you have just claimed. The Great King ordered Kudur put to death without letting anyone have further contact. Such knowledge is forbidden. The priestesses would never describe the knot spell to someone like you. Your knowledge *is* a crime."

Tesha tapped her fingers against the chair. She counted on him not knowing the hierarchy of magical knowledge permitted to the priestesses. The invocation *was* allowed to priestesses, but only healing priestesses. She'd stolen the invocation from the healing priestess Anna, and Anna had only come around to granting approval after the fact, more or less. None of that authority would mean much if the current Great King became aware of this old, forgotten magic. He wouldn't care how useful it was to the healers.

She must silence Utar with this threat, both to keep her magic secret from Hattu for now, and to keep it secret forever from the Great King.

"No! You are twisting this." The physician paced around the hearth. "Your magic is the problem. You are the one who dispersed a curse monstrous enough to consume a battalion of men."

"Saving the king and his soldiers was a problem? Hattu would not agree, nor would the men I dragged from that suffocating cloud."

"No one will call that act of sorcery a problem when you so bene-fitted the royal family—unless you fall out of favor there. But I see the evil in it, the forbidden magic. You could use spells to debilitate King Hattu."

"I have always given Hattu strength. I told you what his time in prison did. That is the truth. Ask him. He will hate you for knowing his weakness and never forgive you. But ask him. Ask the soldiers you spoke to how their king behaved when he first came out of that dark hole."

Tesha rose. She stepped closer to Utar, and he stopped pacing. "Hattu loves me and will reject these absurd accusations. I don't fear speaking to him. Shall we call him? Tell him that you know forbidden magic? Warn him that you must be isolated and executed as the Great King did to Kudur?"

She signaled to Henti as if to send her with a message. Poor Henti stood rigid against the wall. This confrontation must terrify her. She gave Tesha a small shake of her head, a warning not to pull Hattu into this. Tesha had no intention of doing that. Her hands were sweaty with fear. She had to carry on until this man agreed to silence.

"That isn't necessary," Utar said.

Tesha released the breath she'd been holding. "You are the one who must explain the source of your magical knowledge. From whom you learned. Not a temple as I did. So who taught you?"

"I'm no sorcerer."

"No, I don't think so, but you have gained forbidden knowledge from someone." She paused and thought. "Kudur learned from the Paskans. He confessed that much before his execution. Paskans live so close to Alpara. How convenient."

"Why would I have anything to do with Paskans?"

She smiled. Her wild guess had been right.

After Kudur's capture, she'd gained the tantalizing awareness that the Paskans retained outlawed magic to use against their Hitolian foes. She'd taken and hidden two vials of a disguising potion from the pretend seer. He'd been executed before she could find out how to recreate it. Marak was the only other person who'd seen virtue in dragging more magic out of the old man—not that Marak would use magic, but he believed in knowing one's enemies. She'd pretended that was her goal also.

But magic called to her in a way that felt the same as when Ishana reached into her soul. While turning aside Utar's accusations, she might open a door into this remnant of magic the Paskans had preserved over the generations.

"Why would you seek Paskan magic?" Tesha said, "There are reasons. To learn better cures. The healers among the priestesses use some allowed magic to great effect. I can imagine the temptation you face if you learned of some beneficial sorcery. I wouldn't necessarily wish to prevent its limited practice. I know the healing priestesses did no harm with it. But I would need to understand fully what you are doing. Tell me who taught you. Show me that this knowledge of yours is not, in fact, criminal. That is the only way I can keep your secret."

"My secret?"

Utar had drenched his voice in outrage. She heard the lie. "My husband has soldiers trained to force men to tell their secrets. But I believe in your good intent. Who taught you?"

"You wouldn't ask me to reveal forbidden knowledge if you your-self hid nothing," Utar countered. "Just by listening to me, you would acquire a dangerous secret. It is death to know, as you say."

"You speak to a priestess for whom these are permitted rites. These secrets are far more dangerous to you. Tell me who taught you. That is your safety. Tell me or I'll have you put to death."

"I have a way to protect myself if you tell others," Utar said. "Be forewarned. More your undoing than mine will follow."

"Then you have nothing to lose if you answer my question. Who taught you magic?"

"My fears about your sorcerous power and your spell I witnessed —I'll keep those to myself. You must in turn tell no one my secret."

So he did allow that he had one. "That sounds like an alliance. I agree."

Utar ran his fingers through his beard. He twisted his torso back and forth. "My mother was Paskan, and not any Paskan, but one of their magical healers. When the Great Kings of past generations wiped away magical knowledge among the Hitolians and killed all the sorcerers, the Paskans hid away what they could. I do not side with my mother's people. My father fought the tribe where my mother lived and removed me from that misery when I was nine years old. He raised me as a Hitolian nobleman. I have no desire to return to a Paskan village, herding sheep and fighting everyone all the time. Whatever I can do to stop the effectiveness of Paskan magic, I do, but I know very little. My mother taught me a great deal about healing and almost nothing about her magic. She died in the attack. So, yes, I recognized the knots and the glow of magic around your hands. My mother performed something like it."

"Alliances rest on mutual assistance," Tesha said. "I need to know more. I only wish to understand the extent of the Paskans' sorcerous capabilities so that we can defend against them. I don't care whether you are capable of performing the magic or not yourself, describing what you observed will still be useful to the kingdom's defense. There's more than your mother's knot-tying. Tell me."

"She didn't teach magic."

"But you watched. Tell me. If you truly are on the Hitolian side and not the traitor you sound like, you will give me all the knowledge you can so that I can protect this kingdom. I cannot fight with a sword against the Paskans, but no one is better prepared to fight this magic of theirs. Arm me."

He didn't speak.

"Your fears about my powers? That is what you would reveal to Hattu? The same power that saved Hattu? You will suffer, not me. But I can perhaps save Hattu again from the Paskans if you share what your unusual childhood gave you."

Utar grunted as if in pain. He renewed his pacing around the hearth. Annoying, but it seemed to help him find his voice. "I once saw a man's face change its look to such an extent that he no longer appeared like the same man. Horrible to see, and from his cries of agony, horrible to experience. I do not know the manner of casting that spell."

So others knew how to blend Kudur's potion—if she could find another of these magical healers among the Paskans. Marak would be the one to help her, if only the Paskans returned him alive.

"What else? My willingness to keep your secret grows with each memory you share."

"My mother had spells to help a woman laboring in childbirth, but I never witnessed any of those. She also did something with broken sticks and resin that helped broken bones heal. There were words and a mixture, but I don't know them."

"None of these pose a danger to us. Did she do anything that I should be forewarned of? Anything their warriors might use against us. Their curse nearly defeated us."

"If she knew of something like that curse, I never saw it."

Tesha tapped her foot at this limited information, purposely signaling her impatience.

Utar pulled a stone tied to a leather thong from underneath his tunic. "In the battle to take me from the Paskans, my mother gave me this just before my father's soldiers seized and killed her. I had heard she could use it to put a person into a sort of dream in which he would answer questions truthfully without realizing it."

"Really? That sounds useful."

"If I could make it work, but I can't. I don't think anyone's left among the Paskans who can."

The physician glanced down as he said this. In his mother's desperate last moment, she gave him a useless stone? Tesha found that hard to believe.

"You must have had some idea how she brought on this truth dream."

"I wish I did. That is all I can bring to our alliance, so to speak. I am, as you noted, needed elsewhere. A physician is always busy. I came to be certain that you were not using magic to harm the king. You have persuaded me. I hope you see no advantage in revealing my interest. As I said, that would be a mistake." He gave a curt bow.

"I will keep the secret of your maternal origins."

"Good day to you, Priestess." He hurried out the door.

18

Tesha rubbed the carved lion's paw under her fingers, a fierce-looking chair arm. The claws curved down so her sleeves or skin wouldn't likely catch on them, but running her finger underneath, she found a sharp point.

"Priestess?" Samsi stood in the doorway.

He'd appeared quickly after Utar's departure. Pushing aside the thought that he might have been listening, Tesha beckoned him forward.

"You have been left all alone. I thought you might want some company," Samsi said. He gave her a respectful bow, although as second in line to the Great King's throne, he outranked her. She would rule only this rocky outcrop and the embattled lands surrounding it, and she wasn't queen yet—only after Hattu's official declaration and her coronation.

Tesha rose. "You can show me the way back to the great hall. I should see to court business while your uncle attends to his duties with the troops." She straightened her veil, pulling out a stick pin and reinserting it. She'd chosen her usual red veil and gown, the marks of her role as priestess.

Samsi gave her his arm. Stiffness lingered in her legs, and she needed his polite support. No wonder Nerik had trouble competing against him. Nerik was all thorns and thistles.

They wound through the narrow corridors.

"Do you like staying at your Uncle Hattu's palace?"

"I like Uncle Hattu, and his court is a friendlier place than Father's. While Uncle was away, Shatim acted like a father to Nerik, and he was nice to me, too. My father's counselors are always too busy."

A double door opened into the great hall. A few scribes knelt in one area, writing on clay tablets. Several well-dressed men talked quietly together, and servants scurried in and out, delivering messages.

At the far end, a single gilt-edged throne stood on a dais painted deep red. Precious stones of many colors set in a rosette pattern shone brilliantly across the curved top of the throne. The decoration would frame the head of whoever sat there.

When the time came, would she sit on a throne of her own beside it? Or was her husband's insistence that they would rule together an illusion?

"Samsi, are those noblemen over there court advisors?"

The child nodded.

Tesha tugged Samsi toward them. Perhaps they could orient her about what matters of the kingdom she should attend to. She had a great deal to learn as she stepped into her role as queen. The largest temple in the empire and its treasury had been a good place to learn. She'd maintained its central role despite her father's less than adept leadership, but she still felt the gap between what she had done and what she would need to do.

More importantly, she wanted to consult with the commander of the scouts who searched for Daniti and Marak. In the midst of the Paskan attacks that distracted Hattu, she would see to that most important of jobs.

Before she reached the courtiers, Shatim, the advisor who'd befriended the prickly Nerik, came into the hall with an elderly, dark-skinned man of distinguished appearance but dusty from travel. The man's gait showed the stiffness of age, but his eyes scanned the room with intelligent interest.

Shatim drew the man toward Tesha. "It is good to see you recovered, Priestess. Is King Hattu here?"

"He is busy dispatching the troops."

Shatim hesitated and then he turned to the man he'd led in and said, "This is Priestess Tesha, King Hattu's wife. Priestess, this is Ambassador Ahmose. He comes from Gerose's court."

Tesha stepped back, alarmed at being near anyone sent by Pharaoh Gerose of Egarya. Even Samsi looked concerned. His eyes darted between the three adults.

Ahmose gave Tesha a respectful obeisance. "Despite the past battles between our empires, I come entirely as a friend. I realize that has not always been the case with visitors from Egarya sent by the Pharaoh. I apologize for that. The Divine Gerose did not speak publicly about the man he sent, nor will I admit to knowledge of him if asked about it, but my Pharaoh did not take such action on my advice. I promise I mean no harm to you or your husband. I wish to leave that battlefield far behind us. I am here to maintain the peace between our countries. Urgent business brings me this far."

"I will send for King Hattu," Tesha said.

"I'll find Uncle," Samsi said.

Tesha lifted her hand. "No, let me send a servant. Nerik must be enjoying his time with his father. He won't be pleased."

Samsi sagged a little. Tesha shook her head. He shouldn't enjoy annoying Nerik. She beckoned to a servant and gave the order.

Ahmose's veiled acknowledgement of the assassin Gerose had sent reassured her. He'd be unlikely to remind her if he came as one himself. Based on his demeanor, her first instinct was to like him, but he was Gerose's man. Kety had voiced concern that Gerose might be involved in Daniti's kidnapping.

But here he was. Tesha wondered about the protocol of receiving an ambassador from the Pharaoh. Even as recent enemies, the importance of Egarya would indicate far more honor and pomp than she'd given him so far.

"I apologize for the simplicity of this welcome," Tesha said. "King Hattu and I have only returned yesterday, and I did not know of your arrival." Tesha gave a confused look to Shatim. He shrugged, as caught off guard as she.

"Do not concern yourself with this, Priestess. I did not send word in advance. I have need of quiet discussion, not ceremonial pomp." He glanced around. No one stood near them. "Although my journey is on behalf of Egarya, Pharaoh Gerose did not directly send me. I am hoping to accomplish a benefit for both our empires in a manner my Pharaoh will appreciate with time."

This was not entirely reassuring.

"Another skirmish may be closing in on us, but I hope we'll be in agreement about the enemy this time."

Tesha sorted his words—a common enemy? "I don't understand."

"Nor would I expect you to. I'm speaking riddles." He glanced around again. "It would be best if what I have to say was not widely heard."

Riddles and secrets. Tesha scanned the room filled with courtiers and guards. She lowered her voice. "That sounds worrisome."

Ahmose glanced at Samsi. He seemed to be calculating whether the child could stay.

"This is Samsi, Great King Muwatti's son."

Ahmose's eyebrows rose. "Here? In Alpara? There's a story. It's an honor to meet you, sir." Ahmose made a polite bow to Samsi.

That seemed to settle the question of Samsi's presence. Tesha felt relieved. Whatever this puzzling man had to say, he did not mind if word reached the Great King. A safe secret.

Tesha clasped her hands at her waist to keep them still. Otherwise she'd tug a strand of hair, and that wasn't how queens behaved.

They waited for Hattu in an awkward silence.

"Congratulations," Ahmose said, "on your marriage to King Hattu. It was the news of the capital."

Tesha smiled, wishing Hattu would arrive.

"I heard many versions of what preceded your nuptials—sorcery, poison, and the return of old enemies. I would have thought I was hearing an Egaryan tale if I had not been in Great King Muwatti's court. You had an important role, I gather. Not one young brides usually play, but admirable."

"I was guided by Ishana. I sought to uncover the truth, and in doing so, freed King Hattu from false accusations. It is by the goddess's command that King Hattu and I married."

"I wouldn't have thought any man would need a goddess's command to choose a bride as lovely as you, Priestess. I confess when I heard the part you played in releasing Hattu from suspicion, I did not picture you as a beautiful young lady. Odd how men assume a quick mind and a gracious form cannot go together. I am glad King Hattu has such a queen. He will need you."

This ambassador was rather forward with this compliment, although Tesha heard nothing untoward in his tone and his old age granted him some forgiveness. Tesha did not add that she was not yet Hattu's queen. Much as she wanted Hattu to need her, she didn't like the sound of Ahmose's warning.

Hattu entered the great hall with a full complement of body-guards and several courtiers. Nerik was nowhere to be seen.

"Ambassador Ahmose. It is good to see you again. I would have made preparations for your welcome if I had known you were coming. I did not realize Pharaoh Gerose wanted to discuss anything with me. He seems displeased with my existence."

A sizzle of surprise ran through Tesha. Hattu knew this man already and felt comfortable enough with him to refer to Gerose's desire to assassinate Hattu.

"I started at your brother's court, but his illness precluded the kind of discussion and result I hope for, so I came here. You are Great King Muwatti's most trusted general." Ahmose glanced at the group of men surrounding Hattu.

Tesha understood his meaning. "Ambassador Ahmose has trav-eled a long way. Perhaps we could offer refreshments and a quieter place for discussion." She looked pointedly at the men clustered around her husband. He'd brought them to be kingly, but if she and

Hattu were to hear the ambassador's secrets, they would have to give him privacy.

Hattu smiled at his wife. "Of course. It is far more comfortable in my quarters, and it will be a pleasant place for us to share food and drink." He turned to the men he'd gathered. "I will not interrupt your work further. Carry on as we discussed on both projects."

Tesha nodded at Hattu's discretion. He must mean continuing the defense against the approaching Paskan forces and attempting to free her sister and Marak. There was no need to let this Egaryan know about those problems, but Hattu's men must be stretched thin to cover these crises. Most of the men hurried out. One approached the scribes.

Hattu took Tesha by the elbow and led her toward his private quarters with Shatim and Ahmose. Hattu wanted Shatim in on this discussion. As Tesha learned her new world, she stored away knowledge that Shatim was Hattu's most trusted advisor in Marak's absence. Samsi fell in behind, apparently engrossed in untangling the fringe on his sash, but Tesha knew he was listening.

19

Hattu took Tesha's arm as they went to his quarters. She gasped when they entered, and he gripped her arm more firmly in concern. But then he understood. His unusual reception hall.

"Oh my," Ahmose said.

Tesha broke from Hattu and stepped toward the eye-level windows that spanned one wall. The low, wide openings made his hall chilly and windy on all but the hottest summer days unless he closed the shutters, but the view far into the distance over the pine forests, rocky crags, and the river valley below—his kingdom—gave him the freedom of a bird in the air.

Hattu indicated a seat for his guest among the many chairs and side tables scattered around the circular hearth. Ahmose and Tesha appreciated the panorama, so he sat them on either side of him, facing the windows. Shatim sat himself off to one side, keeping back in an uncharacteristic way. Perhaps his king's long absence had disrupted the sense that they could rely on each other. In court business and diplomacy, Shatim served Hattu better than anyone, even Marak. Marak was a man of action.

Hattu commanded the servants to bring food and drink, and soon cups of beer, fresh bread, cheese, and olives appeared beside each of them. He explained to Tesha how he and Ahmose had met. They'd negotiated for the release of Egaryan noblemen taken in the war between Egarya and Hitolia. Hattu had taken a sizable ransom and let them all go, so they'd gotten along fine.

"I appreciate privacy for this conversation. We have a difficult task," Ahmose said.

"You mentioned that Pharaoh did not send you," Tesha said. "Must you hide this visit?"

"Not if we accomplish what is needed."

Hattu studied Tesha's expression. Smart of her to share that, although Ahmose calculated all his comments, so he wouldn't have let that slip unintentionally.

As he watched Tesha, he rubbed the rash hidden under his tunic. When he'd dressed that morning, he'd found a series of long raised bumps on either side just below his shoulders. They stung painfully at times. Like now. He yanked his hand away and turned his attention back to Ahmose.

"Pharaoh will take out his anger on you if he finds you're working behind his back," Hattu said. His hand crept back to the sausage-like lump on the left. When he put on his armor in the dark before the gorge battle, he must have tied it so it rested incorrectly against his padded tunic and inflamed his skin. He was too experienced a warrior for such a foolish mistake. He'd hide it.

"Pharaohs do not countenance anything that diminishes their divine stature," Ahmose said, "but they turn a blind eye to many essential compromises. The Divine Gerose knows I bring him the results that he cannot actively seek himself. I am safe enough and Egarya will be far safer, as will your brother's empire, if we solve this between us."

"And what is it we must solve?"

Ahmose took a drink of beer. Tesha tapped her foot in impatience. Couldn't his wife understand how thirsty a man gets after a trip up the mountain? But Ahmose's visit delayed their attention to Daniti's release. She'd be upset by that—as was he.

"I'm afraid we have a trickier problem to work through this time," Ahmose said. "There's a pro-Egaryan faction in the lands you settled for your brother. They aren't as settled as they seemed. A faction in Amur seeks Gerose's support in overthrowing the vassal king you Hitolians put on the throne there."

Hattu leaned forward in his chair. "That would mean outright war." A disaster, but not so surprising since Amur had for a long stretch been under Egaryan control and retained a strong Egaryan community. He'd warned his brother.

"A war Pharaoh can't afford and doesn't want. No more than your Great King does. I was in your capital. Great King Muwatti lay too ill to receive me, much less lead troops into war."

"So, what do you want from me?"

"We want you to wipe out this Egaryan faction in Amur without anyone knowing we asked you to. Keep this unruly kingdom in Hitolian hands and thus Pharaoh out of a war. Everyone would save face."

"Why doesn't Pharaoh support the Egaryan faction?" Tesha asked.

Ahmose turned to her. "As your husband said, a fight over Amur —which we lost in the great battle between our empires, although you won't hear Pharaoh say that—would bring our two empires back to full-scale war. Pharaoh is torn in two ways. He certainly won't admit to the men in the Egaryan faction that he cannot defend their interests. He won't say that outright and look weak. So those men still hope and will cause trouble. But both our empires spent too much on the war. Gerose can't afford another war so soon. It is best not to weaken ourselves when jackals wait on the sidelines to attack whenever our empires appear vulnerable."

The lumps under Hattu's skin writhed. He fought to keep his attention focused on the problem Ahmose presented and worked to keep his face blank, his hands still in his lap. Hard to think clearly.

Too many crises demanded his attention. How could he sweep eastward to Amur with his army and leave his own kingdom to be taken by Paskans? But the whole empire could collapse if it faced war with Egarya right now. By all the gods, where was Marak? Finding Marak was what he needed to do.

Ahmose continued, "I bought some time. I made sure to delay the departure of the men who made their appeal to Pharaoh. But I had not counted on your brother's illness. You'll need to lead out your troops immediately."

Shatim opened his mouth as if to say something, but Hattu spoke first. "It's not a bad plan, but some matters here will delay me." A gust of wind blew through the open windows and washed over him. He had always loved this room and often did his best thinking here. "Perhaps we can come up with another way to prevent war between Egarya and Hitolia. We will discuss this in more detail after I see to some pressing business. As you heard, I only returned to my kingdom yesterday."

Tesha rose. "Ambassador, you must need a rest after your long journey." She beckoned to two servants by the door.

Hattu gave Tesha a nod of gratitude for taking care of Ahmose. He heard her giving directions to bring the ambassador to the guest quarters.

He stood and shifted his shoulders under his tunic. The irritation of his rash was quieting—like the hush that comes when a squalling child falls asleep. A welcome relief in an otherwise miserable day. He had too many problems, and Marak, whom he needed most, remained in enemy hands.

When Tesha finished sending the Egaryan off with a servant, she drew him aside. "Is there any news from the scouts?"

"None that I've heard, but—"

"Let's go speak to the commander. Perhaps he's heard something."

20

Tesha wouldn't let Hattu call the scout commander away from his work, so she made her legs carry her. They wobbled after too many steps, but she managed the walk into the courtyard in front of the palace.

The huge courtyard operated more as a road, given all the buildings clustered around it and the broad gates at one end to let through wagons and chariots.

Cobblestones bumped unevenly under the soles of her sandals, and she held tighter to Hattu's arm. At least her vision had cleared. Gone was the disturbing gray mist around Hattu.

On one side, Hattu pointed out the archive building with scribal workrooms. The nearest building on the other side, Tesha discovered, housed the officers' quarters. Hattu kept his army leaders close.

The mud-brick officers' barracks rose in three step-backed stories. On each level, a flat roof terrace formed the front section with a ladder giving access to the level above. There was nothing out of the ordinary about this arrangement, but Tesha sighed in relief when Hattu led her through the doorway on the ground floor. Climbing a ladder might still be beyond her endurance.

Scouts wore dull greenish-brown tunics so they blended into the forest. A man dressed in one stood talking to a gray-haired noble with an officer's short cape over his yellow tunic. He must be the officer directing the search for Daniti and Marak.

The officer bowed to Hattu as they entered.

"Any news?" Hattu asked.

"After more than fifty reports from scouts, we still haven't found them. But a lot of the men who are checking farther out haven't reported back."

Tesha asked, "Have you told your scouts to watch for the unusual flying creature who may have found my sister?"

The officer suppressed a smile. "Your maid told us this idea. If anyone sees your pet, they'll capture it for you. But we have more important things to do."

Tesha sighed. "He could lead us to her."

"Yes, Priestess."

Hattu squeezed her hand, telling her to hush. No one understood what Kurala could do, despite his small size. There were other things to accomplish here, so she'd let this be for now.

Hattu said, "Keep up the search. Throw every scout we have into it." He turned toward the door, but Tesha pulled him back.

"Do the reports form a pattern?" Tesha asked.

"A pattern?" The officer puckered his lips.

"A pattern that would reveal the best places to send scouts next."

"We moved outward from the place they were taken," the officer said.

So he hadn't followed the kind of thorough plan she would in deploying the scouts. She could fix that. "Will it take you from your necessary tasks if you or one of your men describe for me in detail the search thus far?"

The officer looked to Hattu with a question. Hattu gave a curt nod.

The officer answered, "Let me act on this latest report, and then I can go over the reports with you."

The scout and officer talked some more. Tesha considered how to proceed, how to turn what he'd tell her into something useful.

"I need some scribal clay and tools," she told Hattu.

He raised his eyebrows.

"To see the pattern. Like a game of Sphinx and Griffin." Patterns like those in the game were exactly what they needed in sorting out the scouts. She saw Hattu's face light up at the reminder of that first challenging game they'd played when they fell in love.

When he looked at her, Hattu's eyes sparked in a way she hadn't seen since before the curse. She loved him best in moments like this, when their minds together became more than they could be alone. He beckoned one of the guards on duty by the door. "Go to the archives building and bring back—" He turned to Tesha in question.

"Enough clay for several tablets, a roller, two reeds, and a line rule."

The soldier repeated her list with some prompting from Tesha and soon returned with the correct items.

Tesha's work with the officer clearly tried the Commander of Scouts' patience. She asked detailed questions of each report. The officer's scribe who had recorded the reports on tablets proved more helpful than the officer's memory.

Hattu sat in silence most of the time, although he occasionally told her to add areas in between the ones in the reports. She realized he moved in memory through the surrounding areas and kept track of the gaps. Very useful. He understood what she was doing and contributed what she couldn't, even if the officer stayed confused.

Tesha pursued an extended process of placing onto the clay the signs for mountains, valleys, streams, and other landmarks from the reports. These helped her see at a glance where rivers ran, mountains ended, and the like. She'd covered the entire big worktable surface with tablets abutting each other.

Tesha sat back and studied her work. She'd never done anything like this before. It looked like the most complicated game board she'd ever seen. Now what to do with it?

Hattu hunched forward and studied it also. "I wish I'd thought of this."

They sat in silence. Tesha reached under her veil and wrapped a strand of hair around her finger, alternately pulling and releasing it. The rhythm of the tug, tug, tug focused her thoughts.

"Where would you have taken them?" Tesha asked.

"Somewhere I could reach before it grew too dark."

"Not far, then."

The officer interrupted, "We looked in all the places reachable by dark."

"The gaps between reported areas are all far off," Tesha agreed.

"Be sure to send scouts into those missed areas," Hattu commanded.

"Yes, sir. I see the advantage to this . . . I'm not sure what to call what Priestess Tesha has done here."

Tesha turned to the scribe who had helped by reading the reports aloud. "Find the report for this mountain." She touched a sign on one of the damp tablets. "It's one of the earliest ones, maybe the third you read to me. Read it aloud again."

He did.

"The scout's report is different on this mountain than the others," Tesha said. "Doesn't it sound like high up on the mountain, he only looked at one side?"

The officer answered, "Many of the peaks have sheer rock faces on parts of them. That's why the scout wouldn't have gone there."

Tesha gave Hattu a questioning look. The officer's answer seemed shoddy to her. Hattu had said the Paskans navigated with great skill in these mountains.

"Let's send a scout back to that peak," Hattu said. "Have him look at all of it, even if he has to climb over rocks."

The officer shrugged. "They were riding horses and forcing the captives to go along with them. They wouldn't have climbed over rocks. But I'll send a scout."

"Thank you," Tesha said. "We should be extra thorough in these closer areas."

"This method of yours"—the officer waved at the tablets—"*is* useful. I don't think I could repeat it, but perhaps when we're not in the middle of a crisis, you can teach me."

"I will be happy to." A surge of pride filled Tesha. Maybe next time Hattu raced off to discuss problems with his commanders he wouldn't leave her behind.

But Daniti was no closer to home. Maybe one of the scouts would find her.

There was nothing else to do to speed the search. At least not with the scouts on horseback. They needed a hawk. Kurala was a sort of hawk, but he wouldn't be able to give a report even if someone found him. And there was nothing to be done about the ransom negotiations until that envoy returned. Tesha wanted to scream.

Accompanied by Ashu, Tesha made her way to the palace kitchen. Hattu had given her the task of putting on a royal feast in honor of Ambassador Ahmose. The best way to hide the ambassador's true purpose in coming was to be as public as usual about this diplomatic visit. Hattu and Ahmose provided the excuse of negotiations on the accepted boundaries between the Hitolian and Egaryan lands. She could do nothing more for Daniti, so she threw herself into taking command of her new household. She'd heard Hattu complain about the meekness of his first wife. She would never make that mistake.

In the kitchen courtyard, near a cluster of rounded mud-brick ovens, Tesha found the head cook, a woman as round as her ovens, with huge muscular arms. Tesha watched her. The cook's sureness in her kitchen became clear. She knelt by the fire pit to tend a roasting spit and then reached into a bread oven to snatch out the flatbreads at just the right moment. With her strong arms she lifted a heavy pot off a tripod over the fire without calling for a helper. The smells of fresh bread and meats spiced with cumin and garlic wafted from the woman's domain and enticed Tesha.

She had time to observe the cook because the woman ignored her presence. Finally, Tesha resorted to having her maidservant Ashu announce her. The cook turned toward Tesha with a downturned mouth. Tesha glared back.

"King Hattu and I have an unexpected honored guest from Pharaoh Gerose's court, and we will host a state feast this evening. We must discuss what can be done on such short notice to provide the proper courses."

"Lady Agat has already discussed the feast with me. I don't need to talk to you."

Tesha stood dumbfounded. What did this servant mean by speaking to her that way? Lady Agat, indeed. The woman was a glorified nursemaid, a wet nurse. She might have come from a noble family originally, but she'd given up a decent marriage when her family pushed her into a bed without a wedding first. It might have bought her family some political influence, but Agat herself lost out, and these servants had best understand who deserved respect and who didn't. Making an enemy of the head cook would be a mistake, but Agat's reign over this household would come to an end now.

"Ah, of course," Tesha said. "You are accustomed to having the daily household plans directed by a woman of no rank. That unfortunate circumstance is over, thank Ishana. I am accustomed as a Priestess of Ishana in Lawaza to supervising kitchens far more extensive than this one. You will find my orders helpful in all aspects of your duties."

Tesha gave the woman a practiced look that had caused many serving women at the temple to cower. The cook had the good grace to drop her eyes and nod.

"Time is short. It would be foolish to make major changes to whatever menu you have planned, but tell me what you have chosen, and I will repair any insufficiencies as best we can with the time available."

Tesha added a few dishes that would not cause undue difficulty and were possible with the supplies available. In precise detail, she went over the seating arrangement for Ahmose, her husband, Nerik, and the nobles who would attend, as well as the assignment of proper drinking cups, knives and platters—important emblems of honor that each guest would have at his place. There was a hierarchy to these things, and Tesha would not insult any of her guests through carelessness. If she and Hattu were convincing the kingdom and any spies that Ahmose's visit was entirely official, she would see that each detail confirmed that story. This time spent examining the gold cups and other royal serving pieces clearly annoyed the cook, but Tesha had little patience for the cook's mood.

Tesha marched back to Hattu's private quarters. She had business to discuss with him. He continued to avoid the subject of those women. He owed her an apology, and he owed Agat a firm putting in her place, one that Agat actually listened to. He had to repair the damage he had done to their marriage. She wasn't sure how.

Two servants were clearing away the dishes from Hattu's hall, but he was not there. Tesha slipped past them into his sleeping chamber. It lay empty. She returned to the great hall, but Hattu wasn't there either. Shatim was, however, and she hurried toward him. He was talking to some other nobleman, their heads close together.

She interrupted them with her approach. Shatim looked up. She said, "I am looking for King Hattu."

"He rushed out to lead another contingent of soldiers, Priestess. Scouts have reported a band of Paskans coming down from the northwest—a small group but they cannot be allowed to roam into Hitolian territory without a response."

"More Paskans?" The pressure in her head mounted. Unrelenting threats filled their lives in this kingdom.

Shatim turned to the nobleman he had been speaking to. "This is Lord Narizu, the head of one of Alpara's most important families." Shatim paused. His lips pressed together, and his shoulders lifted a hair. "He is Lady Agat's father."

Agat's father. An important family. Agat would not be shunted aside easily. Tesha studied his face. It was narrow with hollow cheeks and eyes shaped into off-center triangles by drooping skin. She saw a resemblance to his daughter. They also shared a similar strained tautness.

She couldn't escape that woman. And now Hattu had left her while he dealt with more Paskans? "Could this band be the same tribe that took my sister and Marak?"

Shatim nodded. "Yes, it could be, although there are many tribes. I encouraged King Hattu to accompany his soldiers in case this band approaches with negotiations or other news of the captives. These may be the Paskans we most want to speak with."

"That would be good news. Will the king return by evening?"

"I doubt that very much. He'll want to be certain this group is not responding to your offer."

"So many? Why not send their envoy again and prevent the misunderstanding of being seen as raiders?"

"Paskans make decisions differently than we do. If there is a disagreement about how to proceed, they may have wanted to send a far larger group. That would be good. They'll have more decision-making power."

"I see. That would be an improvement. Wouldn't Hattu bring them directly back here?"

"Not into the city. A group like that will negotiate in the field. They'll feel trapped here."

"Did Prince Nerik go with Hattu?"

"No. He wanted to, but Hattu told him to take his place at the feast so Ahmose would not feel snubbed. He said something about learning an important part of being a king. Nerik would have preferred to go. I tried to persuade the king. Nerik should be with him."

"Nerik looks forward to learning war from his father, but it's appropriate for him to stay." Tesha had not imagined her newly married life would be this unpleasant. She would be holding her first state feast with a young man who clearly hated her. *Please, Ishana, may this band draw near in order to release my sister. Make Hattu's absence worthwhile.*

Agat's father nodded. "I told him the same when he grumbled. It's best for him to stay here tonight. He's a fine young man. During King Hattu's absence over the last year, I have mentored him. He has learned all the necessary skills as a warrior and statesman. I saw to that."

Tesha looked at him in surprise. *This* man thought he could fill in as father to Nerik? Nerik didn't seem to feel his fighting skills had developed to what Hattu could offer. And statesmanship? Nerik certainly had a lot to learn about diplomacy.

Narizu must have seen her doubt.

"Of course he is eager for his own father. I only stood in while Hattu had to be away." He cleared his throat. "We are all glad that Hattu has returned."

Tesha frowned. Both the father and daughter preferred to have their influence unimpeded. Narizu did not seem pleased to hand the job of mentoring Nerik back to Hattu. She wished Hattu had taken Nerik and kept him safely under his wing.

Narizu gave her a curt bow. "I must go." He hurried out of the court hall.

Tesha turned to Shatim. "So Hattu will not return for the state feast accompanied by Paskans?"

Shatim laughed. "Fortunately not, although I gathered from listening today that Ahmose has seen many things. Even sharing a meal with barbarians might not upset him. He doesn't seem to stand on form, does he?"

"Do you trust him?"

Shatim paused in thought. "I think I do. He made it clear he knows our weakness in Muwatti's illness, but he did not hide that Gerose also fears a renewal of war. He gave us some very useful information in that. I, for one, will feel better knowing Gerose isn't planning a new season of warfare while our Great King is indisposed. Since he's dealt with Hattu before, he knows Hattu's smart enough not to miss that information as an offering of friendship—a gift in return for what Ahmose wants Hattu to do."

"If Ahmose told the truth. Couldn't he be tricking Hattu, and Gerose is in fact readying for war?"

"We have spies in Gerose's court, and from the reports Muwatti's scribes send up here, Gerose is not gathering in his men or preparing the supplies he would need. That supports Ahmose's information. And if I were Gerose, the last general I would want to face is Hattu. Muwatti has several generals. It would not serve Gerose's purpose to push Hattu to return to the area if he were starting a war there. I don't think Ahmose lies."

"I will prepare to honor Ambassador Ahmose without my husband's assistance. It will be worth it if he brings news of my sister and the commander."

"I agree. We can hope." Shatim bowed and left her.

Tesha rubbed the sides of her head. It ached, and the long evening still lay in front of her. She had little enough time to dress for the dinner, but first she would see to an important duty she had neglected.

22

————

Tesha climbed down from Ishana's sanctuary where she had prayed with all her heart to her goddess to protect Daniti and bring her home. That, above all, had to happen. Those women, Paskan incursions, the remaining vestiges of the conspiracy she'd uncovered for Hattu while he was imprisoned in Lawaza—she felt assaulted by it all, but somehow she and Hattu would overcome it. If only she had Daniti by her side. She sent her deepest wish again to Ishana. *Bring Daniti back safely.*

As she came down the sanctuary stairs, she heard boys' voices and recognized Nerik's. She put her hand up to signal her maids to be quiet, and they stopped inside the stairwell and out of sight of the two boys.

"At least he sent out troops to kill them," the other boy said.

"He'll be begging them to make peace. He always does," Nerik said.

"He fought Pharaoh face-to-face."

"So he claims. I wasn't there. He didn't think I belonged. You watch, you'll get to go on the next raid, but I won't."

"Well, you're—"

"When I'm king, I'll massacre the Paskans. Put an end to that trouble like he should have."

"That long? Your father is still a young man."

"You never know."

What response Nerik's friend might have made to that, Tesha couldn't hear because they walked farther down the hall and out of earshot. She glanced at Henti with a disgusted look, and her maid shrugged. Tesha shook her head at Nerik's disrespect for his father. He had some growing up to do. Tesha was nearly the same age as Nerik, but she felt a great deal older. As a priestess she'd been forced to learn how to behave so others respected her and so she could get from them what she needed—what the temple and goddess had needed. Hattu should not have sheltered this young man from the hard duties he must learn.

Tesha hurried back toward her rooms. The chore of introducing herself to Hattu's nobles at the feast alone lay ahead. No, it was worse —she wouldn't be alone. She'd have Nerik at her side. She practiced a diplomatic smile she did not feel.

Sounds of children's laughter greeted her at her doorway. She froze. Two older children, a girl and a boy, chased after a roly-poly toddler of about two. Hattu had said the role of those women was to provide children. She knew he'd sent the oldest son out with the troops this morning. These were the royal family's quarters. No other children would play here.

She stared at them. They seemed happy and carefree. Her hand went to her belly. Could there be a child in her womb already? She would be the mother of many children. More than . . . Tesha caught Henti's knowing look and sympathetic smile.

The older children caught sight of her and stopped short, hunched defensively with sudden shyness. The boy took the older girl's hand. Both had dark hair and Hattu's distinctive nose and olive coloring.

She had always liked children. She could understand how a king would need many, and these children would always be part of his life. They were *his children*. It wasn't their fault who their mothers were.

She should be able to get past that. She took a deep breath, balled her fists up, and released them. She could pretend for now. For the children.

The toddler let out a piercing shriek of delight at the loss of her pursuers, and then careened directly into one of the carved ebony chairs around the central hearth.

Before the child could start to cry, Tesha lifted her into her arms. A red mark showed on the little girl's forehead. She needed to be distracted from it. Tesha brushed the toddler's hair from her sweet brow and gave the hurt a kiss. "You are a fast runner. I bet you like adventures. My sister and I did, too. My mother says we nearly killed her with worry."

"Her mother says the same," the older girl said. "Her name is Amma. It's my job to chase after her. I can run fast."

"Who is her mother?" Tesha asked.

The girl looked confused as if everyone would know such a thing. "Lady Pasul. My mother is Lady Ija."

The boy spoke up, "I am Humie, and this is my sister Gashal. You are the priestess Father brought home with him, aren't you?"

"I am his wife, Priestess Tesha. You have your father's handsome features. You are quite a big boy. What do you most enjoy doing?"

The shyness didn't leave his cautious expression. "I'm learning to shoot a bow."

"Would you like to go hunting?"

"I'm too little, Father says."

"He's probably right. I've never been hunting, but it does sound both dangerous and exciting. If you keep practicing with your bow, when you are old enough, you'll hit your quarry. Show me how you stand when you shoot. It must be hard to keep your eye on the target."

Humie let go of Gashal's hand. He moved as if notching his arrow, stood very still with his imaginary bow pulled taut, and stared at a point on the far wall.

"You're very good. I can see the bow, and your arrow is going to pierce that dancing woman's chest, isn't it?"

Humie giggled. "I had to aim at something."

"Good choice. She might be a secret Paskan spy."

Humie's eyes grew wide.

Gashal stepped closer to Tesha. "Girls can't be spies."

Tesha pointed to the wall. "But she is. Your brother is keeping us safe, though, so don't worry."

The children looked at each other, puzzled by this joking. Tesha was enjoying herself. A pleasant surprise.

The toddler in her arms gave another screech. Tesha swung her high in the air so that she laughed and then returned her to the ground. "Gasul, you'll need to run after Amma again. Lucky you're fast."

The dark blue curtains burst open, and the two younger concubines came through.

The one named Pasul said, "Children, out of here. I told you that you couldn't play here anymore."

"They are fine. I like children," Tesha said. "I have no problem with children."

She glared at the graceful beauty. What was she going to do about these women? What did she want Hattu to do? Banish them from her existence. But you couldn't send mothers away from their children. Or children from their father. This was complicated. Why hadn't Hattu told her before?

"We didn't think you'd like our children. Agat said—"

"Do you always listen to Agat? I'd ignore what Agat said about me. She doesn't know me. But I am Hattu's wife, and you are not. Your family chose this life for you, I'm guessing?"

Pasul nodded, her face flushing pink.

Ija stepped forward. "It is a good life. We have everything we want. And Hattu loves us."

"Does he? You did bear him children. Fine children." Tesha sighed. "He loves me as his wife. As his only wife. You need to understand that now."

Ija answered, "You have things to learn also. Agat likes to give the orders. Ever since the news of Hattu's marriage reached us, she's been telling Nerik you'll displace him as Hattu's heir with a son of your own. We don't fight with her. It isn't worth it. She loves Nerik. She raised him as her own son. You have to understand. It's just the way things are."

Tesha sighed. "I've realized today that Agat will struggle to accept me and her changed role. But she has no choice. She may have raised Nerik, but he is grown now, and she must step back." Tesha looked Ija in the eye. "You will all have to step back. Now excuse me, I have to dress."

Tesha turned and left the room.

23

Dressed in an elegant green gown with russet braided trim sewn onto the bodice and hem, Tesha felt like the queen she would soon be. Henti and Ashu fell in step on either side of her to escort her to the feast. She would have preferred Hattu's company, but she pressed back her shoulders and stood straight. Nothing Nerik said would unsettle her—not that she'd let show, anyway.

She led the way toward the feasting hall. Oil lamps in wall brackets lit the shadowy corridor. Ahead, light coming through the open doorway of Hattu's private quarters cast a brighter square on the floor. The servants must have lit lamps there despite his absence.

She drew closer and heard soft footsteps inside. An overzealous servant who should be told to douse the lamps not light them? Hattu? Curiosity pulled her into the room.

Ambassador Ahmose stepped out of Hattu's sleeping chamber.

What was he doing here? Nothing good. He had no business in Hattu's rooms.

He didn't look agitated at being discovered, but his snooping in her husband's private rooms sparked alarm in her.

"Priestess, you look lovely this evening. I am searching for the king, but he must already have left for this fine feast you are holding in my honor because he is, as you see, not here."

"The servants should have brought you to the feasting hall. Guests do not seek out their hosts in their rooms." She steadied her gaze at him. Let him give a better explanation than that.

Instead, Ahmose offered her his arm. "May I accompany you in Hattu's stead? I am eager to discuss the state of affairs between our empires with him. He has a good head for such things. I might as well accomplish as much as I can while here."

She shook her head. A more direct question would be openly offensive. Hattu and she had to delay sending the troops Ahmose wanted. She couldn't afford to offend him right now. "Unfortunately, King Hattu will be unable to attend the feast. Duties have called him away."

"Duties? Something dire, I fear."

Why didn't Ahmose have a guard escorting him to keep an eye on him under the guise of protection? She'd see to that. "A minor foray by a hostile tribe. They need to be shooed away with a small show of force."

"Shooed away? Hostile warriors rarely shoo. Would these be Paskan warriors?"

Unpleasant surprise rose in her chest. Better for one enemy not to know about the other. "Yes, nothing out of the ordinary. Hattu will soon return."

Tesha turned away from Ahmose to hide her discomfort. He asked too many questions.

"I sense neither of us likes war, Priestess. It is a shame your husband has been called away against these Paskans. I had heard from others of these nomads. We have some similar peoples in Egarya, although they live in a flat land of sand, not these mountains that are trying to reach the gods. They also are a troublesome people. Hard to destroy an enemy who is always moving, isn't it so?"

Tesha nodded, caught off guard. Had he insinuated an insult about her husband's inability to finish off the Paskans? No, that wasn't his intent. This man liked private conversations too much.

"I've come at a difficult time for you and your husband. Let me be honest. It is best between friends."

Tesha nodded again. What did this man want?

"That pleasant Shatim—the one who introduced you to me—pulled aside a soldier who'd just ridden back to the city. I should not have listened in, but . . ." Ahmose shrugged. "Shatim asked if there was any word about the hostages."

Tesha wanted to escape the company of this spying old man, but she should find out what he had overheard.

"Hostages!" Ahmose said. "Not the word I wanted to hear. I need Hattu at the head of his troops on the road to Amur without delay."

Tesha tried to hide her scowl, but if he had any ideas for freeing Daniti—

"So, I pretended to know all about these hostages and tripped Shatim up. Pardon my small indiscretion. All for a good cause. Yours and mine."

"And what did you find out?" Tesha frowned at Ahmose, but he did not seem put off.

"That the hostages are your blind sister and King Hattu's best commander. Your sister is a tragedy for you, but that commander is just the person Hattu needs if he is going to be able to leave his kingdom in safe hands. Because, of course, these unfortunate Paskans have launched incursions—two, I now find out. And yet I want to pull him from this troubled land. You must hate my very presence. I regret the pressing nature of my request. King Hattu understands that he cannot allow Amur to be overthrown. But that does not make my calling him away any easier for you or him. In these circumstances, we should help each other as diplomatic friends. You are surrounded by troubles and I am an old man used to solving troubles." Ahmose laughed. "Pharaohs are even more troublesome than this mountain kingdom."

Tesha found Ahmose's willingness to trick Shatim distasteful, although it was only a minor misrepresentation to further his necessary cause. Clearly, he could dissemble when he needed to, but he wasn't dissembling now. She believed his appeal to her for cooperation.

"How would you solve our troubles? The return of the commander and my sister would speed Hattu's departure for Amur. But the trail has disappeared as though a sorcerer hides them." She laughed lightly as if she did not mean this seriously, but she watched Ahmose's face. She had heard that Egaryans knew sorcery, but was that true?

"A sorcerer? Magic troubles?"

Ah, he didn't take it as a mere expression.

Tesha shrugged. "When you heard about Paskans, did you learn they sometimes use magic? If they are now, that would explain how they can cause trouble for the much greater power of the king and his army."

"I'm not sure how you could tell. I have no magical knowledge. But small forces often trouble empires, just as a tiny mouse gnaws at the full bag of grain so that all the grain slips out, slowly but surely."

No magical knowledge? She sensed a lie and wished Daniti were here. Her sister always heard the lie.

"Your help with recovering the hostages will be welcome, although I'm not sure what you can do," Tesha said. "If there's something, do tell me."

"I will think on your hostage problem," Ahmose said.

That would have to do. "We should go to the feast." She stepped toward the doorway.

"To quiet any rumors that I'm hiding from the Pharaoh in Alpara? This is an entirely official visit, isn't it?" Ahmose winked at her and fell in beside her. Tesha's serving women followed close behind.

It had been a very full day. She missed sounding out her thoughts with Daniti. Daniti always told her when she was wrong, but they loved each other enough for that. The loss of her trustworthy source of advice cut deeply. Tesha studied the old man. He was frighteningly good at spying. Did he know she'd spent the day battling a concubine?

They entered the feast hall. Tesha's smile tightened. The noble guests were already standing by their chairs. But that wasn't the trouble. Hattu's chair sat in the center of the arrangement on the men's side of the hearth. Either the servants had not heard of his absence or they prepared for him just in case. It was honorable to have his place prepared, except the servants had not matched the correct drinking cups with the proper chairs. Both the size and ornateness of the chairs and the drinking cups marked the rank of each of the men. Hattu's cup and Nerik's had been reversed. Had Nerik thought to increase his honor with his father's cup and somehow arranged this switch? Was it a way to take over Hattu's role as she'd overheard him say to his friend in the hall? It would be a petty means to make himself feel important. She would put an end to Nerik's grudging mistreatment of Hattu.

Ahmose glanced from her face to the arrangement around the hearth. His head tilted slightly as if he was considering something.

Just then Nerik entered and Tesha turned to greet him. She'd have to deal with the cups at some other moment. She wouldn't let word get back to Egarya that the Hitolians didn't understand decorum.

She looked again at Ahmose. She'd enjoy discussing the problem of Nerik with him, but airing family tensions would be disloyal to Hattu.

Right now she had to greet each of these nobles in the room as if they were trusted courtiers rather than complete strangers, introduce Ahmose, and somehow include Nerik in such a way that he felt flattered. Sitting down to the meal seemed a long way off.

24

Hattu had driven the Paskans back, and his men were returning safely. They thought he'd outsmarted the Paskans and considered the day a success, but he didn't. He was still missing something. That feeling nagged at him.

Hattu signaled his nearest officer. "What are the Paskans really up to?"

The wrinkles around the man's eyes and lips turned down. He shook his head. "We've dealt with them for now."

They had. Maybe that was all that mattered. He needed to talk it out with Marak.

He had hoped that the Paskans came to negotiate about Marak. Shatim had also been sure of that and persuaded him this was their chance to win the release his friend and Daniti. He'd taken his best veterans as parley escort. They'd have also done fine in a battle against the invaders, but once his men neared the Paskans, the raiders had turned and kept ahead of his soldiers no matter how fast he drove them. No negotiations and no battle.

"Your majesty?" the officer asked. "Are you . . . ?"

"I'm fine." Hattu knew what his soldier noticed.

If he could get free of the lacerating agony in his chest for long enough, this run wouldn't kill him. He might even figure out what the Paskans were up to.

Running beside his soldiers, he'd struggled all afternoon with the wriggling pain as it burst alive again. The hot raised welts under his skin disgusted him. These were not the marks of hastily fastened armor. This was a living torment—centipedes that had crawled over and through his skin. He had to face the truth to rid himself of this lingering curse. He would fight it.

The men around him showed no struggle beyond the challenging run.

He heard the Paskan's voice again. *Your weakness. Yours.*

Your weakness let curse in.

Unforgivable.

His secret shame.

He had to fight it and conquer.

There had been times of quiet, but he didn't know why. The creatures' slumber hadn't been under his control. He would fight and silence them once and for all.

He needed a battle plan. The centipedes were moving down on either side of his chest like soldiers executing a pincer attack to surround an enemy. Aiming at his center. He held them off and pushed back. For how long? He must arm himself better.

At first the struggle of keeping up with his men had distracted him too much, but eventually he and his troops had come to a meadow open to the sun, and he gained a moment of clarity about the layout of the land and the direction of his foe's progress.

He hadn't been watching their route, not carefully enough.

The Paskans might be keeping ahead rather than attacking because they sought advantageous ground for the fight. They'd know the territory even better than he did. He assessed the landscape to avoid such a trap.

The energizing scent of pines had filled him. The chill mountain breeze flowed around and into him, bringing a cooling calm.

Was there something else in play?

Like the landscape plan Tesha had drawn on clay that morning over the scout commander's table, the details of the route around him had fallen into place.

He was driving toward Paskan-controlled territory with a small contingent. He'd brought his best fighters and a lot of them, but there was a limit to what they could take on and win. Why had the Paskans initiated this raid if they only meant to turn and run without gaining anything? It wasn't their way. *This* was a lure.

Hattu had signaled his men to halt, then climbed a boulder and stood above them.

"We've driven the rats back. They won't be raiding my kingdom today. But they might be drawing us toward a larger contingent of their warriors. Let's disappoint them and march back to Alpara. How does dinner in your barracks sound?"

They'd cheered. Misgivings shadowed him, lure or no lure, but turning back seemed best. What else was evading him?

Now they were making the return journey. His drained body moved awkwardly, and he slipped on the pine needles shifting under his boots. But with no danger to anticipate—or none that he could identify—the return seemed shorter than the march out. The creatures quieted again for no reason he could discern, but he breathed freely in relief.

If he gave himself a quick wash and change of clothes, he'd make it to at least part of the feast. Best to keep an eye on Ahmose. The ambassador could juggle more than one mission at a time, so what else besides stopping war in Amur? A loose thread, one among several, from that damned conspiracy against Hattu in Lawaza was the letter Kudur sent to Pharaoh identifying ways to undermine Hattu's rule. It had been pure spite, but it was the sort of hint Ahmose could follow up on. The Egaryan could keep the peace as he said, but also weaken his Hitolian foe in secret.

Keeping track of the threats that surrounded him exhausted Hattu. He groaned under a surge of squirming.

He'd keep an eye on Tesha's attitude toward Nerik also. The boy had rough edges, but he was his son. *His* son—not hers, of course.

After changing, he entered his feasting hall. Tall-backed chairs with matching side tables curved around the hearth in rows. Beside each stood a nobleman. His court had responded admirably to this hasty formality, this ruse to hide Ahmose's real purpose in coming to Alpara. The room felt overfull to him and crowded.

The stuffiness of the warm room surrounded him. With a shrug, he shifted his clean tunic, trying to ease the way it sat on the cursed welts underneath. They'd awakened again. Like a large room full of too many loud voices, the hundreds of wriggling pricks under his skin drove him mad.

Tesha and Nerik greeted each of the attending nobles, stiffly pretending to be polite to each other. Tesha had taken the lead, yet Nerik was the one who knew all the guests. Couldn't she let the young man practice being a king?

The first libation hadn't yet been made, so he wasn't very late. The steward hurried to him and announced his arrival. The guests turned their attention to him. He could end the awkwardness and get things moving along.

"Dear friends, I will not hold up the enjoyment of the feast with further greetings. It is good to be back home after more than a year away, and to honor our guest, Ambassador Ahmose. First, I will pour the libations. Especially to Ishana. I owe her thanks for the victory she gave me over Egarya." Let his nobles hear that—Ahmose visited as the losing side, not the dominant. And it had been under *his* generalship.

Hattu turned to the gold cup placed ready on a table next to his chair. He was glad to see the servants had set his place, even though he hadn't expected to return in time.

But before he reached out for the cup, Tesha slipped next to him, blocking the table with her body. The smell of sour milk crowded his nose. She had his usual gold cup in her hand and set it on his table, removing the smaller one and putting it in Nerik's hand with a respectful bow.

His secret bane squirmed across his upper chest. He tried to hide it, but the torture made him twitch.

Tesha bent close to his ear. "Are you all right?"

He drew away from her and stood upright, although searing stings lunged downward. He frowned at her. Why couldn't she let him be?

And this business with the cups—some servant had given Nerik his father's cup. Perhaps they'd heard of his absence. Tesha should have let it be. Why did it matter?

Worse, her stiffness around Nerik showed what really bothered her—Nerik being treated like the king.

Tesha blinked hard several times. Apparently, he'd offended her.

He grabbed the gold cup and raised it to the gods. He stepped to the circular hearth, said the prayer, and poured the first libation to the city's protective god, the Stormgod. The splash sizzled against the coals.

Then he lifted the cup again. "To Ishana, the goddess who has always stood by me." He searched within himself for the confirmation of her blessing that he always felt when he offered to Ishana, but he felt nothing. He frowned, disoriented, and poured out the wine. A sudden flaring of the fire forced him to jump back. He shook his head. This wasn't right. Had the goddess refused his offering?

He scanned the room, looking for any unwelcome reaction.

Tesha watched him too closely. It wasn't his fault the goddess did not accept his prayer tonight. All these distractions were pulling him in too many directions at once. He couldn't find the necessary quiet. Tesha should understand.

Hattu caught Nerik glaring at Tesha. Couldn't those two get along? She shouldn't provoke his son.

Hattu sat in his chair and ate the portions his servants brought to the table beside him. He made conversation with the nearby guests, telling the story of the elusive Paskans he'd driven off.

The strain of maintaining public pretenses with Ahmose exhausted him. The wily old man exuded charm and talked mostly with Tesha. They seemed to have spoken while he had pursued with his soldiers. She acted as if nothing were wrong. A good performance. She'd worn one of his wedding gifts, a close-fitting gown covered in exotic trim woven, he'd been told, on some far-off island.

Regal. She wanted to be queen, beautiful and ambitious. The curving swell of her breasts and that mysterious valley disappearing between them worked on him. He shifted in his chair to hide the effect she had on him.

The feast dragged on, but when Nerik's words began to slur with too much drink, Hattu put an end to the evening. The farewells with his guests took too long. He was tired and irritated. He needed a good rest away from quarrelsome family and the painful gnawing inside.

25

———

Tesha followed him as Hattu returned to his quarters. He was too tired for her. Being alone would be easier.

His hand went to his chest, his fingers digging in to stop the burning. He thought of the dagger on his belt. He should use it to cut them out. And die in the process, but it might be better.

He stumbled into his room. He heard Tesha gasp. She noticed his unsteadiness. Couldn't she leave him alone?

Servants slipped into the room to light the lamps and close up for the night. At least he could be rid of *them*.

Hattu waved away the servants. "Leave us alone. The shutters can stay open. Attend to the lamps in the hallway. That's enough here."

It wasn't enough light. It was never enough light now, but he had to be rid of the servants and their watching. He wanted to be the man he used to be before the prison cell, before the curse. A man with nothing to conceal.

"I'm glad you returned for the feast," Tesha said. "You must be proud of what you accomplished today. You outsmarted the Paskans."

Proud? Anything but proud. He groaned. "Ishana has left me."

Tesha drew him over to the windows. The cold air caressed his face. She pointed up into the sky. "Ishana shines down on us. She's there." Tesha's hand rested on his arm. He shook it off, but she tightened her grip. "The goddess loves you. She blessed our marriage. Remember. You haven't lost her."

"But I have."

"No, you only think that because we've lost Daniti and Marak." Tesha lifted his hand and raised it toward Ishana's stars. "Feel the goddess. May her sacred light fill you. I am her priestess, as you are her priest. Let her love and blessing come into you through her light."

Tesha didn't understand how lost he was. He should tell her about the fight inside of him. She'd cast out the curse, and yet he had these squirming welts and the onslaught of their ripping claws. Why in him but not his soldiers? *His* weakness. His fault. The curse. Ishana worked through Tesha, so why did the goddess leave this inside of him? Only him? How could he admit that to Tesha? He should tell her if he could make his tongue say the words.

How he wanted to believe Ishana still loved him. He cried out, "Ishana!"

From the twin red stars flowed some gentle sparks. Not a strong sign, not like the one she sent on their wedding day. Not the full force of Ishana's love he yearned for, but for the time being, this sign was enough. Tesha wrapped her arms around him, and he gave himself over to her embrace.

"See, she's with us," Tesha said, her breath soft against his cheek.

He took her hand and pressed it against his heart.

She smiled up at him. "She's always with us."

How could he contradict her? But for now, with Tesha near, Ishana was with him.

His body no longer burned, and the crawling under his skin had ceased. He touched his chest under his tunic and felt only cool, smooth skin.

Tesha turned, holding onto him so they both leaned out the window. She drew his arm around her.

Even in the dark, the view from these windows stretched out wide. Moonlight lit the peaks and pooled in the fertile river valley far below, the heart of his kingdom. The openness out there echoed that in his heart, giving him strength.

He pulled Tesha closer. She also suffered. It had been a long day. They needed each other.

"You are wise to tell me to watch the stars," Hattu said.

"Perhaps Ishana will send us soothing dreams when we turn our eyes to the heavens." Tesha snuggled against him as a cool breeze blew through the room.

The familiar delight in their bond overwhelmed him.

Exhaustion showed even on her young face. Lines of worry that he'd never seen before fanned out from her eyes.

"This hasn't been the welcome to your new home I'd hoped for," he said.

She pressed a kiss on his lips, lingering until he relaxed the tension holding her out. Their tongues explored each other in languid swirls. She nibbled his earlobe.

He slid his fingers into that delicious dip between her breasts.

"It wasn't easy today," she said. "Those women . . . You should have told me."

That was her concern? When so much else . . . She was right. He should have told her. The words had been in his mind to say so often.

"I meant to tell Agat to be pleasant to you, but I had to chase Paskans before I got the chance."

"Agat was not pleasant, but the cook now knows she should listen to me, not her."

"That bad?" He ran his hands down her back. "I've never had much courage when facing a woman."

"I'll keep that in mind."

Tesha stood still, unresponsive to his caresses. There was more. He hoped she couldn't bring herself to ask.

"What did Agat mean when she said you broke promises to her?"

He dropped his hands to his sides. "She sees promises where none were made. As you know, I had a wife, and later, when I no longer did, Agat knew perfectly well why I could not elevate her in such a way."

Tesha crossed her arms.

He shrugged. "It's none of her fault, but her family opposed me early on in my kingship, part of Runda's branch. I could not make them powerful by marrying her, even if I'd wanted to. When I was married, she chose the life of a concubine. Nothing changed after my wife's death."

He stepped back to the window and leaned out. He didn't want to talk about his concubines anymore. "All those tablets laid out this morning, marking the scouts' locations—patterns—it makes so much sense, but none of us thought of it before." He turned and loosened her hand from where she'd crossed her arms over her breasts. He lifted it to his lips.

Tesha smiled. He tugged her into an embrace, grasped her bottom with both hands, and lifted her hard against his loins. If only he could absorb her into himself.

"I thought we were going to watch the stars," she murmured into his neck.

"There are more stars than those in the heavens." He buried his face in her neck.

A clattering sound came from the hallway.

Tesha pulled away from him. "What was that?"

"Probably a servant refilling the oil lamps. It's nothing." He reached for her.

It didn't sound like nothing, but Tesha shook her head and stepped over to a table to untie a cord from around her neck.

"What are you doing?"

She didn't answer but came back beside him and slid his hand under her bodice, tight against her flesh.

He shuddered and loosened the clip at her shoulder so that one side of her dress slipped to her waist and revealed her bare breast. He took her firm nipple in his mouth and sucked, twirling his tongue over it and cupping her bared breast in his hand. "Now you can be like an Amazon warrior queen."

She gave a little gasp of pleasure and shifted her body back and forth against his in a way that nearly loosened him. Not yet. He wanted more—for him, for her. He owed her that much, so he shifted his hips away and pointed to the sky. "Do you see that bright cluster of yellow and blue stars over there?"

She nodded against his chest.

"I like to think of them as my heavenly courtiers twinkling outside my window. They shine brightest this time of year, so they are welcoming you as . . ." His throat constricted. A flash of the painful claws darted across his chest. He cleared his throat and gasped. ". . . their queen."

"Are you ill?" Tesha tipped up her face, watching him.

He shook his head. He should tell her. His tongue went numb.

"You have so many troubles to worry about." Tesha brushed her lips along his jawline. "It's hard to recover when each moment some new crisis strikes you. All day I missed Daniti. You need Marak. I understand."

She understood enough. She'd help him get through the exhaustion from everything without knowing more. He was much better here in his quarters with her. Ishana had sent him a star fall. He was free of it—for now.

26

Tesha let Hattu draw her into his sleeping chamber. Next to his bed, she pulled his hips close. He untied her veil, and her black hair cascaded in silky heaviness. He buried his face in it, then he ran his tongue down her neck and over the shoulder he'd bared, gently biting her skin.

Tesha slipped away from his caresses and bent to unclasp her sandals. She kicked them off, then undid her belt so her skirt puddled around her feet. Hattu pulled her loosened tunic over her head and nuzzled in the valley between her breasts.

Tesha drew back and ran her eyes up and down Hattu's still-clothed body. She raised an eyebrow and received a low rumble of Hattu's laughter. He hunched to pull his tunic off.

With his arms still stuck in the sleeves, defenseless, Tesha ran her hands over his rippling back and down around his front, drawing his starved groan as she caressed him. Hattu disentangled himself and leaned his weight against her so they fell back onto the bed. He stretched out her arms, then nudged her knees apart with his legs. She sprawled out under his admiring inspection.

His fingers, lips and tongue brushed over her collarbone and down her arm, sometimes kneading into her, sometimes brushing so lightly it felt like her soul being conjured from her flesh. She lifted her other hand to caress his head.

"Don't move." He caught her hand and kissed it as he laid it back onto the bed.

His fingers played over her body, lighting fires so demanding her hips arced up against whatever part of him they could touch. His tongue pushed into her navel and then downward, wafting her into elated oblivion. When her need for him grew unbearable, he relented and joined their bodies in a rhythm that opened her heart and body wider. She turned liquid under the firmness of his muscles.

They lay with their limbs entwined. Tesha's breath gradually slowed. She held Hattu's love securely. He could not want those other women. Once they rescued Daniti and Marak, her new life would be good. *Thank you, Ishana, my goddess of love and war.*

"Does that make up for some of today?" Hattu asked.

Tesha lifted his hand to her lips and kissed it. "A little. I can't stop thinking about Daniti, though."

Hattu sighed. "I don't know what else to do."

The silence grew long. She knew how to comfort him. Would it be enough to keep him from his dark moods?

"The scouts will find them," Tesha said.

"Maybe with your new plan," Hattu replied. "I really thought the group we chased today had something to do with Marak's capture. Shatim had me convinced. That's why I went out and left you to cope alone. But they made no attempt to communicate."

"We'll get them back."

"I'll give up lands if I have to."

"You don't really have to go to Amur, do you? It's too much."

Hattu smoothed a lock of her hair, rubbing his fingers down it. She liked when he did that. Her hair entranced him.

"How can I let war between us and Egarya break out again? The Paskans whittle away at the empire, but they'll never take control of more than a small part. War with Egarya now? We'll weaken each other so much that one of our vassal kingdoms will clear away the rubble and take over."

"So, you might go?"

"I'll have to."

"Perhaps you should take Nerik with you."

Hattu's fingers stopped and he fell back against the pillow. "I'm sorry you don't like him. He's always been quick to anger. He's not ready to go on a mission like this one. You'll have to manage. You can keep him out of your way."

Tesha slid her arms around him and pressed her body against him. "That wasn't—" He didn't understand. She wanted to like Nerik. Nerik didn't make that possible. "I just meant you—"

"It's fine. You and Nerik will get to know each other better." He tugged her closer, and his fingers brushed along her hair, down her arm, and across the small of her back.

"Who will secure your kingdom while you are away?"

He nuzzled into her neck, and then ran his tongue downward and into a delicate circle around her nipple, drawing up another wave of liquid desire. She arched up toward him.

He lifted his head and looked down into her face. He gently kissed her lips while his hand rested over her heart. "My queen. You can rule for me."

Tesha gasped.

"Rule alone?" Her voice had an uncharacteristic squeak to it. "You will first need to make me *your queen*."

27

———————

In Tesha's dream the woman's screams grew louder. Because Ishana sent her divination dreams, Tesha had taught herself to attend to her dreams even in her sleep and to hold onto them when she awakened. But she could not identify the source of the screaming. How could she determine the meaning without knowing who screamed? Her first thought had been Daniti, but this shriek wasn't from her sister. Some frantic, terrified woman needed help.

Movement woke Tesha. Hattu jumped out of bed. The cries continued. They hadn't been part of a dream. The screeching came from close by—across the hallway in the rooms where Hattu's children and concubines lived.

Hattu grabbed his tunic from the floor where she'd tossed it. Hattu's attention last night had been focused entirely on her, she'd made sure.

Hattu rushed into his outer room. She stumbled after him, collecting her clothes from the floor. The scent of Daniti's perfume lay heavy on the air in the hall. Her mind must be tricking her. The near sound of a woman's distress brought her sister's danger into her awareness.

Someone must have reached the screaming woman. The sounds

changed timbre and now Tesha heard Nerik's name and calls for help. Tesha pulled her skirt up over her hips and tied it, then shrugged the tunic over her head. She struggled to close the clasp at the shoulder so she was decently covered. Hattu had frozen at the window.

"What is it?" Tesha asked. She stepped beside him.

He pointed. "Ishana preserve us."

Dark figures, two hundred or more of them, marched up the switchbacks. The line of men disappeared behind the cover of trees or buildings in places, but elsewhere on the road the moonlight picked them out, moving rapidly forward like a giant serpent sliding forward. Already the front group of invaders had passed through the second to last gate and climbed the ascent toward the final gate. None of the defensive walls had held them back.

Hattu opened a wooden trunk along one wall. He pulled out a sword belt and strapped it on. "Go to Nerik's room. Find out why Ija screams. Take care of Nerik like your own son. I'll stop the Paskans. Someone has betrayed the city." He finished tying on his boots and shot out the door.

Tesha looked once more at the advancing attackers, then she ran across the hall. Hattu had recognized the woman's voice. Ija. If Tesha's instincts were correct, Ija was the young concubine with the most interest in Hattu's presence in her bed. Now she was screaming from Nerik's room in the middle of the night.

Tesha didn't know the layout of the maze of rooms that made up the concubines' and children's quarters, and no lamps shone. Dim moonlight came in from the rooms that had windows, but Tesha had no sense of where she was supposed to go. The first room she looked into lay empty, the bedclothes thrown back. She followed the agitated voices down the hall past other doorways. She went through an empty receiving hall, down a corridor, and into the sleeping chamber beyond.

Nerik lay sprawled across Ija's lap, and Agat kneeled on the bed beside him. The children pressed against the wall in fear. Nerik's body shuddered and jerked as if controlled by some unseen force.

Agat whipped around at the sound of Tesha's entrance. "Where is Hattu?"

"Fighting off a raid. What has happened?"

"A raid? Now?" At a groan from Nerik, the older woman turned back to him.

"My poor boy," Ija said, cradling him.

Pushing at Ija's hands, Agat told her to get out of the way. Nerik's shaking made it difficult for the young woman to hold him. She slid him off her lap and crouched next to the bed.

Tesha leaned over. "What is wrong with him?" His eyes were closed, his face red and sweaty.

"Bring Hattu now." Agat didn't even look at her.

Pasul hurried in, followed by the healer. "I've brought the physician."

"Thank goodness," Tesha said. Utar had threatened to expose her magic, but he had genuine healing skill. Hattu told her to care for Nerik like her own son. He already blamed her for Nerik's dislike, so why not for any harm his son suffered tonight? Not fair, and not like her Hattu, and yet . . .

Tesha pulled the physician toward the bed. Utar's sleep-bleary eyes immediately focused on his patient.

The concubines shifted to make room for him.

Kneeling, the healer touched the prince's forehead and cheeks. "What happened?"

Ija spoke. "When he returned from the feast this evening, he'd had too much wine. He was unsteady, so I helped him undress. When he asked that I stay, I lay beside him."

The youngest concubine, Pasul, groaned at that admission. Tesha glanced at Agat. She did not look concerned at this shift to the son's bed, but her attention stayed on Nerik.

Ija's brow furrowed. "He needed me, and he fell asleep immediately. It was lucky I was there for him because I was awakened by groaning. He held his stomach and said his gut burned. Then this shaking started. I screamed for help. I fear he is possessed by some demon."

"Or too much wine," the physician said. But he shook his head. Even Tesha knew wine alone did not cause these convulsions.

"Ija's cries for help woke me," Agat said.

Holding the boy by the shoulders with the sureness of a person used to taking control in difficult situations, the physician asked Nerik, "What hurts? Do you know why you're ill?"

His head lolling, Nerik muttered something incomprehensible. His eyes fluttered open, but they didn't seem to see the physician.

Utar leaned back and studied his patient. He turned to Agat. "Has he had loose bowels or vomited? Some of the slaves have been sick like this recently. It passed safely for them. Well, not for one, but . . ."

That didn't sound entirely reassuring.

Nerik's mouth moved. He struggled to say something and they all turned their attention to hear. "Poison."

Tesha gasped. Utar jerked back at this word.

"Poison?" The physician leaned closer to Nerik's face to hear better.

Another spasm overcame Hattu's son, and vomit flew from his mouth onto the healer. Ija jumped away from the bed. Tesha covered her nose with her hand and stepped closer to the wall.

The healer lifted his patient forward. "Help me so he does not choke."

Agat grabbed from the other side. Tesha did not intervene.

The healer shoved his fingers down the sick boy's throat, making him vomit again. "If his gut burned, perhaps it is poison. We must get it out of him."

Tesha watched in horror.

They made Nerik vomit twice more until only some yellowish muck came out. Tesha kept her eyes off the disgusting pile on the floor. She desperately needed fresh air or she would lose her own stomach. But Hattu had commanded her to take care of his son. She couldn't leave.

"We'll wash him out with water." The physician pointed to a clay pitcher and cup on a table. Tesha grabbed the cup and filled it. Carefully she handed it to him, avoiding the mess beneath his feet.

He held the cup to Nerik's mouth, but the boy drew back. "You must drink."

When Nerik balked again, Utar handed the cup to Agat and took hold of his jaw. Together they poured some water down, and Tesha could see Nerik's throat struggling to swallow. This time the older woman held the cup to Nerik's lips and he drank, although his eyes were still closed and Tesha wasn't sure he knew what he was doing.

The water did not stay inside. Soon Nerik spewed watery scum. Then a liquid sound came from his lower region, and an even more terrible smell rose. Tesha moved back to the doorway.

Agat looked up at the youngest concubine. "Get serving women. Clean bedding. Water to wash him."

Pasul ran out. Tesha wanted to follow. She could be useful doing that.

Agat and Utar stripped off Nerik's filthy clothes. The woman who had served as his mother used the linen sheet to wipe the worst mess away.

Tesha saw what was needed. She braced herself and carried the pitcher of water to Agat and the physician. The older woman grabbed it from her and wetted a corner of the sheet.

Two servants stopped at the doorway. Pasul held a pile of unfolded bedding. It looked like she'd pulled it off someone's bed.

Agat yelled at them, "You, take away these dirty linens and wipe that up on the floor. And you, spread the clean ones so we can lay Nerik down."

The serving women did as ordered, and the smell diminished when the unlucky servant left with the dirty linens in her arms. They laid Nerik back on the clean bed. He still shook, but the way a person does when he is too cold. Tesha picked up the wool blanket the serving woman had dropped when she spread the clean bedding. She laid it over Nerik's feet and was pulling it up to cover him when Agat yanked it from her hand. Tesha stepped back. Agat had earned the right to cover the boy. She had certainly cared for him like a son and Tesha had not.

Tesha wished Nerik's face was not such a deathly white. All the red color she'd seen at first was gone. The sheen of sweat looked like it covered marble. The stench of sickness hung in the air.

Agat knelt beside the bed, her hand covering Nerik's.

On the other side, Utar sat next to the prince. He had acted with speed and confidence, and yet he looked shaken. Tight lines fanned out across the small part of his face uncovered by hair. "Can you hear me?"

Nerik's eyes opened.

"Did you say poison?"

Nerik nodded. He turned to Agat. Her eyes stretched wide.

Tesha looked up at the sound of someone running toward the room.

28

Hattu shouted orders to the soldiers rallying around him. "Form up twenty across. We either drive them back through that"—he pointed ahead to the final gate—"or we lose the city." To fight off the Paskans bursting through the upper gate, he had only the men from the uppermost barracks. This treachery had separated him from most of his remaining army and fragmented the defense of Alpara. Here at the critical location, they were outnumbered with one chance to save the citadel and palace.

His body felt sluggish, and his armor pressed hard against the burning welts that had returned much worse than before. He glanced up to find Ishana's twin red stars, but he could not see them in their customary place in the sky. By the windows only hours before, he'd felt a reprieve under her star fall, but he'd sensed that it was only temporary. Even monsters must rest sometimes.

The abeyance had helped him. He'd regained essential strength to fight this lethal betrayal of his city, but their slumber had reinvigorated the curse creatures, also. How long could he hold up under their renewed assault? It reached deeper into him with overpowering force. Their scrambling legs maddened him. The piercing claws stabbed at his core. He sucked in the cold night air and threw himself into the battle.

His soldiers muscled forward against the Paskan onslaught. How, by the gods below, had the Paskans slithered through every defensive ring? Had Hitolian traitors bribed the guards? He'd known some conspirators remained to root out, but this—

He called out the necessary commands. "Second Battalion, break through on the left. Third Battalion, on the right. Surround them. First, you're with me, straight ahead. Push them back."

He raised high the spear he'd grabbed in the barracks when he'd roused his men. The king himself giving the alert. That was a new experience. He'd sent the soldier who served as his horn signaler up onto the citadel wall to blast a warning to the barracks near each gate. He could only hope the trustworthy among his soldiers would overcome the curs who let in this snake and retake the walls from them. He hated being cut off from direct contact with the rest of his army, or what he had left of it in the city after sending most of his forces to fight the Paskan incursion to the north. This was a coordinated assault. These night invaders were only a part of a larger whole. Damn the Paskans.

Leading a block of soldiers, Hattu shoved forward. In his head, he heard Ija's cries about Nerik ringing over and over. He shook himself. Not now.

"Spears launch!" He wouldn't let these demons reach his family.

He launched his own spear. A Paskan fell—the one who'd been giving orders. Others collapsed under a rain of spears.

He drew his sword and used his shield as a battering ram. The soldiers on either side followed suit. The Paskan advance slowed.

Only the frontmost of the Paskan attackers had burst through the final gate. The narrow gates acted as funnels slowing any advance. He and the men around him had to shove this invasion into the field of death on the other side of this gate. Then the soldiers on the lower wall would have to prove true and do their job to close the Paskans in on that side. The trap only worked if he had control of both walls.

He glanced at the armed men around him. They had followed his orders so far, but were they also traitors? No—these were his veterans just returned with him. The bribed men must have been among the few who did not march to the Egaryan war with him. He'd been gone from his city too long.

A Paskan leapt toward him, sword swiping in a blow aimed at his neck. Hattu threw his shield arm up and dove low with his sword, hitting above the man's shin greaves and felling him like a tree. His arm felt like deadwood, but he forced himself through movements so familiar he shouldn't even have to think about them. Inside his chest, the worms gnawed at him.

Hattu's bodyguards stepped up on either side to protect him, but he hacked with his sword and yelled orders. To grasp the pattern of the battle around him, he pushed aside the muck that slowed his mind. It felt as if someone pulled his thoughts out of his reach as soon as he formulated them.

"Back lines of the Second and Third, position yourself inside the wall to turn the fight to the inner side. Make the Paskans understand why we call it the field of death."

At the front of their push, Hattu drove the Paskans against the wall and narrow gate opening. Now they stumbled to get back through to avoid the oncoming line of soldiers under Hattu's command.

His runners had come forward with more spears for the First. As soon as he saw his men rearmed, he bellowed, "Launch."

The Paskans scrambled over their dead as Hattu and his men drove them backwards. If only the other side of his trap was closing in as tightly, just the way he'd designed it.

But at least he'd driven the enemy from his palace. Just in time. His thoughts spiraled in confusion, and each movement was like lifting stone. But he'd taken the fight away from his family, his children. Nerik.

Please let Nerik be unharmed. Goddess, hear me.

He'd taken the fight away from Tesha also. A foul taste rose up his throat and a sour smell filled his nose. He'd left her there in the palace where his family was.

No. He wrenched his thought around. Tesha *was* his family. He tried to think that, but the image of her that filled his head was shadowed and hostile. The relentless curse gnawing in his body blocked out the memories he reached for.

He shook himself. The battle was everything now. "Gate holders, close the gate. Second and Third Battalions—all of you to your positions on the wall. First Battalion, kill the Paskan fiends left on this side of the gate."

When he was sure they'd killed every one of the Paskans not yet trapped inside the field of death, he dragged himself up one of the hidden staircases inside the wall. Coming out at the top, he looked down and across. His men at the other gate had not failed him. They'd closed that gate also, penning in the Paskan warriors. Whoever the traitors were, they'd been overwhelmed by his veterans, and his men had sprung the trap as he'd trained them to do.

He propped himself against the shield wall on the walkway. He'd turned aside the disaster, but he felt confused instead of elated. The Paskans had inside help. He'd been betrayed. Thank Ishana he'd turned his men around that afternoon and returned with his tested veterans. That ploy to remove him and his soldiers must have been part of this invasion. Now he saw what he'd missed. If he'd followed the retreating Paskans back to their border, Alpara would be in Paskan hands—or some combination of traitorous Hitolians and Paskans. Who could he trust?

He pulled up on his armor straps to lift the weight off his chest and tried to get more air.

Hattu looked down into the field of death. All the warriors of a Paskan tribe were gathered in one place to be slaughtered. Already numbers of them dropped as his archers shot down arrows.

He pushed off the wall and called one of his officers over. "Don't let the archers kill them all. Live prisoners will be useful to negotiate in exchange for Marak. Fill my citadel cells. I'll get something useful from this nightmare."

The officer grunted in agreement. "Yes, sir. I'll capture enough prisoners to get Commander Marak back."

Hattu staggered toward the stairwell. He had to get back to the palace. Nerik. Ija's cries kept ringing in his head.

His son. His heir. What had caused that screaming? Ija wasn't always sensible. Beautiful, but not much else. He had to trust she overreacted.

He called to a soldier to accompany him as a precaution. They shouldn't run into any enemy, but he wasn't sure who the enemy was anymore.

His limbs barely responded at first, but he struggled onward and ran toward his son. His footsteps and those of the soldier behind him echoed in the empty street. The reassuring crowd of his men had vanished. The dark walls on both sides closed in. He jumped back as the deeper shadow cast by a wall appeared in a flash as a cave-in. The familiar suffocation from the cell overcame him, and the cursed wriggling intensified beyond endurance. The clawing tore and ripped. He gasped and stumbled.

His soldier grabbed his arm. "Sir?"

"I'm fine. Just tired."

The dark abyss that cell had created in him acted like an open wound, bleeding him into weakness. The curse vapor and centipedes had lodged into that wound, eating him alive.

But his son. He had to reach Nerik. His strained exchanges with Nerik since his return rubbed wrong, increasing his alarm. He couldn't lose his son while they were at odds. He'd had happy moments with Nerik since his return, hadn't he? He tried to remember through the incessant turmoil inside of him, but he choked on a rancid smell. All that came to mind was Tesha standing stiff with dislike near Nerik, then her face grew misshapen with hate.

That was how she felt? He lost his footing and tumbled toward the ground, but the soldier behind caught him. "Sir?"

He shook off the soldier's hand and plunged toward the palace.

Hattu passed the wall surrounding the Stormgod's temple. He'd win back his son's love soon enough. If Nerik was alive.

A footpath ran between the temple and the adjacent building, his armory storage. As he drew up next to the path, the sound of footsteps bounced off its close-set walls. With his soldier at his shoulder, he glanced down the path. A man ran toward them. Moonlight caught his armor enough to reveal that this wasn't one of his soldiers running with a drawn sword. Hattu slid his sword from its sheath.

To the soldier at his side, he said, "Enemy intruder."

The man turned to flee.

Hattu sprinted to catch him. *Oh no, you don't. That way leads to my palace and my family. To Nerik.* He swung his blade and caught the man's back with a shallow slice.

He signaled to his soldier, and they put on enough speed to come up on either side of the man.

"Halt," Hattu yelled. Blood ran from his first blow and both he and his soldier were positioned to kill the man, so they left him little choice.

Hattu stood with the point of his sword on the man's chest. "Who let you into Alpara?"

What was a Paskan doing this close to the palace? They'd stopped the invasion before anyone had a chance to get this far.

The man groaned and slowly slid to the ground. He glared at Hattu. "Don't know."

Hattu grabbed his veteran's arm. "Stay with him. Find out how he got here—whatever it takes. Report back. We're hunting a traitor."

"Yes, sir," the soldier said.

Hattu pumped his exhausted legs back down the path and up the wide ramp to the palace gates.

The guards he'd left to secure the palace saw him, and one raced to meet him. "Your Majesty?"

Out of breath, Hattu answered, "Attack contained. Not finished, but . . . Word of Nerik?"

"Nerik?" The man shook his head, confused.

Hattu pushed past him without clarifying. At least the trouble Ija had screamed about hadn't been widespread enough for it to reach the palace's outer doors.

Ishana, keep all harm from my son, now and always. I don't care what else I lose, just not my son.

Hattu dashed through the palace. All seemed quiet. Anxious servants huddled in their nightclothes, but they didn't stop him or say anything. They hadn't lit lamps. He supposed they avoided drawing the attention of the enemy, but their concern seemed all for what lay outside. Darkness veiled every room Hattu ran through. His palace felt like a siege tunnel underground—or a windowless prison cell. Couldn't they have left lamps lit in the hallways?

He turned into the corridor leading through the women's quarters toward Nerik. He panted with the exertion of pushing forward through the silent shadows. His son still lived in his childhood rooms. In his memories, Hattu heard the echo of his son's complaints of being treated too much like a child. He wanted his son to experience only shelter and protection, the safety of love Hattu had so missed as a child. The intensity of that love in his heart felt like a saving hand. He tried to use that feeling to shut out the frenzy the darkness loosed in him and the clawing at his innards by those creatures. He had to fight the panic, or he'd roll up in a defensive ball.

From ahead, Hattu could hear voices. He peered down the hallway into Nerik's bedchamber, but he couldn't make out anything through the gloom. Had this corridor always been this narrow? The air hung too dense and choked him. The prickling in his chest sharpened into knife stabs.

He stumbled the last paces into the room, rubbing his eyes and shaking himself. The stench of vomit hung in the air. He could make out a group clustered around Nerik's bed—Tesha, the physician, Agat, and the other women and children. Nerik lay there, his eyes open. *Thank you, Ishana.*

He staggered to Nerik's side, falling on his knees beside the bed. Nerik had been saying something. He'd missed it.

Tesha stood near.

Nerik turned his pale face toward him. "Poisoned. By her." Nerik raised one finger aimed at Tesha. "Clear way *her* sons."

Hattu's gaze moved back to Tesha and he screamed. A dark

shadow stretched out. It rose behind Tesha, hovering over his son like a demon.

He threw himself over Nerik. "Get away from my son."

She jumped and the darkness shrank, flitting toward him. But he felt nothing from it.

It was gone. Had he imagined it?

29

Hattu had lurched into the room. Now the gray haze Tesha had noticed around him previously had expanded and deepened. It was not produced by her faulty vision. Something evil bound him.

He fell on his knees by Nerik's bed.

Before she could kneel next to him, the darkness that encompassed him stretched toward her like a darting shadow. Hattu screamed. She leapt back.

Hattu fell over Nerik as if to protect him.

She reached out for him, but he ignored her. "My beloved, what has happened to you?"

Hattu looked into Nerik's deathly pale face. "How can this be?" Then he looked at her. "Explain."

She was supposed to explain? Far more important than Nerik's bizarre accusation was the darkness that possessed her husband. Had she failed to drive out some remnant of the curse and now it resurged? She couldn't ask that in front of Utar and the concubines. Hattu's reign would end if Utar spread rumors like that.

No one else had reacted. They hadn't seen the dark cloud around Hattu. Her power with sorcery must allow her to see it.

Tesha crossed her arms and pressed into the wall behind her. Hattu's chest sunk inward. His hands shook. Beads of sweat ran down his face. The familiar signs, but worse now with whatever held him. She stepped toward him to calm him, but something in his eyes made her stop.

"You poisoned my son?"

"I would never harm Nerik. He's ill and doesn't know what he says." Tesha looked into Hattu's eyes. No warmth. Not even the confused plea for help she dreaded but could answer. He'd never looked at her like that. She reached out her hand, then let it drop when he did not take hold of it.

Hattu sat on the bed beside Nerik and pressed his son's hand against his heart. Tesha clenched her own hands into fists. Everybody in this palace wanted to take Hattu from her.

Hattu's knuckles went white with the pressure on Nerik's hand. "How are you? What happened?"

Nerik groaned.

Utar, the physician, described Nerik's symptoms and what he had done. "Nerik could have been poisoned, the way he was sick. After we got him to vomit it out, he's better. I think he'll recover. But your new wife's training as a priestess . . . She would know poisons."

"She did it." Nerik's eyes fluttered, but they seemed too heavy for him to keep open.

"No!" *Ishana help me.* "I don't know anything about poisons. Why would you . . ." Tesha fell on her knees by Hattu. She willed him to realize he needed her even more. She had to help him. *Ishana, Ishana!* "Of course I didn't poison your son. If somebody has, we must figure out who it is, but—"

Tesha turned toward Utar. She'd make him speak the truth. He suspected her because of her sorcery, but this was different. Completely different. "You said others were sick like this, slaves. You said one didn't get better. Isn't this the same?"

Utar tugged at his beard. "The one who didn't get better was a groom. He showed signs of worms, so I'd given him dried tansy to make into tea, not the tincture which is far more potent. I told him how to brew it and how much to drink. Not a harmful amount. Tansy is dangerous enough, so I'm always careful. But somehow he got too much. I don't know how. He died. I . . . I can't explain it. But Nerik's jerking shudders, vomit, the rest. It is similar." Utar touched Nerik's shoulder. "You were at the stables at the end and saw your groom's death. He was worse than you, but . . . You didn't drink tansy for some reason? You haven't been that foolish, have you?"

Nerik shook his head. "No. Saw my groom. Horrible. That woman did this."

"No, I didn't. Stop these lies!"

"It would be easy enough for her to get hold of tansy," Utar said. "It's only harmful if someone drinks a great deal, and it's quite useful. Any healer would have it, even in a temple."

"And easy for anyone else too," Tesha cried. "Why me?"

"Nerik?" Hattu finally spoke up. Tesha sobbed in relief. Nerik had no reason to accuse her but his own spite.

Nerik's broken voice gasped in spurts. "She wants me dead. Gain . . . everything. Throne for . . . own son. You must have worried, Father. Everyone . . . talked of this before your return. She did it. During feast."

Nerik's hate ran much deeper than jealousy over sharing his father's attention. Tesha glanced at Agat. Her head was bowed, and she'd stepped away from the bed—the first time the concubine didn't claim a central place for herself.

Hattu's brow pulled into deep lines. "At the feast?" He shook his head.

Tesha waited for Hattu to put an end to these lies, but he seemed stuck. His back hunched, curling his shoulders downward, nothing like her strong Hattu.

"This is ridiculous," Tesha said. "I love you, Hattu, and so I honor Nerik as your son. Nerik, you have no reason to think I made you sick. All I've thought about is finding a way to free Daniti and Marak."

"But . . ." Hattu struggled for words. He leaned closer to her, then wrinkled his nose and drew back. "You don't honor him. Poison him?

That's hard to believe, but you've made it clear how little you like Nerik. You're lying about that."

"You're confusing Nerik's dislike of me as if that were my feeling," Tesha said. "You know me."

"Do I?" Hattu stared at Tesha, and she could see his rising alarm in the expanding whites of his eyes. His muscles were taut like bowstrings, worse than any of his fits on the journey. She thought of his scream and the darkness that had moved out from him toward her.

"Hattu, my love. I am not evil as your son and concubines assumed before I ever came here. You know that."

Hattu's shoulders twitched. "But last night . . ." His voice rasped. The gray haze bloomed around him again. "You made a point of switching Nerik's and my cups. You tried to hide what you were doing. I thought it was only so he wouldn't have the bigger one, another sign of your disrespect for him. You hate him. But that's when you put in the poison." He rubbed his hands over his face. "You do want him out of your way. You said so last night."

This wasn't her Hattu. "I didn't say that, and I've never possessed tansy. My training didn't include herbs and cures. How can you accuse me? My darling, consider. This isn't like you."

"Thrones and stepmothers. I should have known. You were so eager to be queen. And yet, it doesn't seem like you."

The gray fog hung around Hattu like vine tendrils clinging to a lattice. These traces of dark magic were persuading Hattu of what he should never have been able to believe. She had driven away a noxious curse vapor from Hattu and his soldiers, but here it was, still tormenting her husband.

Hattu fidgeted at his breastplate. He pulled at the ties that held it in place and swayed on his feet. He seemed about to collapse. He wouldn't want to be seen in this state.

Hattu turned to the physician. "Blessings on Ishana that you saved my son. Take good care of him. He will rule long in Alpara when I am gone." He glared at her. "Whatever happened, go to your rooms and stay away from my son."

Hattu stomped out.

Everyone stared at Tesha.

She lifted her chin and walked out.

She went in the direction of her rooms, but after winding down the dark hallway, she stopped. This was a cruel misunderstanding. Hattu needed her. Only she could wrest him from this evil vapor. She could understand a father's fear, but this? This panic was similar to the fits that had come over Hattu since her father imprisoned him, but he had always trusted her and seen her as his helpmate. She had never felt so cut off from Hattu. She should have tried harder to show Nerik she accepted him, even if he hated her, but no one could call her a poisoner. She wouldn't go to her rooms. She swung around. Hattu would see all of this. After all, he knew what it was like to be falsely accused. He wouldn't turn around and do the same.

30

Hattu staggered into his hall. Why hadn't his servants lit some oil lamps? Was he meant to rule in darkness? He looked around, but the servants had scattered.

Nerik was so sure, but Tesha a poisoner? His bride wouldn't have done that, would she? She did hate Nerik. The tension between them was painful. And that demon shadow had risen from Tesha and threatened Nerik. The sorcery she'd commanded to free his soldiers hadn't worked on him, and now it aimed its power against his son through her. He needed time to think. He was so tired.

He lit a stick of kindling from the banked coals in the central hearth and held it to several lamps around the room.

He pulled loose the knots holding on his breastplate. It clattered to the ground. He looked at his tunic, expecting it to be soaked in blood from the ripping of the centipedes, but he saw only the normal wet marks from his sweat. The agony hadn't let up. There were no quieting periods now. Would it kill him from the inside out? He would have turned to Tesha for help, but not now. Sorcery polluted her more than him. She turned it to her own purposes and controlled it. She wanted his son dead. Each time he turned from this disturbing realization, he was forced back to it. He slumped into a chair to release his greaves.

He'd feared for Nerik all night. Every Paskan he ran through with his sword was a danger attacking Nerik. He'd fought back against them all. Throughout the last year of his absence from Alpara, he'd endured panic whenever he'd thought of Nerik alone and without his father. The time in prison facing execution had been the worst. He'd blamed himself for not preparing Nerik for the throne. How could the boy hope to hold onto such a disputed kingdom without any training? He'd come home to repair that damage, but slowly, safely. And then he'd heard those screams about Nerik and seen his city under attack.

Nerik said Tesha had a good reason to kill him. Hattu thought of the selfish woman his own father had married late in life. She had threatened Muwatti's sons in order to put her own sons on the throne.

Hattu heard footsteps coming toward him. If it was Tesha, he didn't want to see her. He had to think. He kept his back to the door even when someone entered.

"You and I must talk. This is a misunderstanding."

Hattu stiffened at the sound of Tesha's voice. She came near. He reeled from a wave of nausea that overcame him at the rank smell that coated his nose and throat.

"I did not poison Nerik."

Hattu stood and paced the room in a wide circle, heading away from her.

"You must have heard how much Nerik's view of me was poisoned in advance."

Hattu recoiled at Tesha's repeated use of that word. Pain and the incessant twitching inside dragged him down. He'd be able to think better if it would only stop and give him peace.

"Before I arrived, he'd already assumed that I wanted him dead. But you know that's not the woman you married."

That was what Hattu didn't want to answer, who Tesha really was.

She'd commanded powerful magic against the curse. She'd released his soldiers but not him. He had watched the dark shadow rise from her to seize his son. She claimed her magic came from Ishana, but that must be a lie.

He hunched around the clawing in his chest.

"Are you ill, Hattu? Does the curse linger?"

On one of the tables, a shiny object caught the light. Hattu stepped closer and peered at it. A vial. He'd seen Tesha wearing it and had wondered why. He grabbed it.

"Is this yours?" He held it up.

Tesha looked confused. "Yes."

Hattu pulled out the stopper and sniffed.

"Give it to me." Tesha reached for it.

He pulled away from her hand.

"It's Daniti's. I was wearing it to feel her near me. I took it off so you wouldn't crush it when . . ." Tesha wrapped her arms around her waist.

"Daniti's?"

"Yes, her perfume vial. Didn't you ever notice her scent? If I closed my eyes when I opened the vial, I could imagine her right beside me instead of in the hands of the Paskans." Tesha bent over, sobs wracking her chest. She slid to the ground.

"You're lying again. This isn't perfume. Do you think tears will trick me?"

Tesha raised her head. "What?"

She couldn't fool him with this pretense, using her sadness about Daniti to hide her hatred for Nerik. He hurried back toward Nerik's room. The healer would tell him for sure. But Hattu recognized the smell of tansy oil. He knew Tesha was clever and ambitious. Nerik was right. What had he brought into his home?

THE HEALER'S certainty silenced the voice in Hattu's heart that had hoped his nose deceived him. It confirmed what his mind kept forcing him to face no matter how much he didn't want to believe it. There could be only one reason for Tesha to have a vial of tansy.

At the doorway of his quarters, he stopped. Tesha hadn't moved from the floor where she had collapsed. A good show.

"You said you'd never possessed tansy, and yet you wear a vial filled with the tincture. Utar confirmed it. This is not perfume. I certainly never smelled this around Daniti. Such clumsy lies won't work on me. You're smarter than this, even if your heart is made of bronze."

Tesha looked up at him. Her eyes glistened with tears, the curves of her lips eloquent with sadness. Her presence used to draw him, but he didn't feel that. It was as if a wall stood between them. He'd broken free. It had been a delusion, that glow that drew him out of the darkness. A sorcerer's trick.

Tesha's brows drew together. Contrived confusion. A pretense. "It *is* filled with Daniti's perfume. I found the vial in her jewelry box after the kidnapping as I prepared to lead your army. I didn't say anything because you were discouraged enough about Daniti and Marak." Her voice caught.

She had to remind him that his rescue attempt failed, didn't she?

"But I needed a sign of Daniti close to me." She rose from the ground. "How could Daniti's perfume smell like some poison?" She held out her hand.

He stared at it. The gold puzzle ring he'd given her glinted at him. His pledge to her. Twisted loops that required a clever mind to bind together. Cleverness they shared. A familiar, sustaining echo from the blackness of that prison cell came to him. *A sign from Ishana. A sign from Ishana.*

Venom from those claws burned across his chest. *No. No. No.* He shuddered at the movement inside of him. He was so tired.

Tesha was a clever liar. He handed her the vial. Let her lie her way out of this. He wished his hands weren't shaking.

She opened the vial and sniffed. "That isn't the same. There's something else in it now."

So that was it. The best she could do when faced with the poison she'd used.

Tesha looked at the vial in the palm of her hand, shaking her head. "This is her vial, but Daniti's perfume is no longer inside. I don't understand."

"Enough. I should have seen this side of you." He snatched the vial away from her. "Your father was heartless and greedy. Like father like daughter. Only unlike him, you are smart enough to hide your true form. You hid your sorcery and your selfish ambition. Thank the gods the healer's quick action saved Nerik."

"I didn't poison Nerik. Hattu, I see the vapor around you that was there when I drove off the curse. Are you—"

"Don't speak. I won't listen to your lies anymore." The evidence lay in his hand. He'd seen the dark sorcery rise beside her. "There will be no coronation. I do not choose to make you my queen. My brother would never approve of a sorcerer as queen. I may have married you, but there is no need for you to remain a first wife or even my wife at all. I will divorce you and send you away where you cannot harm anyone. Agat, with her sour ways, is a better woman than you are. I do not want to see you. I cannot countenance locking away another human being in a cell like I was. That was your father's way. But I will arrange for you to live in banishment in one of the mountain garrisons. That will be remote enough to keep you from threatening my children. You'll be under guard for the rest of your life. Be grateful for that—your life. If Hitolian law permitted, it would be easy for me to order your execution." A lie, but he had to wound her. He had to strike back for this incomprehensible evil she'd done.

Hattu stepped closer to her. Wounding her made him feel less defeated by . . . He would overcome his weakness. He would. On his own.

He didn't need strength to put her in her place. Just words. "How will you like that life? Trapped in a remote fortress with no one but surly guards for company? Even Ishana will abandon you. I'll make sure the goddess knows your crimes in full. Ishana will never come to you in your dreams again."

Tesha stepped back from him. She should be crying after what he'd said to her, but instead the set of her mouth looked hard. He turned away.

"When I take my men to Amur, I will leave my kingdom in Nerik's hands if I cannot win Marak's release in time. But before that, I will arrange your banishment."

31

———————

For another day Daniti sat or paced at the back of the cave hideout, trapped there by Paskan guards. Their captors provided dried meat, stale flatbread, and water. It was enough to survive, but barely.

They talked to fill the time. She learned that Marak's parents had chosen a wife for him early on, but the girl's family had broken the betrothal over a dispute about the bride price and dowry. The disgrace that fell on his family from this breakdown had slowed their search for another wife.

Then his father and mother died of a fever within days of each other. He'd been in shock by the unexpected loss. Taking his father's place as the family patriarch when he was still young hadn't felt right, and his sister had to prod him to take care of the necessary duties. Fortunately, she was already married, and the death in infancy of their only other sibling left him mostly unburdened. His lands were farmed by peasants who gave him a portion of their crops each year. He left them to it. He never got around to arranging a marriage for himself.

Instead of marriage, he'd chosen a soldier's life with Hattu—and that of a spy. Marak had secretly traversed the Paskan territory, assessing strengths and needs. No one among Hattu's nobles understood these nomads, and Marak believed he could conquer the Paskans only if he grew familiar with their ways.

"They do not actually want all that much," Marak said to Daniti while they sat leaning against the rough wall of their cave prison. "Just land and to be left alone. Fighting between themselves, one tribe against another, they prune back their own strength and keep themselves from growing powerful enough to become anything like a rival empire."

"But they've terrorized these lands, and nobody's been able to stop them," Daniti said.

"Not Hattu or me, it's true. Their conflict with the Hitolians could be avoided if they didn't see particular lands as theirs. You wouldn't think a people who move around to keep their herds fed would identify themselves through the land, but they do. Their movements are contained in very important boundaries. For each tribe, it's this patch of dirt or death."

"So besides mistaking me for an important queen, they kidnapped me because I crossed one of their precious boundaries?"

"Something like that. Don't worry, I'm still watching for a way to escape. We'll get out of here. But with Paskans it's always about land. I'm afraid Great King Muwatti, for all his intelligence, does not quite grasp that it's pointless to try to budge them. We either let them herd and dig on the patch each tribe identifies with, or we'll fight forever. I'm not sure it's worth it. Let them work the land and be done with it. But then they make that solution unworkable by raiding constantly—and kidnapping, although that's new. No one wants neighbors like them. No easy way with the Paskans."

"You're more sympathetic than I would have guessed after all the battles you've fought against them."

"I like the strategizing and daring that war demands, but it'd be far better if I didn't have to kill anyone."

Daniti thought about the man who'd attacked her and how quickly Marak had responded by trying to strangle him.

"Some men deserve to die," Marak muttered as if he'd heard her thoughts.

Daniti reached out and found Marak's hand. "I never thought being blind would protect me, but being a witch in the minds of these men suits me just fine."

He cradled her hand in both of his. "Don't worry. Something will change soon, and we'll get out of here. One way or another."

Angry voices carried back. They both fell silent.

Daniti listened. She sat up. "Riam has returned."

"Riam?"

Daniti squeezed his arm. *Yes.*

"Not surprising he's the Hitolian traitor. I disliked him at first glance. He was taunting Runda's son in a tavern. That poor kid made a very bad murderer, but not for lack of courage." Marak brushed Daniti's shoulder. He'd adopted the comfortable language of touch her sister used. He must have been watching them on the journey.

Daniti shuddered, remembering the bad feeling Riam had given her when she'd first been in a room with him. He'd come to her father's house disguised as a merchant. It wasn't only that he'd run down Tesha and spread false rumors about Hattu in order to seal Hattu's execution, it was something in the man himself. "Runda and his son convinced themselves they acted for their honor. But Riam, he's . . ."

Marak said, "His blood runs evil."

That was it.

From the voices Daniti counted, there were six new Paskans who must have accompanied him.

"You told us there'd be no one to defend the city." A Paskan. One of their previous guards.

"That wasn't my fault." Riam's voice again. "You were supposed to draw Hattu and his men out of Alpara."

Daniti felt Marak's hold tighten on her hand. They'd attacked Hattu's city?

"We did. Our scouts saw him. We drew him deeper into the mountains. But somehow he was there to defend the city."

"He trapped our warriors and picked them off like fish in a bucket."

Daniti felt the tension in Marak's arm release, and the weight of his hand relaxed against hers.

"You led them into that bucket. You betrayed us, Hitolian."

Marak gave a soft laugh and Daniti clasped his hand. Riam's comeuppance.

"I hate Hattu even more than you do. I told you there were risks. You had to get Hattu out of Alpara. You can't out-general him in his own city."

"He slaughtered our men, but you put them there."

There were sounds of a scuffle. Riam getting his reward as a traitor?

"You still need me," Riam rasped.

"How's that? You don't look very useful. You can't even lift your right arm. You're pathetic and a traitor. We'll avenge our warriors. Kill you and those two Hitolians in there."

Marak was on his feet. How he manage it so quickly, Daniti didn't understand, but she scrambled up and stood behind him. Tensed energy vibrated off his skin.

"I should have seen the game of treachery you played with your sorcery," Utar said. He kept his voice low, still intent on hiding his Paskan birth, but his whisper hissed with anger. "I should have exposed you immediately."

Tesha rose from the chair in the women's hall that she'd fallen into in despair. A weak glow of dawn came through the high windows, fading out before it reached the tricolored squares of the stone floor. How long she'd sat in numbness, she wasn't sure. But she would not take these accusations from the physician. He'd gotten past Henti by saying he'd come to see to Tesha's health. Ha!

She glanced at the blue curtains into the concubines' quarters. The yellow edging showed no movement. "I saved Hattu. There's no treachery."

The physician approached her by the circular hearth. "Preserving Hattu's life serves your purposes, but you have no use for Nerik. Nerik has identified that threat correctly."

Tesha shivered with the room's chill and the man's certainty. "But that groom—this started before I arrived. Tell Hattu. Make him see."

"An ignorant slave took too much of the medicine I gave him. An ugly death I regret, but it seems hearing that tale inspired you to use your vial of poison."

"I cannot explain the vial, but I did not use it." How could *she* be accused of poisoning? In Lawaza she'd been too slow to recognize that poison had been at the root of the conspiracy against Hattu. Now lies and poison stuck to her in her new home. *Ishana, where are you? Unbind me from these accusations.* But the goddess remained silent.

"I will not be persuaded by your lies," Utar said. "I should never have believed that any form of sorcery was beneficial. I know better."

"Was your mother evil? You feared that I would expose you. That was the only persuasion I used. I did not lie."

Utar shook his head.

Tesha saw the slight bump underneath the physician's tunic where the stone hung against his chest. "Use your mother's stone on me. Force me to speak the truth. Bring Hattu and let him hear me speak it. You can prove to everyone that I did not poison Nerik. No mother would choose with her final moments to give an empty gift. You *have* to be able to make the stone's magic work. If you try, it will work. Ishana will send the magic you need."

Utar's mouth fell open. He snapped it shut and crossed his arms over his chest. "You would agree to submit to the rite with Hattu present?"

Like the sudden flare of light when an ember is touched to lamp oil, Tesha's head filled with relief. Ishana's hand. At last.

"Yes, yes. Bring him right now. Remove this torment from us both."

"I have the stone but not the magical skill. It was an empty gift from my mother. Even to try would expose her and my birth. I'd pay with my life. Hardly a fair exchange. And useless. I cannot make the stone work."

"Try it on me with no one else present. Persuade at least yourself."

"The vial of poison you possessed is a stronger witness than what you say now. You know I can't make the rite work, so it's safe for you to ask me."

"Perform the rite. Ask me about the vial. You can find a way to tell

Hattu the truth in safety."

"I have no magical skill."

"I will expose you."

He shrugged. "You have no evidence. Think—I have lived at court for years. As the trusted queen, perhaps Hattu would have listened a little, but now?" He laughed and turned to go. "Do not try your invocation on him, or I will be forced to tell him that curse sorcery is not your only magic. I will be watching him for any sign you have tried it. He'll be staying away, in any case."

"Wait." Tesha stepped nearer to him. "Your concern about the Great King's prohibitions against magic is well founded. He fears even the hint of sorcery, which does not bode well for me now. Your suggestion that saving the soldiers and his younger brother would only protect me while I stood in royal favor—well, that seems true enough. But I can bring you down with me. You say no one will listen to me now, but the Great King? This is the one topic about which he will listen to anyone who says they can identify an active sorcerer. That is what I will say you are to Muwatti. I will persuade him just enough with the details of your childhood. You matter not at all to the Great King. The killing of one provincial Paskan-born physician as a safety precaution will cause him not one moment of doubt."

Utar's mouth opened. His arms went stiff, his fingers spread wide. She had his attention.

"I've told you I'm willing to submit to the rite. You must believe me," Tesha said. "At least help me. Give me the stone. Teach me the rite. I will claim the magic. I will hide your role and take the risk." She couldn't work it on herself, but she could use it to force the truth from the poisoner when she knew who that was.

"I can't make it work."

"So you say. But you know the rite. Your mother taught you or you observed her."

"You won't be able to make it work."

"Then there is no harm."

"Why should I give away this remembrance of my mother?"

"To save your life."

33

The mountain peak rose into the heavens. In its shadow, Tesha stood on the terrace of Ishana's palace sanctuary, Henti at her side. Below her, the sheer cliff gave way to a dizzying drop. A waist-high wall along the outer edge provided the only barrier against a fatal plunge.

It felt like her marriage had fallen down that cliff. How could the passion Hattu had shown die so quickly?

The spring sunshine hadn't warmed the day yet. Tesha drew in the clean air, so fresh after the smoky rooms of the palace. Sharp cold filled her nose and throat. That jolt brought her strength.

Hattu had said Ishana would abandon her when he told the goddess about her crimes. But she had committed no crimes. No poisoning, and as to her sorcery, Ishana herself had given her the power to remove the curse from Hattu and his men. He had no right to accuse her of dark magic.

She and Henti had come to the sanctuary to escape those prying eyes and ears at the curtain in the women's quarters. It had been difficult to persuade the guards posted outside her rooms that she should be permitted to pray in the sanctuary under their escort. They kept watch at the base of the sanctuary stairs, showing the loss of her freedom. In the coming days, Hattu would send her to some remote garrison.

Henti scowled at Tesha's tightly closed hand. "Do you trust that?"

Tesha opened her hand and rubbed the physician's gray stone against her palm. It reminded her of the smooth, flat stones she'd sent skipping over the lake's surface back at home in Lawaza—after, of course, a thorough rinsing in the shallows so she didn't dirty her fingers. When she'd succeeded in multiple hops, the patterns intrigued her, the circles spiraling into and over each other. Each disturbance of the calm lake left its traces.

But this wasn't an ordinary pebble. Through her skin, she could feel the spark of power.

"Trust it? Bringing truth to light would be a fine thing."

"But . . . but . . ." Henti's doubt came as a rising shriek. "It's death to use it."

Tesha nodded. "If I don't win back Hattu's trust, it is."

She would have to overcome the curse's influence on Hattu. Maybe this stone would give her magic skills that would release him. She had to try. The curse had to be why he'd cast her off. She wanted so much to believe that, but the rejection stung. The things he had said to her and the betrayal passed into her soul. The hurt would not heal easily.

Henti wrapped her arm around Tesha's shoulder. The warmth brought tears to her eyes. She leaned against Henti and closed her fist around the stone.

"It's banishment from his trust forever if I do not use it. I have to find out who poisoned Nerik."

Henti groaned. "The healer does not believe you can make it work. I don't think *he* can."

"It speaks to me."

Henti shivered, and her lips thinned into a tight line. Tesha forgave her that fear.

The stone terrified her also, but it held an irresistible pull. The flares it sent into her felt kindred to that golden power she'd drawn from the earth and stars, the plants, rocks, and streams. She yearned for the return of the sensations she'd felt while lifting the curse from the army. The goddess had provided the bridge then. Tesha had had no idea how to repeat that experience without such divine access until she'd held this stone. It thrummed with the power she'd been given by Ishana. She needed it more than ever. Now she could fill the emptiness left behind when that golden power had left her and find a way to draw Hattu free, although she did not understand how she had failed to do that before—or even if she had. Had this darkness come into him from somewhere else? She would use the stone no matter the cost.

"I'll need the clean and unclean water for the rite," Tesha said. "No one will know what we do here. It will look like any proper libation." Henti dropped the comforting arm from her shoulder. Tesha added, "Just to see if I can do it. That's all."

Henti's face tightened in uncertainty.

"I have Ishana's blessing." She hoped that was true. She'd ask for it. "We have to figure out who poisoned Nerik. Who would gain by his death? No one."

"They all think it's you who will gain—the throne for your own son."

"I'm not that kind of stepmother."

Henti patted her arm. "Of course not, but that woman Hattu's father took as his wife has set the model for stepmothers they see you through. Nothing to be done about that."

"Except rule here and show a different way. But I can't if I'm banished to a garrison. Who could have added poison to something Nerik ate or drank? Could it be an accident? Although that doesn't explain the tansy in my vial. Some store of tansy left from a dosing that got mistaken as a flavoring herb? The foods served at the feast?"

"But only Nerik got sick."

"He drank more wine than we did."

"But the wine pourers also served the nobles around you, and some of them drank a lot. There'd be word of more widespread illness, surely. The king would welcome news of an accidental problem if no one had targeted Nerik."

Whether Hattu wanted an easy reason to drop his accusation against her seemed a lot less certain to Tesha.

"Go to the kitchen to get supplies for the rite," Tesha said. "But while you are there, observe and ask what you can about who might have put poison in Nerik's food or drink. Sometime before or during the feast seems likely, there in the kitchen or the feasting hall. Doesn't that make sense?"

"I suppose. I don't know what I'm looking for, but . . ." Henti pulled up her shoulders and set off for the kitchen.

Tesha heard Henti's soft voice talking to the guards at the foot of the stairs, but she couldn't make out the words. Henti did not return, so apparently her servants could still move around as needed.

She owed these small liberties to Hattu's unwillingness to recreate the horrors of his imprisonment. That was *her* Hattu. Compassion born of his nightmarish experience.

But *this* man, quick to make false accusations? He was under the influence of the Paskan curse, but how could he abandon everything he was like this? He'd abhorred her father for that. When she'd freed him from the sticky black cloud of the Paskan curse, even in that victorious moment, there'd been something inside him that had pushed her away. She'd felt it but ignored it. That had been a mistake.

But if she told him that the curse still held him under its sway, he wouldn't accept what she said. She'd seen that last night. When she tried, he cut her off. Even without the malign influence of the curse, he hated the fits that cell had brought upon him so much he could not speak about them. Admitting to dark magic inside of him seemed impossible. And if she told anyone else, he'd be overthrown or locked up again, not saved. Nor would she be.

She clutched the stone and the echo of that golden power it sent through her. She couldn't see a direct way to use the stone to solve these problems. She would have to try what she could.

Freeing herself from the false accusations was the first step, then she could regain Hattu's trust enough to help him banish whatever that something in the curse had been that pushed her away.

She had to believe that truth would persuade him if truth came fully clothed in evidence. He'd been convinced by the vial full of poison. Surely he'd believe counter proof he could touch and hear.

Tesha sat on the low wall. If she looked out far enough, she could see the green river valley below. But between lay a rocky cliff face, studded with sharp boulders and offering no shelter.

The familiar rhythm of Henti's footsteps rose from the stairwell. The intimacy of that sound in this strange place opened the wound of Daniti's absence. Every part of her wanted Daniti here with her, safe and free from those barbarians, but Henti's company gave her deep comfort. She was someone Tesha was so accustomed to that she knew who was coming by sound the way Daniti recognized everyone. Tears sprung to Tesha's eyes.

Tesha called to Henti. "Did you learn anything?" Henti had returned quickly, not a good sign for uncovering proofs.

Her maid carried two shiny, burnt-red pitchers with tall, graceful spouts. She set them down on the altar in the niche.

"The kitchen servants will not speak to me. Gossip travels quickly, and everyone knows I am your maid."

Tesha groaned.

"But I did learn two things. Since the king thinks it's the wine cup that was poisoned, I found where they keep the wine. In a storeroom with a wooden door sealed by the steward's imprint on a clay plug. He runs a properly managed household. No wine left sitting around for slaves to steal drinks. So if someone put poison in the wine, they'd do it right before or during the feast, which doesn't tell us much. The other thing I learned that nasty cook revealed by accident."

"What'd she say?"

"When I tried to find out who worked that evening in the kitchen and as servers, she grumbled that everyone had to help with all the fancy food and service you'd insisted on, from the lowest servant to the royal family."

"Hattu's family? She said that?"

"And not a word more. I guess she saw on my face that I found that interesting."

"That's something. If we had a way to ask more." An idea sprouted. They might get some questions answered. And it would be a useful errand in two ways since it would take Henti away again. Henti shouldn't be present while she tried the stone.

She explained and Henti's face lit up. Off her servant went.

Henti's news that the wine was carefully stored hardly mattered. Hattu insisted she'd put poison in the wine, but that was no reason to suspect the wine in particular. Nerik could have consumed tansy in anything—something only he ate or drank. A late snack in his room? That didn't sound likely. Ija had said he'd gone to sleep immediately. Unless she was the poisoner.

Then Hattu's accusation rang in her memory. *You made a point of switching Nerik's and my cups.* What if they were looking at this completely wrong?

No one gained by Nerik's death except Tesha's future children—that point kept stopping her. But if Nerik wasn't the intended victim .. . Hattu had enemies in abundance, all of whom needed him dead. Paskans, the Hitolian nobles who'd participated in the conspiracy against Hattu but remained cloaked, the Egaryans—Pharaoh Gerose. How many assassins had Gerose already sent?

Ahmose. Why not send one more and hide him behind a pretend diplomatic crisis? Poison Hattu, and if that failed for some reason, stir up plenty of trouble by removing Hattu from his own fragile kingdom to solve a non-existent emergency.

The Egaryan ambassador had Hattu's trust from past encounters, but what if that trust was misplaced? She'd caught Ahmose in Hattu's rooms before the feast. He hadn't offered a real explanation of his presence, only a flimsy lie anyone would see through, but she'd dropped the question because he didn't seem dangerous, just intrusive. At the start of the feast, Ahmose had stayed by their chairs, near the cups, while she had labored around the room greeting nobles with Nerik, the most unpleasant social duty she'd ever performed. That left Ahmose with plenty of time to put the poison into the cups.

And then she'd switched them at the last moment, casting suspicion on herself and saving her husband. And the city—Hattu would not have fought off the Paskan invasion if he'd been as sick as Nerik. Could Ahmose have worked in coordination with the Paskans?

An intense danger still threatened Hattu and the kingdom. Circles swirling outward, blurring each other's patterns.

34

Footsteps sounded on the stairs again—a man's, slow and uneven. Had Hattu reconsidered his rash accusation?

At the top of the stairwell, the Egaryan ambassador's head appeared. Tesha's chest shook with wild thumps of her heart. To confront one of Pharaoh's assassins alone? She hadn't had time to figure out what to do about Ahmose.

But then she decided. She put on her most gracious smile and bowed courteously to the old man as he stepped onto the sanctuary terrace. A skilled diplomat—spy—like Ahmose could never be tricked into revealing his role in the poisoning. She patted the stone in her pouch. Magic wasn't a trick.

"Greetings, Queen Tesha."

That startled her. She ignored the misused title. "I was starting a prayer to Ishana—for calm and peace. After the attack last night, we could all benefit from a clear mind. Will you join me, Ambassador Ahmose?"

"This is a stunning temple. No artisan could craft a building as magnificent as this." Ahmose's hand swept toward the forested slope on the mountain opposite. "I feel the holiness. I have not worshipped your Ishana before, but I am happy to give her obeisance. We do well to respect the gods, even those of our enemies. Perhaps those most of all."

His enemies. Tesha's hands went damp. She surreptitiously dried them on her skirt. "All gods require respect."

She stepped up to the altar niche where Henti had placed the two pitchers. The creamy stone of Ishana's image glowed in the morning light. The gold leaf on her breasts and on the tips of the arrows the goddess held sparked like fire. The goddess held sway over two realms, love and war. She would invoke Ishana's name as she worked the spell to divert Ahmose's suspicion. If she erred in using the Paskan stone, Ishana would know of her crime and stop her. The one open hand of Ishana's statue gave Tesha an idea about how to proceed.

Tesha placed the polished stone in Ishana's palm. "Ambassador, for this prayer I ask you to look steadily at this stone the goddess offers to you."

"At a stone? But the goddess herself is far lovelier to gaze upon."

"Yes, but the stone is necessary. Do not let your eyes shift from the goddess's gift. Through the stone, she will fill you with clarity and calm."

Ahmose gave a small bow of his head. "A worthy divine gift. You are a powerful priestess to bring such prayers into being." He directed his focus to the stone.

Tesha began the song of adoration to Ishana, watching Ahmose to see if his eyes remained locked on the stone. The physician had said gazing for some time without distraction was key. It required willingness to participate.

But Ahmose watched what *she* was doing, not the stone.

"Ambassador, if you would prefer not to participate in this prayer, I will wait for you to leave the sanctuary. For this rite, you must look only at the stone."

"My apologies. My attention swandered."

Tesha chanted the familiar song several times. Now Ahmose showed no signs of wavering. She could begin.

"Feel Ishana's gift reaching you from the stone. The goddess fills you with soothing waves." Tesha had to force her tongue to form these words, as if her mouth belonged to some other person. "The calm begins . . ."

While Tesha struggled to speak, instead of the calm body of water that should fill her mind, a wild tempest crashed, each successive wave reaching a higher crest and plunging with destructive force into bottomless troughs. She felt no control of this storm inside her. She received the goddess's message to leave off and not use the stone.

She glanced at the old man standing beside her. Ahmose appeared untouched by her inner turmoil. He rocked gently back and forth, his eyes never leaving the stone.

Goddess, give me permission to work this stone's power. Allow the magic of my enemies to become a source of strength for your devoted priestess. Do not fear that the Paskans' evil will overcome me through it. Trust that I will use it to pursue your plan. If you want me to uncover the truth, as with your assistance I did once before in Lawaza, put your divine power inside of me so that it can flow into this stone and beguile Ahmose.

The clashing image of storm waves gave way slowly to tranquility. She continued and the words flowed easily from her mouth, "The calm begins in the center of your chest, and like the gentle lapping of waves against a lakeshore, calmness ripples outward. Each wave pushes away fear that clouds your thoughts. Trust the goddess's gift and let her fill you with goodness. Breathe in as each wave gathers, and breathe out as each wave releases more tranquility."

The first step of the spell gradually took hold. She had won the goddess's blessing. The golden glow under her ribs, Ishana's presence inside of her, brightened with each word she spoke. The stone gave off light like a full moon. The lines of Ahmose's face relaxed. His shoulders drooped as he breathed in and out.

"When you are filled throughout with Ishana's calm, lift up the stone that the goddess offers to you, press it to your forehead, and then to your lips."

Ahmose reached for the stone. An ecstatic gasp slipped from his lips when his fingers touched it. Sparks arced outward as he pressed the gray stone to his forehead and then his lips. He did not react to the sparks, and perhaps he did not perceive them.

"Replace the stone in Ishana's hand and allow her presence to fill you with calm and clarity."

After Ahmose followed her instructions, he stood still beside her with a blank gaze.

Tesha lifted the pitcher of water Henti had made unclean with a handful of dirt from the ground around the ovens in the kitchen courtyard.

"This pitcher is full of water mixed with dirt. The water has become unclean and must be thrown out. So also a man's mouth may be full of unclean words, lies, and falsehoods meant to deceive."

Tesha lifted the pitcher above her head and stepped nearer the rectangular basin full of ash and bone.

"Now I pour out the unclean water and free the pitcher of this pollution. As the pitcher of dirty water is emptied, so may your mouth and tongue be emptied of lies."

Tesha poured out the dirty water and stepped back to the altar. She lifted the other pitcher.

"As this pitcher is full of clean water, so may your mouth and tongue be full of true words and clear speaking. As I pour out water, so you will pour out true words."

What should she ask first?

"What was Ahmose doing in King Hattu's rooms before Priestess Tesha discovered him there before the feast last evening?" She dribbled a small stream of water.

"In the king's rooms . . . I went there because . . ." Ahmose spoke with a flat, expressionless voice. "I searched for a token. Hattu has one from Amur. He sends it with his messengers as the guarantee that the messenger comes from Hattu."

Her spell worked.

"Why did Ahmose search for this token?" She poured out a thin stream.

"If I can . . . speak to Amur with Hattu's voice, perhaps . . . I can stop a rebellion."

"Did Ahmose take this token?"

"I did not find the token."

"Did Ahmose put poison in a wine cup at the feast?"

"No."

"Did Ahmose poison Nerik?"

"No."

"Does Ahmose want Hattu dead?" Tesha tipped the spout to form a continuous trickle puddling in the ash of the offering basin.

"I want Hattu strong . . . While Hattu leads Muwatti's army, Pharaoh Gerose will not . . . dare war."

"But if Hattu died, couldn't Egarya defeat Hitolia?"

"Perhaps . . . but still bleed to death. Empires weaken through war."

"Does Hattu need to go to Amur?"

"If Hattu does not go to Amur, there will be war between Egarya and Hitolia."

"Who poisoned Nerik?"

"I do not know."

The pressure at her forehead and temples released. But relief that Ahmose wasn't an assassin gave way to frustration.

"Do you want to know who poisoned Nerik?"

"Yes. Hattu cannot go to Amur until he knows."

"Hattu believes I poisoned Nerik. Does Ahmose suspect Priestess Tesha of poisoning Nerik?"

"No. This false accusation is an unfortunate distraction."

For her it was far more than merely a distraction, but it was good Ahmose saw it as unfortunate for his plan to send an army to Amur. He might work to undo the accusation. Her first instinct to like this man had not been misplaced. He might prove useful but not in this trance. Utar had said a person who answers in the truth rite will not remember that they spoke.

"Ambassador Ahmose. Please close your eyes. I will seal the goddess's gift of calm with her stone."

Tesha lifted the radiant stone from Ishana's hand. Sizzling power arced up her arm as if she'd been possessed by lightning.

She steadied her feet against the mountain bedrock underneath her.

She tapped the stone against Ahmose's forehead and lips. "You will awaken filled with Ishana's peace. Open your eyes."

Tesha slipped the stone into the little pouch she wore on her belt.

Ahmose blinked a few times. Lines of confusion bunched around his eyes.

"Did the goddess bring you calm through my prayer?" Tesha asked.

Ahmose straightened up a little. He nodded. "I do feel calmer." He looked out at the mountain slope where rays of morning sun overlaid the treetops with yellow light.

Ahmose turned toward Tesha. "I feel calm, but I should not."

Tesha braced her hand against the chilly stone of the altar. "We all benefit from divine calm."

"I do not question the value of your goddess's gift, but last night's events work against the great need that brought me all this way from Egarya. Why has suspicion fallen on you?"

Tesha clasped her hands together. "Who else would gain from the death of the Crown Prince?"

"Ah. When I was at Great King Muwatti's court, I heard similar accusations against his and King Hattu's stepmother."

"I am not like her."

"You must persuade your husband of that."

"I tried."

"When Hattu goes east, he will need a strong ruler to leave in his stead. You are such a leader, an intelligent queen. I've watched you."

She didn't entirely share his confidence, but it was good to hear. "I am no longer even his wife, certainly not the queen. He announced he will send me away. Nerik will rule while he is gone."

"Nerik is very ill, I heard. First the Great King, and now Hattu's substitute. Sick kings. I will never get an army off to Amur."

"And I will live alone in a horrible place. My husband does not love me."

"You are the queen."

"I never was."

"You are. It is who you are. You must rule. Your husband may or may not love you, but your duty as a wife is not what matters. Your kingdom matters. You must fulfill what the gods—or goddess—placed inside you."

"I can't unless I prove I did not poison Nerik." Ahmose had shown a disturbing ability to dig out secrets. Let him put that to use.

"A plan, then. That's what you need."

"I don't have much time. Hattu will send me away."

"A plan. Is there anyone in the court's inner circle you suspect? Poison is an intimate weapon."

"Nerik's death does not seem to benefit anyone." She left it there, wondering if the wily old man would jump to the same conclusion she had—that the poisoner aimed at Hattu. She didn't trust she was right about that. The cup might not have been the source of the poison. Only Hattu had decided that, and Hattu wasn't thinking well.

Ahmose hesitated and pursed his lips for a moment. "None-theless, you should consider his family and others near the prince. You can accomplish that, even restricted to the women's quarters as you are currently—and you may find ways around that. Do not ignore the women, anyway."

"The women have not been friendly."

"You don't need friends," Ahmose said. "You are looking for an enemy. Poison is a close weapon that anyone can wield. You already know from your experience in Lawaza that Hattu has trouble among his nobles. Find out who was near that night."

"I don't know where to start. Hattu never told me about the important families here."

"Then you will have to ask someone who will."

She could do that. Henti would already be helping her start one path to these answers.

"Do not forget Hattu's family—the foulest foes are kin, but the commonest also."

"I don't see anyone in the family who would harm Nerik." Or Hattu. Either of them. If only those women were to blame. That would be satisfying. And appalling. They'd raised Nerik, acting as his mothers.

"Since you are restrained, I'll hunt for the outside foe. Paskans attacked last night—why not them? That would be a welcome discovery, wouldn't it? The favorite enemy in this city. Though it will take some unraveling to show the way they snuck poison into the young prince."

"Difficult to see how they could."

"We both have work to do. Use all your skills."

Did she imagine his eyes flitted toward the pouch at her belt?

35

———

Hattu held back in the door to his son's sleeping chamber. He watched Nerik, propped up by pillows, his eyes closed. The boy's coloring was all wrong, tinged with a sickly, yellowish shade. Hattu had asked the physician about that color. Utar confessed that the people he'd treated with this color in their skin had died slowly and painfully, but he was doing everything he could to save the Crown Prince.

Tesha had done this. He couldn't believe it, and yet it was true.

Even dozing, lines of tension tugged at the boy's eyes and neck. If only he could recover. No one would attack him again. He didn't need to worry. Hattu would see to his safety from now on, no matter the cost.

Nerik's eyes opened. His gaze caught Hattu, and he looked down.

Hattu came up to the bed and pulled a stool close. "How are you feeling?"

"Not so good."

Hattu's hands wrapped tight around the seat of the stool. If he could feel steady, maybe he could think more clearly. "You'll get better. Give it time. You've been through a lot."

The stench of sickness still lingered in Nerik's room. It'd be more pleasant if he opened the shutters on one or two of the windows. He stood up and reached for the hook on a long stick that was used to open them.

"Leave them closed."

Hattu turned in surprise. "But the sickness—"

"I like the shutters closed."

For him the walls felt too close. Hattu fought down panic and sat again.

Fiddling with the edge of the linen sheet covering his chest, Nerik looked up at him. "Father . . . it's good to have you back. I missed you."

Warmth radiated through Hattu. "I missed you terribly. Especially when I thought I would be executed without ever seeing you again. There's so much I need to teach you so you can be a good king from the start."

"Me? You'll help me be king?"

"Of course. It's my dearest hope." Hattu wrapped his hands around his son's hand. He had a happy idea. "I've given orders for a second throne to be carved. When you're well again, you will sit in that place of honor at my side as Crown Prince."

Hattu assumed that Nerik would realize that the second throne had been intended for Tesha, but maybe he'd ignore that. Young men yearned for outward signs of authority.

"Really? I get to rule with you?"

Nerik looked alive for the first time since Hattu had run into this room to find his son poisoned.

"How else will you learn to be king?"

The boy kept asking to be given military command. Even when he was healthy again, Hattu preferred to introduce those duties slowly. But an important role in his court would both satisfy Nerik and train him in statesmanship. At his age Hattu had also thought it was all about taking down enemies in battle. Time the boy learned there was more to it—without losing men, the way Hattu had.

"But . . . a throne. Like yours?"

"You're my son. Why not?"

Nerik hung his head.

"You'd like that, wouldn't you?" Hattu leaned forward to see his son's expression.

Nerik's eyes had filled with tears. "Yes, very much. Thank you." He mumbled something else that Hattu didn't quite hear.

"What was that?"

"Nothing."

He thought Nerik had said he didn't deserve it. How sad that his son felt that way. Hattu had neglected him too much. That would change.

He offered Nerik the cup of water the healer had left on the table beside the bed. "Some water?"

"No. My stomach hurts."

"I'm sorry I brought Tesha here. I didn't understand her true nature. I'm sending her away. But you're safe now. You'll heal."

Nerik's face contorted in an unattractive way. "I saw her selfishness the first time I looked at her. Lying in that wagon, she lorded over everyone in Alpara as if she were queen already."

Hattu tried to see their arrival as Nerik had seen it. Is that how she'd looked? She *had* acted like she already ruled.

"Samsi told me stories about your stepmother," Nerik said. "Even the Great King fears she'll kill his sons. Your stepmother was a princess before she became queen, but Tesha is a nobody. She needed to act faster. Get her out of the palace, Father."

Hattu rubbed his chin. "They're not the same. My father never should have married that woman. It was the foolishness of old age."

"Tesha's my age. It's obvious why you took her. Look at her."

"It's still different. Besides, I'm sending her away."

"You wanted her body. That's all you could think about."

"That's not true." Hattu rose from the stool. He didn't want to fight with Nerik. They had been getting on well again.

He stepped into the hallway and nearly ran into Ambassador Ahmose. Gods below. Hattu shook out his shoulders and tried to appear relaxed. "Ambassador, good day to you." He'd remembered to assign one of the palace guards to keep an eye on Ahmose under the guise of protection. He stood a few steps back.

"Excuse me, King Hattu. I should watch where I'm going."

"I would have thought an older gentleman like yourself would take advantage of this quiet afternoon for a nap. You must be tired from your travels."

"Your thoughtfulness is appreciated. I am distressed to hear of your son's ill health. I hope he is doing better."

"Thank you. I am sorry you have come at this difficult time."

"We must pray to your Ishana to return him to good health. I was just doing that with Priestess Tesha. I gather you blame her for this accident that befell your son. You may be mistaken in that. It's best to think carefully about such things. She is an intelligent and strong woman. As queen she would give you the freedom to leave your kingdom while knowing there would be a firm hand guiding your realm."

"I would hardly endanger my son by leaving her in charge."

"We do not always understand where the real danger in our lives comes from. Are you working to get your Commander Marak back?"

Hattu frowned. This man poked into business where he had no right to. "I am. Good day."

"I won't keep you longer. Perhaps a nap is for the best."

Hattu scowled when the old man walked away. He wasn't headed toward his rooms, but his guard followed close.

36

Daniti pressed her hands flat against Marak's back so she could sense his movement and react with him if the Paskans closed in. Their guards wanted to sink daggers into them both, as well as the betrayer Riam.

The scuffle between the Paskans and Riam ended with Riam bound but not gagged. His frantic voice carried to their prison at the back of the cave.

As the Paskans argued with Riam, she could hear the ragged grief in their voices, the ripping of their hearts. The scale of their loss, most of their tribe's warriors, was too much to absorb. Daniti realized what drove them, and her fear rose. They had good reason not to kill her and Marak, but she doubted they'd remember that. These remaining fighters struggled against both grief and guilt. They were the survivors when most of their comrades were dead. They needed some action like slitting her throat to gain redemption for being alive.

Riam's voice rose. He kept saying it wasn't his fault the invasion failed. He was on their side. The hostages were too valuable to kill. Daniti hated the man, but she hoped the Paskans listened.

"Why should we trust you?" The fury in the Paskan's voice mixed with sorrow.

Marak moved up next to the doorway, keeping her behind him. Riam wasn't making a good case. His scheming had already cost the Paskans dearly. It tainted whatever he said.

Daniti reached up on tiptoe and whispered into Marak's ear. "Should we try to sway them?"

Marak breathed into hers, "Maybe."

Daniti could hear Riam's panting. He knew this wasn't going well. "Hattu will kill off your whole tribe, women and children included, now that he has the chance. You need me to stop him."

"You? How are—"

Marak strode into the main chamber of the hideout. Daniti clasped his shoulder. He had reared back when Riam said Hattu would kill the women and children. A defense of his friend wouldn't be the best idea right now. Daniti tensed.

"You have battled King Hattu for many years," Marak said, his voice surprisingly soft.

Even without eyesight, Daniti knew everyone had turned to watch him.

"You know him to be a smart and effective general—to your sorrow. He does what is necessary to win battles, as he did the other night when you invaded his city. He did not choose that fight. You brought it to him. But winning battles has never included harming those who cannot fight."

"You're Hattu's man," Riam shouted. "Don't waste our time singing his praises. We hate him."

But Daniti thought Marak made a good start. She edged forward. Marak pulled her close against him, his hand firmly at her waist. She took in a breath, raising the courage to speak. These men needed to see how to turn their grief into a useful weapon, a salve to their self-inflicted reproach for being alive. Marak's fingers pressed her in silent agreement that she take over. The heat where her hip touched Marak's came to her like a promise of trust.

"You underestimate your strength." Daniti heard sharp gasps from the Paskans facing her. They'd taken offense.

She went on. "King Hattu is indeed a clever leader. The battle you described inside Alpara, and the trap your warriors fell into show that Hattu regained control despite the stealth and treachery of your attack. So, what would he do then—a man of strategy such as that? Indiscriminate slaughter serves no purpose. He would take prisoners, as many as he could, for bargaining later with you. He wants us back, and he wants peace. Captive warriors give him the power to negotiate for both those things. But you have power also—two hostages that King Hattu wants very much. Turn us to good use. Not all of your warriors need to die. They can come home safely to you if you buy them back with us."

A Paskan cleared his throat. "Hattu has fought against us for years. It will be too tempting to finish us off. Even if he hasn't killed most of our men already, he won't allow them to return home and face him in battle again."

Riam started to speak, but the Paskans shouted him down.

Daniti used the opening. "But if you seek peace instead, your restored warriors will not pose that threat. Strength does not always come from a spear."

Daniti heard a disgusted grunt.

"This woman talks of peace with Hattu." The man spat.

Daniti tried again. "If Hattu gave you only two men in exchange for our two lives, would that be worth forgoing the empty revenge of killing us? Would you choose to sacrifice the lives of your comrades for a moment's satisfaction? If you were among the captives, is that the choice you would want your tribe to make?"

Marak stepped forward. "You *are* stronger than you realize. Negotiate well and you will save more than two of your men. What do you have to lose? Send an envoy immediately, before Hattu decides you have given up and do not want to redeem your comrades. We have not always understood each other very well in the past. Don't let Hattu come to the mistaken conclusion you do not value the lives of your brothers."

"Yes, send an envoy," Riam said. "But send me also. I will sneak into the city and get your hidden allies among the nobles to argue on your behalf in Hattu's court. They will do it in such a way that they will seem to be recommending what is good for Hattu. You need my help. Even that Hitolian snake told you you'll need to negotiate well or you'll only get two men. I'll get your men back, lots of them."

Daniti wondered what Riam aimed at with this. Probably nothing more than a reason to leave this cave alive. Maybe he planned to put the returned Paskan warriors to use in future battles. No Paskan would follow his lead again.

"Do not trust this man," Marak said. "He only cares for himself."

"The ally he got for us did let us through the city gates. The Hitolians who hate Hattu enough to overthrow him are real enough. Why not use them again?"

"He'll run. It's just an excuse to escape from us."

"Possibly. But Riam's a cripple. He can't even use his right arm. He'll never get away. But he's right. Hattu will be hard to convince. Have you ever known the jackal to back off when he had us in a corner? All I see for us to take to the bargaining table is a mouthy blind woman and a commander we've beaten in the field more than once. Hattu will find someone else to lead his dogs. I like the sound of getting lots of our men back. Send two Paskans to keep an eye on this traitor, but send him also."

Daniti shivered. Growls of assent arose from the Paskans. If Riam snuck into Alpara, he'd cause trouble that would not work for her good. She did not mind how many Paskans Hattu handed over, but she wanted this process over soon. At least the Paskans seemed willing to postpone killing her—for a little while.

37

———————

The woman Henti showed into Tesha's hall exuded goodwill, none of the cautious disapproval Tesha expected. Her pretty face had rosy cheeks and a wide smile. She was shorter than Tesha and rounder, about the age of her mother.

Tesha beckoned Katte to one of the chairs around her hearth and sat beside her.

She had sent a polite invitation to Shatim's wife, anticipating a rejection. She'd pretended there was no accusation about her and no reason not to have a social visit, and for some reason that pretense had worked. Ahmose advised getting to know those inside the palace, the nobles who were present at the feast. Katte fit that description. She must know everyone. This step in her plan was easy so far.

Tesha turned to Henti. "Will you bring us some wine?" Ashu stood next to the curtain where the concubines spied. She would signal if anyone came near on the other side.

Katte leaned over to Tesha's chair and took Tesha's hands in hers. "I saw you briefly while I stood among the crowd when you arrived, but I am so glad to be able to talk with you."

It was as if no accusation had been made against Tesha. This gracious woman was going to ignore that, at least for now. A swelling of gratitude filled Tesha's chest. She had seen Shatim's diplomatic manners. His wife shared this quality. Perhaps she'd get answers without using the stone. That would be safer by far.

Tesha held Katte's hands. "I am pleased we can meet. Shatim is a good counselor to my husband."

Katte held Tesha's hands another moment. "But some counsel he may not listen to as well as others."

"Thank you." Here was another ally, and Shatim too. There were people besides Ahmose willing to believe that she wasn't a poisoner. If only she could break through the malign influence of the curse—that had to be why Hattu grasped at the ridiculous accusation.

"What are you going to do?" Katte asked.

It was a direct question but a confusing one. "Do?"

"Ah well, of course there isn't really anything you can do. We'll wait and see what Hattu decides." Katte patted her hand and then leaned back in her chair.

So Katte's support was rather half-hearted. "But you don't think I tried to poison Nerik?"

"You are a young girl and only just arrived here. Why would you do something like that?"

"Do you think any of the nobles who were at the feast could have put the poison ... somewhere?" *This* is what she would do.

"A nobleman? Oh, surely not one of Hattu's friends. They wouldn't harm Nerik. I grew up with these men and women. They aren't poisoners."

"Did anyone look uneasy to you?"

"Uneasy?" Katte shook her head.

"Someone who might have had some part in Runda's conspiracy?"

"How are you getting on with ..." Katte wrinkled her nose and glanced toward the curtain where Ashu stood watch.

A question, not an answer. "Not well," Tesha said. Katte didn't want to discuss guilty nobles. Hard to blame her, but how was Tesha to find the poisoner? "Did you arrive early at the feast, by any chance?"

"I don't recall being early or late. But what will you do now?"

Ahmose's plan came to mind—studying the possible inside foes while he pursued the outside foes. She wouldn't mention that. This conversation felt like cupping water with her hands. The drink she needed kept slipping away. It was annoying. Katte might be too empty-headed to help, although that didn't seem quite right.

"How do *you* get on with Agat?" Tesha asked, returning to the topic Katte had brought up.

"Well enough. I have no need to get in her way. But for you, it will be more challenging."

"Agat hated me before I arrived. That's how Nerik's dislike of me arose. She certainly doesn't want me running the household. I suppose I can't now anyway."

"Life has been hard on Agat. No excuse for being rude to you, but still. Do you know her story? Did Hattu tell you?"

"Hattu forgot to mention Agat and the others until after we'd arrived in Alpara."

Katte's eyes went wide at that. "Oh dear."

"What *is* her story? Hattu only said he couldn't marry her because her family opposed him early on. It seems strange that she ever became . . . close, if that was so."

"You know that Hattu's wife, his first wife, was a timid girl? They were both very young when they came to the Upper Lands. We all were. But she did not seem to have the courage to grow up."

"Hattu mentioned something like that."

"Agat filled in for her. At the time it seemed a blessing. Agat was smart and gave Hattu the support he needed. His wife did not. Those were difficult years. Hattu had to learn to rule. But over time, Agat's role has grown to be less of a blessing. She likes to have everything under her control. She seeks more and more ways to display her power, although the life of a woman in her position makes that difficult. Do you want to run the palace household, or would you prefer Agat continue?"

"I've made it clear to the servants that I am in charge. Well, I was until . . . this trouble."

Katte waved her hand in a little dismissive gesture. "I understand." Katte smiled at Henti, who put the cups of wine on the tables next to their chairs.

"It is hardly Agat's fault," Katte said, "but her family will be held against her even more now that Runda's been arrested for leading this conspiracy against Hattu. Runda and Hattu have been enemies for years, but now—well, no one related to that traitor is going to fare well in Alpara." Katte was happy enough to condemn Runda even if she'd dodged Tesha's questions before.

"Is Agat Runda's daughter?"

"No, not that close. Runda's father and Agat's father were brothers. Agat's father was the younger of the two," Katte said.

"So Runda and Agat are cousins?" Tesha shook her head. "Why does Hattu trust her if she's from that viper's family?"

"They've lived . . . familiarly for more than fifteen years. He must have reasons. He's never minded her bossiness in the household or any of the other roles she took for herself. She may not look like much now, but they are close—*were* close."

"Tell me more about Agat. If I'm to be banished, I suppose she'll reestablish herself."

Katte brushed back a strand of Tesha's hair and cupped her cheek in one hand for a moment. It felt so much like her mother's gesture that Tesha had to bite her lip not to cry.

"If she's in Runda's family, could she have been in the conspiracy?" Tesha asked.

"Agat part of that conspiracy? No, she's always loved Hattu. She had real hopes of marrying him until the news of your wedding arrived. Agat's sympathies would lie with her father, not her uncle. You heard about her father, I presume?"

"Her father? I met him briefly, but what do you mean?"

Katte looked surprised. "No? Well, this is a sad time for her. Her father was found among the dead this morning. He was one of the nobles who came out with Hattu to defend the city against those treacherous Paskans. Treacherous, indeed. One of those barbarians ran him through from the back. Agat has been seeing to his burial rites. Her mother has fallen ill at the news and is no help. I know Agat can seem bitter, but she's suffered. She's always tied her path to Hattu, and it wasn't always a smooth path."

"Tell me."

Katte settled back into her chair. She took another drink of wine. "I think it started with love. You can understand how hard that can be to resist. She fell in love with Hattu and it was so easy to persuade herself that his timid mouse of a wife could be pushed aside, divorced. Agat made herself indispensable. But she did not press quickly enough for her marriage. The mouse became pregnant. That must have hurt. Hattu was in both beds. I watched. He was so joyous at the idea of an heir. Agat lost her chance. Despair. Worse, she was pregnant, further along than the mouse. She couldn't extract herself and pretend no relationship had existed. It might have worked, but then she had to accept the formal status as concubine. She, who had been born into the highest family in Alpara. But she'd done it to herself. No comfort there. Her son was born. Two months later, Hattu's wife died in childbirth. Agat thought she'd been saved. But Hattu feared any challenge to his heir, and Agat's son was older. Hattu had already taken Nerik into his heart, and he was leery of Agat's ambition. You can see why Nerik's accusations rang true so easily?"

Tesha frowned. "And then later Hattu and Nerik witnessed the evil stepmother's plots against the Great King's sons when Samsi arrived for safekeeping. Conniving mothers seem expected in this family."

Katte shrugged. "Mothers love their sons. Sons need power. It's just the way of things. But the final blow was the fight between Runda and Hattu. In their first confrontation, Runda did nothing criminal, but he lost a great deal anyway. It looked to him like Hattu had embezzled funds from the treasury, and he made the accusation before the Great King. He was wrong, and then Hattu had more reason not to advance Agat's status. She's Runda's cousin, and Runda made the accusations to bring down Hattu."

"And somewhere along the way, he added Ija and Pasul to his household. More hurt," Tesha said.

Katte laughed. "You'd think, although to be honest I think part of his goal was to give Agat a small kingdom to rule over. Two subjects who had to follow her orders. They do."

"So I noticed."

"I think Agat has always believed her devotion to Nerik would bring Hattu to marry her. It could have been that Great King Muwatti would require some dynastic marriage, but when he didn't, well, I think Agat truly believed it would be her turn after the war with Egarya concluded and he came back. They had many experiences together and two fine sons, even if one wasn't fully hers. But then word came of you—"

"Not a smooth path for Agat."

"And now she's lost her father. They were close."

"I'm sorry for her."

"Me too. She's grown bitter, fair enough, but she's a good person. I hope you will not become another sad woman in Hattu's life. Something will turn up."

Tesha didn't think she'd wait. Katte gossiped readily about Agat, but she'd slipped away from topics that might lead to the poisoner. The stone rested in Tesha's pouch. Its sparking power penetrated through her wool skirt and heated the skin underneath. She could use the stone to force out Katte's observations during the feast. She might have seen something revealing, even if she didn't realize it. She seemed unwilling to speak badly of any of the people surrounding Hattu. The truth rite would change that.

Then again, if anyone reported her use of the stone to Hattu and he recognized it for magic, it would be fatal before she had won back his trust.

And Ahmose might have seen through it, so Katte . . . No, that wasn't what that glance of his had meant.

"It would be a great comfort if you would pray with me to Ishana," Tesha said. "There's a short rite that brings me such calm."

Katte twisted a ring on her left hand, one set with a swirling design in agate. "A rite? Goodness, I'm sure it's very powerful, given your reputation. But I'm sorry. I can comfort with gossip, but I've never been any use with praying to the gods. It's time I returned to my duties, in any case."

38

Flanked on either side by her maids, Tesha set out for the baths. She'd sent word ahead for the attendants to prepare.

The palace itself didn't have any baths, but Henti had discovered that the palace residents used a bathhouse just below, placed where the closest spring provided sufficient water. She could properly wash away travel filth and gather gossip about the feast and poisoning.

Tesha got as far as her doorway. The two guards Hattu had posted outside her rooms stopped her. She had known they would, but she hoped to talk her way as far as the baths with them as escort.

One asked, "To the sanctuary again?"

"I am going to the bathhouse—an essential activity. I will return directly. You may escort me and wait outside the baths to be sure I do not do anything else."

The guards looked at each other. She wished she knew exactly what their orders were, although she suspected Hattu hadn't set clear ones. He avoided thinking about imprisonment of any kind. Her father's cruelty had seen to that.

Tesha tugged at Henti's arm, and the three of them stepped into the hallway. The guards would have to forcibly restrain her. It would be far easier for them to follow her as escort.

Tesha hurried. Henti pointed to a side hall she'd learned as a shortcut, and they turned down it. Ashu pulled open a heavy wooden door, and they exited into sunshine and a footpath between tall mudbrick walls. Peeking down an intersecting path, Tesha realized they walked roughly parallel to the main road that ran from the topmost gate to the palace. They still had one guard at their rear. The other had returned to the palace, probably heading to Hattu for clearer orders.

She broke into a near run, eager to get inside the bath before the guard changed his mind. Henti and Ashu stayed with her, Henti guiding their route.

Although she wanted a bath so much, when she pictured sinking into lovely heated water, guilt and worry about Daniti overcame her. Going without washing—and even the threatened banishment— seemed insignificant next to Daniti's danger. The Paskan attack and the poisoning were distracting Hattu from the main thing they needed to accomplish—rescuing Daniti and Marak. At least she'd consulted with the commander in charge of the search before Hattu, curse-rattled, lost faith in her. Would Hattu include her when the Paskan envoy returned? She'd made more progress with that giant than he had. Nerik's ridiculous accusation interfered with what mattered most. It showed all the more the need to find the true poisoner. Without the accusation, she'd be at Hattu's side, in a better position to root out the curse, keep their kingdom strong, and save Daniti.

Henti jerked her arm, and they veered through an open gate into a courtyard surrounded on three sides by a low building with several wooden doors. They came to a halt. The odors of steamy dampness and scented oils pervaded the small courtyard. Tesha glanced back at the guard. He took a stance on the far side of the footpath, across from the gate. She shared a secret smile with Henti—they'd made it before his fellow guard came back.

A servant stepped forward. Her tightly blank expression

suggested she'd heard the gossip about Tesha's fallen status. "The bathing room for the royal women is over here."

For the royal women. Much as private bathing suited her far better, Tesha had hoped to cross paths with some of the noblewomen who might have been at the feast.

The servant pulled open a central door. "Please enter here. As your maidservant requested when she brought word you were coming, the attendants have heated the water and laid everything out for you. Do you prefer they stay, or will your maids care for you?"

"My maids will be plenty, thank you." If there were no attendants, Henti and Ashu could bathe also. They had just as great a need.

The bathing room was laid out much like the one in her parents' house. A stone tub, a corner hearth for heating the water, benches for setting things on and sitting. Piles of linen towels and small jugs of scented oil. It was a private setting. She'd get clean, but any gossip gathering would happen only if she met someone in the courtyard on the way out.

She gave in to the pleasure of a hot bath.

The aching pressure in her head receded a little under the influence of soothing warmth and the feel of her clean, wet hair dripping down her back.

Feeling stronger, she dressed and wrapped her hair in a wool drying snood, then covered that with her veil. While Henti and Ashu finished their bathing, she slipped out into the courtyard, ostensibly to sit in the sun.

She looked around the stone-paved courtyard in hopes that her timing would be good.

The person who appeared almost immediately in the open gateway shook her confidence.

Ahmose strolled toward her. She saw the palace guard assigned to protect him at the gate, waiting at a respectful distance.

"Ah, Queen Tesha, I heard I might find you here. I thought you might find some way to escape from the women's quarters. I was hoping to have a quiet talk. Best to do without the audience listening from behind the curtain in your hall."

How did this man know she was here? How had he gotten his timing so precise?

Tesha shifted her shoulders. She hadn't rubbed enough water from her hair before wrapping it up. A drip tickled down her back. "You have news?"

"I suspect King Hattu has not told you all of his experiences during last night's Paskan invasion. There is one part that may help us find our outside foe, the poisoner."

"Outside?" She'd made so little progress with those close to Hattu.

"Yes. I overheard King Hattu ordering one of his soldiers to bring a certain Paskan captive to him for questioning. While he waited, I asked what made this Paskan interesting to him. Your husband is reluctant to talk to me. He wishes I'd be gone from his court, and I do not blame him. But he does not want to offend me, either. He told me a remarkable thing. Last night after the battle against the Paskans was mostly over, he headed toward the palace to check on his son. It was at that moment that he was attacked by a Paskan. Imagine my surprise. I had asked many soldiers about their brave deeds and the course of the battle. They all stressed the brilliance of Hattu's trap that contained the Paskans just as they stole through the final gate. So where did this fellow come from? How did he come to be *leaving* the palace?"

With a quick tightening in her chest, Tesha asked, "What did Hattu say?"

"He doesn't know. That was why he sent for the man to interrogate him."

Tesha twitched away another droplet down her neck. "Well? What did the man say?"

"He isn't well enough to speak, unfortunately. That is the message the soldier returned with. Hattu wounded him while taking him prisoner. Hattu ordered the physician to see to his wound immediately, and the moment he is able to croak out a word or two, your husband will be on him like a hawk. I will find a way to listen in, you can be sure."

Tesha leaned toward Ahmose. "Bring me news as soon as you

have it. Perhaps that Paskan was close enough to poison the prince. Or this Paskan may reveal the traitor among the nobles. It is possible the poisoner intended to kill Hattu, not Nerik. Their cups were rearranged early at the feast."

Ahmose nodded. "I did notice your small restoration of proper protocol. Not so significant at the time, but you do raise an important point. I had already taken it into consideration. Hattu may have been the target."

"I should warn Hattu."

Ahmose nodded. "But he is unlikely to listen. His mind seems trapped in some way."

Yes, trapped. But how had Ahmose noticed?

"At this point, we know only that a Paskan came in or near the palace? Nothing more?"

"Hattu found him coming down an alley that leads to a servants' entrance of the palace. But I just took a walk along that road, and there are other homes and shops along the way. He could have been leaving the palace, but it could have been one of the houses."

"Homes of the nobility?"

"Large and luxurious homes, but whose, I have not learned."

"So, we need more information before this revelation is useful?"

"I'm afraid so. I will continue my explorations."

Ahmose bowed and left her, his guard trailing behind. Some clouds had crept in to cover the sun.

Another Paskan treachery, or a Hitolian traitor among the nobles? No one would be sad to discover the poisoner was a Paskan. Hattu might even believe it. She hoped Ahmose brought her further good news soon. It felt odd for one of Gerose's men to be such a friend to her.

Ashu and Henti came out of the bathing room. Tesha peered out the gate. Both the guards who'd chased them waited there. Their stances did not speak of patience.

One of the guards called out as they came onto the footpath, "You are no longer allowed to leave the palace. Your serving women will bring bathing water to you. King Hattu's orders."

Henti patted her arm. "We'll bring plenty of water, Priestess."

"Lucky we ran when we had the chance."

Henti nodded.

"But I keep thinking about Daniti whenever I enjoy some luxury. Do you think they are hurting her?" Her voice caught on the last words.

Henti's only answer was to wrap her arm around Tesha's shoulder and pull her close as they trudged back to the palace.

Heavy clouds burdened with rain massed above them.

Something occurred to Tesha. Ahmose had never been in her hall —not while she was there, and certainly not while the concubines leered at her through the curtain. How did Ahmose know about those spying women?

39

"How quickly do you think Riam and the Paskans will get the negotiations done in Alpara?" Daniti leaned against the rough stone wall of the cave. She shifted, trying to find a place where the uneven wall didn't poke into her back.

"The Paskans will rush," Marak said. He enveloped her hand inside his. As usual, he sensed her frustration and comforted her. "They'll want to negotiate the release of the rest of this tribe's men as fast as possible. When the other tribes realize this one has lost so many of its warriors, they'll attack. The Paskans feed on each other."

"But what will Riam do?"

"That is what worries me." He gave her hand a squeeze.

"He'll cause trouble once he's inside Alpara."

"I'm even more worried about what he'll do before they get there. I'm guessing he'll try to escape."

"They said he's crippled."

"I heard that also. He was tied up, so I couldn't tell what they meant. He certainly used his right arm when I fought with him, and he nearly killed me. But your sister held off his attack on your mother. I've never . . ."

"She won't speak of it. She had something in her hand that she used. I felt it. Wooden and evil. The moment my fingers touched it, I sensed a life inside. A demon. Like the ones I sang to in the cave of the Underworld to make them release Runda's son. Tesha had trapped a demon in that figure."

"A demon? And you can sense that?"

Daniti felt Marak quiver. "From outside in the courtyard, I heard Riam's wail of agony. Tesha did something to him that caused extreme pain."

"And the loss of his right arm."

"I think so."

"Even without his right arm, I would never turn my back on that man. He fought with skill and had no honor. He'll do anything."

"If he kills the envoys, there will be no negotiations. We'll . . . they'll kill us if Hattu hears nothing and chooses to push them further to get a response. They feel the loss of their comrades too much. They aren't thinking clearly."

"No. You calmed them for a while, but with Riam out there, we need to escape."

Escape, however, was proving to be far easier said than done. The Paskans had increased the number of men guarding them. If either of them so much as appeared in the opening, they were driven back at sword point.

They slumped in silence. Marak gently tucked her head down to rest on his shoulder and slipped his arm around her waist. There was a freedom in this imprisonment that they would never have found otherwise. She no longer ignored the voice inside that whispered to her that she was dear to Marak. He'd told her in the language of bodies that she had always understood best.

She let herself drift into a dozing state, easily awakened if trouble came. Marak's shoulder made a soothing pillow. She lingered in a near sleep that allowed some of the tightness of her fears to relax.

"Do you hear me? Are you near?"

Daniti lifted her head. Who had spoken to her? The voice had come from inside her head.

"A man gave me food and water. I'm stronger now. Do you hear me?"

Kurala. Her sweet pet wasn't dead. She sent her thoughts to him, "I do hear you. You're alive. I thought I'd lost you."

"I was too weak to move. I could not send to you. A darkness knocked me from the sky."

"Where are you? I'm a captive of the Paskans in a cave. What man helped you?"

"A bad man. He will not let me go. He only gives me a tiny bit of food. I'm so hungry, but I am strong enough to fly now. I want to come to you. I can't. He tied me. He put me in a sling on his back. He doesn't share his food."

"Can you escape?"

"I have tried. He only uses one arm, but he tied the knots so tight."

"What do you mean, only one arm?" Daniti's panic for Kurala flooded her insides.

"He has two, but one hangs dead."

"I know who this bad man is. But he is supposed to be on his way to Alpara with two other men to negotiate for my release."

"He is alone, and he does not walk to Alpara. The sun is behind us, not in front of us. He goes the wrong way."

"Then he has betrayed the Paskans again." Perhaps she could give the Paskans another reason not to kill Marak and her.

Kurala added, "The way he walks, I come closer to you."

"Yes, I feel that too. When you send, I can also sense how near or far you are." She'd never been far enough away from Kurala to discover this sensation so clearly. It was akin to the way she sensed what was around her from her clicks and humming, but like their conversations, it did not involve sound. Another wondrous thing about her pet.

She'd use it.

She explained to Marak. He didn't like it. It would be too dangerous for her.

"We will die if we do nothing. The Paskans have to know about this at the very least."

"They'll never believe you."

"I think I know how to persuade them." Daniti stood up.

40

———————

Pounding rain forced Henti and Tesha to close the shutters on the high windows in her hall. Henti built up the fire in the circular hearth. Her dear servant was trying to bring cheer to the room, and the receiving hall did look bright and well-ordered now. Tesha didn't want to go live in some remote garrison. But mostly she wanted Daniti safe and her husband in her arms with that quirk of his lips that warmed her from the belly up. How was she going to extract either of them from the snares they'd been drawn into?

Her heart rebelled, but she couldn't see any way to help Daniti. That had to change. She and Hattu *had* to work together again for that goal. Proof of the real poisoner would help bring Hattu back to trusting her even as he struggled inside with whatever piece of the curse still clung to him. *That* she also had to fix.

But how? She knew so little about magic. She had driven off the Paskan curse without understanding what she was doing, and now she didn't know what else to do for Hattu. The stone hadn't given her the right sort of power for that. She had waited, thinking Ishana would show her, but nothing had come. She must find it herself. Time was running out.

She could consult with the physician about the knowledge he had from his mother. A Paskan witch to remove a Paskan curse. She assumed that was the source of whatever held sway over Hattu. If she told the physician Hattu was under the control of dark magic, he'd turn against him. The need to hide his childhood nearness to magic made him as zealous about rooting out magic as anyone she'd met. Unrevealed Hitolian traitors still lived within the court and would provide too easy a choice for the physician to turn to as alternate rulers if he feared the sorcery inside Hattu. She couldn't destroy Hattu in the process of saving him.

Ishana had given her all the true sorcerous power she'd ever wielded. Hattu was dear to Ishana. Somehow she had to entice Ishana into driving out whatever evil magic lay in Hattu. If she were in Ishana's temple in Lawaza, she would go to the archives and hunt for some mention of a rite or spell that could be adapted for this purpose, probably multiple rites to borrow from and combine. The tablets with magic knowledge had been destroyed long ago, but she could sometimes hear remnants in safer rites that had been left intact. She'd read the oldest tablets in the archives and listen for what they did not say directly.

But she wasn't in Lawaza. Did Alpara's archives have such rite tablets, the old ones from before magic was banished? It was the capital of the Upper Lands. There would be treasury lists and royal correspondence with the Great King and other administrators, but what she needed wasn't as likely. Would the Stormgod priests here need to refer to such rites?

"Henti? Can you go to the archives building? Hattu pointed it out to me in the main palace courtyard. Slip inside and see whether it's divided into small storerooms or just one large one. If they have a room set aside for tablets with sacred rites, I could see if I can find one to protect Hattu. It will be hard to sneak there, but if I thought it was worth it, I would try. If there's only one big room, it will mean they only keep current correspondence and treasury lists and I shouldn't bother. But I need to find a way to save Hattu."

Henti's brow creased. "I can try. But I don't see how you could get there even if I find there are many small rooms. The guards won't let you."

"I'll find a way. One step at a time."

Henti shook her head, but she wrapped her shawl over her head and shoulders and left the reception hall.

Even if she really had lost Hattu's love forever, Ahmose had a point —he kept addressing her as the queen. Hattu had learned to rule. She could too. Being a priestess at the most powerful temple in the empire had taught her about negotiating, about changing people's minds without their noticing, and about winning over people who mistakenly thought they did not like her. Perhaps even more relevant to learning to rule, she'd spent years putting her interests second to Daniti's and tending to Daniti's needs without annoying her determined sister. There were many forces pressing hard against Hattu's kingdom, but she saw them in her mind like the pieces of an interlocking puzzle ring. Their proper places could be found with time. If Hattu never overcame the damage her father had done, if she could never quite remove the dark magic that plagued him, then Alpara needed her as queen. She had to prevail against the accusation and step into her rule.

Daniti, that's who she needed right now, her intelligent sister who ignored the social rules and perceived what Tesha didn't notice. She wrinkled her nose and pressed her tongue against the top of her mouth. She ached for her sister, but she would not cry. *Get on with it.* She clutched the arms of her chair and willed back the tears.

Secretive footsteps came from the concubines' wing. Tesha frowned. Not those women again. She stood and closed her eyes. The footsteps retreated. She tried to listen like Daniti. Very light footsteps, and now they were creeping back to the curtain. Shallow breaths trying to be silent, far too low to the ground for a full-grown person. She looked through her lashes, pretending her eyes were still closed. She saw no telltale eye at the curtain. Someone did better spying than those women. She took a guess.

"Humie, I'd be happy to talk to you if you came out from behind that curtain. It's warmer by the fire."

The curtain slowly drew back, and the little boy stepped through. "Am I in trouble for spying?"

"I don't think so," Tesha said. "Do you like to spy?"

"Commander Marak goes on spy missions for my father."

"He brings back very important information for Hattu. I like Marak."

"Yesterday you told my sister that girls can be spies. I didn't know that."

"Women are very good at spying."

Humie nodded. His lips turned down and he shifted his weight from one foot to the other. "They shouldn't."

Tesha caught a hint of sympathy in his voice. "Were you practicing your spying? Like Marak?"

He nodded. "But I wouldn't tell on you."

Tesha smiled. No one had turned this child against her. "Thank you. I don't have very many friends here."

She could see his confusion. Children weren't friends with grown-ups. "I realized you were behind the curtain because I heard your footsteps, but I couldn't see your eye at the opening. Most people wouldn't have noticed you at all. Pretty good spying."

Humie's face brightened. "It's fun to sneak around the palace as a spy. I want to be like Marak when I grow up."

Tesha studied his rounded cheeks and turned-up nose. His eyes had depth to them. She had an idea. "Have you seen the Egaryan ambassador who has come to your father's court?"

Humie nodded. "He asked permission to be introduced to all King Hattu's children and concubines. Visitors don't do that, but he did. His name is Ambassador Ahmose. He came into Nerik's receiving hall—the one we use. We aren't supposed to use this one. Remember?"

She smiled. "I didn't mind you playing here. But did you like the ambassador?"

Humie drew back a little. Tesha didn't think people asked his opinion very often, not about adults.

Humie fiddled with the hem of his tunic. "He said nice things to us and gave us presents. He gave me a wooden animal that he said was called crocodile. It has an open mouth and a long jaw with teeth carved into it. I wouldn't want to see a real one, but I like the toy."

"Are you allowed to walk in the palace wherever you like? Maybe into the town here or there? Or does your mother think you are too little for going out on your own?"

He pressed back his shoulders, and Tesha restrained her smile.

"I am big enough to go wherever I like—as long as I don't go outside the walls of the city." Humie stood very straight. "Mostly I stay in the upper part of the city where my friends live. Games are more fun when we can run in the streets and squares."

"Would you like to play a game of spying for me? I'd need you to do it by yourself. It's a secret."

"Spying is always secret. Is it dangerous spying? Marak might be dead."

Tesha slipped to her knees in front of Humie, eye level with the boy, and held his hands. "Marak will come back safe. He has to. We all need him so much. My sister also. The spying I mean is just a game. It isn't dangerous at all. Will you do it for me?"

The tension released from Humie's face. "I would like that."

"I want you to see where your friend Ambassador Ahmose goes, whom he talks to, and what he learns. Then come tell me. If he sees you, wave and tell him thank you for your crocodile. That you like it very much. Then come home and don't spy anymore. But see if you can be a master spy like Commander Marak. See if you can track the ambassador without his ever knowing. Does that sound like fun?"

"Very fun. Should I start now? Tracking?"

She nodded.

Humie trotted toward the door to the women's quarters. He turned back. "Priestess Tesha?"

"Yes?"

"I won't tell anyone what you said, but when I spied through the curtain, you wanted to know about the archive. You needed to read something to keep my father safe. I could help with that too. If it's for my father."

"I love your father very much. How can you help?"

"My father makes me learn writing at the scribal school. When I grow up, I'm to serve as one of his diplomats, and it's better if I can read. At first it was boring and I hated it, but I like it now. I can read whatever I want from the archives. But I'm still not very good. You can read, can't you? None of the others can."

She assumed "others" meant the concubines. Of course they couldn't read. "Do you ever take tablets away from the archive to practice reading?"

"Every day."

"Could you bring one to me so I can read it?"

"Any tablet?"

"No, a special tablet. Is the archive organized into separate rooms or compartments?"

"Yes." Humie chewed his lip, and she could practically see him trying to remember all the names.

"Is there one that the Stormgod priest uses? Rites for the gods, healing, that sort of—"

"Yes, I like that room. Some of the tablets tell stories. Not like the boring lists of what's stored in the treasury, like a lot of the other rooms."

"Did you hear what happened on your father's journey back to Alpara?"

"You mean after Marak was kidnapped? The scary part the soldiers talk about?"

"Exactly. The scary part was some kind of bad curse. I helped the soldiers get away, but I'd like to understand it better. I don't want that to happen ever again. Can you bring me any tablet that might help me with that? If there is anything . . ."

"There are old tablets about things like that. The signs are strange, and I can't read them. But I can read their labels."

"That's good. I don't think you should read those tablets anyway. Not those old ones. I'm a priestess, so I know how to keep safe."

"No one told me any of the tablets were dangerous to read."

"Your teachers may not understand."

Humie's eyes narrowed in concentration. "I've never studied with the priest of the Stormgod. He might know."

"Probably."

"But I like you better. I'll bring you some tablets. I'll only read the labels. If there's a good story, you'll tell me so I can read it? If it's safe?"

"I promise."

"This is part of my job as your spy. Bringing secret information." Humie's chest expanded.

Tesha hoped no one caught onto their friendship. He'd lose this enthusiasm quickly if his mother or Agat got to him.

"One more thing," Tesha said. "Don't tell your mother or—"

"Agat or Pasul."

Tesha nodded. He was a smart child. This might work.

He disappeared behind the curtain. He stopped on the other side, and she sensed he practiced stepping lightly so no one would hear him.

She hadn't expected to make it easy for Humie to find Ahmose, but before the soft padding of his boots faded, a rap and a greeting sounded from her doorway. She heard Humie return to the curtain. Ahmose announced he had something to tell her.

But she did not like at all what Ahmose told her. She didn't even wait for him to leave before she headed toward Hattu's great hall. Her two guards cried out.

She dodged their awkward attempts to stop her.

"I'm going to the great hall, not leaving the palace," she said and raised her skirt to run even faster. "I'm following King Hattu's orders. Come with me if you must."

41

Hattu pressed his fingers into his forehead and temples. The incessant twitching in his chest reverberated through him. He could collect his thoughts if it would go still like it had before. It never went quiet now, though. There was no more slumbering.

He must form a plan to save Marak. What would work? If he had Marak here, they'd overcome this Paskan treachery inside him. Marak understood Paskan tricks. Marak, not Tesha. She'd betrayed him.

If he could only have a moment away from the incessant scrabbling of those creatures. He pressed them back, held his defensive wall. Despite the exhaustion dragging him down, he held against them. Soon Marak would help him. But there was never silence inside him now. The goddess needed that emptiness of silence to speak to him. That must be why he felt so lost from her.

He'd keep attacking, that was the thing to do. Strike the Paskans. He was good at that.

He sat on his throne at one end of the expansive, mostly empty room. Ishana looked down on him from the fresco where she stood, beautiful but armed in the manner of a man, leading soldiers into battle. His goddess would tell him to strike back if she answered his prayers and spoke. The face on the fresco seemed to scowl at him instead.

Shatim stood next to him, watching and waiting. He offered nothing. Why couldn't he help?

A plan. Marak. Attack. The maddening advance wriggled downward, pressing. *Push back, push back. Don't give in.* He had to find the strength to drive it out of him, but first he needed Marak.

"We'll force the Paskans to give him back," Hattu said. "We have plenty of captives. I told you."

"Yes, sir?" Shatim asked. Hattu wanted to strike the man and his deference. Advice, he needed advice. He'd already told Shatim about his way to force Marak's return. Why was Shatim acting like he hadn't heard and hadn't already objected? *Give me a better plan.*

"Paskans. We took prisoners. We'll use their methods. Blind two warriors and send them as a warning—give back Marak or we'll blind all the captives. Just like they do."

"We've never done that before," Shatim said. He sounded so unsure and incompetent.

"We'll attack them the way they attacked us and get Marak back as fast as we can. I need Marak. Treat the captives the way they do—blind them."

"You don't think it might provoke them to treat Marak in the same way if they haven't already? Or kill him in revenge?"

"Or give them a reason to hold off."

"Why don't we negotiate a trade—Marak for the prisoners you took last night? Send an envoy."

"Negotiations? More negotiations?" Hundreds of scratching legs wormed their formation tighter.

"Your position is stronger now. We'll make progress."

"Too slow—"

A commotion drew Hattu's attention to the great hall's entryway. Tesha stalked across the room toward him, two guards trailing uselessly behind. She had no right to come here. Did she want to provoke him into locking her up in some dark cell? He looked away.

Her pull, her body. He didn't trust himself. He forced himself to picture that vial at her neck, her hands around Nerik's cup. If it'd been anything but his son's life. He could have forgiven anything else.

But his eyes stole back to her. She acted as if she were the queen, holding herself regally indignant, her back straight and chin up, which only emphasized the softness of her hips, the generosity of her breasts. He shut his eyes.

When he needed her most, she'd betrayed him. If they could fight together, he would win. But they couldn't.

Marak. Get Marak back. That was what he needed. He must ignore her. Fight her.

He'd be able to think again if he could have a moment of stillness.

She walked close and stood in front of his throne. He rose and stepped down from the blood-red dais. He wouldn't let her take the role of beseecher before the throne and turn sympathy to herself. But the spark in her eye and the flush lighting her cheeks looked too beautifully fierce for a petitioner. Perhaps he should draw his sword. There was more than one way she could overthrow him.

"You are considering a way to force the Paskans into giving back Marak and Daniti," Tesha said. She kept her voice low, a conversation between the two of them, although her tone had the keen edge of a blade to his throat.

A public scene would have been easier to resist.

"That is no business of yours. I will conduct the affairs of this kingdom without interference from poisoning traitors."

"Traitor? Don't you remember how recently you were unfairly called that?"

Hattu tried to shrug off her taunt. He could only twitch and shudder. She weakened him. *Fight her.*

She glanced around and whispered, "You are not yourself. I can help you more than anyone else can."

The smell of sour milk drove him backward. "Return to your rooms. No one should be talking to you about my plans. I will cut off your access to gossips." He crossed his arms over his chest and tried to press the frantic creatures into stillness.

"Your Majesty." Ambassador Ahmose stepped forward.

Where had *he* come from? He wished the ambassador would return to Egarya and leave him to handle the Amur problem. He'd told Ahmose he would. That should be enough. He should stop popping up everywhere, watching.

"I mentioned your decision to Priestess Tesha," Ahmose said, "as a kindness to reassure her that her sister might soon be free."

Hattu glared at Ahmose. Tesha didn't need kindness. He'd been kind *enough* to leave her in her rooms until he shipped her off. These idiot guards would follow his orders from now on. Lock her in. He'd started the arrangements for her banishment. She'd be gone soon. He hadn't been able to bring himself to send her to some wild garrison of soldiers with no warning or preparation to receive her.

"I'm sure you meant well." Hattu waved his hand in dismissal. He should be more polite to the man, but Tesha's presence threw him off balance.

"A kindness?" Tesha's voice rose shrilly. "You are planning to blind the prisoners. It's horrific. Informing me that you would consider such a thing is hardly kind. You cannot go through with this. This is not who you are as king."

"Who I am as king? And you know better than I do?"

"Use the captives to negotiate a trade without this abomination."

"You and Shatim would have me delay and drag this out. That's your advice. You know nothing about negotiating with Paskans. They blind prisoners all the time. This is what they'll understand. Go back to your room and leave this to me."

"I helped you negotiate with their envoy. I made more progress than you did, and I did it without becoming a barbarian."

He braced his palms on either side of his head. "This is war." She was no warrior and had no experience with battles like last night's. "I have to use the tools war hands me or I'll lose."

"Use the captives, by all means. You *have* the tools you gained in the counterattack."

"It's not enough. We've run out of time. Think of all their men who died last night. Revenge is all they'll be wanting unless I shock them and show them how much worse it can get."

"With so many already dead, that means they'll want their remaining warriors back as quickly as possible. They will know they cannot risk losing more. They'll negotiate without you sending blinded men. In your offer, if you must, threaten to blind the captives if they do not release Marak and Daniti quickly. You don't have to *do* it."

"An empty threat if it is not accompanied by the demonstration that I mean what I say. You've admitted to the power of this act."

"I've called it an abomination. We don't want to escalate the violence or encourage them to harm Marak and Daniti."

"Escalate? Last night I killed what must be most of the warriors from this tribe. Killing's all they'll have on their minds. I've left the tribe defenseless. They won't even be safe from other Paskans. The tribes turn on each other whenever they see a moment of vulnerability. They're like rats who eat their own weakened kin. If I don't pull Marak from their clutches fast, he'll be killed when one of the neighboring tribes attacks."

He watched the horror on Tesha's face. Good, he was getting through to her. She had no idea. She shouldn't be here. "Leave me. Stay in your rooms. Or—"

"Has your scout commander made progress? You might be able to rescue them without this."

Gods below. Tesha knew how to twist the knife in him. His scouts should have found them. He should have been able to swoop in with a rescue.

Shatim glanced at him. Hattu closed his eyes. Why did he need to tell his traitorous wife about this?

Shatim cleared his throat, the diplomatic pause asking for Hattu's permission to speak. Fine, if it would silence Tesha. He nodded.

"Your assistance with the commander's search plan is much appreciated, but so far it has not borne fruit. The Paskans appear to be killing our scouts now. We've had to send larger contingents for protection."

"Is there a pattern to where they've attacked the scouts?" Tesha asked.

"Silence!" Hattu said. "There is no time for patterns and scout searches. I need Marak now. I will send blinded captives. I will get fast results. Go back to your rooms."

"You don't need to show them blinded men," Tesha said. "The Paskans blind prisoners, so they know exactly what the horror is like. A threat is enough. I love my sister. I want her with me more than ever. But don't do this. Not like this. Offer the captives in return for Marak and Daniti's safety. If they are as desperate as you say, they will cooperate with speed."

"You've been to a Paskan village and know how they react when you kill off most of their men? They'll slide a dagger up under the ribs of the one source of revenge they have. The only safety for Marak is to shock them out of taking quick revenge. Blinding's the only safety. Your sister dead or your sister alive. That's all I can offer."

Tesha's hands covered her mouth. Tears gathered in her eyes. Just what he needed, a sobbing woman. She could at least understand how little he wanted to do this. He wouldn't lose his friend because he didn't have the courage to do what was necessary.

Tesha wasn't leaving.

Hattu pointed his finger at her. "Do you want them to kill your sister? Is that what you want? Marak's the only one who matters to me."

She gasped at that. "Save Daniti. Please. Do what you have to, but save her."

"Get out."

She turned and walked toward the doorway. Finally.

Then she stopped. Without turning around, she said, "I did not put poison in anyone's cup, but you should consider, for your own safety, that I exchanged your cup and Nerik's. If someone did put poison into it, they intended to kill you, not your son. If you agree with Nerik's idea that he drank poison at the feast, then you must find the true culprit who may be aiming at you. There are Hitolians who have wished you dead. I saved you from one of them."

"More excuses to throw off blame. You are the poisoner. You had the vial. You aimed at Nerik." There were Hitolians who wanted him dead. Someone let the Paskans in. He'd have to consider that much.

Tesha walked out.

Hattu staggered onto the dais and sank onto his throne. Free Marak at any cost. He nodded to Shatim. "See to the preparations. Get the two ready."

42

"He isn't himself. And when you're a king, it's terrible." Tesha covered her face with her hands.

Henti sat next to Tesha on the bed in her sleeping chamber. Tesha leaned against her maid.

"He says it's the only way to get Daniti back, but he isn't thinking. He looked so frightened. I'm afraid for Daniti and Marak too, but this will provoke the Paskans, not bring them to reason. Why can't he see that?"

Henti comforted her, but she didn't have an answer. Of course her maidservant didn't have advice about this. But she couldn't talk to Daniti or Marak. That's who could help. That's how hopeless her life had become.

"It's the vial of tansy that convinced him. Even now, I don't think he really believes I did it. But the vial is such solid proof. And his son, his heir, is so sure I poisoned him." Tesha leaned her head on Henti's shoulder. She was tired. It was the worst and longest day of her life. "And now he insists on doing this horrific thing. Blinding men on purpose. As if that would save Daniti." A tear wound down her cheek.

Henti handed her a clean handkerchief. "He knows these Paskan demons better than you. Perhaps you should trust his judgment about this."

"While he's accusing me of murdering his son? Such good judgment."

Henti looked shocked at that. Not the way to talk with servants, even one she'd known her whole life. *Daniti, I need you.* Usually her sister made the rude criticisms. Her tears flowed. Tesha blew her nose.

She and Henti huddled on the far corner of her bed so they could talk without being overheard. Agat must still be taking care of her father's burial, but Ija kept slipping up to the curtain and got ruder each time Henti sent her away. Ashu had grown too fearful of the rebukes to even try to shoo the concubine from the doorway.

Henti patted Tesha's arm. "You've had too many troubles for a woman in your condition."

"My condition?"

"You can't hide these things from me, child. You've been married three months already. You're going to have a baby. Early days, but you are."

"I did consider that, and for some reason Daniti said I might be. In the morning . . ."

"Just like your mother. Don't worry, though. That'll pass soon, and your mother never had trouble carrying or birthing either of you girls. You saved the aggravation for later."

Tesha tried to smile at this gentle teasing.

Henti rested her hand against Tesha's cheek for a moment. "You need some rest. Take a nap."

"How can I sleep? I have to figure this out."

Henti sighed. "You said that vial was Daniti's. Why did she have tansy?"

"She didn't. Daniti kept perfume in it, and that's what was in it when I took it from her jewelry box. It never had tansy in it until Hattu found it on the table in his quarters when he accused me."

"If that's so, how did the tansy get in it?"

"That is a very good question." She'd wondered about that, but how could she track it down? She considered the sequence of events. "When I came from Hattu's sleeping chamber into the receiving hall, I smelled a hint of Daniti's perfume. I thought it was the woman's screams that made me think of Daniti. You know, another woman in distress. But I did smell it. Someone had opened that vial in Hattu's hall."

"And poured out the perfume?"

"Yes! Probably out those big windows. It left its trace in the air. But there was no one there. Not then anyway."

"No way to know who," Henti said.

"There might be. Hattu's quarters are right across the hall from the concubines." Tesha thumped her fist against her leg. "And the children."

"You've already sent Humie to spy. You could ask him when he comes back if he heard anything that night. But children tend to sleep hard."

"I saw Humie in Nerik's room that night. He looked like he'd just been dragged from a sound sleep, all disoriented and fearful."

Henti frowned.

"Now that I think about it, the child I didn't see was Samsi. Yet he's the one who is always listening in. He'd have made an ideal spy except he might tell his father the Great King someday. That wouldn't do."

"Samsi is a nice boy. He likes you—or he did," Henti said.

"I think he might still. He dislikes Nerik, after all."

"He wouldn't like a murderess." Henti waved her hand as if to brush away a fly. "Sorry. You know what I mean."

"But he wouldn't be likely to believe Nerik's tale."

"Would you like me to look for Samsi? Is there any harm in asking him if he heard something that night?"

"No one's going to let me talk to Samsi. What if you sneak into the children's rooms and find him? They've been using the hallway to spy on me. We'll use it for our purposes."

Henti reached for the veil Tesha had removed.

Tesha held still while Henti stabbed the pins back in place to hold her veil. Then they sent Ashu out where the guards kept watch.

While Ashu distracted the two soldiers with a request to go to the kitchens for food, Tesha and Henti checked that none of those women lurked in the hallway to the concubine and children's quarters, then they slipped past the curtain. Tesha stayed hidden in the hallway while Henti went to bring Samsi.

43

———

et Marak back. With Marak he could fight and win.

He and his old friend had fought many battles together. None like this one. But he was losing ground, and Marak would understand. When a battle went badly, a general had to bring in reinforcements.

Time was running out, so he had to do this.

He would take responsibility. He'd do that much, at least, so that he could live with himself. He would be there when they did it. The men being blinded would not value his presence. They'd see it as an insult and viciousness on his part. But *he* would know that he acted honorably if he watched this brutality.

He called for the commander of his tower keep. A servant ran off with the message.

He had no choice. Everything hemmed him in. He'd lost track of all the threats. The relentless attack inside confused him. All his strength went into pushing that assault back. Marak would think for him again. They'd strategize as they always had. He'd be himself.

Get Marak back.

Shatim had already gone to implement his orders, but he would shift them somewhat. This was torture, and such things took place in the bowels of his citadel dungeon, down dark, dank steps into the mountain itself. Just the image in his mind, much less the actual descent, gave force to those creatures feeding on his wound like maggots gnawing on his weakness, enlarging it, consuming him. Anything that took him back into the darkness of that cell added to the curse inside him. No, he'd tell the commander to do this thing in the light of day. It would be the last sunlight these men would ever look upon.

The tower keep commander arrived. Hattu gave the new orders.

"Very well, Your Majesty." The commander bowed. If he thought his king's orders strange, he didn't show it.

How far had his rule been undermined already? Word of his . . . fits, that's the word Tesha had used, had spread. He knew that. And what of this cursed taint that squirmed through his insides? If only he had Marak to help him. *Oh, Tesha, why?*

He marched from his hall to the courtyard outside the tower keep. The cruel tools were ready, laid out on a table. The cauterizing bronze shimmered in the coals of a brazier. They'd tied the two prisoners to chairs, their heads fixed by leather bands against the back of them. The man who would do the work was skilled in this, he'd been told. He was also a Paskan prisoner. He could do it without killing a man in a way that would heal. Hattu couldn't grasp such words. The victims had been fed poppy syrup. Their heads would have lolled if not held in place.

Everything was ready.

Still, the guards and the gruesome workman looked to him for the signal. They would only proceed at his word. He must choose. Lucky Tesha, she could lay it on him.

Even through the poppy haze, the two men's faces contorted in terror. They were whole. He would make them shells of men. He'd seen such men. In the early days of his rule, he'd been ambushed by the Paskans and lost too many men. When he had finally overrun the Paskans and taken back his captured men months later, they were blinded and broken. Perhaps this wasn't—

Again, the razor claws seized at his flesh. They outfought him. He groaned and braced a hand against the stone wall of the keep.

The rough stone held firm, propping him up.

He snatched his hand back and stood straight, his hands soldier-like at his sides. He glanced around. They still waited for his command. His alone.

He gave a minute nod.

It was enough.

The sharp tool did its duty and the molten bronze its sealing. The smell of burnt flesh sickened him. The men screamed, roused from any poppy solace. One of them sunk into the darkness that extreme pain could bring. But the other, poor soul, shrieked like one possessed, his body shaking violently. Blood and yellowish shreds ran down his cheeks.

Hattu did not look away.

When it was done, he commanded, "Dress the wounds and prepare these men for transport immediately. Let one of the sighted Paskans take them back home. Choose the least of the warriors to act as guide. Give them the fastest horses that can manage the terrain. I need them to reach the Paskan assembly as soon as possible. Be sure the sighted one understands what will happen to all the others here in the tower if Marak does not return immediately. I do not give them much time. Be sure they know that."

He turned away from this business.

"Sir?"

Hattu stopped. What now? He'd made his choice. Marak, at any cost.

"The guide should demand the woman back also, shouldn't he?"

Hattu balled his right hand into a fist. "Yes, of course. We demand the release of both Commander Marak and Lady Daniti."

It would be like Marak to refuse to leave unless he had Daniti with him. Hattu had seen how closely Marak watched Daniti. Hattu had no quarrel with the blind woman. It was her courage to live without her sight that gave him some shelter in his own heart.

His commander and the guards were still looking at him. He signaled their dismissal. He wanted them to leave him alone.

Hattu's body quivered. He saw through a blurred, narrow tunnel. His hands shook. His weakness must show. He needed to get away to a place where everyone did not watch him. He'd go to Ishana's sanctuary. Maybe she would help him as she had yesterday with her star fall.

He remembered Tesha invoking the goddess then, before he cried out in desperation. Each time he'd prayed to Ishana since, she'd been silent.

44

Daniti clicked her tongue against the top of her mouth to guide herself. She walked fast, and it took concentration to avoid rocks and trees. The midday sun still fell directly down on her. She wanted to reach Kurala. She'd told the Paskans she used magic to "see" where she went, so the faster she moved, the more they believed her. They had to trust that she was a powerful witch. Marak had told her that magic was far more active among the Paskans and witches were something they knew about.

They hated Riam. She'd warned them that Riam had killed more of their men, yet another betrayal. They didn't want to believe her, but they had to find out. They overcame their terror of her witchcraft to pursue the traitor. She hadn't convinced them she needed Marak to come with her. They'd made him stay under guard at the cave.

She moved past a tree and darted around an obstacle in front of her, boulders or something. The sound from it came back too hard to be another mound of bushes. She clicked and found an opening between the trees ahead.

The Paskan warriors talked between themselves, releasing their fury. That, too, drew her attention.

"He's a broken man. We should have killed Riam right away when he approached us with his 'plan.'"

"That worm thought he was in charge. Telling us what to do. Just because he knew when the jackal king and his queen would come north and where we could kidnap that woman."

"We used *him*. He couldn't even get revenge on a woman without our warriors."

"But if what the witch says—"

"I'll rip his heart out of his chest if he killed the envoys we sent him out with."

"We should have known better than to trust him when he said he'd get us into the city. It was a trap."

"He didn't know that. Too stupid."

"*We* should have known. The men he told us to contact in Alpara were too desperate to kill Hattu once their conspiracy had been uncovered. Men that desperate are losers. The jackal king outsmarted them. *We* knew the enemy we faced. Hattu's never been tricked."

"He's got witches helping him now. He brought them with him. We had no way to know that. We thought we had all the magic."

"We have one of his witches now. Maybe another curse would work. Maybe they couldn't—"

"Look at her. She casts her power far."

Daniti gasped. Her plan might undo her. She'd made herself too valuable. They'd never give her back, or they'd kill her out of fear.

"Shut up, both of you. She's listening."

Daniti swept the area ahead and headed down the slope, following Kurala's guiding thoughts.

She'd also told the Paskans it was she who'd made a demon figure that crippled Riam, and she could track him through that demon. That wasn't true, but it was a good story for now. Persuading them that Kurala would lead her would never have worked. This story had enough truth to it. It was easy to believe an evil spirit haunted Riam.

They were getting close.

Kurala sent to her over and over, "I'm here. I'm here."

She sent back, "I'm coming. I'm coming."

As clearly as she sensed the closing gap, Kurala's joy at being reunited came to her. "Did you bring me food?" Kurala's voice and happiness at her approach was unmistakable.

The close-packed trees offered cover for her and the Paskans. The warriors moved almost noiselessly now that they'd stopped talking. She whispered to them and pointed the direction to creep up on Riam.

She heard the warriors spreading out on either side of her, some moving ahead. They'd surround Riam. Kurala was very close. Perhaps they could see Riam.

A surprised yell. Riam. He'd seen them.

"Where are the men we sent with you?"

Silence after this question. Daniti smiled. Riam didn't have a quick lie, and even these Paskan louts would realize he was struggling to come up with an explanation that wouldn't get him killed.

"They attacked me," Riam finally said. "They didn't agree that I should go to Alpara with them. But I got away. I don't know where they are. On the way to Alpara, perhaps."

"We'll make you show us where their bodies are."

She'd led them to him, and he was alone. They didn't doubt her now.

She edged toward Riam. He'd bound Kurala, and she would free her friend.

"You're here! I can see over the bad man's shoulder. I'm in a sling on his back. Come free me."

"I'm coming."

"These ropes hurt. They cut into me." Kurala's complaint broke her heart. How could someone hurt so sweet a creature?

She should have told the Paskans about Kurala so they wouldn't hurt him when they attacked Riam. "Stay back," she yelled to the Paskans. "The creature—"

"You brought that witch." Riam's voice shrieked in fury. "Don't let her near me."

Daniti hesitated.

"She tracked you down, traitor," one of the Paskans said, laughing. "It's all her fault that we've caught you. She told us how she over-powered you with a demon. You can't even defend yourself against women."

"Take us to our dead and maybe we won't let her at you."

"Or we'll just watch her use more magic on you. What limb will it be this time?"

Daniti sent out, "Kurala, how can I protect you? The bad man will fight these—"

One of the Paskans yelled, "Get back. He carries the demon on his back now. She called it out of him."

Kurala screamed silently, "Dagger. You, at you. Dagger out."

Riam yelled and lunged toward her, his boots thundering down.

Kurala screeched the piercing cry of an eagle killing its prey.

Riam's battle cry distorted into a scream of agony, and his forward movement stumbled. "My eye."

Riam and Kurala tangled in a skirmish. She imagined Riam's dagger in a fight against Kurala's eagle beak—a sharp hook but so near his vulnerable feathered neck.

She screamed, "Kurala. No!"

Suddenly Kurala squawked, and from the movement of that angry sound, Kurala had worked loose from the sling and thudded against the ground.

"Dagger. Toward you." Kurala's desperation shrilled in her head.

She threw her clicks in an arc to pinpoint the movement of the dagger and dodged away from the ringing back of metal. Not far enough.

His shoulder struck hers. The force threw them both to the ground. His body crashed against hers. A metallic ping on stone marked the flight of the dagger from his hand toward her.

Riam bellowed, "My eye. My eye." He curled away.

The dagger. It was near. She felt for it before Riam could find it. Her fingers touched the sharp edge. She clasped the hilt.

Riam flipped over, and his knees knocked the wind out of her.

She reached with one hand and found the fabric of his tunic and his belly underneath. Her other hand held the dagger tilted up. She yanked him closer. He didn't expect this, and he fell toward her. She shoved the dagger with all her strength and let his falling weight push it further into his belly. He tried to draw back. She worked both hands onto the hilt and yanked upward, twisting the blade, some instinct of violence showing her the way to kill. Warm blood ran over her hands. It smelled metallic and rotting. A gurgle came from him. She imagined the feel of blood filling his throat. She kicked and wrestled out from under him.

"Witch, you are a warrior." A Paskan stood over her. "Kill that demon for us. Riam bound it, but it still lives."

Kurala sent her a terrified cry.

"No, don't harm it. That's not the demon," Daniti said in a clear voice.

"Kill it. That is no animal of this forest."

Daniti dragged herself over to Kurala. She found the knots and worked at them as quickly as the sliminess of blood on her fingers allowed.

"I'll see to it," she said to the Paskans, trying to reassure them without an argument. They would take their swords to her poor friend.

"Fly away," she sent to Kurala.

"I'll bring my friends to free you."

"Yes, bring them. You can find me again, lead them to me."

"I will. I promise."

The last knot broke loose. "Fly." She stood and raised Kurala up on her open hands, and he took off into the air. *Bring Hattu's whole army.*

The Paskans cried out.

She spoke to them, "The creature needed only to be free. He wants no trouble with you."

"He was fierce enough when he pecked out the traitor's eye."

"As I said, he wants no trouble with you. You cannot complain when he defended me against that traitor."

"He is your creature, witch. See that he does not come near again or we will kill him."

45

"Uncle Hattu says you tried to kill Nerik."

Tesha saw hesitation in Samsi's face. He'd been so friendly before.

They stood facing each other in the hallway between her quarters and the concubines' rooms. Henti had snuck into the children's quarters without being noticed by anyone. She'd found Samsi and convinced the polite boy to come with her without attracting the attention of the children's guards. As a servant, no one paid attention to Henti.

Tesha had hoped Samsi would be on her side, but that was too much to ask. He adored Hattu, the kind father he'd never had. He barely knew *her*.

"But I didn't try to kill anyone," Tesha said. "It is important for Hattu and Nerik's safety that I figure out who put that poison in Nerik's cup. It could have been meant for Hattu. It would be terrible if whoever is the poisoner tries again and succeeds."

Samsi frowned.

"You can believe I am the poisoner, but I'm not. Meanwhile I have a murderer to uncover before he kills my husband and my stepson. To accomplish that, I want to ask you a question."

"A question?"

"Did you see anyone moving around the women's quarters or Hattu's rooms the night Nerik was poisoned? Either a stranger or someone who had every right to be there, like Ija or Humie, but you saw them at some point that night."

"If there had been a stranger, I would have called the guards. You'd already know about that."

Tesha nodded. "That's true. I don't think there was a stranger."

"Why would I tell you if someone was walking around where they should be?"

"It will probably mean nothing. But we need to know where everyone was. You can help with that. I didn't see you that night in Nerik's room with the other older children."

Samsi's frown deepened and his brow drew together. "I didn't poison Nerik."

"Of course not. That isn't what I meant."

"Ija's screaming woke me up. I heard Humie and Gasul run into his room after Agat did. He didn't need my help."

"Was everyone asleep before Ija screamed?"

"I don't know. I was sound asleep by then. I went to bed late because I was worried for Agat. She doesn't talk to me much. I think seeing me makes her think about my father and how he might arrange a marriage for Uncle Hattu. That was her big fear until you came. So she doesn't talk to me, but I was watching for her." He shrugged.

Tesha liked the return of the talkative, observant Samsi.

"You're much prettier than Agat. When I heard you talking to the Paskan envoy, I knew Agat was going to lose her place. Agat knows it also. I liked you, but it didn't mean Agat didn't matter anymore."

"You're right."

"While you were feasting with Hattu and Nerik and the other nobles, Agat paced around the women's quarters. Each time I got a glimpse of her, she looked very sad. Nerik came back. He could barely walk. Agat told Ija to take care of him. That was the saddest thing of all. Nerik is like her own son, and yet she felt she had lost him also. She sent Ija in to be his mother."

Ija as his mother? That hadn't been Ija's plan. She'd gotten into bed with Nerik. But Agat sent her in. Agat knew Ija.

"What did Agat do after she sent Ija in to help Nerik? Did she go to bed?"

"I thought she would, but she stood in the hallway near Nerik's room. I could see her if I looked out from the dark of my room. It was as if letting Ija take her place was too much."

"She just stood there?"

"For a bit. Everything fell quiet in Nerik's room. Then I could hear Hattu's voice. He gave some command to the servants. Agat went out that way. I guess she thought she should make sure the servants were doing what they ought to for the king. She's like that."

"She's good at supervising servants."

"She didn't come back for a long time, so I guess the servants didn't do what Hattu asked and she had to. I couldn't go to sleep. She'd looked so sad that I couldn't get her out of my mind. She did come back eventually. I was going to greet her when she walked down the hallway past my room. To cheer her up. But I didn't say anything. As I watched her go past my doorway, this sweet smell came to me like a kind of blessing, and Agat was smiling. All was well with her."

Tesha clasped her hands in excitement. A sweet smell?

Samsi's shoulders hunched up toward his neck. "Agat doesn't deserve all the misery you brought her. Now her father's dead too. I answered your stupid question. I didn't see anyone else. Uncle Hattu wouldn't like me talking to you."

"Thank you for speaking to me. What you told me is very helpful. I don't want you to get in trouble with Hattu."

Samsi turned and hurried down the hall back toward his room.

46

————

Tesha paced around the hearth in her hall. The angle of light in the high windows showed evening approached. Her maidservant Ashu had brought food from the kitchen, but Tesha didn't feel hungry.

More important was the news Ashu had also brought. She'd seen Kety in the kitchen, stirring a big cauldron suspended on a tripod over a hot fire, unpleasant work that he'd cheerfully taken on himself. In his broken speech he gossiped with the cooks, the plan Tesha had sent to him through Henti.

Samsi's reluctant description of what he'd seen last night pointed at Agat, although he didn't understand it that way. It was probably best not to have Samsi talk to Hattu. Samsi might refuse to repeat what he'd said, and she'd do a better job of revealing the significance of what Samsi observed.

Would Kety bring her more information that would make the pattern accuse Agat more surely?

Kety had nodded at Ashu in a way that Ashu thought meant he'd come soon. Ashu wasn't very clever, but Kety was, so Tesha would wait for his news before trying to speak to Hattu. Persuading him would be hard unless she had solid evidence.

Tesha heard one of the guards at her door call out a challenge. She turned to see who was there.

"I bring food for priestess," Kety said. He carried a tray covered with a linen napkin.

Henti hurried forward. "Oh good, you brought what I asked for. Please carry it in here."

Kety entered and placed the tray on a table as far from the doorway as the room allowed. She came over to him away from the guards.

He bowed to her. His boney limbs poked out of a loose tunic, making him look even more frail than usual.

"Were you able to find out anything from the kitchen servants?" Tesha kept her voice low, although, unlike the concubines, the guards didn't seem to spy on her. Keeping her restrained in her room seemed to be all they viewed as necessary.

"Kitchen easy make friends. Many job to help. Easy talk and do job."

"Good. So?"

"I ask what slave make food only Prince Nerik like. Special him." Kety shook his head. "No one make. I not see slaves happy about Nerik. Not do just for him anything."

Tesha smiled a little. It did her good to hear that even the slaves didn't care for Nerik enough to spoil him with special treats. "A bristly young man none of the slaves like."

Kety dipped his head in agreement. "So we not need who made food. All ate. Only prince sick. Find who near Nerik dish."

Tesha nodded. "I've already thought about each of the nobles near Nerik's seat, but I can't remember anyone leaving their seat to approach him."

"I say to pretty girls who serve how good they do. Trays heavy."

"Good idea. And what did you learn when you flattered the serving women?"

"They show how. Tray here." Kety modeled carrying a tray on one upturned arm held out straight. "Spoon here." With his other hand, Kety clasped the air as if it were a serving spoon. "Girls go this way."

Kety leaned down in a way that kept his arm level and he scooped with his other hand. "Hard hide poison. Priestess?"

"I agree. I can't see how any of the food servers could slip poison into Nerik's food. What about the wine? Nerik certainly drank plenty. That wine bearer is impressive. After he mixes the water into the wine pitchers, he goes around to each guest in turn. I wonder if he could have added something to Nerik's?"

Tesha closed her eyes and pictured the wine bearer swooping gracefully between the guests that night. Showy. He'd enjoyed his work, holding the pitcher higher above the cups than necessary so the wine cascaded down in a red stream but not so high that it splashed.

Tesha looked at Kety. "He did stop a couple times that I remember and put down his pitcher to wipe up small spills. He had a linen napkin on his arm for that." She sighed. "But not near Nerik. Not at his table, nor the ones on either side of him. I had my eye on Nerik, watching for chances to win him over. I think I'd remember."

"You right. I make little friend. Small boy like my son. He like make story. Talk much about people at feast. He hide in back to see swords high people wear."

A spurt of hope flared inside Tesha. Someone who'd spied on the feast and wanted to talk about it. Bless Kety and his ability to win over others. A child like his son whom he'd never see again. Poor Kety. "And what did you learn from this boy?"

"He like big arm of wine man and wine go." Kety demonstrated the flowing of wine from up high with a drop of his flickering fingers. "I ask where strong wine man put down. Not Nerik or king."

"That makes sense. He'd put on the best show for the royal family, I imagine, and not take a rest near them. So not a servant. I didn't really expect it to be unless someone bribed them. Did the boy notice any nobles stopping near Nerik?"

"He like swords. Keep eye there. So I say, tell each sword me. Go from king chair each sword in . . ." Kety marked a row with his pointer finger. "Kety ask if any sword man walked from chair. Two go . . ." Kety's brow wrinkled.

Tesha thought he searched for a word, but then she realized he didn't want to discuss men relieving themselves around her. "But none of the men with swords went near Nerik?"

Kety shook his head. "Boy say no. I hear what many sword have." Kety acted out a sheath and hilt and what Tesha guessed was meant to be jewels or inlaid designs on them. Nerik hadn't been run through with a sword, unfortunately. No one could have blamed that on her.

What if this boy had been more observant than Katte about early arrivals? "Did the boy see if anyone approached Hattu's and Nerik's cups while everyone was arriving?"

"Boy come after. Cook give many jobs."

Tesha stomped her foot. "Someone must have seen something useful. Anything about the cups?"

"I hear who put cups. Fancy cups like for king and prince." Kety uncrossed his arms and then crossed them again.

"Oh! That's good."

Kety rocked on his legs, his weight shifting from side to side. "Cook not like priestess. Say . . . I not like say what cook say."

"I won't be angry at you, Kety. I need to know what the cook said and who put out the cups."

Kety scrunched his nose. "To me cook say priestess give too much rule how to make feast. Cook make voice sound like bird squawk 'Put this cup here. That cup there.' Before feast Agat there with cook. Cook made the not kind bird sounds to Agat about priestess. Many sound. Agat like cook. Say she put cup for her. So cook not do. Agat do."

"Agat? That's who put out the cups?"

Kety nodded.

Agat, who also put the tansy in Tesha's vial. Hattu would have to believe her now. Agat loved Nerik with the devotion of a mother. That much Tesha had observed, so she must have targeted Hattu. And Tesha had saved him when she restored the proper order of the cups. Had Agat felt all was lost now that Tesha had arrived and Agat's marriage to Hattu would never happen?

But Agat had gotten the order wrong. So much for the concubine's knowledge of royal protocol. Or had she intentionally mixed them up? And if so, why?

Tesha could extract the truth with the rite using the Paskan stone Utar had given her. Agat wouldn't cooperate enough without pressure from Hattu, but her husband would want the truth now that she had uncovered such strong proof.

"Henti, you must go and persuade Hattu to come speak with me. You heard what Kety said?"

Henti's smile indicated she had. "I'll bring him to you, Priestess."

47

Hattu ran toward the sanctuary he'd built for Ishana. He'd find his goddess there, with its air and wide-open distances. He kept his head down and passed through the palace hallways without greeting anyone. Flecks of color passed across his vision, blocking it, and darkness blurred at the edges, narrowing it. The snatches of sight he caught confused him. The floor pavers seemed to jump. He reached for the walls, and his hand swam through air. He fell. Crawling, his head struck the wall and he dragged himself up, solid stone under his fingers.

All the while, the curse built up its forces. The centipede legs pricked more and more. When the enemy piled on, strength upon strength, a general had to respond with his own. He placed stone upon stone on his defensive wall. Keep them out. Push back.

He clung to the rough stone under his fingers and dragged himself down the corridor toward the stairway to Ishana.

Marak, he'd done that to those men so Marak would come. He'd acted with courage. But Marak wasn't here. He wouldn't come soon enough.

He looked up the stairway. Narrow. Dark. The stairs shifted when he reached for them. His foot missed. He stumbled and braced himself. He'd get to the top, out onto the sanctuary.

"Excuse me, sir." A woman's voice came from behind him.

He found another step and pushed himself up. It was so hard to climb a single stair. That's how much these things inside had drained him. He'd lost control of his own body.

"Excuse me. Sir, when it's convenient, Priestess Tesha would like to speak to you."

What? He held onto the wall and turned slowly around. He blinked and peered at the woman bothering him. Something about Tesha. This was her fault. Why bother him now?

In between blinding patches of color, he made out the face of Tesha's maid, that ferret-faced Henti.

"What?"

"Priestess Tesha hopes she has helpful information about the source of the illness that struck Prince Nerik. She would like to speak to you."

He didn't say anything.

She stepped into the stairway and looked up at him. "May she come to the sanctuary?"

Hattu shoved her back. "Can't you see I want to be alone?" He kicked at the ferret so blindly his leg didn't connect, but it drove her away. He turned back to the stairs and the climb.

Finally, he stepped onto the terrace. He stood in the bright midday light, so strong it hurt. Disorienting bits of colored light still floated across his vision. He walked forward a few paces, unable to see the surface he stepped on. Dizzy, he crouched down and crawled to the low wall at the edge. He sat propped by the balustrade.

"Please, Ishana, help me. Strengthen me. I'm here in your holy place. Find me."

In their final preparations against a city, armies swarm with activity. The curse hordes marshaled in his chest. Time ran out.

What should he do? Traitors hid around him. He had to find them. Someone let Paskans into his city. Someone guided them when they kidnapped Daniti and Marak. His son had been poisoned.

They'd planned to take his fortress capital. He'd won the battles, but somehow he was losing what mattered. Ahmose drove him to take his army east. How could he do that? But another war with Egarya? Fatal. Muwatti was too sick. Everything fell on him. Always on him.

He was so tired. Who could he trust? Tesha was so perfectly matched with him, but she'd done an unthinkable thing. She used her sorcery against him. Marak was lost to him. Shatim? He was so cautious and slow. But was he right? Something felt different about Shatim ever since he'd returned home. Shatim used to be so helpful, but not now, and then Tesha said the same about those men. Not to do it. She'd called it an abomination. The attacks came from all sides. What next?

"Ishana!" He screamed the divine name, but that wasn't how the goddess listened.

For the goddess, there must be room inside of him, sacred emptiness. Instead he felt them inside, scrambling and scratching. Filled with evil.

What if the horror of those blinded men angered the Paskans and sent their revenge out of control? Shatim said something like that. What if he'd killed Marak with that act? He had to get Marak back no matter what. It'd been courage to choose that. He'd felt courageous.

But what if the curse controlled him? Blinding men, the horror. He'd never done it before. He'd behaved like a Paskan. He'd used a Paskan to do it. He couldn't see the stones in front of him, but he could see that grim, hard face of the prisoner who'd done the cutting and the burning, the blood spurting, all done to men tied and trapped in place. There was no honor in that, just horror. What else would he be unable to resist? So feeble now. He'd always seen what to do—the right thing, even when it was hard. The choices, the patterns. There was no pattern to these patches of color blinding him, none he could find among all the betrayals and threats. Everyone from every direction in a blur he couldn't distinguish.

His flailing served his enemies. He was useless now. Or worse, a danger to his kingdom. If he continued to rule, stripped of his capacity to make sound decisions, he would destroy his lands. He feared when those things ripped one more bite from his flesh, they'd strip him down so bare he would no longer care. He would feel nothing. He had to act now while he could still care.

The wriggling soldiers tunneled under his walls. He knew the clack of siege ladders hitting the battlements, but he was in the center this time.

They breeched the walls. Hundreds crawled over the piles of rubble to the last piece of himself.

Their claws tore into the bloody flesh of his center, ripping out gobs to feast on. Like the bloodied eyeballs he'd watched burned out. Their work. Their control.

They wouldn't make it easy and kill him, but he wasn't alive as himself anymore. Just a thing. A weapon for the curse to use.

He had to save his kingdom.

He had nothing left to give except his love for his son. He would leave Nerik his kingdom. His son's deepest wish. He would do it now before his debilitation destroyed the realm. Before he became only a Paskan tool. Before it was too late—

He rose with his hands on the top of the balustrade. He dragged himself onto the wall. The stone cut into his knees. He could see only through flashes of yellow, reds brighter than carnelian, patches of blue broken from the sky. All sent to confound him. He peered far below at blurred green of trees. He caught a glimpse of bristly pines and hard, rocky outcroppings. He would send himself down onto that and break into pieces, break free from the inescapable inside and save his kingdom.

That was courage. He hauled himself up to stand. To stand straight before he died. Dizzy, he wobbled.

Ishana, is this right? Is this my only choice?

Silence. Divine silence louder than he'd ever imagined.

He waited.

"No! My darling. Come down."

He jerked at Tesha's voice. His balance wavered between the air and the stone under his boots. *Make her go away.* He knew what he needed to do. Find the courage to jump.

He heard her step closer. "Go away. You torment me."

"I only want good for you. Henti said . . . I'll go away, but first, step down."

He knew how to escape. Fly off. Down, down onto the rocks. Break open and spill out the worms inside. He leaned out.

Tesha's arms closed around his legs. She screamed as they both fell.

He hit hard but too soon. They fell backward onto the terrace. His torso crashed onto Tesha, and he heard a crack against the stone pavers.

She had betrayed him again. He'd found true courage to undo the curse, to save his kingdom, but Tesha stopped him. Of course she would stop him from making Nerik the king, from freeing himself of dark sorcery.

He pushed up on an elbow. She lay still. Her eyes didn't open. She couldn't be . . . He leaned over her. Her chest rose and fell. He felt her head. No blood. Her eyes fluttered. He drew back.

He hated her. She forced him to be a creature of his enemies.

Shatim appeared at the top of the stairway and hurried forward. "Your Majesty, let me help you up."

"No!" Hattu pushed up.

Behind Shatim, guards climbed the stairs with Agat. Everyone watched him. His shame. His failure.

Agat pushed past Shatim and grasped his arm. Her eyes were red and puffy. She'd been crying. She looked so old and tired. Like him.

"Hattu, did she attack you? You fought her off?"

"Attack?" He tried to pull away from her toward the balustrade.

"Just like she poisoned Nerik."

"Nerik?"

Agat dragged on his arm. "Come with me. Let's check on Nerik."

He yanked his arm free and stepped onto the balustrade again. He faced the mountain. The blotches of light were floating away. He could see better.

"Hattu! What are you doing? Come with me to Nerik. If she tried to hurt you, she probably harmed him again. I couldn't keep watch. I've been attending to my father's pyre. Nerik needs us. Hattu?"

Standing on the edge felt free and dangerous. He could leap out.

Nerik had almost done that. The memory jarred him. The shock of that moment years ago had been etched into him. Holding his toddler son in his arms, he'd stood right here, but before the balustrade had been built while the sanctuary was still under construction. He'd carried Nerik up and told his son to listen for Ishana because this was the place he could find her. That was why he built this place. Nerik's eyes had gone wide, and he seemed to understand about listening. Hattu whispered that Ishana was there with them. Nerik had leapt out of his arms as if reaching for the goddess on her mountain. Somehow Hattu had caught him by the legs. Nerik didn't fall. Hattu's heart had pounded with his son clutched tight against his chest. He had never felt his heart beat so hard as then. He'd never felt such a lurch of terror and then such relief.

Hattu looked down the same sheer drop. Nerik hadn't fallen. He'd kept his son safe with the goddess's help. The memory prodded him. The same relief to live. Ishana had never spoken to him like this before, but the message felt clear. He stepped down from the low wall.

He understood the message. *Protect Nerik.* As Agat said, check on him. Keep him safe from Tesha. His dear son would be his help, his trusted supporter. He wasn't alone and never had been. He glanced at Tesha. She was sitting up with a dazed expression.

He waved back the guards and Shatim. They looked worried, but they didn't understand what had happened. They didn't realize what he'd tried to do.

Agat pressed her arm around him. "Come with me to Nerik. We'll make sure he's safe, and together we'll consider what to do."

48

Tesha refused to permit the guards to touch her, but she couldn't rise on her own. Her head throbbed, and wooziness kept her on the ground.

She could only watch Agat pull Hattu out of the sanctuary and down the stairs. Clever strategy. If she'd been Agat, she would have done the same.

At least he wouldn't jump off. No one else understood. Once again they saw *her* as the danger and missed what mattered.

As soon as Agat and Hattu left, Henti came up the stairs and ran over to her. "What happened to you?"

Tesha looked at the guards. They were hanging back, but still stood on either side of her. "I hit my head when Hattu and I fell."

The guards had let her go up to the sanctuary by herself, as Hattu had allowed before. Henti had told her Hattu had been desperate to get to the sanctuary and warned her that it was worse with the king than ever before. She assumed the guards didn't realize Hattu was already on the sanctuary terrace—or perhaps they hadn't thought a woman posed danger to their warrior king.

But now they'd accepted Agat's explanation of why she and Hattu were on the ground—she'd attacked him. If that fear stopped them from letting her approach Hattu now, she couldn't make him understand who Agat really was.

She caught their attention and pointed to the balustrade. "Did you see King Hattu standing on that wall? The concubine Agat called him down from it, as she should have. You saw that?"

Both guards nodded, but their frowns and narrowed eyes weren't granting her anything.

"That was the second time he climbed onto there. When I came up, I saw him standing on that edge." She hesitated. "I'm not sure why he was there, but it frightened me. Perhaps I startled him and he lost his balance. He seemed to be falling. I grabbed his legs and pulled him off that wall. I acted to protect him."

They didn't look persuaded.

"What attack would I be able to make on King Hattu?" She gestured around her. "I don't have a weapon. He's far stronger than I am. Other than pulling him off that wall, what could I have done to end up knocking him to the floor? I'm the one who got hurt."

Tesha leaned on Henti and gradually stood. The floor wobbled. The walls and mountainside spun. She bent over. Henti guided her back to the floor. She said softly to Henti, "I need to talk to Hattu before . . . before Agat takes control."

Henti looked doubtful.

The foulness of vomit rose in Tesha's throat. She crawled to the ash basin, and waves of nausea brought up a disgusting mess.

Henti gave her a handkerchief, and she wiped her mouth.

"Help me up," Tesha commanded.

"Are you sure you're able? Think—"

Henti was thinking of the baby, but dark Paskan magic had taken her Hattu. She had to save him. Their love might be tattered beyond repair, but it was the only way to save herself.

She got her knees underneath her. Henti wrapped an arm around her waist and drew her up.

Tesha and Henti staggered to the steps and down, the guards following close. When Tesha turned toward Nerik's rooms rather than her own, they didn't stop her. Perhaps they thought she was too ill to cause trouble. There was some use for her revolting, pathetic sickness.

The stone that could wring out the truth hung in the pouch at her waist. Using it would reveal her as the sorcerer everyone feared, a sorcerer who should be executed. Her favored status as savior of the Hattu's soldiers wouldn't protect her anymore.

The stone only worked if Agat cooperated. Could Hattu force Agat to participate? Why would he?

She'd have to persuade him first. The hallway spun. She closed her eyes and let Henti guide her, but the dizziness didn't let up. She willed the heaving in her belly to quiet. Agat had Hattu in her grasp. *This* Hattu did not see the hidden treachery around him.

"Where are you going?" one of the guards objected.

Both guards stepped in front of Henti and her.

"You must see I am unwell. I can barely walk. But I must speak with the king. I must be sure he is safe."

They didn't look like they had expected that.

"I'll just stand in the doorway and speak to him. If he asks me to leave, you can take me back to my rooms. He is my dear husband. Please. Only a few words."

With Henti's support she made it through the children's quarters to Nerik's sleeping chamber. Ija sat on the bed on one side of Nerik and Agat knelt on the other side.

Hattu hunched at the foot of the bed, facing his son. The way he stood was all wrong; his shoulders curled in so much that he bent forward like a crippled old man. Around him hovered the gray haze that she now realized arose when the curse dominated Hattu, the part she'd failed to drive from him. It was a sign only she saw, shown to her by magical power she had to hide or be killed for. Fixing this crisis was up to her, but she didn't see how she could other than making Hattu understand she wasn't the enemy and thus giving them time to work on the curse.

They all looked at her when she reached the doorway.

She thought about what she'd learned. The scent that

condemned Agat was going to be hard for Hattu to believe. She'd start with the poison in the cup.

Agat spoke first. "Guards, do your job. This traitor should be kept away from the royal family."

"I saved Hattu's life—more than once. And his soldiers. Is that the behavior of a traitor?" Tesha turned her gaze entirely on Hattu. "You accused me of putting poison into Nerik's cup when I moved your cup from his spot and gave him back his own. But I know I did not put anything in the cup, so I have been figuring out who did."

"It seems obvious it's the person who was carrying around a vial of poison." Hattu's harsh voice didn't offer any room for understanding. The curse cloud intensified around him.

Tesha stepped closer to him. "That wasn't me, either. But I know who put the tansy in that vial."

Tesha glanced at Agat. She was washing Nerik's forehead with a cloth.

"You wore the vial around your neck," Hattu said.

Tesha clenched her hands in frustration. She felt Henti shifting her legs to brace her more strongly. "I've thought about the night of the feast. No one approached Nerik's cup during the feast except the wine bearer, who did nothing unusual while pouring for Nerik. So if the cup was poisoned, it happened before the feast began. I had given careful instructions to the cook which cup to put in each place. It seemed odd she got it wrong."

Hattu pointed his finger at her. "You're concerned with putting cups in order, but you don't think poisoning your husband's son matters in the least. I loved you, but I will harden my heart to protect my son."

Tesha closed her eyes and gripped Henti's arm to steady herself. "Can't you listen? Use the intelligence I fell in love with. This is the trail to the truth, like I followed in Lawaza to free you."

"This is nothing like that."

"Someone wants to kill you. If it weren't for me switching the cups, you'd have been the one vomiting."

"You'd have liked that."

Her head swam, but she had to make Hattu listen and think the way he had before the curse. She realized there had been times since the curse that he had seemed free of it. They'd had some lucid conversations. She had to push for one now. "I'm trying to save your life again. Someone tried to kill you the same night the Paskans planned an invasion. It wasn't the cook who put out the cups. It was Agat, and she put tansy in the vial."

Agat stood up. "Never!"

"Stop this," Nerik cried.

Hattu's eyes looked blank, empty. "What are you talking about?"

Tesha stepped toward Hattu, but he backed away and raised his hand in warning. If the guards thought she posed a threat, they'd take her away. She let Henti draw them back to the doorway.

"The cook was annoyed by my instructions. Agat used that as an excuse to volunteer to put out the cups. She put in the poison then."

"You're blaming Agat because you made the cook angry?"

Why couldn't he make the connection? She glanced around the room. Nerik had closed his eyes. Underneath the yellow tinge, his face had gone pale. Agat and Ija stood on either side of his bed. Ija looked delighted, and Agat was angry. Her hand tightened around the cloth she'd used on Nerik's brow.

Tesha tried a new direction. "Agat's love for Nerik is clear, but is her loyalty to you above reproach? She's bitter about the promises you broke. She's Runda's cousin. What about family loyalty? He certainly wants you dead."

"Agat poison me? She wouldn't do that."

Agat flung the cloth across the room. "Get this woman out of here. Isolate her. You know I never sympathized with Runda. He should have accepted the Great King's decision to make you ruler long ago. In this latest plot of his, he revealed what an evil man he is. I've never acted in loyalty to him."

Tesha jumped in. "No one else besides Agat was near enough to put in poison."

"After twenty years of devotion, Agat's turned vicious? Poisoned *me*?" Hattu's lips twisted in disbelief.

"*Her* devotion? I love you and chose to defend you, even when my city and my family named you a criminal. *I* am devoted. How many times must I save your life to convince you of that?" This rejection fractured the fragment of love for him she'd clung to despite it all.

"I don't know who you are." Hattu's chin thrust out. "Agat didn't put poison in any cups. Why would she? I told you, she knows I never promised her more than she has. She likes her life."

Hattu believed his own lies, or the curse made him believe them. He couldn't hear the truth that went counter to this self-deception. Tesha sagged against Henti.

She raised her head and tried to break through the blankness of Hattu's eyes with her direct gaze. *That* was the curse at work inside him. "But did she still like it once you brought me? Isn't that what's changed?"

"What's changed is that I brought into my home someone who views Nerik as an impediment to be moved aside. You will never be queen."

"You need me as your queen. You're struggling. I can help you. On the balustrade—"

"You conniving liar. I've ruled for years without your interference."

"How can you be so willfully blind? You of all people, falsely accusing me just as was done to you."

"Like you're accusing Agat?"

"I have proof. The kitchen staff told Kety Agat placed the cups. And—"

"Never!" Agat lunged at Tesha, then held herself in check.

Hattu rubbed his chest. "So Kety cooked up this idea that Agat decided to kill me? That's where you're getting this nonsense?"

Ija shrieked. "That skinny man? Hattu's groom?"

No one answered her.

Ija pointed at Tesha. "He came to see her. Yesterday he came right into the women's hall and handed her the poison. I saw. He told her it would help drive away problems in her new home by making people sleep—he meant die, that's the sleep he meant." Ija turned toward

Agat. "You watched with me. That Egaryan killer is working with her."

Agat shrugged. "He did come to the women's hall yesterday and give her something."

"This is ridiculous," Tesha said. "Kety didn't bring me poison. He handed me a bag of chamomile. He said it helped his children fall asleep. His *children*."

"Silence!" Hattu shouted them all down. "The healing priestess in Lawaza told me Kety has knowledge of medicines. He knows which can be used as poison. He brought you tansy, did he? He was always loyal to you."

Tendrils of black fog had crept out of the haze and wrapped around Hattu. She'd pulled him free of their grasp on the hillside. She'd do it now. He'd hear reason. Her Hattu was in there somewhere.

"Kety is loyal to you. You know that," Tesha said. "Agat is the one who put tansy in that vial, not me. Your hall smelled of Daniti's perfume when we were awakened by Ija's screams. She switched it to make it look like I had tansy. When Samsi saw her returning earlier, he said she smelled of Daniti's perfume. Samsi didn't realize the smell was important, but he mentioned it. Two of us smelled it."

"Smelled it? Now there's proof. An imaginary whiff of something. Samsi didn't think it was important because it isn't. Stay away from my brother's heir. You are lethal to heirs."

"It was real." That wasn't how she'd meant to bring up that up. It didn't sound real.

"Agat's been very busy with poisons, according to you. Pouring them in cups and vials all over the palace. You're too clever." He turned to one of his guards. "See to it that Kety cannot leave the stables. He's harmless when this woman isn't misleading him." Then Hattu looked at her guards. "You will be punished if you let this woman get near me ever again. She'll be taken to the garrison tomorrow. Keep her in her rooms until then. Do I make myself clear?"

49

———————

Tesha had not slept well, but she rose at dawn. Her head and body still hurt from her fall with Hattu, but she could ignore that. She had things to do.

Her attempt to persuade Hattu of Agat's guilt had gone terribly wrong. She had thought she could speak to the man she married, the man who understood conspiracies and plots against him, who could strategize and see patterns. But that man was gone. The Paskan curse controlled him. She would find a way to pull him out, but she didn't have it now.

If she did, would she ever again find the intense love she had treasured? It was the curse at work, but it was still Hattu's voice that rejected her. It was Hattu's arms that tossed her aside and embraced Agat as the one to trust. She could not love this Hattu.

Please, Ishana, I know you commanded us to love each other and marry. But my love has been burned away by his hate. You are the goddess of opposites, love and war. Bring the Hattu I loved back and cleanse the curse out of him, or forgive my empty heart.

She should never have chosen this life. She wanted to be back in Lawaza with Daniti safe beside her, not married. But she was trapped. She was married to Hattu, and the only escape was banishment. Or

she could save Alpara and the Upper Lands by convincing Hattu she
was not evil and he should let her rule. She didn't have to love Hattu
to be queen. Hattu showed he was no longer behind her or even clear
thinking enough to be a true king. But she suffered no such impairment. There were others around Hattu like Shatim and Ahmose who
would listen when she brought the conclusive proof. They would talk
sense into Hattu even if the curse blocked her from doing that. But
she had to find more proof.

She needed more connecting Agat to the tansy.

All night she had considered some way to trick Agat into falling
under the truth stone's spell. She would have to perform the rite
while Hattu observed, or it would be useless to persuade him.
Neither he nor Agat would let her near them, much less permit a
prayer or conversation of the length she'd need.

She remembered the physician's unguarded comment at Nerik's
bedside about other people who had been sick. It was all she had.

If, with the help of others, she could wedge enough doubt into his
thoughts, he might allow her to speak to Agat with him present. She
could persuade him his presence was needed to protect Agat. He
trusted prayers to Ishana. She might work it out and hide the rite's
true purpose as she had with Ahmose. Her heart sank at the unlikeli-
ness of any of this.

Ahmose hadn't brought her any further news, either, but he
might. There was that.

She had to take action to shore herself up against the despair of
last night. She pulled herself straight. She had a future as queen, even
if she had lost her dream of a loving marriage.

First, she needed that solid proof. And she could not leave her
rooms—not as Priestess Tesha.

She pulled open one of the wooden chests she'd brought from
Lawaza. She slid her hand below layers of clothes to the bottom. Her
fingers grasped a small wooden box and drew it out.

She laid it open. Nestled in soft wool were two vials. They did not
contain poison, but it was death to possess them.

She did not know what they contained. She only knew their power and the pain they inflicted.

Tesha took one vial out and returned the other to the bottom of the chest. The magic inside the vial pricked her fingers. Powerful magic.

Before she lost her courage, she pulled out the stopper and swallowed it down. She had already dressed in one of Henti's tunics and skirts so she could pass herself off as a servant. Her distinctive hair was bound inside a plain brown veil. A loose cloak hid her form. Only her face gave her away, a face everyone had seen.

She crumpled onto her bed as it began. The torment started with her nose. Her bones cracked, her skin stretched and strained. She touched her shifting skin. The sockets around her eyes fractured under her fingertips and reformed narrower. The force she'd given herself to mangled her lips, twisted her teeth, pocked her skin, and bloated her cheeks. She choked back screams. The guards stood at her door.

Her torso cramped in response. Her hand flew to brace her belly. *Not there. Not there. Please, Ishana, not the child. I thought this potion only changed my face.*

She hadn't been certain that she carried a child, but now she knew. She felt a separate response inside to this evil she'd welcomed, and in that otherness, a fight. *If I must pay for this, let the price be mine alone, Goddess.*

The spasms in her belly did not disappear, but they did not grow worse.

Marak had told her about the limited time Riam had stayed transformed by this potion. The moment the torture subsided enough to let her stand, she rose. With shaky arms, she gathered a bundle of dirty laundry into her arms and walked through her hall and out the door, past her guards.

From the corner of her eye, she saw one of the guards frown in confusion, but they didn't stop her. She had trusted they would assume she'd come via the concubines' quarters, gathering dirty bed linens as she went. It was what the servants did. The guards on either side of her rooms locked only the priestess in.

She found the side door Henti had shown her on the trip to the baths. She stowed the laundry in a corner, groaning with pain as she bent over, then hurried outside. The early morning light still held a tinge of grayness about it, and the chill felt good against the pain that was her face.

50

───────

This damned Paskan would speak. He'd make him. This was the Paskan who had been close to the palace the night of the invasion. Utar had sent word the prisoner was not improving despite dressing his wound. Hattu would have to pry any information out of him before he died.

The healer had done his best but to no avail. Utar had included a small piece of useful information. He hadn't told the Paskan he was dying. He'd told him if he received excellent care, he might recover. Utar had given Hattu the needed inducement to get the prisoner to speak.

Hattu leaned against the wall. His legs quivered with exhaustion, but he'd done little that morning. His whole body ached.

The prisoner lay senseless, and the stench of death rose from the wound at his back.

Ahmose had trailed behind him when the message arrived that the man's condition worsened instead of improving and he should be questioned. Why was this Egaryan privy to all his troubles?

Hattu knew better than to go into the darkness of those cells below the citadel keep. He'd made the guards bring the man into one of the palace storerooms on a litter.

Now the Paskan lay there to be questioned, if he could speak. Hattu's thoughts shuffled like old men. What was the thing he needed to know from him? A traitor. There was a traitor. Like Tesha.

Ahmose glanced at him and waited. Damn the old man who was always observing. Hattu rubbed his eyes.

Ahmose cleared his throat and bent down over the prisoner. He took the man's jaw in his hand. "Wake up. Your life depends on showing the king you know valuable information. You are very ill. Do you want the physician to stop caring for that wound?"

The man's head lolled back when Ahmose released it. He looked up to Hattu for guidance. Hattu looked away. Ahmose hadn't missed Utar's hint about getting the man to speak. Let him do this unpleasant job.

The Egaryan slapped the prisoner's face. "You will speak, or you will die." The man's eyes fluttered. "You will die unless your wound is cleaned each day. Wake up. I grow impatient."

Hattu watched. If he bent down like Ahmose did, he feared he'd fall over. Leave this to the crafty envoy.

The Paskan struggled to open his eyes.

"What is the name of the Hitolian who let you into Alpara?" Ahmose asked.

Saliva dribbled from the side of the man's mouth. The Paskan lifted his hand to wipe it away, but had trouble bringing his hand to his face. "Don't know. Hitolian secrets? Me?"

Ahmose rose and went to a table where a pitcher and wooden cup sat. He poured a cup of water and knelt by the prisoner. The man spilled when he took the cup, but he drank greedily. His eyes stayed open.

Ahmose asked, "How did you get in?"

"Hidden in a wagon."

"Who drove the wagon?"

"Some peasant. He didn't know. I killed him."

Ahmose refilled the cup and handed it back to the Paskan. "Who made these arrangements?"

"Don't know."

"You must know something." Ahmose put a threat into his voice. Hattu noticed. His own voice felt muffled and weak. Leave this to Ahmose.

"Give me information or we will not bring the physician. Why were you separate from the rest of the Paskan force?"

"Wagon early in the day. At night, I killed the watch. I knew the password."

"How did you know the password?"

"Someone among your court told the Paskans, but I don't know who. No need to know. Some of your guards on our side also." The man closed his eyes, but his face didn't relax. Pain and desperation must be keeping him alert.

Hattu braced his arms against his chest and his own pain. It would be like a Paskan to tell him he had traitors among his men but hide who they were or who commanded them.

Ahmose stood over the prisoner. "Where did you hide during the day? Where did you kill the peasant?"

The Paskan looked like he wouldn't or couldn't say more.

"Shall we call for the physician and have him clean your wound and sustain your healing, or are you going to stay silent?" Ahmose asked.

Hattu wished Ahmose did not act so confident of his authority here. Hattu had ceded too much to him. He had to find some strength. He pushed off from the wall and stepped toward the litter, but the Paskan spoke up.

"In a barn. I buried his body under manure and hid until night."

"A barn? How close was this barn to the gate you were to open?" Ahmose continued.

"A ways."

"Along the main road?"

"Mostly."

"From what side street did you come out onto the main road? Tell me some mark that you noticed."

Hattu watched. He sifted through the confusion in his thoughts, trying to understand why this barn mattered. He should know. He would have known. Before.

"A mark?"

"Yes, like a distinctive building or decoration."

The Paskan shook his head. "It was dark."

"You want to be helpful. Think." Ahmose turned toward Hattu. He tipped his head toward him, inviting him to join in. Hattu blinked hard to clear his sight. He stepped closer.

"A tavern with a wooden hawk on the wall."

Ahmose leaned in closer. "Was this tavern of the hawk on the side street where the barn was or on the main road?"

Hattu knew where the tavern of the hawk was, but he didn't intervene.

"Side street, a ways down. Close to the barn."

"Was the barn on the same side or opposite the tavern?"

"Opposite."

Hattu would send someone to look. He could do something. But how could a barn reveal a traitor? The nobles who betrayed him hid their secret too well. Ahmose wouldn't get what they wanted from this man. No Hitolian conspirator would reveal his identity to a Paskan soldier who could be captured and interrogated.

Ahmose kept on. "You never heard a name or anything else that would hint at who inside Alpara worked with you? Your life depends on telling us."

"You have to believe me."

Ahmose stood back. He turned to Hattu again.

Hattu tried to stand upright. He'd remembered a question. "So why were you near the palace? Your comrades fought below. Did you abandon them?"

"No! A guard whispered you'd come back. Wasn't the plan. I went to kill you, but guards watched the back servants' door. I drew them off with a distraction, but it took too long. I heard your troops. Too late."

"How did a Paskan know where the back door of the palace was?" Hattu asked.

"Our commander told me. Paskans have been in Alpara before."

"You were inside the palace? Earlier?" Ahmose asked.

Hattu clamped his arm tighter against his chest.

"No. I told you, I couldn't get past the guards."

"Where else besides this barn did you go?" Ahmose asked. "You couldn't have stayed there the whole day."

The Paskan looked confused. "Go? Nowhere until I slipped out to kill the watch." He sounded sure.

Hattu thought of Marak. "And what of the hostages your tribe kidnapped?"

"Hostages? Don't know what you mean. You destroyed us."

Ahmose shrugged. "Not much use."

But Hattu noticed the ambassador hurried away in a purposeful way, shadowed by that inept guard who never kept Ahmose away from him. Hattu had commanded him to protect and watch the ambassador. He should have given less diplomatic instructions.

51

———————

Tesha smelled the stables before she saw them. She entered through a broad gateway into a forecourt with stable buildings on three sides.

A man with a few tufts of gray hair rising from a ruddy head snorted some words at her that she didn't understand. She tried to look helpful and subservient.

"Could you point me to the groom named Kety? One of the palace staff sent me with a question for him."

"Kety?" The man tugged on one of his tufts. "The palace staff? I hope he isn't in more trouble. He has a way with horses."

Tesha shook her head. "No trouble I know of."

The man tipped his head toward a dark doorway at one side. "In there, last I saw."

The doorway was strewn with manure. Tesha watched her steps. When she entered, everything went black. The sour smell of horse urine and rotting dung made her eyes water. The overwhelming odor disoriented her even more coming through a nose that both was and wasn't hers.

Gradually, dark shapes appeared out of the gloom. Beams divided the area into open stalls. To one side was a pile of manure higher than she was tall. A man shifted forkfuls to a wheelbarrow. Tesha knew they used it in the fields, but she had never been this close to the gathering of it. She tugged her veil around her nose and mouth.

Behind one of the horses, she saw a man's head and recognized the shape of the linen wrap. She stepped nearer to him.

Loudly enough to be heard by the man forking manure, she said, "Are you Kety? If so, cook has a question for you. Something you mentioned when you were in the kitchen yesterday."

"I Kety. But I no go kitchen more. King say here only."

The man with the wheelbarrow trundled out of the stable. Tesha came very close to Kety. "I know. I'm sorry. It was my fault Hattu's angry at you."

Panic covered Kety's face.

"You don't recognize me, but I'm Priestess Tesha." She pulled her golden amulet of Ishana from under her tunic and held it out so Kety could see it. "My face changed for a short time."

Kety took a step back. "Drink like bad man did. Magic bad."

"Yes, but I am desperate. King Hattu accuses me of poisoning his son. Of course I didn't do that. I had to disguise myself to get away from my guards. I need to find someone who can tell me about a groom who died of too much tansy. Has anyone spoken about that? They would gossip about a man's death. He was Nerik's groom, I think. And I think others were sick in the same way but didn't die. The physician said something like that at first, but he suspects me and won't say anything more now. I need to find proof Agat used tansy as poison. It's the only way I can protect King Hattu."

"I not hear about others. I bring to men saw groom die. I not can ask for you. My king think I had poison. I not be near you."

"I understand. I've gotten you in enough trouble. You only gave me chamomile, but those women make up any lie. How about if I go behind you but not as if I'm following, and you go near the men and signal me. I'll speak to them without any connection to you."

Kety nodded solemnly. "I do that."

Kety walked out through a doorway opposite where she'd

entered. Tesha waited and then followed, looking about her as if searching for someone.

Kety perched himself on a low wall. He flapped a stalk of hay idly in the air, pointing it at three men brushing down horses that were tied to a long railing. The horses' coats gleamed in the sunshine. The hard-packed earth was swept clean here. A shelf of brushes and other tools showed under an area protected by an overhang.

"What fine care you are giving these horses," Tesha said, approaching the men. "Their coats are lovely with your brushing." She pushed back the cloak that hid her shapely body. The face she wore was no longer hers, but the body was.

The oldest of the three men paused in his work and thanked her. The other two men looked to be about Tesha's age. She saw their eyes stick on her bust while they pretended to continue brushing.

"I have an important question for you. It's such a sad thing to ask, but I'm sure you can help me." The wrenching pangs pulsated from her face through her body, making this pretense difficult.

The stable hands gave her their attention.

"You see, a member of my family fell sick recently, and I'm afraid it may be the same problem that took the life of your friend who was a groom here."

"That were a terrible death. Not the same, I hope, for your family."

"Can you bear to describe what happened when he died? It would be such a help to me." Tesha hid the quiver in her legs by leaning against the horse railing for support.

"I don't like to say such. It isn't proper."

"I've cared for the sick before. The gods do not spare us when those dear to us are ill."

The old man notched up one shoulder in a half shrug. "He just seemed tired to start. Then woozy. Then everything came out, one way or the other, you know. I thought he'd bring up his guts or send them out the backside. Sorry, but that's the way it was. We couldn't even move him to a house because his body shook so. The horses near us in the barn grew uneasy. I had to order Wanza there"—he pointed to one of the two young men—"to lead them into another barn. They were rearing up on their hind legs and making a racket. Not war-trained, of course, or they'd be easier with a man's dying."

"What do you suppose made the groom fall ill?"

"The healer said it looked like too much of that tansy tea he'd told the groom to dose himself with. Getting out the worms, he was. Gulli—that was the groom's name—couldn't talk much, but he shook his head when the healer asked if he'd drunk more of that tea than he was supposed to. But that's what the healer said it had to be. I guess Gulli didn't remember what he'd drunk. I found the rest of the tea after—to throw out, of course. It smelled strong and had an odd, dark look to it. It's been a lot of years since I been dosed for worms, but I don't remember such a strong smell to the stuff. Maybe something was wrong with it."

"Did you ask the healer?"

"Wouldn't like to suggest nothing to him. When you're sick, you don't want the healer as an enemy. But if your family is using his tea, you might—" He turned his lips down in a frown.

"We haven't used any of his tea, but thank you for the warning. What a shock for you and . . ." Tesha fluttered a hand toward the palace. "A man died. The royal family must have been concerned. Lady Agat wouldn't like to have such a disturbance in her household."

"She didn't at all. Asked us all kinds of questions—how many cups of tea he drank, when. She seemed more concerned with the man's illness than the physician."

This sliver of success strengthened Tesha. "As well she should be. She sees to everything in detail."

"She didn't used to care about us in the stables, but lately she does. She knew about the dosing the physician did for the groom. Maybe that was the reason for all her questions. Felt a kind of responsibility since she had checked on the groom and all."

"How kind of her. She checked on him?"

"That were what it seemed like, anyway. Came asking him how he was. Took a look at the tansy leaves and made him tell her back the physician's directions to be sure he'd got it right. And then he didn't. I guess she felt bad."

"Did anyone else from the palace see her here at the stables?"

"Anyone else? No, just us stable hands. No need for all the palace folk to butt in down here."

"No, that would be unfortunate. I'm told some others have been ill like the groom was. Did you hear of anyone?"

"No one so sick. But for a while, there were a lot of us with troubles in our bellies. Some worse than others."

"Were you sick?"

"Had to stick close to the chamber pot, if you get me."

"But you didn't have any tansy?"

"No. That was before Gulli. Never thought of tansy at the time. But when Gulli's gut went so bad, I did think I'd gotten off easy. I thought it might be the same until the healer felt so bad about his tansy tea being the cause."

"Everyone who got sick—did they work in the stables?"

"No, my wife, she works in the palace. She was the first of us sick. She couldn't keep down food for a week or so. Brought up nearly everything for a stretch. But she mended."

"That's a blessing. Your wife must attend Lady Agat."

"If you call scrubbing floors and such attending. She wouldn't, I reckon. But she does what Lady Agat tells her to, that's for certain."

"Did Lady Agat show the same concern when your wife was sick?"

"Come to think of it, she did come to the servants' quarters and check on her. She's not a stranger to our quarters, of course, but I'd never seen her be so kind before."

Blessings on Ishana—and on this friendly stable hand. Tesha smiled. "Maybe she wanted to win you all over before the king's new wife arrived."

The stable hand laughed and then looked over his shoulder to make sure no one heard them besides his friends. "That just might be. Lady Agat has no kind words about her, that's for sure."

"Your wife, when she was sick, had Lady Agat given her medicine? Some tansy perhaps?"

"I don't remember Lady Agat having anything to do with it, but I spend my time down at the stables. My wife didn't dose herself for worms, I can tell you that. It was something else, not what got the groom. Good news for your kin, since we all did just fine in the end. Gulli was the only exception, and we know what made him sick. Your kin will mend, I'm guessing, even though you don't know why. Don't fret."

"Thank you." Tesha pushed off the railing and found standing without its support extremely difficult. She hid the struggle as best she could. She needed to get back to her rooms. "You've been most helpful. Far more than you can understand."

52

Tesha was coughing up blood before she made it back to her rooms. The bones in her face were shifting again, and the agony had caused her to stumble. Unsure how much of the transformation remained, she had ducked her head and hurried past the guards at the doorway to her hall, mumbling something about an unreasonable demand of the priestess that she had been sent to take care of.

Henti and Ashu had almost carried her into the full privacy of her sleeping chamber, then Henti sent Ashu for warm water.

"What have you done?" Henti had cried.

Tesha gasped out what she'd done. Henti knew about the vials but had clearly never considered that Tesha might use them.

She had found more proof against Agat, but it seemed too little against the harm she'd done to herself. Henti did what she could with cool cloths on Tesha's face and a soothing, steady hand to comfort her fear. Tesha had curled up on the bed, tears dampening the pillow. Finally, sleep had released her.

Now Henti's whisper pulled her back into the room. "Are you well enough? It's little Humie. He says he has news for you and can only stay a little while. He can't be caught slipping in to see you. Shall I bring him in here? Away from . . ."

Tesha sat up. She did feel better. She was still shaky, but she couldn't sleep away the day. How long had she slept? Her glance jumped to the high windows. From the angle of light, it was afternoon, not morning. She'd slept too long. She had to be ready to act before Hattu gave the orders to remove her to the garrison. Either the ruggedness of the place was so truly appalling that he had to give them notice before sending her, or—and she prayed this was the truth of it—some part of him resisted sending her. That resistance had worn thin last night. It could tear to shreds any moment.

"Yes, bring him here. But first help me into my own clothes."

Quickly they changed her look from disheveled servant to the tidy priestess she was.

Henti came back, leading Humie by the hand.

He bowed.

"Good afternoon, Humie."

His young face looked concerned. "I'm sorry I did not come tell you anything yesterday. My mother was very angry about something. I didn't dare sneak out to talk to you."

Tesha knew what had upset Ija. Ija would never let Humie speak to her, so she nodded sympathetically. "Being considerate of your mother is the proper duty of a son."

"I brought you two tablets. The label on the shelf where they were stored had the symbols for curse on it." He pulled the palm-sized tablets out of a satchel and handed them to her.

Tesha scanned the top one. It gave directions for turning aside a curse of infertility used against a queen and involved placing herbs and other things on and in the queen's body. She shuddered at the idea. *May Ishana keep such a curse from me.* Her hand went to her belly. *And may this child be safe.*

This wasn't useful for Hattu's problem.

The other tablet was harder to read. The signs followed a very old style. Even when she thought she'd deciphered the words individually, the meaning of them together didn't join in a clear way. The sentences were disjointed or so cryptic that she couldn't guess what was intended.

She murmured one such sentence softly to herself, "The one cursed must see himself and be stronger than himself." She shook her head. Something to sort out later.

Humie fiddled with the empty satchel in his hands and hopped from one foot to another.

"Thank you. I'll read them closely later. Did you—"

"Spy on Ambassador Ahmose?" Humie's face lit up. "Yesterday he didn't do anything exciting, but today he found a dead man."

Tesha sank back, sitting on the bed. "A dead man? Who?"

"No one important. He was dressed in farmer clothes. A peasant. But Ahmose told the guard who was with him to look under a pile of manure, and there he was, a dead man."

Humie's delight in this disgusting discovery was alarming, but it did sound like something a boy might find interesting. Perhaps he wasn't old enough to understand that the farmer's death would matter a great deal to the farmer's loved ones.

"How did Ahmose know to look under the manure?"

"I don't know. Someone must have told him, but I didn't hear. Yesterday the ambassador and his bodyguard walked back and forth along the path going down from the back entrance of the palace. He asked who lived in each home. He found out by buying things from the people who have shops along there. I thought he was very clever. I'm learning how to be a good spy. But I didn't hear him say anything about a dead man."

Tesha nodded. "Ambassador Ahmose told me he wanted to look there. Your father found a Paskan there, past where all the other Paskan fighters were, so it's important to figure out how he got so close to the palace."

"This morning when I followed Ahmose, he went to talk to my father. So maybe he told him about that. I couldn't get close enough to hear. The guards at father's door would have seen me. After a while, they came out and went along to one of the corridors of store-rooms. I thought maybe my father was going to give Ahmose something he kept in a storeroom. But then guards came carrying a litter. A sick man lay on it. I think he was a Paskan prisoner." Humie's eyes widened and he jumped up and down. "I bet he was the Paskan you say father found near the palace. Father would have struck him down, just like this man had been."

"What happened when the guards brought him?"

"They took him into a storeroom. I heard Ahmose ask one guard to bring a pitcher of water and a cup. But father and Ahmose went into the room with the sick man. They closed the door, and all I could do was wait outside around the corner where the guards wouldn't see me."

"Did they stay inside for long?"

Humie nodded. "When they came out, my father looked like he needed a nap. He turned back toward his quarters, but the ambassador hurried off the other way, and I had to be a very smart spy to catch up and find him again without being caught."

"Where did he go?" Tesha felt confused by this story, but she let Humie tell it in his own order.

"That was the strange part. He asked the guard who accompanies him if he knew of the tavern of the hawk and could they go there."

"A tavern?"

"Ambassador Ahmose could get much better wine and food here at the palace. My mother says I should stay away from taverns when I'm out playing in the city. But I don't think he was hungry. When they got to the tavern—I saw the hawk carved on the wall outside—he went across the street to a barn. That's where he found the dead man."

"Oh, gracious. Someone must have told Ahmose about the dead man while they were in the storeroom."

Humie nodded solemnly. "That's what I decided. The ambassador was trying to figure out something about the dead man. He talked to a beggar who sat outside the tavern, then he went into the tavern and talked to other men in there. I couldn't follow him inside, but I heard what he asked the beggar."

Humie's enthusiasm seemed to grow weighed down by what he'd heard. He leaned against the bed near Tesha, and she put her arm around him.

"There are noblemen who want to hurt my father, aren't there? I have heard my mother and Agat talking about it."

Tesha brushed back the thick dark hair that had fallen across his eyes. "I'm afraid that's true. I helped defend your father from one such nobleman, but I fear there are others."

Humie sighed. "Someone bad let the Paskans in, didn't they? Someone who lives in the city?"

Tesha nodded, but she didn't like that Humie thought of these questions. She hadn't considered that this smart boy's thinking might put him in danger, but she should have. Ahmose would soon come and tell her all this information more fully. Ahmose was doing what he had told her he would. But she had endangered this sweet child by asking Humie to spy. She should have trusted Ahmose and kept the boy out of it. Hattu would be rightly furious with her.

"What did the ambassador ask the beggar?"

"He asked if he sat there often and who he'd seen come and go from the barn the day or two before the Paskans attacked the city."

"What did the beggar say?"

"He said the ones who would know were the men who drank regularly in the tavern, and to go inside and ask them. When Ambassador Ahmose went inside, the beggar ran away."

"What else did you hear?"

"Nothing. He stayed inside for a long time. Then I followed Ambassador Ahmose back to the palace. He's in Father's court hall, waiting to speak to him. I have to go to my lessons, so I came here to tell you first. But I have to go."

"Thank you for all your spying. You can keep bringing me tablets, but stop playing spy. Your mother and father would be cross if they found out."

Humie looked like he might argue with her about that, but then she saw relief push that impulse away.

"Don't worry. Ambassador Ahmose will tell me what he learned."

"You'll tell me about the dead man—anything you find out?"

Tesha shook her head, but she patted Humie's arm and said, "If it's a good story, I will."

53

———————

Hattu turned at the sound of a servant in the doorway of his quarters, hesitant to enter.

What does the winesack want? Hattu pressed his hands against the armrests so he sat more upright. Kings weren't supposed to be alone, slumped in a chair while the kingdom fell apart.

"A soldier to see you, King Hattu. With a report you requested."

A report he requested? The soldier entered, and Hattu recognized the man. He'd sent him down to the barn the Paskan had mentioned to see if there was anything to learn about the traitors who let in the enemy.

"What did you find out?" Hattu asked the soldier.

"We identified the dead man found in the barn. A farmer from one of the villages. He doesn't live in the city. He was bringing a wagonload to his barn. They all do that to protect their crops from Paskan raids. I knocked at a nearby house, Lord Mahuri's, to find out whose barn it was. The lord himself told me it was the farmer's, as I expected."

There was nothing to be learned? Hattu pushed through the fog of his thoughts for a useful question. "What else did you find at this barn? The Paskan hid there, he said."

"There was nothing else to find, sir. It looks like the Paskan tricked the farmer by hiding in the wagon so he'd be brought inside the city. Then he killed the farmer so his presence wouldn't be discovered until it was too late—after the Paskan had opened the gates at night. He had only to wait in the barn until dark."

That had been the Paskan's claim. "You found no indication of Hitolian conspirators?"

"No, sir."

Hattu waved the man out. Useless. There had to be conspirators, didn't there? The Paskan couldn't open the gates on his own. The city's watch would have killed him first. But they'd been influenced, either by bribery or some sort of promise. How could he uncover the traitors?

"King Hattu?" Yet another servant stood at the doorway of his quarters.

He nodded permission to speak.

"Sir? The watch says your troops are returning."

"My troops?" His troops. He had sent soldiers out—when had that been? Before Tesha betrayed him. Another lifetime. He'd sent them to counterattack a big force of Paskans and push them back north. Only two days ago. They'd returned fast—too fast. The pushing must have gone the other way. A defeat. It would finish him.

He lifted his head and looked at the servant. "What is the news from them?"

"I do not know. The watch saw them approaching and sent me."

Hattu dragged himself out of the chair. He went to the open windows that gave him such a long view. Soldiers in marching formation climbed the switchbacks to the city. Their postures from this distance didn't tell him whether they were dejected or not. By their numbers, they had not been massacred.

He leaned his head against the window frame. They would expect him. He had to welcome them, whatever had happened. No matter how exhausted he was.

Hattu turned and staggered out of his quarters. Waiting in the hallway, his bodyguards fell into place around him. He could feel their apprehension. *Let them fight off curses.* He cringed at the accusation his mind shot back. *They did. Only you.* Your *weakness.*

Jerking his shoulders back, he clenched his jaw against the answering pain and burn in his chest. He wouldn't be weak.

He made it down to the field.

His commander stepped forward. The soldiers filed through the gate into the practice field and lined up in their fighting units for inspection. They were not overly bloodied or wounded, but they did look dejected. Had it been a cowardly run from a Paskan onslaught?

The commander saluted Hattu.

"How did the counterattack go?" Hattu asked.

The tight, thin line of the commander's lips and tense creases around his eyes filled Hattu with misgivings. He could not take another blow.

"We were able to outmaneuver them, Your Majesty, and once we surrounded them, we made quick work of it. That tribe won't attack your kingdom for a long while. They will stay out of your lands. Not as thorough a slaughter as what I hear happened within these walls." He gestured to the field around them, the trap between two gates that had allowed Hattu to slaughter the Paskan invaders. "An impressive accomplishment, my king, given how few men you left yourself for the city's defense."

"The men fought well. It was a close thing. Congratulations on your quick success. I have a great need for these soldiers." He thought of Ahmose's hounding to take these men to Amur to stop a new outbreak of war.

His commander did not meet his eyes. "It was your son Luwa and the warriors he commanded who turned it our way."

Hattu jerked at the mention of Luwa. He'd forgotten he'd sent Luwa to his first battle. Agat had been so torn by this honor. It was Luwa's chance to make a place for himself as a commander, but— Hattu scanned the blocks of soldiers gathered on the field, hunting for his son. "Luwa will make a good general." A wish to ward off evil. Hattu didn't see Luwa where he should be among the soldiers.

The commander looked at the ground. "Luwa slipped around the back of the enemy and then, as we agreed, drove them against our main force. His leadership was key, but he pushed forward into the Paskan troops before we could match it and protect his small group. He was cut down and many of the men with him. I'm sorry to bring you such tragic news. You are right. He would have made a great general."

Hattu swayed. To steady himself, he clutched the pommel of his sword in its sheath. Thank the gods he hadn't listened to Nerik and sent him also. But then, Nerik had been poisoned at home. His sons were under attack from all sides. He shouldn't have sent Luwa into battle. He'd shown courage, but also foolhardiness. He'd made a young man's mistake. Hattu had made similar ones himself, but he'd never paid this price. Others had, though. He still felt the weight of their deaths.

Blinding lights darted again across his vision. Crippling dagger points darted within his chest. He slumped forward with a groan. A bodyguard stepped to his side.

He let his guard support him. "You brought back Luwa's body?"

"Of course. It is on a supply wagon and will be here soon."

He must tell Agat. She'd just seen her father on his pyre.

His soldiers. He should tell them they did well, despite . . . despite Luwa. He sagged at the thought of addressing the whole practice field.

"You'll assure the men I'm proud of their fighting?" Hattu said to his commander. "Luwa's death wasn't their fault."

The man nodded.

Hattu turned back toward the palace and stumbled up the hill. Perhaps his men would blame his grief for his inability to acknowledge them. That would be forgivable. His weakness was not.

His head bowed low. His steps fell heavy, and lifting each foot was far too hard.

But through the flashes of color that blinded him, he saw Ahmose hurrying toward him. That slippery Egaryan kept appearing when he least wanted him.

"The return of your troops, King Hattu? A cause for celebration, I hear. They've driven back those problematic Paskans."

How had the man learned that already? "No celebration."

"Now your troops are free to go with you to Amur. First your Paskan victory, and now this one. Your city is secure. So safe you can leave Alpara under the guidance of your son."

The word "son" struck Hattu like a blow.

Ahmose continued, "The physician says your son is recovering. He'll be shaky for a time, but this will be a fine opportunity for the young man to practice his statesmanship. He'll be a more sober-minded ruler for this recent trouble."

"Nerik rule?" Hattu mumbled. He had said something like that. Or had he only thought about giving Nerik a chance to learn to be king? Go to Amur? How could he? "My Commander Marak is not yet free."

"That is unfortunate, of course," Ahmose said. "But Shatim will carry on the negotiations in your absence. A capable man, Shatim."

"Stop. This isn't your decision to make."

"Ah, but it is mine—yours as well. Not a situation either of us has any choice in. You must put the empire above friendship. Show your brother you can lead while he is ill. You can't afford to let him down so soon after . . . the troubles that locked you up in Lawaza."

Hattu wanted to punch the insinuating old man. "I did nothing to deserve that cell. My brother knows that. I will go when I am ready."

"Sadly, you must be ready now—your troops are here. I admire you. You are a tough man to beat in diplomacy and battle. But if your brother's empire collapses under the weight of a war you did not stop when you so easily could, the Great King too ill to lead a response himself, who will he turn to afterward? Not you. Can you afford to lose this hard-won trust?" Ahmose shook his head. "Do not let this sudden infirmity . . ." Ahmose ran his hand up and down as if sizing up Hattu. "Not now. I am sorry. But it is the truth, and you know it."

It was true. Hattu hated that his weakness was so obvious to this old man. He tried to stand straighter and hissed at the agony of it. His brother's trust was a fragile thing. He'd won it back, he hoped. And this was beyond even that. He had to stop a renewal of the war or see the end of his brother's reign as well as his own.

He hated that gesture of Ahmose's, summing him up in a flick of his hand. He hated how visible his weakness had become, but he would find strength and not shirk his duty to his brother and his kingdom. He'd lost one son today. He would grant the other, his heir, the chance to rule. He'd win Nerik over, finally. That would be a strengthening grace.

Hattu blinked away the blotches flitting across his vision and glared at Ahmose. "You will leave my kingdom at first light tomorrow. I will take these troops to Amur."

Ahmose clasped his hands at his chest and bowed to him. "Thank you, King Hattu."

54

"Priestess Tesha," Ahmose said. He bowed to her at the entrance to her reception hall, his bodyguard behind him. "You requested my presence?"

Henti brought him to where Tesha sat. Tesha noticed Henti signal Ashu to stand at the curtain as guard against the spying.

Tesha rose from her chair by the circular hearth. She'd wondered at Ahmose's silence. Before she would try again to persuade Hattu, she must complete her understanding. Agat had a role, but what of others? Henti had brought the news of Luwa's death. Perhaps that tragedy had delayed Ahmose's report to her.

"Thank you for coming to see me. You have news?"

"News? Nothing significant. I'm sorry."

"When we spoke last, you were on the trail of the Paskans, "the outside foe," as you put it."

"I was. I walked up and down that path where Hattu encountered the stray Paskan, but I could not find out why he was there or what he might have accomplished."

"And what else did you find?"

"I am sorry, but I found nothing else."

A lie. The tightness in her chest clamped sharper. "Really?

Weren't you going to listen in when King Hattu questioned the wounded Paskan?"

"King Hattu prefers I stay out of his state business. It is hard to blame him. Our countries fought each other so recently."

"You did not go anyway?" Blessings on little Humie. But what now?

"No, I would not like to offend King Hattu. That would be unwise. I am glad to have this chance to say goodbye to you. I hope your troubles will soon be over. I am leaving early in the morning. King Hattu has asked me to return to Egarya, and I am indeed needed there."

"You will leave?" Tesha steadied herself by grasping the back of her chair. The potion's damage still shook her.

"Of course. The king is a gracious host. Goodbye, Priestess."

"Wait. Since you leave me in the midst of troubles, perhaps you would be so kind as to pray with me again. You brought me such comfort."

"We would pray with the assistance of that lovely stone, no doubt. You are a remarkable woman with surprising skills. I think you will prevail without my prayers."

He gave her a deep bow, then turned and left so quickly his bodyguard stumbled to follow.

The limitations of the stone frustrated her again. A wondrous magic that was nearly useless to her. The Great Kings had abolished magic out of fear of its uncontrolled power. That was not her experience.

Ahmose had betrayed her. What had he learned? Something it no longer served his interests to reveal.

A dead man could not be described as nothing.

Henti hurried over to Tesha and helped her into her seat. She pulled up the footstool and sat close. "Egaryans are untrustworthy."

Tesha rested her head against the back of the chair. "Except Kety, who can't help me anymore. I should not have relied on Ahmose."

"You sent Humie to check."

"A barn across the street from the tavern of the hawk. I wonder who owns that barn? Was it the dead peasant's or some noble family's? The Great King arrested Runda for conspiring against Hattu, but Runda must have allies who remain in the city. They are more likely poisoners than I am."

Henti laid her hand over Tesha's. "If only your husband could see it that way."

"Would you recognize that guard who was here with Ahmose? Like Humie, he follows the ambassador around. Maybe he knows more. Could you find him, get him away from Ahmose, and ask?"

"That's a good idea. We can find out what Ahmose is hiding. That Egaryan sneak has no right to keep these secrets." Henti's indignant look cheered Tesha. Someone fought on her side.

TESHA SPOKE TO ASHU, who laid another log on the fire.

"While I wait for Henti to return, would you go bring me an early dinner?"

Ashu left. The potion had left her tired and not right inside. She didn't feel hungry, but she should eat to get back her energy and feed the child growing inside.

Every time she heard footsteps outside her reception hall, she assumed Hattu's soldiers had come to take her to the garrison Hattu had chosen for her. It must be even farther north than Alpara, deeper into dangerous territory. Even if she could get past the guards, escape now from Alpara or later from the garrison, what would she do? To get anywhere safe took weeks of travel with horses, supplies, and armed guards.

Ashu returned with a tray and put it on a table by Tesha's chair.

Looking at the roasted doves on a bed of early spring greens, Tesha found she did have an appetite. She enjoyed the smell of the cinnamon and garlic the doves had been flavored with.

She beckoned to Ashu to join her on the other side of the table. "We'll leave some for Henti. I hope she'll be back soon."

Ashu sat and served portions for both of them. "Not too soon, I think."

"Why is that?" Tesha looked at her maid with concern.

"I saw Henti on my way to the kitchen. She said she would walk down to that tavern and barn you two were talking about. She wanted to find out who owned the barn—like you were wondering about."

"What? She went off without asking me?"

"Best to stay out once she'd gotten away from your watchers." Ashu's glance took in the doorway outside of which the guards stood, and her voice dropped even lower. They'd grown accustomed to speaking at barely a whisper. "Don't worry about her going to ask questions in a tavern. It's not such an unusual thing for us, not like it would be for you."

That might be true, but unruly men at a tavern wasn't what made Tesha's heart beat like a bird's in a snare. She had never intended for Henti to ask such dangerous questions. Speaking to one of Hattu's guards posed no danger, but that wasn't true of the nobles who had tried to end Hattu's rule with poison and collusion with Paskans. Henti did not realize how lethal her questions could be.

"Could you run quickly and bring Henti back? Stop her?"

Ashu looked up from her dinner with wide eyes. "She's left the palace. I don't know where she's gone."

"I do. It's the tavern of the hawk and a barn across the street. If you don't catch her right now, you'll have to ask people to help you find the way. Go, fast as you can."

Ashu burst into tears. "Why? Is Henti in danger? Are you sending me to be attacked?"

"Collect yourself and go. Right now. Just catch up to Henti and bring her back."

"But I don't know the way. I heard you. That Egaryan found a dead man there. He probably killed the poor farmer himself, and he'll kill me for asking about it. I won't go. Let Henti take care of herself. If you make me, I'll hide and wait until Henti gets back on her own."

Ashu's terror didn't calm Tesha's real fears for Henti. Nor would Ashu be any help. Stupid sheep of a woman.

Tesha tried to persuade herself that Henti would ask nothing obvious. She'd be cautious. But she remembered Henti's trip to the kitchen to question the cook. She'd caused such immediate suspicion even Henti had noticed it. Kety could probably stay safe in this pursuit, but not Henti.

Henti would draw the attention of traitors who could not afford to let her live. There was no denying the truth. Henti had unwittingly put herself in grave danger.

Tesha rose and went into her sleeping chamber. She stared at the wooden chest. At the bottom of it lay the second vial of disguising potion. Her hand went to her belly. The potion had caused damage, but the child in her womb seemed safe now. She and the child had recovered. But to take it again?

Henti would draw the lethal attention of a murderer. Faithful Henti.

She cradled her belly between her hands. *Be safe. Forgive me.*

55

Cold stone poked into Daniti's back. She was rational enough to recognize that there were worse prisons, but she could barely restrain her frustration at being trapped again in this cave hideout. At least Marak sat next to her.

"They're too afraid of you. Being cautious of you was useful, but now—"

Daniti pressed her hand against Marak's arm to quiet him. In his anger, the volume of his whisper climbed.

"Remember Kurala," she breathed into his ear. "He's free now to bring help. That makes the risk I took worth it."

"They're talking about killing you before you send demons after them," Marak hissed into her ear. "That's not what I call worth it."

"They also think I'm a warrior who stabbed the traitor they most hated. They won't kill me."

"You *are* a warrior who did that, but they think you can do sorcery like whatever Tesha did. If they trusted you, that would be fine with them, but—"

They both stopped to listen to a loud outburst from their Paskan guards. Someone had arrived, and they didn't like whatever this messenger had to say.

Marak rose and went to the opening in the wooden wall that separated their back area of the cave from the rest of it.

Daniti didn't need to get up to hear the Paskans clearly enough, and she was exhausted from yesterday's tracking and the fight with Riam. On the way back to the hideout, the Paskans had let her wash in a brook. She'd gotten rid of the blood, but not the memory of it.

She was well aware of the Paskans' two-sided view of her. She was a hero who, even though a woman, had killed their most hated betrayer. Their scouts had found the corpses of the Paskans who had set out with Riam. The fact that Riam wanted to kill her and had attacked her won her praise among the Paskans. But they knew what magic could do, and she controlled demons.

Or so they believed. She could speak to them and sense them—which Marak clearly found terrifying—although she'd assumed that anyone could if they had the misfortune of encountering one. She was still thinking about what she would have to do to control one.

Angry Paskan voices crowded out everything else.

"If we don't release them, he threatens to blind all the men he holds captive, like he did to the two he sent as warning. He oversaw the mutilation himself."

What? Who were they talking about? Daniti pushed herself up.

"All the more reason to kill the witch and his favorite commander."

Marak pulled her close against him. "Hattu sent a message. For our release."

"By blinding men? Not for me. No!" Pressure pulsed against her forehead and temples. She swayed with dizziness.

Marak steadied her. "He has never done this before. He always refused. Other Hitolian rulers did it, and it's the way Paskans treat prisoners. Considering that, they're awfully angry."

"It's horrible. Tesha should have stopped Hattu. I've listened, and he always pays attention to her views. If she had spoken up, he would never have done this. How could Hattu . . . *anyone* do this?"

"In this case, he shouldn't have," Marak said. "Listen to how enraged they are. Not helpful."

"Never!" Daniti stepped through the opening into the large front part of the cave. She felt the attention of the men turn toward her, and, at the same time, she heard men taking steps away from her.

"Get back where you belong," one of the Paskans shouted.

"I want no part of this threat King Hattu sends by mutilating your men. Life does not end with the loss of sight. I have known happiness without my eyes. Even so, I will not seek benefit from this horror. But send us back before they blind the others."

"You claim no benefit, but we must send you back? Hurry, hurry and let you free. For nothing? And what do you think the jackal will do once he's got his sorcerer and commander back? Release all our warriors unharmed so we can carry on the fight against him? He thinks he can trick us into releasing you, that we'd be too frightened about the blinding of the others to think clearly."

"Kill her now before she curses us."

Marak grabbed her off her feet just as she heard the whoosh of a spear's flight and the crack of it piercing the wooden divider she'd stood in front of.

"Stop," Marak shouted. "Your envoys didn't reach Hattu because of Riam's betrayal. King Hattu misunderstood your silence. While you have us as hostages, you can reach a deal for your men. A proper exchange."

"It's too late for that."

A man's shriek of terror came from outside the cave hideout. Then more screams.

"What's going on?" one of the Paskans near Daniti cried out.

"Someone attacked our men on watch."

"Or the witch overcame them with her demons."

Daniti heard the man lunge toward her. Marak shoved her behind him and swung out with an arm, then came the sound of a fist hitting flesh.

"If I could overcome your guards," Daniti called out, "why would I have waited until now?"

"Kill them both. We're under attack."

Marak yanked her into their back area behind the meager barrier of wood.

Daniti whispered to him, "Kurala brought Hattu. Like I said."

"Hattu better act fast."

A piercing screech shattered the air. Then another. A bird call unlike anything Daniti had ever heard. She shrank against Marak's back.

"Bar the door," a Paskan ordered.

From outside, Daniti heard a strange whooshing, not the small, focused sound the spear had made, but a sound coming from something huge. Had a sudden storm brought tempest winds pounding against the hideout?

Great thuds sounded against the outer wall, reverberating through the cave. All the while, the whooshing came in waves.

If these were Hattu's soldiers, they came armed with something strange and terrifying.

56

Ija ran into his quarters. "Come help Agat. Come! Now!"

Hattu had called together his counselors. He was trying to hide his struggles from them. That was hard enough without screeching women. Too many troubles haunted his fogged mind—the trip to Amur, Marak's release, hidden conspirators, unspeakable betrayals and losses. Each plan they discussed skidded from his mind. He felt like a man slipping on ice.

"Agat's been poisoned. She's dying. Come."

Agat poisoned? Hattu jerked from his chair and swerved as he followed Ija's rush back toward Agat.

He entered Agat's room. The same smells of vomit and feces that had haunted Nerik's room assaulted Hattu's nose.

Agat lay curled on the bed, her arms wrapped around her middle. Her body twitched.

The healer sat next to her, trying to pull her up. He had a cup in one hand. "Sit up, Agat. You must drink to clean out the poison. Remember what we did for Nerik. Sit up."

"Leave me."

At least she could speak. Hattu's knees buckled, and he collapsed onto the bed. He tried to help the healer lift Agat.

The healer offered her water to drink, but she locked her jaw tight.

"Do as the healer says," Hattu said. "I need you. You must recover." More poison? He couldn't make sense of this.

Agat's eyes were bleary. Hattu took hold of her jaw and tried to open it. He wouldn't lose any more of his family. She gave in and drank when the healer put the cup to her lips.

She panted and hung her head. The twitching increased, and she vomited into a clay bowl the healer quickly put under her mouth.

She fell back onto the pillows. A trickle of yellow bile clung to her lips. The healer wiped it away with a cloth.

"Will she recover?" Hattu asked.

"Nerik did, but she seems weaker. I suspect she was given more of the poison."

"Tansy?"

"It looks like it."

Ija shouted, "Tesha is the poisoner. None of us are safe. She'll kill all of us and the children. You should have locked her away from us."

Hattu crouched by Agat. "How did this happen?"

"Tesha's maid. Earlier. My wine . . ." Agat raised one hand slightly to point. A pitcher and cup sat on the table.

Hattu stood and went over to the table. He leaned in and smelled the wine in the pitcher and the cup. He picked up the cup and brought it to the healer.

"Do you smell anything here?"

The healer leaned in and sniffed. His face reddened. "Tincture of tansy. Someone's put in enough to leave a scent."

"Agat, why do you think Tesha's maid did this?"

That didn't make sense, did it? He drew his arms protectively over the searing in his chest. Tesha would understand she'd be suspected. Agat's death would not help her. The maddening writhing inside reached a crescendo. He watched Agat, unable to hold onto thought.

Agat's eyes were closed, but she pointed to one of the serving women standing off to one side.

The physician asked, "Do you know what she means?"

"Priestess Tesha's servant, that woman named Henti, came by this afternoon. She acted like she'd been called for, brazen as she is. I shooed her out, but not before she'd stood right by that pitcher of wine. Agat was attending to one of the children and wasn't here then. I didn't think much of it at the time, just the priestess making Agat feel pushed out. But I see now what really happened."

Hattu grabbed the arm of one of the serving women. "Go bring Henti here."

Violent twitching overcame Agat. Hattu and the healer tried to hold her still. The physician wrapped her in a blanket, but almost immediately the sound and smell of violent bowels made him call over two of the serving women.

"Help me clean her again. Fresh linens," Utar said.

Hattu stood back, braced against the wall, disgusted. When he had brought Agat the news of Luwa's death earlier in the day, she seemed to turn to stone. No tears or crying out. She hadn't torn her hair and clothes the way women usually did in mourning. When he asked her about the preparations for Luwa's pyre and burial, she just stared at him.

Fortunately, Nerik had come in. He looked so weak and sick himself, but he'd heard the news from his room and gotten up to comfort Agat. Nerik had told Agat that he always looked up to Luwa and would do everything he could to be a good son to her now that she had lost her true son.

Hattu had backed out of Agat's room. He'd given the job of overseeing the funeral to the priest of the Stormgod.

Now Agat was dying.

The serving woman Hattu had sent off to find Henti returned alone. "I can't find Henti. Maybe she's run off out of guilt at what she's done."

Hattu scowled. "Go look harder."

"I . . ." The servant met Hattu's glare and left the room.

The physician and servants finally had Agat clean and settled. Hattu stepped forward. The seizures had stopped, but Agat lay still and limp. She looked dead. He thought he saw her chest rise now and then.

Hattu sat down in a chair next to the silent form on the bed. He'd told Tesha he would divorce her and banish her. There was no life for her in the Paskan wilderness and no escape. She knew that all too well. She'd tried to blame Agat to stop him and regain her position as his wife. When that failed, she'd seized on deadly revenge.

He had no choice now. Ija was right. He'd endangered his whole family. He couldn't live without his children. It didn't matter who their mothers were. They were his, and he loved them. He'd protect them as he should have before.

Hattu stood. "Guards!"

Four soldiers ran in.

Hattu pictured what he intended and grasped the back of Agat's chair to brace himself. The men waited for their orders. Beads of sweat broke from his skin as if someone had wrung him out.

"Sir?"

Those flashes of light again. He closed his eyes, but it didn't help. He leaned hard against the chair.

"Sir, are you unwell? Sit here." The soldier pulled another chair behind Hattu and helped him sit.

"What are your orders, King Hattu?"

Hattu saw Agat's unmoving body. He forced himself to speak. "Lock Priestess Tesha in a cell so she cannot endanger my family. Restraining her to her rooms is no longer sufficient."

"Yes, King Hattu."

57

Tesha ran down the path from the servants' door at the back of the palace, the way Henti would have gone. The bones of her face seemed to break and twist as she ran. Her skin moved like dough shaped by a baker. She forced herself to stay upright and sent another prayer to the baby in her belly, who again resisted this force she'd taken inside of her. She felt a streak of pride at the fighter she carried in her womb. Maybe all would be well. *Please let this child be safe.* She had to save Henti, didn't she?

As she hurried down the alley, she watched for anyone Henti might have asked directions from.

She called out to two women hanging laundry on the roof terrace of their second story. They shook their heads. They hadn't spoken to any palace servants.

But as Tesha continued along the alley, an old man in a nearby doorway called to her and she went over to him.

"She's in trouble, is she?" The man chuckled. "I thought she might be heading for mischief when she asked me where the tavern of the hawk was."

"I do need to speak to her," Tesha said in a soothing tone she hoped would encourage the man to talk. She hid her face in her cloak and veil as much as possible. The transformation seemed to have steadied, but she understood so little of this process.

"She looked like a very respectable servant from the palace, so I told her to go down by the lowest gate and right on a side street just before it." He gestured out to the main road visible at the end of this alley.

Tesha nodded thanks, but the man said, "It's a goodly walk. You don't look well. Perhaps you should let your friend get herself out of trouble?"

Tesha didn't feel well, but she rushed down the way the man indicated. *Please let me find her before she puts herself in more danger. Please, Ishana.*

Dusk fell, but Tesha studied each person ahead of her as she went, searching for the familiar brown cloak and Henti's posture.

She sped her steps when she caught sight of a figure that surely must be Henti. She hadn't expected to find her so quickly. Her choice had been worth it.

"Henti!" Tesha called. The figure didn't turn.

Tesha ran and touched her shoulder, but the face that turned in surprise was a stranger. "I'm sorry. I mistook you." She hurried on.

Tesha passed through the gates of the upper levels. No one recognized her. The guards at each gate ignored her. The disguise worked.

But fewer and fewer people walked in the streets as evening fell, and none of them were Henti.

She went straight on down the main road, she thought. But no roads ran straight in this mountain fortress. Every road cut back and forth sideways across the steep slope, narrow and winding. Somewhere in the dusk, she must have followed a side road.

It felt like forever before she wound back out and saw another gate ahead. She knew she'd returned to the main road.

And then, yet another gate down there. The lowest gate.

This small street off the main road was where to turn to find the tavern.

She walked a little way down. A crowd had gathered farther on. Given the emptiness elsewhere, a twitch of panic flickered in her chest. What had drawn these people? She caught up to them and mixed in.

A large barn loomed up on one side. A space opened in between it and the complex of buildings next along the road. At first Tesha thought there was a field in this open area, but when she stepped close, she realized with a start that the mountain fell away sheer, and she stumbled back. It reminded her of Hattu on the balustrade.

Tesha observed the people nearby. Some of them peered over the cliff's edge. Nervous exchanges of conversation overlapped around her.

"They pulled a dead man from that barn, and now this. King Hattu will have to station some guards on this street to keep us safe."

Tesha focused on a man and woman talking near her. She didn't like what she heard from the woman.

The man tossed his head scornfully toward the cliff's edge. "That woman was a stranger here. I've never seen her. Probably a Paskan spy. Just as well what happened to her."

Another man came up and added, "She's a stranger, all right. Careless and didn't know you watch your step in this city. I've sent for soldiers to haul her body up, what's left of it. I heard her scream when she fell. I won't be sleeping easy tonight with that ringing in my ears. Stranger or not, it's a bad death."

Tesha made herself lean out over the edge. The last rays of a disappearing sun illuminated the base of the cliff. Jagged rocks thrust out here and there on the way down, but straight below, a dark heap was outlined against the paler granite. Tesha saw an arm thrown out from that heap. The hand looked so tiny from where she stood, but she recognized the hand that dressed her each day, combed her hair, and rubbed oil into her skin.

Henti had not stepped off a cliff out of carelessness. Certainty of that burned through Tesha as surely as if she'd poured a boiling cauldron down her throat.

Someone had ended Henti's life for no reason beyond silencing her questions. Henti, dear Henti, who had been too loyal and devoted for her own safety. Tesha ached with the depth of this loss. Henti had loved her in a constant, unquestioning way that only the closest family could. And she had loved Henti in return. She hadn't thought about that affection. It had simply been.

Her eyes darted around the crowd. That cruel someone must still be watching. The conspirators' need to guard against discovery had not diminished. Someone hid among these people, ready to kill again. Probably another waited within the palace—they'd poisoned Nerik and opened the gates to the Paskans. That seemed like more than one conspirator.

Observant watchers would have noticed Hattu's collapse. They'd be poised to strike. Alpara needed a strong leader. She was the kingdom's only hope. She was certainly the only hope to avenge Henti.

Tesha ran up the road toward the palace. Her goal lay far away. Already sickness overwhelmed her as the potion lost its force. Somehow she must talk sense into Hattu and make him understand the danger that threatened them. She would get justice for poor Henti. Someone had to pay for this death.

Tesha panted in frantic bursts. The wrenching of her insides and face wracked her far worse this time. That potion would kill with overuse. She held her hand over her belly. *Not that, please, not that loss also.* She'd failed Henti.

The road to the palace went up ever more steeply. Evening shifted toward night, and she struggled to see where to put her feet. The bulk of the palace etched the dark sky above her. She knew the right direction, but on the path in front of her, she stumbled into holes and tripped over stones. She needed a torch, but she hadn't thought of that. She'd just hurried and been too late.

She wiped away tears. Henti had been her last connection to home—while the Paskans held Daniti captive—and the only trustworthy friend she had who believed she was innocent.

Another pothole caught her foot. She would have gone down, but she flung out her hand and broke her fall against a wall. She straightened up. Her belly cramped, and she clutched her middle. She stumbled forward despite the pain.

She came around one of the sharp bends in the road. A group of soldiers with torches approached. There were no side alleys for her to cut off onto, and they were coming fast.

She feared they would recognize her. She had escaped—not good for persuading them to let her speak to Hattu.

But they had torches and could speed her journey.

One of the soldiers cried out, "She's there."

The group ran toward her. They'd discovered her absence and pursued her. It was turning out even worse.

She had no choice but to persuade them as best she could.

"I have urgent news for the king. I am glad to have found you. It is dark, and I did not bring light when I set out."

None of the guards spoke. They fell in on either side of her and took hold of her arms. She cried out as a spasm contracted low inside. The soldiers gave her looks as if she were trying to escape and jerked her along.

"Please bring me to King Hattu. I have information essential to protect him."

Still, they said nothing. Her feet barely touched the ground. Their silence grew ominous.

When the soldiers guided her through the palace gates, they turned to the left instead of toward the main palace residence.

"No, this way." Tesha pointed toward the building with Hattu's great hall and quarters. "Unless you think the king is in the citadel keep?"

The soldiers marched her up the steep ramp that led through the massive, bronze-reinforced doorway of the keep. The torches threw jumping shadows against the black stone walls.

Hattu wasn't in this place. She knew that as they plunged into darkness.

58

____

Thunderous blows hit the outer barrier of the hideout. With her hands locked on Marak's shoulders in front of her, Daniti pressed against the cave's stone wall. The next blow crashed through with the sickening sound of wood rending, and bodies crushed, and shrieks of agony. Always, she heard that strange, rhythmic rush of air farther out.

Marak darted forward. He left her. Her hands swam in emptiness, trying to find him. He was gone. Inhuman cries vibrated through the air, the force of them confounding her senses. There was another rending and massive thud.

"Fall back," a Paskan yelled.

Marak cried, "Sorry," then he clasped her arm in momentary reassurance. He kept his back to her, with his front to the Paskans and the . . . what? What launched this attack? Was this what soldiers in battle sounded like?

"I grabbed a sword," Marak said, "from a Paskan thrown back by boulders bigger than men. I don't understand how—"

He pushed them back tighter against the wall. Their cell, partitioned by thin wood from the rest of the cave, had never felt so small.

Men crowded toward them. She heard their panicked tumbling past the meager screen that stood between them and the barrage.

"Stay back or I'll run you through," Marak shouted. Clever Marak. Arming himself just in time. The Paskans wanted them dead *before* this assault. To kill them now would take nothing.

Marak jumped forward, and the sword met flesh. She could hear it. He stepped back to her. The greater foe out there drove the men toward them.

Paskan screams of pain and terror fused with the discordant calls that reverberated from outside and those sweeping rushes of wind.

"Who is out there?" she cried.

The attackers had smashed the outer barrier. She sensed that exposed openness. Something dragged screeching men out of the cave. The noise battered her mind, deafening it.

"I don't . . . I swear I saw . . . a giant lion paw," Marak gasped out. He fought off the crush of men fleeing from the assailants outside.

A giant lion paw? She listened to the unearthly calls, the great whooshes of air, and the pouncing thumps that preceded the ripping of flesh and death screams. None of this violence felt right or familiar, and yet . . .

She ducked her head and clamped her hands over her ears to silence the outer noise and vibrations. She focused on the place inside where Kurala sent his messages. She listened with that other sense, the sense that sang to demons from the world below and conversed with creatures no one else understood. Her own sorcery of sound.

And she heard.

"We have come. Stay back. We will free you."

She sent back, "We thank you."

What had Kurala said? *His friends.* He'd bring his friends to free them. He hadn't meant Hattu.

Who were his friends? She and Tesha had found their pet alone, wounded, and without any friends.

To Marak she called out, "They have come to free us. Kurala sent them."

"What?"

"They say to stay back. They will free us."

"Who, what are they?"

"I don't know."

"Kurala did this?"

"Yes."

The slaughter tore at her soul, even though these men were her captors. Kurala had summoned savage friends. Would she survive?

She heard in her mind reassurances that she would soon be free, the battle nearly done.

But she heard other thoughts passing between their rescuers—not directed at her, but not hidden, either. There was delight in this bloodshed, in digging into men's flesh with powerful claws and piercing with fierce beaks. They gloried in old battle memories and images of revenge for ancient outrages—revenge sought against men.

Whoever Kurala had summoned, they did not like the mass of men. Had Kurala told them what sort of being she was? Did he understand this hatred from long ago?

Eventually, no Paskans confronted Marak. He stood still, catching his breath.

The shrieks from the wounded died away.

"You may come out. All your captors are dead."

She relayed this message to Marak. In his ear, she whispered, "They enjoyed killing these men. I'm not sure we're safe."

Marak took her arm and pressed her to his side. He guided her forward over many obstacles. She did not want to know what they stepped around.

"We are coming. I cannot see. My companion must guide me."

"We know, but you hear and speak as we do."

The sunlight fell on her face. They had passed beyond the cave.

Marak gasped.

"Tell me," she said to him.

"Three griffins, giants with heads like massive birds of prey, armed with beaks that make my curved sword look like a hairpin. Their bodies, paws, and tails are like a lion, but each leg alone is far greater than you or I. Lethal claws curl from their paws, forming a row of weapons that appall my heart. But it is their wings that defy words to describe. No mere bird has such a majestic expanse. They've splattered their bodies with the gore of their enemies as carelessly as if they'd pounced in a mud puddle. May the gods protect us from them. I certainly can't. But they are beautiful as well as terrible. Their tawny coats shimmer as if lit from within. Their feathers shine with iridescence. No one would question the place they hold in the old tales as the most regal and lordly of beings. I hope they come as our friends, or else we are doomed."

She touched Marak's arm. "Perhaps I should go forward alone, at first." She felt him stiffen and added, "I speak with them. There's less chance for misunderstanding."

He squeezed her arm.

She clicked her tongue against the top of her mouth to know what she stepped toward, moving her head and testing her impressions. She sensed the griffins' massive size towering above her like great boulders or trees. She felt the potential for destruction in their powerful muscles and coiled will.

She moved forward. The ground between them was uneven. It took some concentration and sounding to navigate—a blessing to be distracted as she approached.

She held out her hand, preferring, as always, to touch those she conversed with. From high above, a head dipped down and nudged her hand. She stroked silky feathers bigger than the span of her fingers.

"Thank you for rescuing us," Daniti said. She thought it wise to remind them of their saving purpose. "I am Daniti, and my friend is Marak." She also wanted to include Marak in the category Kurala had used.

"I am called Bolthar. We have not visited the realms of man in many of your lifetimes." There was a pause in the thought she received. "We did not part as allies."

"Then I thank you all the more for the help you brought me and my friend now."

"You have been hospitable to one of ours."

"I love him." She hesitated. "One of yours? He is not entirely like you."

A trill of laughter came to her, unexpectedly light from these creatures. "He is his own kind but still one of us. In our land, not everyone chooses to love the others of their own shape. Such love gives rise to new beings."

Another voice, a voice layered with tension, sent, "We do not wish to stay long in the kingdom of men. We will return you to your place."

The feathered head lifted away and moved toward this second voice. Daniti suspected a rebuke.

She took another step and felt rippling muscles under fur that was short and impossibly compact.

"Crenon speaks true, but we do not wish to be . . . abrupt," Bolthar said.

"I took no offense," Daniti said. "I will be glad to return to my . . . place." She almost said "sister"—what other place did she have in the world? But Hattu had ordered the blinding of men, and she knew he would have consulted with Tesha. In the three months of Hattu and Tesha's marriage, Daniti had never seen Hattu disregard Tesha when she argued strongly for something. Tesha had to have agreed to this horror. They always shared decisions of consequence. That was their strength—and now an unforgivable failure. Marak could choose a place for their return. She had no place to call home unless Marak was there.

Bolthar said, "Is it true you sang to demons in the world below and convinced them to take back one of their offspring that had invaded the upper world?"

"I helped release a man possessed of a demon."

"Interesting."

Daniti stroked Bolthar's extraordinary coat, so irresistible to her fingers, and wondered what his question meant.

"As Crenon says, it is time. Mount. It has been a very long time since I carried one of your kind, but as I recall, you will find you can hold on by what you call the scruff. We call that handle of fur the child-carry."

"I prefer that name also. But how do I—"

"Climb up? Here is my paw. Sit on it, and I will lift you toward my neck. You'll have to scramble. I won't be offended. My children pile on in very unruly ways. Pretend you are a child."

"Marak should do this also?"

"Your friend may ride on the back of Lila. She has approached him. Tell him to observe you. He will understand what to do."

She called out to Marak about riding Lila.

"Riding these winged creatures? I was afraid that was next," Marak said. "You have been conversing, but I can't hear anything. You are going first? Are you sure?"

"Bolthar will help me."

She patted Bolthar's powerful leg to signal she was ready. Gargantuan claws protruded from his paw. They were still sticky from the slaughter, but she scooted back from them and fought off the swooning they caused in her head. She almost tumbled off as she rose in the air, but her roll brought her to the wide surface of his back instead of air. She crawled over it, shaking and disoriented.

Bolthar's back was too wide to straddle like a horse. She knelt and searched for his child-carry. His coat and the muscles beneath moved as one, too tight to grab, except right at the base of his neck near where the feathers started. There, she discovered soft folds she could hold onto. While clutching this gathered hide, she reached out to either side to see how far from the edge she perched. She had to lean out a long way to find it. Even if she tipped over, she might not plummet to her death—if she didn't tip too far.

Suddenly the flat surface of Bolthar's back surged into movement beneath her. She wobbled until she spread her knees wide enough to give her better balance as she crouched over his neck. The tempestuous whoosh of his wings rolled over her, and she felt the lift into the air. Her heart thudded at the idea of being high up. She sent some clicks downward but quickly stopped. She did not want a clear sense of that drop. Holding tight to the child-carry, she pressed her body low over Bolthar.

He gained speed so that cold wind roared in her ears and rushed against her face. The muscles along his shoulders glided underneath her with each mighty wing beat, but his back gave her a steady perch, and she lifted her torso and head to revel in the sensations of flight.

She heard Marak's whoop of delight. Then Bolthar swooped in a curve, and for a moment she lost her balance. Her hands scrambled for their hold, and her stomach dropped. But as the griffin swooped in the other direction, she discovered how to sway with him. After two more turns she had the feel of it, and the pure freedom of movement in the sky released the last of her fear.

She knelt upright and let the air currents flow around her. The sense of suspension in the vast, heavenly expanse overwhelmed her with ecstasy.

59

———————

Agat clung to life for now, but as Hattu stumbled back to his quarters, his limbs seemed to belong to someone else. His thoughts swirled and blurred beyond his control. He guided himself with a hand braced on the wall.

What cell in his citadel had they put Tesha in? Did dread fill her when she heard them slide the bar across the door? Did the torch flicker and threaten to die?

He regretted he hadn't ordered Tesha locked up the moment he realized she'd poisoned Nerik. His suffocating experience in that cell where Tesha's father had imprisoned him lay behind this failure. He hated this lingering trauma Tesha's father had inflicted on him, ready to be exploited when the Paskans implanted their sorcery. The curse had crawled into his wound and now it gnawed, slowly eating him alive.

But duty told him to carry on. Root out the traitors, even if that included Tesha. Protect his family and his kingdom. But how? He sensed enemies everywhere. What now? He tried to concentrate.

Once in his quarters, he propped himself against the windowsill and surveyed the darkening skies.

He looked for Ishana's blood-red stars in the lapis lazuli arc above but could not see them in their customary place, a fitting absence. He had been cut off from divine guidance, from that beloved wisdom. He had lost his goddess.

The servants had lit the oil lamps that hung from brackets along the wall, following Hattu's instructions to keep night from his hall. He shuddered. For Tesha, there would be darkness.

It was always night in the citadel prison beneath the tower. It didn't matter whether he'd sent her there as night fell or if he'd given the order at daybreak. Darkness would close around her.

That wasn't what he needed to think about. There were other traitors besides Tesha, and they weren't locked up. He had to plan. Think. He used to be good at that. How he missed Marak!

He turned again to the openness beyond his window. Something glimmered golden in the distance. He squinted. A falling star? Three falling stars? Not falling but flying toward him. Was this some new illusion produced by his fractured body?

Three of them came, borne on a majesty of wings. The royal griffins painted on the wall around his throne were a pale reflection of this grandeur, but he recognized these beings. The mesmerizing fluidity of the movement, the deliberate, leisurely flutter up and down, as if it were nothing at all to sustain their giant bodies in the air. How could divine beings of this gracious form appear to one such as he?

They seemed to capture the last rays of sun that lingered at the horizon. Light glinted off their glory.

They held their heads with the regal curve of birds of prey and the formidable profile of aquiline beaks. But their bodies hinted at deadly pounces on prey.

His soul filled with wonder.

The sound of their beating wings enveloped him. He swayed with the rhythm and felt a swell of wind brush his face, cleansing and cool.

The griffins followed a path laid out by a tumble of yellow stars.

As they drew nearer, he saw the pattern of feathers on their wings in layered shades of gold, more intricate and precise than any mosaic.

Now he glimpsed the smaller figures, mortals soaring on the backs of two of the radiant creatures. How could this be? He recognized Marak. But instead of clinging to the neck of the godlike griffin as it swept through the heavens, wild-hearted Marak had tossed back his head in what looked like elation. Daniti perched upright, her face launched into the wind, perhaps totally free for the first time in her life.

The three griffins glided in a great swooping circle, drawing Hattu's eyes to the center where Ishana's twin red stars shone more brilliantly than he had ever seen before.

The griffins, their giant wings now motionless, hovered in a sacred orbit that highlighted Ishana's celestial signs.

The air around Hattu held itself in reverent stillness.

In the quiet, he felt the soft beating of his heart in his chest. How could it hold his joy?

In the sky, three proud heads bowed in obeisance to the goddess, and three crimson rays sparked outward in a responsive blessing.

No blessing came upon him. But hope did.

The goddess marked the path of these winged rescuers. Her divine choice to bring Marak and Daniti safely home.

In contrast, he thought of the blinding, his hideous, fruitless plan to force Marak's release. He had called it courage.

He could not invoke Ishana now and might never again.

But perhaps he could find a way. She showed her power in this saving of Marak and Daniti. His heart filled with gratitude. She could not help him out of his cursed state, but the battle would be worth fighting to regain her allegiance. She brought the miraculous.

The weapon of the curse was weakness and debilitation. He had not yet found a lasting defense.

He must arm himself in a new way.

If he could find it. Alone.

He looked out the window at the night sky. The griffins no longer bowed to Ishana's stars, focusing that part of the sky for him. They had landed in the courtyard outside the palace to unload their riders. He felt panic when he realized he could not see the red stars at all anymore. His cursed eyes needed the griffins' purifying reverence.

He'd been granted only a momentary vision, but Ishana was there all the time. He could find his way back to her. He could hope. He had seen her stars. He could again.

Hattu was truly separated from his goddess, invaded by those things. But he would run down to the courtyard and find Marak and Daniti whole and safe. He had regained his vision of Ishana's grace, and he remembered himself. A ray of light cracked open inside of him.

It was a battle worth fighting.

60

The soldiers forced her through a trapdoor and down stairs below the tower keep. Tesha heard screams, Paskan captives suffering from their wounds and interrogations or lost in despair. She passed barred door after barred door as the guards dragged her along.

"We're full up," the guard in the lead said. "But we've got a place for you—the last one. Too wet and filthy for the Paskans. We need to keep them alive to trade for Commander Marak."

Tesha tried to slow her descent, to convince them this was a mistake. The sounds and smells gagged her, and the cramping of her insides nearly paralyzed her. Her voice shook when she said, "Please let me speak with King Hattu before you lock me up. For the good of the kingdom."

"Silence. You're a danger."

"I'm the king's wife. A priestess. You can't lock me in the lowest hole in the citadel."

"You don't act like a priestess. You poisoned yet another person—Lady Agat this time. King Hattu's not going to free you. Get along." The soldier pushed her down the dark corridor.

It startled her to be accused of poisoning Agat. Lies piled on lies.

"I have to warn the king about the real murderer. You must believe me. Just let me speak briefly to the king."

"He'll come speak with you if he sees any use in it."

No, he wouldn't. Hattu would never come down into this dark, closed place. This pit contained everything he most feared. Hattu could never bring himself to walk this tunnel, especially not the man she'd witnessed standing on the balustrade of Ishana's sanctuary. Her husband was as good as dead. No one would pull her from this abyss.

"Please don't lock me in here. Hold me in the citadel keep above. Not down here. Please."

A soldier shoved her along faster. She clamped her arms around her ribs against the pain shooting upward.

"Please bring me back above ground. Just until you take a message to the king. I'm sick. Can't you see that I'm ill?"

The soldiers pushed her into one of the cells. The heavy door closed. The dim light left her sightless. What hid in this darkness? What lay in wait to attack?

Blackness closed in all around her. She shrieked. Prisoners' screams echoed back her cry. No one cared or noticed.

Uncontrollable shivering wracked her. The cramping dragged her into despair. It hadn't been this bad after the first time she took the potion. She should never have used the second vial. She'd done Henti no good. She massaged her belly with her fingers, trying to calm the contractions. *Don't abandon me, my child. Be safe. I promise I will never harm you again.* The spasms tightened.

She would die here, forgotten. The only person in the world who would care was Daniti, and she was lost.

As her eyes adjusted, she made out dark walls and a low ceiling. Parts of her prison were cut block, others mountain bedrock. Moisture oozed from stone like monstrous blood.

A tiny open rectangle in the wooden door let in some light from the hallway. Tesha peered at the torch through the opening. Torches didn't last long. She swayed with her trembling and grasped the tiny ledge of the opening in the door to stay upright. She couldn't touch the rock, nor the dark slime around her, above, and below her.

Would her food come through the opening? The very idea of eating in this place made her dizzy. She should have told the soldiers she was with child and that her illness threatened the royal baby in her womb. That was the way to ask for mercy. She cried out and called for the guards, but no one came.

All around her, the dripping water beat an irregular rhythm. This was like the cave of the Underworld where she had banished the sorcerer's curse from a mutilated body. But she had walked out of that cave, and people who cared about her had waited for her outside.

Hattu had trapped her, locked into the Underworld itself, and left her to die.

He had thrown her away into his own paralyzing nightmare. She hadn't believed he could do that to her, no matter how much the curse consumed him. No matter how lost their love was. But he had. He hated her this much.

She hated herself. She'd failed everyone—*please, please don't take from me this little one inside.* But if she stayed too long in this place, they would both die.

Death in her worst nightmare.

Wooziness and waves of pangs from her womb made her lose her grip on the door. She went down. Blackness sealed out everything.

She shivered with cold and opened her eyes to darkness. Her cheek lay against cold, wet rock. She gasped and pushed herself up from where she had fallen onto the black slime. She had lost herself into fear, fallen into a blackness of the mind as deep as this outer filth.

The spasming in her womb had stopped, but the stillness inside ached in a way that seemed more wrong than the cramps.

Faintly, she saw a dirty pile of straw in a corner. Someone must suppose that was for sleeping on. She used the door to drag herself up to standing. A trickle of warm dampness ran down her thigh. Her lips pressed hard together to hold back the cry of despair at what that meant. She would never know the child she'd carried. Never cradle the baby in her arms, suckle it, or see its first milky smile.

The darkness crept close around her. The staccato drips of water sounded loud in this grim solitude.

Her father had never put Hattu in a place this terrible, and yet that cell had left so deep a scar on Hattu.

What would this place do to her before she died in it?

She had lost everyone, even the child she would never hold. She couldn't even find words for a prayer.

61

Bolthar told Daniti they'd landed in a courtyard in Hattu's palace. A cool breeze still brushed Daniti's face, but it was nothing like the embrace of wind she'd felt as she flew on Bolthar's back.

"I'll lift my paw. Climb on and I'll bring you down," Bolthar sent to her.

Daniti didn't want to obey. Riding the massive griffin's back and sailing through the sky had been the most exhilarating experience in her life.

"You were a fine rider, child, but I cannot stay here. Climb off."

She sensed from the movement of muscles underneath her that he was lifting, and she slid across and reached out until she found his paw and scrambled from it to the ground.

Everything during their flight had felt smooth and gliding. The majestic rush of wings on either side of her and the turns and swoops had filled her with joy and raised her to a dignity she'd never imagined. The silly, awkward climbing on and off was just as profoundly humbling.

She heard a thump, and Marak laugh. His experience must match hers. Wings beat the air. The other two griffins had taken flight.

"I want you to stay," she sent to Bolthar.

"That would be dangerous for everyone. I do not think you would choose that if you understood how little I like your kind."

"I'm sorry. People can be cruel. Why did you come to rescue me?"

"There has not been a human who could talk to our kind for a very long time. That intrigued me. There is something else, a pressing need that you may be the one person to help with. You are good at holding onto the child-carry. Would you like to protect some griffin cubs?"

"I would love to, but I don't understand how I could do that as well as you."

"Nor do I understand yet. But you have passed the first test. We will see what the future holds."

His huge feathered head bumped lightly against her.

"A test? I hadn't realized."

"If you had, you would have failed. But my sense of time and yours are wildly out of measure. I have more study before I know if you are the one I am seeking, and by then, you may be long dead. It happens when griffins attend to human affairs. You live such brief lives. But do not be afraid if I return—and tell no one that I might."

"I will not be afraid, but I'm very confused."

Bolthar laughed that melodic trill. The wind from his wings swept against Daniti in rolling waves of air. She sensed his graceful spring into the sky.

"Goodbye," Bolthar sent her. "Your friend Kurala is journeying home. His little wings take longer, but he'll rejoin you soon."

Daniti turned her face up to the sky, trying to follow Bolthar's flight. She hummed and clicked her tongue, but he was soon beyond her reach.

Marak put his arm around her shoulders. She leaned against him.

"I considered at least a hundred different ways of escaping that hideout," Marak said. "But I never came close to imagining anything as glorious as that. I tried to tell the griffin I rode that I would provide her with whatever her heart most wanted if she would stay, but I don't think she understood anything I said. Or I heard nothing from her, at least. I don't have your skill. I suspect no one else does."

"Bolthar told me there used to be other people who could talk to griffins, but not for a long time. And I think a long time to griffins is far longer than we can imagine."

"I envy you. I would love to have spoken to those magnificent creatures. But why is no one here to greet us?"

"I assume they are afraid of the griffins. Remember the battle."

"The Paskans will never forget it. Nor will I. The gods save me from ever fighting griffins. I was very glad they were our friends."

"That might be presuming more than you ought to. But they rescued us."

"Here are guards coming out of the palace now. No Hattu, though."

"I don't want to be near Tesha."

"You should forgive her," Marak said. "She tried to save your life. I'm sure that's the only reason she and Hattu blinded those prisoners."

"I don't forgive her. She should have known that I would never make that choice, nor allow her to on my behalf."

Marak talked to the guards. No one answered his question when he asked where Hattu was or why Priestess Tesha did not greet her sister.

Daniti hissed in anger at that. "Just take me somewhere I can bathe and rest. I will not stay with Tesha."

"To the royal guestrooms it is," Marak said. "Temporarily, I hope," he added, then led her into the palace.

Royal rooms, indeed. Marak clearly brought her to the most richly appointed rooms she'd ever been in. She ran her fingers over the fineness of the carved furniture and the deep pile of fleeces on the bed. The glass makeup jars and silver mirror on the dressing table were similar to those she had handed to Tesha so many times. The mirror made her smile. Not something she had much use for.

She sounded out the spacious rooms and paced them so she knew their layout and could walk around easily. She sensed Marak watching. No one else had ever fully believed in her ability to navigate on her own. Tesha had witnessed it often enough, but she'd never accepted that it worked. She always wanted to hold Daniti close to her.

Daniti was glad she could take care of herself without Tesha. She wondered if it would ever go away—the sick feeling that arose in her whenever she thought about the blinding. Her sister, of all people, should have stopped that brutality.

"I have to find Hattu," Marak said. "The guards and servants are strangely unwilling to answer any questions. I fear his troubles may have gotten far worse. That's something no one would talk about."

"Yes, go find out."

"Are you sure you don't want to have someone bring Tesha to you?"

"I'm sure."

"Then I'll have her send one of her maids. You know them. They can fetch whatever you need."

Daniti placed her hand on Marak's shoulder. "I agree. Send Henti or Ashu. Preferably Henti."

62

———————

Hattu ran down a corridor of the palace. There, finally, was Marak, coming the other way.

Hattu raced forward and fell into Marak's arms. He clasped him a long moment against his chest.

When Hattu finally released him, Marak dabbed at his eyes with the back of his hand.

"How are you?" Hattu asked.

Marak smiled his crooked smile and shrugged. "A few more scars than before."

"The griffins—how did you find them?"

"Find them? I had nothing to do with it. Maybe Daniti understands."

In a blur, Hattu told Marak what had happened. The invasion, the poisoning, and the traitors, known and unknown. He didn't know how much he could trust his own judgment, how far the curse held sway, but he had to act to save his kingdom. And he trusted Marak.

Marak asked questions he couldn't answer—some about Tesha. Hattu's frustration rose. He didn't tell Marak about what lingered inside of him or that his weakness let in the curse. Marak would remember his fits from before. He could see that concern in Marak's face, and he let his friend assume that only the earlier problem plagued him. That was bad enough. Marak would never let him down, but he could not bear to lose his respect.

"The important part is to identify which nobles betrayed us to the Paskans," Hattu said. He remembered the soldier's report about the farmer the Paskan killed. Something seemed off-kilter, but he wasn't sure what. "I shouldn't have relegated the search of the barn to a stupid soldier. We should go."

Marak shrugged. "I would like to understand all this better. If that is the place to start—"

"Yes, let's go now."

Marak walked with a limp. He was filthy. He should let Marak rest, but traitors lay hidden in his city. He had to act. He'd been too slow, too weak. "You're wounded. I should send for the physician first."

"There's time for that later. I've fought off Paskans and ridden a griffin with this leg. Rooting out traitors sounds like a good plan."

He should go alone with his bodyguards and let Marak rest, but he couldn't. Not with those things ruling inside of him. He needed Marak's good judgment. That was at the heart of this. They went, even though it was a struggle for both of them.

They stood in front of the tavern of the hawk and looked across the street at the barn. It presented nothing out of the ordinary. The city was full of these storage barns because that was the only way to protect harvests from the Paskans.

Marak pushed off the wall he'd leaned against and headed toward the barn. "Let's look inside."

One of Hattu's bodyguards dragged the bar across and pulled open one side of the barn door. In the darkness inside, a flare of panic stopped Hattu. He stayed near the door.

Marak limped forward. Hattu peered after him.

"This isn't a storage barn," Marak called back. "That's odd, don't you think? If it was a farmer's?"

Hattu answered, "Hmmm . . . I see horses in stalls, not grain bins."

"Back here must be the pile of manure they buried the man under

—it's been shifted and scattered recently. But no grain. I think we might want to have a conversation with the owner. The soldier said it was the farmer's barn? The poor guy they found dead?"

Hattu waited until Marak came back to the open doorway. He couldn't force himself to walk into the unlit barn. He tried to remember what the soldier had said. "Yes, the dead man. His family lives in one of the farming villages."

"That's a long way. Let's see what the neighborhood has to say about this barn. I've always liked neighborhood gossip." Marak set off down the narrow street. Hattu followed.

A few doorways down from the tavern, an old woman sat on a stool, spinning. Marak caught Hattu's eye and pointed his chin toward her.

As they approached, the old woman stood and bowed. "King Hattu. This is a humble part of your city, but you are welcome. Are you seeing about the troubles in that barn? I'm glad if so. I don't like to have danger so close."

"Of course not," Hattu said. "We need to keep you safe."

"I'm wondering," Marak said, "if you noticed what the farmer used that barn for?"

"Farmer? Oh, you mean the fellow they found dead. I never seen him before. Don't know what brought him there. Unlucky, I guess. Lord Mahuri keeps horses stabled there. It's his home." She pointed to the large house next to the barn. "It doesn't have space off the courtyard for a stable with the steepness of the mountain, so he built it there."

"Ah, then Lord Mahuri is the one we need to speak to. Many thanks," Marak said.

He and Hattu walked away. Marak asked, "Now, why did you think the barn was the farmer's?"

"Because the soldier I sent took a different approach than you did. He went nextdoor to Mahuri's home and asked."

"So Mahuri lied?"

"Seems like it."

"This is fun," Marak said. He didn't look as worn out now.

Marak suggested they send for more soldiers. This conversation could get violent.

When the gatekeeper let them in, Hattu saw from Mahuri's reaction that Marak had been wise in that. Mahuri had been caught in a stupid lie, but there wasn't much room to deny it. *Let this traitor lead them to the others—any and all there might be.*

Finally, under Marak's onslaught of questions, Mahuri broke. "I panicked when the soldier arrived asking about the barn. I said the first thing I thought of to put him off my scent. It seemed to work. I should have acted horrified at what they'd found and brazened it out. But you have to believe me—I played a negligible role in this. Your real enemies used my old sympathy for Runda to force me to go along. They told us you were a sorcerer, doomed, and that supporting Runda was best for the empire. I didn't want this trouble, but once you were cleared and I realized my mistake, I feared you'd uncover our identities. That I'd be mixed in with the others, whether I was or not."

"That may gain you some leniency as long as you tell us about the others. Take him," Hattu directed the soldiers. "I'll finish the—"

"So," Marak said, interrupting Hattu, "you poisoned Prince Nerik at the feast? You must have been seated near enough to put it in his cup. The steward will remember."

"What—" Hattu started.

Mahuri spoke over him, "I will not be charged with Nerik's murder. I had nothing to do with that."

Marak's eyebrows expressed doubt. "You were happy to let Paskans into the city. Why wouldn't you be the poisoner?"

"I was not happy about that. I argued there had to be another way other than a Paskan invasion, but I lost that argument. I didn't even know that they'd used my barn until the dead body appeared. That's why I panicked. None of the others would have poisoned Nerik, either."

"You seem conveniently sure of that," Marak said.

"They had no intention of leaving the city in Paskan hands. They'd use the Paskans to get rid of Hattu, then shove the barbarians out later with a promise of land. They'd return the city to the Great King and be the heroes. Who would the Great King choose to rule after Hattu? Nerik, of course. Once Runda was gone, they saw Nerik as the best choice. Nerik's young and malleable."

Hattu cringed at the man's opinion of Nerik. Unfair, surely. Marak didn't look pleased with this man's explanation.

Mahuri went on. "The Great King would not realize who held the real power. We'd all be safe. No one would have poisoned him. You cannot blame any of us for that. You brought that on yourself, King Hattu, with that woman. I've heard the gossip."

"Gossip often lies," Marak said. "You really wanted only a trade of rulers? Hattu to Nerik?" He sounded incredulous.

"Once they arrested Runda, we had to plan some way to avoid exposure. There was someone at the heart of the conspiracy who believed he'd have full say in how things went once Nerik ruled. I never wanted to know who. Too dangerous. I hated all of this. I only wanted safety. I was never active in this."

"Take him to the citadel," Hattu said to the soldiers. He turned to Mahuri. "You will give the names of the conspirators while a scribe records your testimony."

"If you will promise leniency—let me make up for my mistake—I will tell you those I know. As I said, I had little to do with this conspiracy. You will have to get the other names from someone else."

Gods below. How many of his nobles had turned against him?

63

———————

Daniti stood in her safe, fancy rooms alone.

Her life no longer dangled on a dagger tip, but the heavy dread did not loosen. Tesha needed to understand how vile she'd been, but Daniti hadn't expected to be ignored. She hadn't asked Tesha to come, didn't want her to, but she'd expected Tesha to barge in, wanted or not. Where was her sister? Hattu's troubles, as Marak named them, had been escalating, and perhaps that explained his absence. But nothing made sense about Tesha's absence. She wanted to be angry at Tesha, not worried.

"May I come in?"

This strange voice did nothing to soothe her. "Who are you?"

"A friend of your sister's. She isn't able to come, so I have. My name is Ahmose. I am an Egaryan ambassador."

"Egaryan? How can you be a friend?" His accent made sense as Egaryan, but why was one of Pharaoh's men here?

"Old enemies often make the best friends," the man said in a voice tinged with gentle amusement. She didn't sense deception. "I'm in Alpara to work out some necessary details between our empires, but somewhat separately, I found a sympathy between Priestess Tesha and myself."

"Why isn't she able to come see me? It isn't like her."

"I overheard you telling the newly rescued Commander Marak that you did not want her company. And yet now you are complaining?"

"I don't wish to be in her presence. She ordered the blinding of prisoners. It's unforgivable."

"I found it an offensive choice and even counterproductive since it seemed most likely to lead to your slaughter, not release. But you had something else planned to save you. How did you summon griffins? There are old tales, but truly, I had relegated them to the stuff of children's stories."

"They came. That is enough," Daniti said. She had no intention of telling this peculiar Egaryan what Kurala had done. She wouldn't expose her little pet to the danger of being known as a summoner of griffins. "They left and are not returning. I have no say in any of it."

"You or the commander must have some say."

"What possible say could we have?"

"Your sister has powers that no others have."

"Powers?"

"She's quite influential, shall we say."

Influential? That was one way to describe how Tesha's invocation shifted a person's mood. Had she been up to more than that? "I'd always heard that Egaryans were the ones with magical powers."

"We command far less magic than you Hitolians assume, but your sister practiced some on me and I did sort it out. Did you learn while in captivity that she undid a Paskan curse, a very large curse?"

"No, though we knew their trap had not gone entirely as the Paskans wished."

"Your sister's doing—entirely your sister, as near as I can reconstruct from conversations with the affected soldiers. You can imagine she hasn't boasted about such large-scale sorcery in a public way. The Paskan curse overwhelmed a battalion's worth of men. Her ability to remove such a curse was handy at the time, but sorcerous talents on that level might turn troublesome to the Great King should he ever hear of it."

The backdrop of worry in Daniti's heart leapt to the fore. Had her sister been accused of sorcery?

"Is this curse sorcery—whoever did it—the reason why she hasn't come to see me?"

"I thought you did not want that?"

"I don't, but still . . ."

"A confused heart. I understand. Let me solve this one difficulty, at least."

"Solve it?"

"Would you say the marriage between your sister and King Hattu was a happy one?"

"Yes, quite happy." This man meandered in an irritating way, but still, she heard no deception in his voice, and she'd missed too much while captive.

"Marriages can suffer setbacks, even young marriages. Some force pushed the king away from the priestess. This inclination away from his bride came on only after the curse, which strikes me as more than coincidence, but I am not certain. He accused her of poisoning his son, the Crown Prince Nerik."

"Poisoning his son? Why would anyone believe that?"

"The evidence was quite persuasive in some ways—a vial of poison found in your sister's possession, a clear dislike between the two, and an episode involving a cup, which I believe had everything to do with protocol but which could be understood as committing murder if looked at in an unfortunate light."

"I don't understand any of this."

"The part that matters for you is simply this: once the king rejected his new bride because he considered her a murderer, he made the decision to blind the prisoners. He made that decision entirely on his own. I heard your sister make a spirited argument against the idea, but she was dismissed outright. Forgive your sister. She committed none of the evil you attribute to her."

Daniti found a chair with her hand and slumped onto it. She couldn't sort this out. Such a strange messenger.

He continued, "And most importantly, I believe she needs you. I saw her being taken into the citadel prison by force."

"Locked up? How could Hattu do that? Even if he thought—"

"Surprising, I agree. The gossip among the guards is that King Hattu ordered her locked into a cell rather than her previous arrest in her rooms because she is now also accused of poisoning Lady Agat."

"Lady Agat? Who is she?"

"A lady of the king's household. She is not quite a wife, but she and the king had a son. News of this son's death in a battle against the Paskans arrived just this afternoon. Apparently, the king believes Agat suffers from poisoning, but perhaps it is simply grief. But her sickness, whatever its cause, tipped Hattu into locking up your sister."

"A lady who is not quite a wife? What?"

"I believe the term is "concubine." A royal arrangement. Pharaoh has houses full of such women."

"Poor Tesha. I had no idea."

"That is all I came to tell you. Amid so many other accusations, which may or may not be valid, I thought you should understand a simple truth. Priestess Tesha called the blinding an abomination. She failed to persuade the king from the deed, but not for lack of trying."

Daniti felt a hand on her shoulder.

"Good evening, Lady Daniti. I wish you well. You did manage the most exciting rescue I've ever witnessed—actually the most exciting anything I've ever seen in my long life, even among the wonders of Egarya. Entirely worth overstaying my welcome. I have preparations to make for my departure. I leave before the dawn. I've a long way to go through a dangerous land, having accomplished what I came for. Hattu definitely wants me gone—an Egaryan in a Hitolian court. Not quite right, as you noted."

Daniti heard his footsteps leave. Her sister's life was in chaos. Time to act. She needed Marak.

More footsteps.

"Lady Daniti?" It was Ashu's timid whine.

"Ashu? Is my sister locked in prison?"

"Prison? Oh, I knew she shouldn't go off like that."

"Who is this Lady Agat?"

"Don't call her 'lady' around your sister. It will anger her. Priestess Tesha says Agat gave up any claim to high status when she chose the life she leads now."

That Ahmose must have been right about Agat being a concubine. But what had he said—whether grief or poison? That required investigation.

"Ashu, can you take me to Agat? Perhaps I should speak to her."

"Oh no. We mustn't do that."

"Why not?"

"She hates Priestess Tesha."

"Let's go quietly, then. Perhaps we'll hear something useful." Daniti had always found listening when others did not know you were there was the best way to sort out confusion.

They set off, Daniti's hand on Ashu's arm.

This winding palace challenged Daniti's ability to chart it in her mind. She would have to wander it a few times on her own to learn it well enough to go where she wanted quickly. The mountain, not man, determined the pattern of this place. She liked its wildness.

Ashu whispered, "If we go the back way into Agat's rooms, there is a small connecting hallway behind. You can hide and listen. Henti did."

"Perfect. Take me there, then silently return to this spot and wait for me."

They walked and made four more turns—a left, two right, the last a left. Daniti had the measure of each span charted. She'd have no trouble returning. Ashu departed as ordered—the maid had no idea the noise she made while standing in place. Getting rid of her was essential.

Daniti did hear hushed voices. Voices in conflict.

"But you aren't dead, and you have a reason to live—Nerik." A man's voice was angry, not reassuring despite his call to live.

"Let me be. Isn't it enough that Luwa is gone? My son, the son of my womb." The woman's voice sounded raw and weak. "My father bullied me like this. If I'd known you—"

"You will poison Hattu. It's the only way to assure Nerik's place on the throne, and if you don't, I will expose you when Hattu uncovers what happened and arrests me. Use the real poison this time."

"How did you—"

"You must rid us of Hattu."

"Hattu won't displace Nerik now. I've made sure of that."

"Have you? Did you see the way Hattu hungers for her body?"

"I'm dying, there's nothing I can do."

"Ah yes, dying. Another charge against that woman. Clever of you. Hattu will come to you. He's locked her up for now. You hold his sympathy. Offer him wine, and be sure you make it his last drink."

"I won't kill Hattu. He's my husband."

"He's not. That's the point, isn't it? You failed your father. You say he bullied you, but you deceived him."

"You are—"

"Don't you fear your father's spirit reproaches you? Even when you meet him in the Underworld, your father will scorn you. Do not die with that on your soul."

"That woman is finished. Nerik will rule. I will die. It is enough."

"You can recover. You never intended the tansy to cause serious harm. Nerik certainly is recovering. With Nerik on the throne and Hattu gone, you can have the life you wanted. The life you deserve."

"No! Stay quiet and they'll never connect you to Runda's conspiracy."

"That meddlesome Egaryan may have poked around too much. Hattu must die. The priestess's servant asked dangerous questions until—"

"You'll see that no harm comes to Nerik?"

"We need Nerik. I'll take good care of him."

"You'll have to get rid of that woman. Hattu says he will, but as you say, his judgment can't be trusted."

"That will be arranged. He's ordered her to be sent to the garrison tomorrow. She will be greeted by one of ours. Her stay will be short—very short."

Daniti gasped involuntarily.

"Someone's near," the man said.

Daniti did not wait. She fled back to Ashu.

64

"Ashu, take me to the tower keep," Daniti said. They stood in some hallway or other of this confusing palace.

Ashu wailed in horror.

Daniti hushed her. "Don't argue with me. Find the way."

"I won't go down with you. It's underground. All dark and nasty. The other servants said so. It's where they locked up the Paskans who wanted to kill us all."

"Be a coward if you must. The dark means nothing to me, and I've faced Paskans."

Ashu took her to the keep. Walking with Ashu was infuriatingly slow. The maid acted as if blindness affected the limbs.

They entered the tower. Daniti considered how to persuade the soldiers to let her visit her sister alone so they would not accompany her. She'd have to make it easy for them.

Ashu whispered, "There's a trapdoor in the floor. I'm not going down there."

"You can stay up top," Daniti said. She smiled. "Guards of the keep? The king asked me to check on the priestess. My maid will stay here with you."

Daniti pushed Ashu toward where the men stood, an offering of sorts. Ashu's choice, after all. Ashu considered herself very pretty—Daniti had heard that often enough. "I do not wish to bother you. If you direct me, I'll go along by myself."

The plan worked. Daniti guessed the idea of a blind woman going down alone into the bowels of the prison excited these men. They had no idea how easy it would be for her. She'd left them such fine entertainment that they did not care how long she wandered lost. But they'd said to go down the stairs and straight on to the end of the tunnel. Simple.

They'd also warned her not to even try unbarring any cells. She wouldn't be able to—they were too heavy, and it made a racket. They'd hear, and they'd allow the Paskans she'd loosed to have at her before they went down to restore order.

They'd never usually be so rude to a noblewoman. Her blindness stripped her of her rightful status, and being Tesha's sister no longer offered protection.

Daniti put her hand on the wall and took the measure of the first step and then the next with her foot. She clicked her tongue against the top of her mouth and judged the size of the space around her and the obstacles in her way. Her hand grew wet from running against the wall. Seepage. She tried to imagine this hallway in Tesha's view. The filth would undo her sister.

She called out Tesha's name softly at a door when she thought she'd reached the end. A despairing moan told her she hadn't found her sister. She went a little farther.

"Tesha?"

"Daniti? Is that really you?"

"It is."

"I thought I would die here. I have come close."

"No, no. You're alive and I will get you out."

"Did you come alone?"

"Ashu wouldn't come, and I can see better than most in the dark. I'm told it's dark, anyway."

"You're free of the Paskans? Unhurt?"

"I am. It's a long story. It's you we need to worry about."

"Hold onto my hand," Tesha said. "Over here. Through a small opening in the door." A soft tap on wood told Daniti where.

Daniti clasped Tesha's hand. Tesha whimpered when their fingers touched as if she had not believed it could happen.

Sobs jolted Tesha. Her sister had never been undone like this.

"I was pregnant. You thought I might be and I was, but I lost the baby. I know it. It was my fault." The sobs grew more violent.

"Shh, shh. It can't be your fault. Perhaps you haven't really lost the child. In this horrible place, you could think anything."

"No. The baby is gone. The signs were unmistakable. It was my fault. I took the disguising potion. I needed to, but . . ."

A heaviness settled in Daniti's soul. She hadn't realized Tesha had kept the potion.

Tesha finished in a cracked whisper. "It acted like poison to the infant inside me."

Magic always had consequences they couldn't imagine. Even during her wondrous escape by griffins, a degree of violence had loomed in a way no humans could threaten.

"It wasn't your fault. You didn't realize what would happen," Daniti said. "But now we need to concentrate on getting you out of here and safe." She clasped Tesha's hand between both of hers. "You are strong."

Tesha's shuddering quieted.

Daniti said, "Let's figure this out. I've heard a confusing story about a curse, some sorcery you did, poison, and concubines. What under the skies has happened, Tesha? And you are in great danger. We have to get you out of here."

"You must be careful also. Someone killed Henti. She went asking questions for me—I didn't send her. I wouldn't put her in such danger, but she went. I took the potion to go after her, but not quickly enough. Someone pushed her off a cliff."

"Henti?" Daniti's heart deafened her with its blows. "What can we do?"

"Marak came back with you?"

"Yes. He's with Hattu right now."

"Thank the gods. He's the only one Hattu will truly listen to. The curse hasn't turned Hattu against Marak. We have to convince Hattu that I am not a poisoner. We have to make him listen when Marak tells him he is in danger and not from me."

"I overheard a conversation that may help. It doesn't make sense to me, but it may to you."

"Being with you again, I've never felt a greater blessing. I thought the Paskans would kill you."

"I'm glad to be near you." Daniti felt guilty about her unfair anger at Tesha. It wasn't the time to explain and apologize. She quickly explained about the warning Ahmose had given her and why she'd gone to listen at Agat's rooms.

"Ahmose betrayed me, but what he said to you was true." Tesha described Agat's role in placing the cups and how Tesha had switched them. "I don't know who the intended victim was. What did you overhear from Agat? I thought she was the poisoner, but now that she's a victim also, I guess she can't be. The guards said Hattu thought I poisoned her."

"She *was* the poisoner. The man I overheard said as much, only he said she should use the real poison this time on Hattu."

"Do you think this man had poisoned *her*?"

"He implied she'd done it to herself to get you accused of another crime. She didn't deny that."

"Do you know who the man might be?"

"A conspirator against Hattu, a noble from his speech and manner toward Agat, but other than that, I can't identify him."

"He said to use *real* poison?"

"I'm sure that's what I heard."

Tesha described Nerik's illness, the discovery of Tesha's vial full of tansy, and the substitution of Daniti's perfume. "Nerik's recovering, I think. So Agat used tansy instead of whatever this real poison was. She claims to love both Hattu and Nerik. Maybe she didn't want to kill anyone. But she's still the poisoner, not me."

"The man said he would arrange for you to be killed the moment you reach the garrison. You'd be greeted by 'one of ours' he said, and your stay would be short. I have to free you."

"We need something that will prove without a doubt that I am innocent. Did it sound like Agat would still have the real poison?"

"The man told her to use it. He thought she did."

"If we found it and showed it to Hattu, explained it came from Agat, that would convince him, especially now that Marak is back. Hearing from Marak is essential."

"Marak's worried about him."

"He should be. I removed the curse from the army but not, I think, from Hattu. I don't understand it, but Hattu suffers far worse than before."

"That was bad enough. You really freed all those soldiers from a curse—that much sorcery? It's . . ."

"Dangerous for me. If Hattu comes to his senses, it will be much less so. I can't believe he won't appreciate access to such power, although I have a great deal to learn before I can command it on my own."

"If he doesn't feel it is a threat."

"Trust is everything. Right now, he does not trust me."

"I must find that poison."

"Searching for something in Agat's rooms isn't a job you are well suited for. Sorry."

"Marak will help me."

"Hurry. I don't know how much longer I can stay here without going mad."

65

Daniti chafed against Ashu's plodding, hesitant guidance as they left the main reception hall. It was noisy with courtiers and servants, but they hadn't found Marak or Hattu there.

She had to find Marak and the *real* poison. Would it be in a vial like her perfume or a powder in a box or . . . She tried to imagine all the possibilities so she'd recognize it when she came upon it.

"Where else should we look for Marak?" Daniti asked.

"The king's quarters, I think. It's near."

Thank the gods for that. She might strike Ashu if she had to go much farther led by her.

They turned into a silent room. Not a good sign.

"The commander's not here, either," Ashu said.

Daniti huffed with impatience. Ashu shifted awkwardly next to her. She hadn't missed Daniti's mood for once.

"I can go faster by myself," Ashu said. "You wait here. We're right across the hall from Agat's rooms. That's the front entrance that goes into her sitting room. This is the right place. I'll run. I promise I'll bring Commander Marak back as quick as I can."

"Go, then. Interrupt whatever he's doing. Don't let anyone make you wait."

Ashu left her.

Across the hall was Agat's sitting room? Agat probably lay in her bed in the sleeping chamber where Daniti had overheard her before, sick with her self-inflicted poison. If Agat hid the poison under the fleeces of her bed or near there, even Marak would have trouble retrieving it. He'd have to give some unpleasant orders and would probably have to get Hattu to cooperate. But taking a dangerous poison into one's bed seemed unlikely.

Not well-suited to the job of searching? Tesha's mistake, that. She'd never trusted Daniti's skills.

No harm in listening at the door of Agat's sitting room to see if it was empty like this one. Daniti could move more silently than anyone when she wanted to. If she was caught, she'd apologize and say she was searching for Tesha's rooms. The poor blind girl was lost, that was all. Agat and her maids did not know her. They wouldn't suspect her of anything but blind bumbling.

From the doorway of Hattu's quarters, Daniti sounded across the hall to find Agat's doorway. No noise from inside. She went in.

Softly, she clicked her tongue as she turned around the room and learned the layout. She slipped to the opening that must have led to Agat's other rooms and listened intently. Another empty room. She crossed it and heard an uneven, ragged snore. Agat's sleeping chamber. If someone kept vigil with Agat, they were utterly silent.

Daniti returned to the sitting room. Her hands explored the objects on a table, then a bank of shelves—nothing likely. She moved around the chairs set around the hearth to a large chest. She lifted the lid, knelt, and rested her hands on the contents. Gowns. From the richness of the fabrics and ornamentation, she'd found Agat's court clothes.

Daniti felt within the folds of each dress. Nothing. People always hid things at the bottom of chests. She slid her hand below the gowns and felt a soft woolen shawl. Buried in its folds was a vial wrapped in linen.

Daniti put the vial into the sack she wore on her belt. She heard footsteps entering the room quietly. She closed the chest lid and readied her lie.

Could it be Marak? No, that wasn't his sound. He would have closed the distance between them immediately.

"I'm sorry," Daniti said. "I think I'm lost. I was trying to find Priestess Tesha's rooms."

No response.

She expected an outburst. One of Agat's maids would be startled to find her here. Anyone would.

Daniti heard only the breathing of someone else in the room. A man's breathing, she was sure. There were a few slow steps toward her.

"I didn't mean to intrude. I'm blind," Daniti said.

No response. The man's breathing sped up.

"It was you," he said.

The anger in his voice made her cry out. It was the same voice she'd heard talking to Agat.

He plunged across the room toward her.

She screamed and ducked away from the sound of movement coming at her.

His hand grabbed her arm and yanked her back. She screamed again and twisted sideways, breaking his hold. She turned and stumbled backward, but suddenly pain shot through her shoulder. "Help!" She lunged away and fell to the floor.

There was a familiar cry in the background, outside the room but coming toward it. She screamed again.

"Daniti!" Marak's cry.

"Damn you!" The man ran out through the other rooms, away from Marak.

She lay on the floor, her blood sticky and warm, soaking through the fabric of her sleeve.

And then she was in Marak's arms.

"Are you hurt?" Marak lifted her. "You're bleeding." He grabbed some fabric and held it hard against her shoulder with both hands.

"Who did this?" He pressed his cheek against hers. "We escaped those wolves. You will not die now. I won't let you." And then she didn't mind the stabbing pain in her shoulder.

She thought of when she'd thrust the dagger up and through Riam's flesh. Someone had done that to her. It was only luck that she'd turned sideways so the blow did not go straight into her heart.

66

The pigeon lay dead. The squawk and wheeze of its death had followed almost immediately after Marak poured some of the contents of the vial down its throat.

The search for Daniti's attacker had turned up nobody marked with blood. The man had run before being found close enough to identify him as her attacker.

Agat could barely speak. For now she claimed she knew nothing, and the physician prevented anyone from forcing more from her. He seemed to believe fully that Tesha was the poisoner. He kept saying there was more evidence against her than he would discuss and any more questioning would kill Agat. Only Hattu could order that.

First, they must persuade him.

Marak had caught a pigeon and brought the cooing creature into the royal guest room where Daniti lay on soft fleeces after the physician cleaned and bound her wound. After days of the hard ground of the cave, this luxury almost made up for her aching shoulder. If she didn't move, the gash was merely agonizing. The cooing of that bird and then what followed had disturbed her. A necessary evil to get through to Hattu, but it had been dramatically gruesome.

Marak started by explaining to Hattu where they'd found the poison.

"Hattu, listen to me," Marak had said. Daniti heard Hattu's fidgeting. He acted nothing like himself. Some force pushed him—that was what the Egaryan ambassador had said—some force that coincided with the onset of the curse.

"You are the friend I value most. I'm listening."

That was all very well, but shouldn't Hattu value Tesha most? What had happened?

"No, I don't think you really are listening. Or you're not thinking like the Hattu I know. We found this vial in Agat's rooms, hidden in her clothes chest. Whatever is contained in this vial is fully Agat's responsibility. Do you see this?" Daniti had never heard such bitterness in Marak's voice. He was pushing through something inside his friend, something that disgusted him.

Then Marak had picked up the pigeon. She'd heard its alarmed screech and death gurgle. But loudest of all was Hattu's cry when the poison did its work. At first, Daniti wondered if Marak had struck him, but that wasn't it. Marak's demonstration had made the truth unavoidable for Hattu and had loosened a path in his mind. His horror arose from seeing his own actions with sudden clarity.

Marak quickly explained about the two poisons and how this one, a truly fatal one, had been in Agat's possession in order to kill Hattu and that she had admitted to setting Tesha up as the poisoner in order to prevent Hattu from having any future sons who could displace Nerik.

"Agat did this?" Hattu asked. "She didn't trust me to protect Nerik?"

Daniti spoke up. "I overheard her speaking to some nobleman. She agreed to kill you to ensure that her plan to displace Tesha continued without a doubt. She admitted to making Nerik sick. Tesha is absolutely innocent. I don't know why you would ever think my sister would murder your son."

"She hates Nerik," Hattu said.

"Tesha?" Marak said. "She was nervous about meeting him because she wanted him to like her, but someone has tricked you into thinking she hates him. We weren't here, but that isn't how Tesha would behave. You know her better than that."

"Do I? The idea that she hates Nerik came so strongly to me. But . . . Agat hurt Nerik? That's who made him sick? You're sure?"

From the sound of it, Marak had thrust the dead bird at Hattu. "What does this dead bird tell you? Why are you incapable of seeing what is so obvious?"

"I kept telling myself I just needed you, Marak. Then I would understand everything. You are my most trusted friend."

"Then believe me. Believe the solid proof that we took from Agat. Agat, not Tesha, is the poisoner."

Hattu groaned. "What have I done?" Daniti heard him slump to the floor.

It had been a brilliant way to persuade Hattu, almost too cruel in its effect.

"We didn't catch the man who ordered Agat to give you this poison," Marak said, "but that's how he wanted you, like that bird. And Agat agreed to it. She chose Nerik over you."

"Do you know where they imprisoned Tesha?" Daniti asked. "A dank, slimy pit at the end of a tunnel of cells under the citadel. You complain of my father's treatment of you, but—"

Hattu rose from the ground. "No! No! I never ordered that. I never intended for the guards to put her in that cell. Just locked up. I thought she was a poisoner, a danger to my family." He paced around the room. "I was a fool. How can she ever forgive me? I believed others over her. I did not trust her. I have to win her forgiveness. Ishana help me. How can she ever love me as she did?"

Hattu ran out of the room.

"I should go with him," Marak said. "I don't like to leave you—"

"No, he must do this by himself," Daniti said. "If he can't, then he is lost and so is she."

Marak sighed. "But down there? You went there—he'll never

make it. The fear that has gripped him since his imprisonment—the bowels of the citadel contain everything that set off his terrors."

"Can you think of a better proof of his love to win her forgiveness?"

67

Weighed down as if he carried the armor of his entire army on his own shoulders, Hattu forced himself forward. The wooden door of the citadel keep emerged from the darkness. Behind it lay the trapdoor leading into the bowels of the mountain and the dark cells where he must go to bring Tesha out. He threw all his endurance against the vision that filled his mind with crushing walls and the suffocation that would overwhelm him there.

The moving light of the torch by the entry made the door's beams waver in front of him. He closed his eyes, but the wavering sensation continued. He opened them and reached out to brace his hand against the rough wood.

The Paskan's words rang loud in his head. *Your weakness let curse in. I can't stop it now.*

His weakness. His wound to seal. Only then could he beseech Tesha to cleanse him of the curse—if she could bring herself to forgive him. The first insurmountable task was his alone. He must close the wound his prison-born fears had dug into him. Once he did that on his own, perhaps Tesha could drive out the wriggling that tormented him inside and turned his thoughts against those he loved. The griffins' gift to him, Ishana's shining light, had pierced into his soul once again and granted him that much understanding.

But first he had to conquer the darkness. His fight against his deepest fear. By himself. Without Marak, without Tesha, without Ishana.

He had led men in battle. He had not hesitated to face the forefront of the enemy, even the Pharaoh himself with his best fighters around him. *I will be strong. I am strong.*

The door still wavered. It was a trap. If he entered the cramped chamber of the guard tower, the stone walls would push him into the pit below. Crush him.

I am strong.

He moved with layer upon layer of bronze crippling his limbs and chest.

He wrenched his arm up and pushed open the door, startling the two guards inside. They jumped from their stools.

"King Hattu." The guard looked confused. "It is late."

"Late?" Hattu repeated. Sweat ran down his face. The guards' eyes went wild. They saw his terror and shame.

He pointed at the trapdoor. He couldn't speak. One of the men pulled it up, and a black hole opened in the floor.

The guard lit a torch and moved as if to precede the king down to the cells.

"No. I'll go alone," Hattu forced out. His fight. His alone. It was the only way to win.

The guard objected.

"The Paskans are locked within cells?" Hattu said.

"Yes, sir. If you do not open them, there shouldn't be danger. Priestess Tesha—"

"Has been fully exonerated."

"She's free?" The guards bowed and looked at each other.

She was free of his accusations, but *he* was not free until he felt her forgiveness. He had to earn it by overcoming the fear that had paralyzed him ever since Tesha's father had imprisoned him in that dark hole. Then perhaps, with his weakness sealed and barred, she could free him of the curse as she had the other soldiers.

First, he must go through the abyss to reach her.

The guard handed him the torch—a good weapon, but his arm sagged at the effort.

He moved to the top of the stairwell. Dank air rose from the blackness. *I have a torch. The darkness cannot harm me. I can breathe. The walls will not crush me. I am strong.*

He used memory to fill his legs with the strength he'd had when he'd thrown his spear into Pharaoh's shoulder. That invincible power had flowed through his veins on the battlefield.

In that fight, Ishana had granted him strength, but now he had to restore it himself, draw it up from his own soul and seal the wound that had festered there.

Each step lowered him further below the earth. The walls closed in on him. Stone blocks piled above his head, chinked with sharp shards. He looked up. The trapdoor opening was lost above him. Darkness reached out on all sides, but he kept on. The more he conquered his panic, the more strength he regained. Somewhere in this godsforsaken hole, Tesha endured this nightmare on his orders. He had to bring her out.

He edged forward. His fingers clamped hard around the torch. The low ceiling and blackened walls narrowed. If he went forward, he'd be pulverized between them. No, that was the lie, the delusion. He shuffled his feet toward death, arming himself with the hope for life.

A drop of water fell onto his face. He howled and jumped back. His body shook, and he cried out for help. "Ishana!"

"Hattu? Is that you?"

The drop grew into tears sliding down his face. Tesha's voice sounded empty and desolate. His name on her tongue used to ring with love. But she was there.

His fingers faltered around his torch and it fell. The flames snapped when they hit the edge of this constricted passageway, then sputtered out, doused by the seepage dripping down the wall. Even as the light failed, he felt the old wound seal. Darkness closed in tight around him, but he stood upright. A torch in a wall bracket flickered near the end of the abyss. Tesha must be there. His light. He would win back her light.

He moved forward. He was no longer ruled by shadow fears.

The wall torch and her voice still lay ahead. His goal. His steps were sure. He pushed forward through the murky gloom.

He had crossed the abyss of his greatest terror.

But even as the old wound sealed, the creatures rallied for attack. Thousands of squirming centipedes flared into action inside. He could not fight them himself. He had prepared the way for Tesha, done what he alone had to, but magic must fight magic. Would Tesha forgive him and free him from these vile creatures? Could she, even if she wanted to?

"Tesha!"

The man she had called her husband walked—or stumbled—down the tunnel outside her cell. She heard him. To come into this place himself—Tesha quivered at what that meant for him.

His howl reminded her of the demon shrieks she had endured in the cave of the Underworld. She understood. Terror enveloped him. Terror had filled *her* in this place where he had locked her away and she had lost her first child. She'd lost herself until Daniti had calmed her.

But Hattu came through his greatest terror so that she wouldn't die here.

The hardness that covered the place where her love had been did not soften, but she could not deny his courage and the greatness of what he did.

His plunge into this darkness was a promise to her that he would save her, and that ebbed her own terror now like embers put aside to cool. But nothing would hold back his terror in this place.

His steps moved toward her. Fear was the hardest warrior to defeat.

This prison under the citadel brought him into the darkest hole, the narrow, closed-in walls, the worst place imaginable for him. He braved his greatest fear. All to get to her.

"The one cursed must see himself and be stronger than himself," Tesha murmured, repeating the cryptic curse tablet Humie had given her.

She heard his feet against the stones. He called her name. He had faced this place. She closed her eyes and tried to feel his love, but that inner place was dead.

Tesha peered through the small opening in the door. A torch flickered in the bracket across from her cell, giving enough light to see the horror that held her husband in its grip. Dark curse vapor spiraled around him. The curse grew strong. Mucous whips lashed out and grabbed his legs, but he still lurched forward.

The door shook as Hattu yanked the bar across. She stepped back and the door swung open. Hattu fell to his knees. All over his body, spills of black vapor wrapped around wriggles of blood red. They seeped from Hattu's skin like a thousand cuts.

An otherworldly voice rang out, "He has done his part. You must do yours."

Tesha fell onto her knees beside Hattu, but she shook her head. "You, Goddess, allowed him to break the connection of love between us. How can I free him when I cannot reach into him?"

Tesha heard an angry roar from above.

Hattu braced his hands against the floor and held himself steady, even while the outer marks of the curse increased.

He held her gaze. "I betrayed our love. Even before the curse took control of me, I let you down. To blame the curse is not enough, although I shudder at the thought of what I did to you under its vile influence. I failed you. But a love renewed in wisdom is stronger than a love that's never been tested. Is a new covenant between us enough, my unbreakable vow founded on my deeper love? Can you find a new love for me? Will you forgive me?"

The divine roar rocked the stones she kneeled on. Could she?

She searched in her heart and saw the sorrow in his eyes. It softened the bitterness in her heart. The curse creatures fought with him, knocking him to the ground, but he clutched at the rough stone floor and hauled himself to her.

He reached out and took her hand. His hand shook so that he struggled to place hers against his heart. Ishana did not shine a beam on them this time. The goddess didn't need to. Tesha's chest surged with its own inner warmth as her love for Hattu ignited. Its strength sustained her.

"I can forgive you if you will trust me."

"I do. I pledge my trust forever more." Around him blackness swirled and hissed. She barely caught his words, but the promise came through as sure as anything she'd ever heard.

The charged air between them reminded her of the first time they met, the bond they'd effortlessly formed. In their gaze they exchanged the old connection of trust. It was the connection she needed to save him.

"Only you can help me," he gasped in a strangled groan. "I'm ready, but only you can drive out this curse."

She trembled. He'd fulfilled what the curse tablet required. If that ancient prophecy proved true, he had done his part. Now, as her goddess commanded, she must do hers. They were connected, but she did not command the power from all things that had driven out the curse before. Her own illness in body and heart remained, and her strength foundered. What did the goddess mean?

She stood, extended her arms wide, and set her feet in a firm stance. "Goddess, show me how to rid my husband of this evil. You command me to do it, but you must give me the skill and the power."

And then she felt it. Ishana's beacon lit inside her, surrounding the golden light under her ribs, which now burned brighter than it ever had.

She focused her inner gaze and willed the glow to spark and expand, to reach into the sacred potency in the earth and sky. For a moment, she hesitated. This power might kill her, but what remained for her if she failed?

Through the stones surrounding her, she felt Ishana's beam fire into an answering echo of power.

"Please Ishana, guide me. Drive out this evil. My husband has destroyed the shield the curse hid behind. Through me, strike now and obliterate the curse. It grows stronger. Do not hesitate. At whatever cost, free my Hattu."

Hattu flailed on the floor below her.

Tesha called out, "Ishana, do not abandon my husband. Shine your blessing upon him."

The beam inside her crackled like lightning. Power flooded into Tesha. Her body was a star whose beams linked to distant sparks of energy. The room grew brighter. In response, what poured from Hattu's skin writhed in a death struggle. She brought her hands together and concentrated the golden light on him as a piercing spear.

Hattu scratched at his flesh, tearing off his tunic to rid himself of the things oozing from his chest. Whirls of black bound him, strangling him and contorting his limbs.

Blood-red carcasses littered the floor like a field under the onslaught of locusts.

Divine energy streamed out from her body and into Hattu, striking down the curse. She was winning the battle, but she'd loosed the floodwaters and now her life-force flowed along with them. She tried to grasp shreds of herself and hold them back.

Tesha fell to the ground, her chest exploding in pain.

A piercing shriek reverberated against the low ceiling. *That* was a demon's cry, and it was a cry of defeat.

Hattu's straining fingers clutched her leg. "I'm free."

69

Hattu marveled that his skin showed no marks, but his body felt like he'd fought the longest battle of his life.

Marak had seen the disgusting carcasses thick on the floor when he'd burst in, but by the time anyone else had come, they'd vanished. Convenient for hiding what had happened from his men, but . . . An oversized opponent with a sharp sword didn't bother Hattu all that much, but this magic terrified him. He'd promised to trust Tesha. He would. But he wished solid things did not vanish into the air.

Without Marak, he and Tesha would still be lying on the floor of that cell, too spent by the battle against the curse to stand and walk out.

Marak found them and brought servants with litters to carry them up, calling for the physician. Then he disappeared, saying he had to speak to someone. He hadn't said who. Strange, but Hattu couldn't delay confronting Agat any longer. Those cursed worms didn't befuddle his mind anymore. He'd stop this man that Daniti had overheard. Marak hadn't been able to drag his identity from Agat. Hattu knew that was his own fault. The physician protected Agat on his orders. He would no longer.

Hattu lay on the bed next to Tesha. He pressed her hand to his lips. "Are you well enough to come with me?"

The bags under Tesha's eyes and her body drooping into the pillows didn't reassure him. She hadn't lost her ability to move as she had when she drew his whole army out of the curse, but whatever sorcerous power she'd called upon had drained her in dangerous ways.

"I want to hear what Agat says. She hates me. She caused all this."

"The poison, yes," Hattu said, "but there were others involved. I will force her to tell me."

Tesha rested her hand on his chest. "I have a way to make her speak the truth. You only have to ensure she cooperates with me. A man wants to kill you. Let me uncover him."

"A way? More sorcery?" He'd had more than enough of that.

"Sorcery, yes. A magic the Paskans held onto. I've been learning things."

Tesha told him about his physician. Utar had hidden his Paskan mother well.

"I think Utar serves you honorably," Tesha said. "The magic is useless to him anyway. The goddess does not give him power. But she does give it to me—a great deal of power. That is something we must hide from your brother, who does not understand Ishana as you and I do. He'll never overcome his distrust of magic. But you? Either you want to rule in partnership with me, who I am, or . . . You said you would trust me. You knew I used sorcery to free your army. Why would I never access such potential again? Will you trust me, even now?"

"I pledged that I would trust you, and I will never challenge that pledge. Ishana's love is the blood in my veins—as is your love." He took her in his arms and held her tight. "I do not know how I could be turned against you. I must learn and understand about my enemies. If you have magic that can accomplish that, use it."

Hattu kissed her. The longing for her engulfed him. He pressed her close.

She pulled away. "Let us go now."

70

---

gat lay propped on pillows, her eyes closed, stretched out in her grandiose bed. She'd ordered it built with the winged sun disk of the royal family carved into the headboard and overlaid in gold. Hattu had never liked it. It was for him, she'd insisted, as if these weren't her rooms. It wasn't what he wanted in a bedroom, but it had made her content.

The linen sheet over her chest rose and fell. Her limp hands lay on top of the sheet. She wasn't dead yet. Her face, yellow and flaccid, hadn't shriveled in on itself the way a corpse's did, but she no longer looked like the living woman he had known. Utar said she'd taken too large a dose of tansy to recover. She faced a slow, painful death.

Tesha settled into a chair Hattu had ordered brought close to the bed, well cushioned with pillows. Near her, the servants set a table with two pitchers of water and a bowl. The pitchers were the type for sacred libations. Any priest or priestess would use them. Maybe he did not need to fear this spell.

A rule of warfare was not to engage the enemy while your own troops were wounded, but Agat looked even more ill than either Tesha or him. Tesha's eyes had a new spark of fury. Even the final fight with her father hadn't lit that in her. He loved her for it.

"Agat, wake up," Hattu said in a loud voice. "Utar told me you can speak. I will not be ignored." She didn't open her eyes. He shook her shoulder. "You claim you want what's best for Nerik. Speak to me if you care for his future." He knew Nerik was the one link to life that Agat still had. He'd use that to gain her cooperation, much as he disliked the strategy.

He saw small movements in her face. They'd shared a long experience of life together. She'd been attractive once, and she was always clever. "Agat. Do not betray Nerik as you have betrayed me."

Agat's eyelids opened slowly. Her lips moved. No sound came out. She tried again. "I was a good wife to you. I did not betray you."

"If you did not betray me, you have nothing to hide. You are dying, Utar says, but you are strong enough to perform a rite with Priestess Tesha. You need only look at a stone that she will hold up for you."

"Concentrate on this." Tesha held a smooth gray stone in front of Agat.

Agat's eyes focused on him, not the stone. "You will hold Nerik in your heart always? And preserve him as Crown Prince?"

That had always been Hattu's intent. Why wouldn't he love his son and see him to the throne? "Help me now and I will. Do what Tesha commands. I know how hard that is for you. Consider your cooperation with her as the compelling proof you did not betray me. You want me to believe that, don't you?"

Agat shifted her eyes to the stone.

"Do not let your gaze shift or waver," Tesha said. "Stare at the stone and let calm fill you. This rite will help you. It may give you strength."

Tesha said many soothing words. Even he felt a healing glow inside, although he kept his eyes away from the stone. He'd never stare at it. For him, getting information from prisoners was a bloody process, ugly and dishonorable. It was a king's duty he hated. Tesha's magic had advantages, as long as her sorcery stayed away from him.

After a long stretch of prayers, Tesha put the stone in Agat's hand and instructed her what to do with it. When Agat touched the stone to her forehead, then kissed it, an exclamation burst from her that sounded happy. Tesha took the stone from Agat's limp hand. Hattu studied Agat's movements. She did look stronger. There was healing power in this spell. Truth could heal.

The words Tesha said over the unclean and clean water echoed prayers he'd been taught in Ishana's temple during his priestly training. This magic had a familiar feel. Long ago, the priests and priestesses—those who could access magic, as Tesha could—must have used prayers as his wife now did to accomplish far more than Hattu's prayers had ever done.

For generations, the Great Kings had slaughtered every sorcerer they found—priests and priestesses might be more accurate, Hattu realized now. And once the kings had stripped away the holy power, the forms of the prayers had stayed the same, preserved by tradition long after they'd become hollowed-out shells of their former divine connection.

He felt cheated. Tesha was right. She should pursue this power she'd found. And he would protect her.

Tesha poured a slow trickle of water into the bowl while she asked, "Did Priestess Tesha poison Nerik?"

Agat's eyes were blank. "No. Priestess Tesha did not use poison." Her voice came out even and calm.

"Did Agat poison Prince Nerik?"

"Not poisoned." Agat grew agitated. Her eyes stayed unfocused. "I used a small amount of tansy. I tested the dose on some of the slaves. Nerik shouldn't have gotten so sick. He drank too much wine. I hadn't counted on that. I would never harm Nerik."

"Who gave Agat the real poison?"

"My father." Agat seemed to shrink with the effort, and Hattu drew back at the despair in her voice. "He joined Runda's conspiracy after Hattu was arrested in Lawaza. I didn't know. I would have stopped him. When news of Hattu's wedding to Priestess Tesha reached us, he brought me poison. He said that I'd been rejected as Hattu's wife again. I must kill Hattu when he arrived. I thought by substituting tansy, I'd convince him I had followed his orders but failed. I couldn't defy him openly, and by agreeing, I stopped him from forming another plan. I did it to protect Hattu." Agat shriveled even further into her pillows.

Agat had been loyal in her own foolish way. For a clever woman, she'd made a mess of this. Although how else she could have protected both her father and him, Hattu couldn't see. Tesha, on the other hand, had chosen to protect him at great risk to her father.

"Besides Agat's father, who else ordered Agat to poison Hattu?"

"My father did not tell me who the other conspirators were. I thought no one else knew about my father's plan to poison Hattu—because I was his daughter, he thought he could make me do it, but he didn't betray me to others. But one man revealed himself today. He knew or guessed that I hadn't used the true poison. No one suspected him until that Egaryan ambassador asked too many questions. Shatim saw Hattu's death as his only safety."

"Shatim?" Hattu jumped from his seat. "How can it be Shatim?"

Hattu bellowed for his guards. Their heavy boots pounded from the hallway.

"Arrest Lord Shatim. Hurry. Take a large force. Do not let him escape."

The soldiers ran out.

His old friend? The man whose advice about diplomacy had always served him well? Hattu sank back into his chair. Truth stabbed deep.

Tesha reached out and held his hand. She understood what betrayal felt like. Far too much. Hattu sighed.

Tesha said, "Send Shatim to the cell your soldiers put me in. Let him rot there. He thought to hide hate behind friendship. He took a dagger to Daniti."

Hattu squeezed her hand. "I will. That is justice." He turned back to Agat. Her eyes had regained a normal focus. He'd disrupted the spell, but she had revealed the one traitor she knew.

Agat looked flustered. "What did I say?" The flaccid yellow turn reappeared in her face.

"You said Shatim wants me dead," Hattu said. "Soon he'll be my prisoner."

"And that your father gave you the poison," Tesha added. "How could you let your father and the others turn over the city to Paskans? You *did* betray Hattu."

"My father is dead. Now you take his honor as well. I didn't know about the Paskans. If he allied himself with them, they repaid him by spearing him in the back. If I had known, I would have warned Hattu."

"Did you put it in the cups?" Hattu asked. "Was Nerik right about that?"

"Yes, that came out as I hoped. I realized before the feast that I could place the blame on your new, very young wife." Agat's hate apparently still ruled her. She reveled in this tale, and her resentment toward Tesha bolstered her. "No one liked her. Some good would come from the terrible thing my father forced on me."

Agat's color grew more like a corpse. She was using up what life she had left.

"Go on," Tesha said.

"I listened to the cook's whining about your fussy instructions. I left it to the gods and that priestess's bad nature whether it would be you or Nerik who drank the tansy."

"And you don't think you broke faith with me?" Hattu's disgust at Agat grew unbearable. He wanted to know what had happened, but listening tormented him.

"It suited me best if she switched the cups. Then I could accuse her, and my father would be so overjoyed that the poison did not kill Nerik—he'd never know I intended the switch—he'd be less likely to question why his poison failed."

"Why would your father care so much about Nerik's health? You treat him as your son, but—"

"Since you left, he had mentored Nerik. For the good of the kingdom."

"The same kingdom he wanted to hand over to the Paskans? He no doubt sought influence over the next king once he'd killed me."

Tesha pushed upright in her chair. "You worked hard to hide Shatim's name. If you loved Hattu, why not tell Marak right away and protect the king from Shatim? You claim you suffered trying to protect Hattu. You're lying."

"No, I don't think that's it. Is it, Agat?" Marak said. He stood in the doorway, supporting Daniti with gentle care. He brought her to a chair and helped her sit.

Agat's eyes had gone wide. She lay very still. Hattu was minded of a rabbit when a hawk flies overhead.

71

———

Marak drew up a stool near Hattu's chair. He stretched out the leg the damned Paskans had sliced. Hattu saw that the wound was freshly bandaged, at least.

"You protected Shatim," Marak said, looking straight at Agat, "because of what he might reveal if we questioned him. You held off, hoping he'd be smart enough to flee. But that doesn't matter. I spoke to Nerik."

Agat jerked under the linen sheet.

Nerik? Hattu felt like he had stepped off a cliff.

"You forget," Marak said, "long before Shatim and your father weaseled into Nerik's confidence, I was the one Nerik trusted and confided in. I got to thinking about the way Hattu described Nerik's behavior. All I had to do was ask Nerik a direct question. Did you poison your father?"

Hattu jumped from his chair. "Agat confessed. She's the poisoner."

"You are standing here, so no one actually poisoned you. But what Nerik wanted to do is another thing."

Hattu slumped back into the chair. "Even my son wants me dead? He conspired along with the others? For *him* I accused Tesha?"

Marak scooted his stool closer to Hattu. Marak's green eyes could skewer a man when he needed them to, but Hattu saw only compassion.

"It's not quite as bad as that. Nerik said he never tried to poison you, but it turns out he did talk a lot about wanting to kill you. He told Agat."

This betrayal by own son ran too deep for Hattu to absorb. Had Agat turned the boy against him? He wanted to see Agat's expression, but she'd turned her face away from him.

"How can this be?" Hattu heard the thinness of his voice.

"I don't think Nerik's talk was meant . . . How seriously? Well . . . Conspired against you? No. He clearly did not know about the nobles conspiring with the Paskans, although I assume that without his knowing it, he figured in those men's plans as your successor."

"So he does want me dead," said Hattu.

"Not anymore. His sin lay entirely in his uncontrolled emotions, not his actions. He told Agat weeks ago that he wanted to poison you and take the throne because that was the only way he would ever hold military command. Your cautious protection was not appreciated, Hattu. I did warn you."

Hattu half rose from his chair, his hands swerving in front of him to ward off any more revelations. "But look what happened to Luwa. If I'd sent Nerik as he wished . . ."

Marak put up a hand to stop Hattu. "I think his anger is not so different from many young men's at their fathers. The desire to be recognized as grown and independent. He wants to be the master of his world. But in his case, that world is a kingdom, not a farm or a workshop. A kingdom is too big for such anger to be harmless."

"He had to kill me to prove he'd grown up? That's ridiculous."

"If you put it that way."

Marak's searching look stopped Hattu. He'd better listen to his friend. He shook out the tension from his shoulders.

Marak continued, "Nerik raged at Agat about getting rid of you, that's true. But when he came face-to-face with you, felt your embrace, and saw your love, he changed his mind. He didn't want to admit it and he acted wretchedly, but he didn't want to kill you."

Agat stirred. "He . . . didn't."

Hattu could barely hear her words. Her cheekbones etched lines through skin that had grown too brittle to stretch over them. A wave of sadness surprised him. He remembered watching her suckle both his sons at the same time, juggling the two infants with affection. So long ago.

Marak continued. "So that was why Nerik was so shocked when he came down sick, remembered the switching of the cups, and assumed Agat had stepped in to be Hattu's poisoner for him. He was clever enough to think of accusing Tesha on his own. He certainly didn't want the truth to be known, and Agat had taught him to hate Tesha."

"She'd made sure I had no chance of winning him over," Tesha said.

Marak's lips pursed in disgust. Hattu wondered what was next.

"While Nerik was recovering from the poisoning, Shatim wormed out of him what Nerik thought Agat had done."

Tesha asked, "Did Nerik know about Agat's father's part in the poisoning?"

Agat mumbled a denial.

"I agree with Agat," Marak said. "Nerik couldn't have told Shatim about that or about the real poison. He found out some way or other. Probably a servant who overheard something. Shatim often put otherwise meaningless pieces together like that. I always admired Shatim's ability to find out everything—when I thought he was on our side."

"So Nerik trusted Shatim with his darkest secrets?" Hattu asked.

"Oh yes. He was stupid enough to tell Shatim how much he'd wished for his father's death and how much he now regretted it. He thought, no doubt, Shatim would make him feel better."

"And Shatim took this trust and ordered Agat to finish me off?" Hattu groaned. He rocked back and forth in his chair. "You are right, Tesha, let him molder in the worst cell in the citadel."

"It was unfortunate," said Marak. "Before that, only Agat, who is his mother more or less, heard that idiocy, and she only tried to hush Nerik. From the so-called friendship with Shatim that Nerik described, I'm guessing Shatim saw himself as the man Nerik would lean on as a young king, and he used this confession to deepen Nerik's dependence on him."

Hattu cried out. He hunched forward with his arms locked over his belly.

Marak muttered under his breath, "Gods' balls. What a mess."

Daniti grasped Tesha's arm. "Doesn't it strike you as surprising that Agat's father pushed Agat to poison Hattu, and during the same time, Nerik was also carrying on about poison? That coincidence is hard to believe. Is this palace full of poisoners?"

Hattu made a bitter sound, part laugh, part growl. "Only when I'm around. I sprout enemies like weeds along a riverbank."

He stood and leaned over Agat so he could see her face. Her eyes were open, but they had a glazed look that had nothing to do with Tesha's spell. Marak had taken away the last prop giving her strength. Her darling Nerik's true self was revealed.

Hattu poked Agat's shoulder. "Nerik is loud and incautious when he's angry. You were close to your father, weren't you, Agat? He visited often. The guards would not feel any need to send a servant to announce him. He was family. So Nerik gave him the idea when he overheard one of Nerik's rages. Your father's fellow conspirators probably thought letting the Paskans kill me would suffice. He had a surer plan."

Marak placed his hand on his friend's back. "Nerik never intended to go through with anything against you. And Agat did what she could to protect both you and Nerik while not undoing her father. Your family may have flaws, but they are not your enemies. Nerik needs to learn wisdom, and he must be allowed to make some big mistakes of his own. He'll grow up, given time and experience."

Tesha turned to Marak. "How is Nerik's health today?"

"He's much better. The yellow color that so worried the healer wanes. Nerik's still weak, but apparently Agat knows her dosages of tansy. She's done no lasting harm."

A moan rose from Agat.

"He should be here to face his father," Tesha said.

Hattu staggered up from the chair, stumbling and tipping over the chair with a crash. "But—"

"It is time," Marak said. "I'll get him."

Marak left.

Hattu righted the chair and sat down. He jumped when Tesha's hand rested on his shoulder. She ran her fingers soothingly over his arm. He caught her eye, and she gave him a small smile. He could go forward.

He waited. The gap between each rise of Agat's chest grew longer.

Tesha squeezed his arm. "He's your son. You won't lose your love for each other."

Nerik entered and stopped short. Hattu rose. Marak slipped in behind and went to stand next to Daniti. Hattu stepped toward his son.

"Father..."

"You wanted me dead?"

"No. I was angry. I thought you would never respect me, never give me what was mine by right. I'm not a small child."

"I don't treat you like a child."

"Yes, you do. Or did. I would like to learn to rule, like you said. It isn't easy, is it? If you had been sick instead of me that night..."

"It isn't all fighting. Or it shouldn't be."

"I know it's not all battles, Father." Nerik's voice cracked. "Luwa's dead. My brother."

Hattu took Nerik by the shoulders. He sighed and wrapped Nerik in an embrace. "Luwa's gone. Isn't that unbearable enough? I could never let that happen to you."

Nerik pulled Hattu toward Agat's bed. "Is she...?"

"Not much longer. Say whatever you need to."

Nerik knelt by the bed. He laid his head next to Agat's and wrapped his hand around one of hers. "I'm sorry." His voice sounded so young. Agat's eyes remained closed. "Forgive me." Then he whispered something Hattu couldn't hear.

Tears streaked Nerik's face when he stood. "I did tell Agat that I wanted to kill you. But I never imagined what that would be like. If I had . . . I didn't mean what I said. The moment you were really there with me again, back home, I . . . I'm sorry. I acted childishly. As unready for command as you thought. Please forgive me. I will do my best for you while you are away in Amur. Give me a chance."

Marak stepped forward. "I don't think your father should be the general who goes to Amur. I can knock some sense into the locals and round up the pro-Egaryan faction just as well as the king. All that's needed is some tact and a sufficient show of force." Marak glanced at Tesha and then Hattu. "There's . . . business for you here, Hattu."

Tesha twined her fingers through Hattu's. "Take Nerik with you, Marak. He wants to learn statecraft and help with military actions. This trip will provide both. Don't you think, Hattu?"

Hattu found accepting Nerik's apology difficult. Nerik's presence must be even harder for Tesha. "You both need a few days to recuperate. Ahmose will have to accept that—if he's still around here. But then . . . with all speed. Do you want to go, Nerik?"

"I would. Marak will take care of me."

"Fine. But listen to me. I do not want to sow in Amur the kind of bitterness that Runda harbored here in Alpara for twenty years. Deal gently with this uprising."

Nerik pushed out his powerful chest. "I'm not being gentle to those Egaryan rabble. We'll rid the empire of them."

Hattu wanted to slap Nerik, but instead he laid a hand on his son's shoulder. "Listen to me. You will have to execute a few of the most vocal of the Egaryan supporters, but do not cut off their families and allies. Access to trade is the source of power in Amur. Share that even among the followers of these troublemakers."

"Why should we march all the way to Amur to help the troublemakers?"

"Because they will be less likely to be troublemakers in the future if they get what they want without the Egaryans. You have to show them we are their valuable friends. Just make the punishment of the few clear enough so everyone knows the Hitolians are never giving up control. But no extremes. Do you understand, Nerik?"

"I guess so."

Nerik had that familiar sullen look. Marak was going to have his hands full.

"Listen to Marak. And hold your temper."

Nerik bowed his head. Hattu wondered if his son would ever be able to follow that last piece of advice.

Hattu watched Marak lean in to touch Agat's neck. He didn't see her chest rising. Marak stood and shook his head. Agat and her bitterness were gone.

72

Tesha stepped into Hattu's room. She had slept after the long unraveling at Agat's bedside. Fighting curses was a deadly art. There was much more for her to learn about magic to expand her powers.

Hattu's broad shoulders and chest were outlined against the light coming through the expansive windows of his reception hall. The remembered feel of those muscles under her fingertips overwhelmed her for a moment. She shivered in the chill air. The scene outside the windows puzzled her.

From the doorway, Tesha watched white flakes float down against the pines and boulders of the surrounding mountains. Hattu seemed always to have the shutters open, even in a storm.

Hattu spoke to her from across the room. "We've arrested the others. The owner of that barn, Mahuri, gave us some names, and those led us to the others. He knew more than he thought he did. A sloppy conspiracy, fortunately. Except for Shatim. We would never have caught him except for Daniti's cleverness and your magic with that stone. It was Agat's father who gave them the password that allowed the Paskans to take down the watch at each gate. The deepest traitor of them all. Even the Paskans recognized him for a traitor and stabbed him in the back for it. Paskan honor is a strange thing, but it has its code. He was the man who boasted that he acted as father to my son while I was away. Hah! I have so much to repair with that boy."

"He's a man, not a boy."

"You're right. He's your age. You reminded me of that and I ignored you. You are far wiser than he is, experiences or no. But he's my son."

She knew he waited for her to come to him. He still hesitated to reach out for her, to trust the forgiveness she had given. There was substance to his doubt. He had wounded her deeply. She wanted to put the bitterness aside completely, and she believed in the love Ishana had rekindled inside her. But still, her heart had been hurt. Hattu offered a love renewed in wisdom, but wisdom brought scars that must heal.

But their love was better now. They were stronger. No one would ever succeed in breaking them apart. Not Paskan curses, not petulant crown princes, not angry concubines—although what to do about them was still a question to Tesha.

Hattu rested his hands on one of the windowsills, staring out. It was a sight worth attending to, painfully beautiful.

Tesha went to the window next to him and leaned out. Down in the river valley below, the snow wasn't sticking yet. Tesha hoped it wouldn't. Such a late spring snow could harm the newly sown crops. She wrinkled her brow. She didn't actually know if it would or not. She ought to. The well-being of the crops was now her responsibility, so she'd remember to find someone to teach her.

"Do you know whether this late snowfall is bad for the crops?" Tesha asked Hattu.

He turned in surprise. She smiled. That wasn't the question he'd expected.

He shook his head. "I'm not sure. I will find out. If I we must import more seed for a replanting, I'll have to be quick. The farmers only put aside what is needed. The rest gets eaten. I guess it's good I'm not setting out to Amur."

"And even better that Nerik is, although Daniti will complain about Marak's departure. But where would the extra seed come from?"

Hattu leaned back against the windowsill. "There's the real question. Perhaps my brother has stores in the capital. Between drought and the loss of men to work the fields, it's possible there isn't any."

"Starvation—that's all we could offer?"

"Peace with Egarya has many advantages. One of them, I hope, is grain. Their river supplies them with the most fertile soil. Perhaps Gerose or one of his subordinates would send a shipment."

"I'd hardly call the current situation peace."

"Neither would I. Something to hope for."

They stood in silence, watching the snow fall.

"I was vile to you," Hattu said, "More than an apology can atone for. When I came to you in that cell, Ishana left you little choice. Do you truly love me again? The hurtful words and actions came from me, even if I was filled with the curse."

The goddess *had* given her a choice, or at least her rekindled love for Hattu had driven her forward, not the divine command.

Tesha snuggled against Hattu for warmth, and he wrapped his arm around her. "Do you remember the first day we met," she said, "our conversation in the temple in Lawaza?"

"The game of Sphinx and Griffin?" Hattu's face lit with happiness. "I could say anything to you then. I barely knew you, but somehow I could speak as I never had been able to with a woman. But I lost that again."

"My father saw to that. He took the shine off our courtship."

Hattu looked out the windows again. "But I must learn to talk to you again. I want the ease we had."

"The gods do not let us undo what has been done. Ishana gave us that conversation so you could woo me. Now we must live with what we are."

Tesha reached out and caught a snowflake on the palm of her hand. It felt both soft and intensely cold, an odd contradiction. Then it melted and disappeared.

She reached for Hattu's hand and pulled it outside so that a flake fell on his open hand. The whiteness shimmered on his skin. When it was gone, he turned to her in question.

"Does the snow disappear?" Tesha asked. "One moment it is white and vivid on the skin, then the body's heat melts it. But it has only turned into water—water that will feed the fields and nurture the seeds. It isn't gone. Our love never vanished. It has become something else, more sustaining."

Tesha brushed away a tear that insisted on tumbling down her cheek. A small smile crept onto Hattu's face. He closed his arms around her. She slipped her fingers under his tunic and traced the muscles of his shoulders.

"Love is not the easy thing I imagined," Tesha said into his chest. "I thought that I, the loving wife, could hold you and all would be well. But I am more now than I was."

She lifted her head and placed her hand on Hattu's chest. She pictured the daily honesty, even the hurtful honesty, she had learned to trust with her sister. "As you say, you must learn to talk to me again. You will tell me the uncomfortable things, even if it causes you unbearable pain. Hidden concubines, unhappy sons, past mistakes that leave a trail of hurts, your suspicions of me, your dislikes, whatever you must do that you fear I will not like. You must swear to me to speak about all such things. And I will hide nothing from you. That must grow as our habit."

Hattu's eyebrows had come together. Tesha put her hand on his cheek, shaking her head. "Speaking to me will come to be less harrowing with time."

He laughed. "Are you sure you wouldn't rather run me through with a sword each day? It'd be less painful."

A gust of wind blew a snowflake flurry at them. Hattu enveloped her when she shivered. "I will talk everything out with you. I promise."

"There is something I have to tell you. It's terrible." A wave of grief caught her, and she moaned.

Hattu held her tight. "It cannot be worse than what I did to you. Tell me. I love you."

"I carried our child in my womb." The sudden light of joy in Hattu's eyes cut her. "I lost that baby. The potion Marak took from Kudur? I used it to disguise myself from the guards so I could escape from my rooms. That magic killed the baby."

Hattu's face sagged. The spark in his eyes died out. His arm around her loosened. He wouldn't forgive her for this. Not this.

"Escape from my guards? That was my fault, not yours. No queen should have to hide from her own guards. My brother didn't allow you or Marak to question Kudur. You couldn't know what that potion would do."

Tears ran down her face. "No, I didn't know. But I drank it two times, and I did know that I was ill the first time. I . . . believed I had to protect Henti . . ."

Hattu wrapped her in his arms. "My soldiers brought Henti's body back to the palace. One of the conspirators killed her. That's what happened, isn't it? My men said she fell, but I questioned that. You tried to save her. I forced that choice on you. One more sin of mine. Forgive me."

"We have to forgive each other."

"There will be other children. Many of them, my beloved," Hattu said, his lips pressed against her hair.

They pulled apart and leaned against the windowsill side by side. The snowflakes glowed white in the dusk, falling more thickly now and silencing the world outside.

"It's sticking," Tesha said.

"Enough to hide the dirt underneath. You ought to like that. A tidy kingdom." He stroked her back.

"It is the spring melt that feeds the land."

"Sometimes the spring takes longer than expected to arrive."

73

———

In the large stone tub, Tesha slid her head below the perfumed water, letting it cover her whole body. Bless the gods for requiring such generous ablutions before a woman was ritually clean enough for them to lift her in their divine hands and transform her into a queen.

She raised her dripping head out of the water. The sheen of rose-scented oil floated around her breasts and arms. She ran her hand down her wet hair and felt the smooth slickness of it.

Immediately following the confrontation with Agat and Nerik, at Hattu's command, the head priest had taken the omens to ascertain if it would be propitious to hold the queen's coronation in the morning two days hence. Both the hurri bird and the swimming snake divinations showed the gods agreed.

Tesha had risen in the middle of the night to prepare for her coronation, and now her sleepy senses gradually awoke to the pleasures of this bath. Dawn was the divinely sanctioned time for the anointments of rulers, so this purification had to start while darkness still held the city in its embrace.

Tesha sat more upright to allow a priestess to run an ivory comb through her hair.

"I comb away harm, impurity, and sadness," intoned the priestess. "As the servant cards all knots, dirt, and uncleanness from the lamb's wool, so let this comb take away confusion, defilement, and illness from our queen."

The priestess signaled to Tesha to stand in the tub, then ran a silver scraper down each of her oiled limbs, belly, and back. She poured water over each from a pitcher of silver, the pure metal. With each part, the priestess repeated her plea for the gods' blessing upon Tesha.

It was lovely. Never had a rite so filled Tesha with well-being. The holy stream repaired the drained breach she'd carried inside since her battle with Hattu's curse. Ishana's light nestled under her ribs. She'd watched it regrow after the first curse confrontation, but still, its dimness since she'd freed Hattu had disquieted her. She did not wish to step into her reign without Ishana's power glowing inside. She knew now that she had enough skill to rule, but her goddess must be with her. Even if she didn't have all the understanding she would need, the queenship itself held authority, and she would grow into it.

Before the gods and her people, she was ready to be a queen.

Tesha stepped out of the tub and dried the fragrant water from her skin. The priestess pressed her waist-length hair into one linen towel after another, then combed it again beside the fire in the wide corner hearth where the heat would dry it. Lined up against the wall were bronze cauldrons for heating bath water. The coals still burned intensely around the empty tripods that had held the pots used to heat hers. Tesha sat down in a chair with a headrest cut into its back. Wrapped in a linen towel, she tipped back her head against the chair with her black hair cascading behind her. She closed her eyes and let the holiness of the day fill her.

A soft knock on the doorway and Daniti's greeting brought a smile to Tesha. Daniti had asked to be one of her dressing assistants, and Tesha had overridden the priestess's objections. Daniti entered the room by herself. Tesha heard the soft clicks and knew how Daniti walked so confidently toward her, but she enjoyed the shocked look on the priestess's face in watching a blind woman move with such ease. It showed, as Daniti intended, how skilled an assistant Tesha had chosen.

Words had to be chosen carefully on such a consequential day, so when Daniti dragged a stool near to her sister, they sat in companionable silence. Every once in a while, Daniti ran her fingers through Tesha's hair, spreading it before the heat and checking its dryness.

After a while, Daniti laid her hand on Tesha's belly. The sorrow for the lost child flowed back in. Tesha wished Daniti hadn't reminded her. She tried not to think about that loss. Then Daniti laid her head on Tesha's stomach.

Tesha pushed her away. "Leave that be. It makes me too sad."

"You don't understand," Daniti said. "I hear a voice. Let me listen."

"Stop it. Babies don't speak from the womb. It's mean to pretend. I saw the blood and felt the cramps. I called for a midwife yesterday and discussed it with her. I lost a child. Let me be."

Daniti cocked her head and Tesha knew she was concentrating like she did when she claimed she spoke to Kurala. That had turned out to be true. Kurala had guided her across countryside to find him. Her conversation with Kurala had brought the griffins and rescue. But a baby in the womb? Daniti should stop provoking her sadness.

"The midwife was right. You did lose a child," Daniti said. "But you carried two. The remaining one has strong magic. She can't speak, not with words, but I can sense her feelings. She grieves for her twin. She is proud of her fight."

"Are you sure? Don't give me false hope."

"I would never do that. I am sure. A child lives inside you, and she has magic like mine."

Tesha had never thought of what Daniti did as magic, but there had been a great deal Daniti did among the Paskans that she had not yet heard everything about. And it would explain much about her unusual sister.

Tesha cradled her stomach and smiled. She still carried a baby. Truly. Hattu would be overjoyed. She shared the child's grief that the other one did not survive the harm she'd subjected them to, but the continuing life was a blessing beyond any expectation.

And she wasn't the only family member with magical power anymore. Daniti and the infant inside her shared in that. What made Daniti think the child was a girl? Sons were supposed to be better, but Tesha felt a growing warmth at the idea of a little girl, a little girl with strong magic. Now that would be a challenging child to raise. Her smile grew wider.

The priestess would soon return for the dressing, and the coronation would go on. The last piece of grace had fallen into place for Tesha. For now, she let the healing of these quiet, relaxed moments wash over her. She kissed Daniti's brow and treasured this happiness with the most familiar person in her life.

She loved Hattu and had forgiven him. Could she say for certain that a curse could never drive her to denounce those she loved most? Shadows remained, but they had both chosen to embrace light over darkness. The panicked terrors he had confronted had not been his fault—she hadn't forgiven her father for that. But even so, in the end, he had defeated them. And as to the curse that had taken hold in him because of those fears, they had battled it together, and Hattu would never question her use of magic again. They had a new, stronger bond. She was no longer the girl he'd married. They had a balance between them that she preferred to the relationship they'd enjoyed at first—balanced in heart, balanced in home, and with Ishana's help, unbreakable in justice and peace.

74

———————

Hattu stood ready in his royal robes. He placed the sacred double axe in the loop on his belt. It was a beautiful thing, carved of smoothly polished white marble, its handle contrasting in ebony. Raising it high in ceremonies symbolized his military might as king. Today he'd take a side role. He held in his right hand the spiraling ivory and gold crook, more graceful than the practical ones the shepherds used but meant to recall them. He must be a wise judge and protector of his people. He did his best.

He went to one of the side doors of the temple and peered out. Too early for the ceremony to begin. The sun must reach with her fingers for the sky. The Sungoddess's blessing was as important as the Stormgod's and Ishana's. Those central three would speak for the whole pantheon. Tesha's preparations weren't likely to be finished anyway.

Hattu had the urge to look out over his people. Despite the early hour, they'd be gathering now in the plaza and streets of the city. He'd ordered the news of the coronation to be spread throughout the city and surrounding farmlands. He wanted his kingdom to witness Tesha's blessing by the gods as their ruler.

This side of the temple was built close to the fortification wall.

The alley outside the royal dressing room was empty because its only other purpose was to provide access to one of the defensive towers. Hattu signaled his bodyguards, and with them, he slipped out and climbed the stone steps into the tower.

Through the dim gray light, he looked out and saw men, women, and children climbing the road, and others already in place on the plaza in front of the Stormgod's temple. Servants herded the sheep and cattle for the sacrifices into an alcove where walls on three sides contained the frightened animals. Following the coronation ceremony, sacrifices would satisfy the gods' hunger and ensure their blessings upon the queen. The feast would also feed the people, just as the acrobats and musicians would entertain both gods and their subjects. A line of temple servants kept open the area in front of the temple's portico where the ceremony would take place. They pushed back those eager to get closer.

The crowd of townspeople and peasants would be all the bigger for the curiosity Tesha had sparked. Their king had been without a queen for fifteen years. Then he'd arrived with a prostrate beauty, and there'd been rumors, an invasion, a victory over the Paskans, and more arrests of conspirators against Hattu's rule. The coronation meant all was well now, but they wanted to see Tesha for themselves.

Tesha would win them over and calm the storm.

Hattu adjusted the heavy lion skin draped over his ceremonial robes. The large turnout suited his purposes.

He took one last look over his city and out to the surrounding peaks that were beginning to show in the dawn light, the bend of the river that he could glimpse from this tower, and the fields that spread out from the riverbanks. Today he gave his kingdom a queen greater than they could have hoped for.

Descending the steps, he rejoined his men who waited for him. His royal guard were resplendent in their saffron tunics, leather kilts edged with gold, polished bronze helmets trailing many-colored ribbons and glistening spearpoints flashing in the sun. He reentered the temple to wait for Tesha.

The priestess who oversaw Tesha's preparations informed him all was set. Marak and Daniti waited by the main temple doors into the plaza. He went to greet them.

"I'm glad the gods consented to a speedy coronation," Marak said. "This I do not want to miss."

"I do not want to miss *you* while you go off to Amur," Daniti said. "I find the call of royal duty annoying."

Marak planted a kiss on her head. "You're going to be annoyed a great deal. I hope you grow used to it." The joy in Marak's eyes completely undid any sting in this conversation.

"Slip out and take your places," Hattu said.

A guard opened the side door, and they passed through.

His bodyguards formed up behind him. Two guards swung open the great doors.

Hattu marched through them into the plaza. The crowd cheered. He greeted them and stepped to one side. Marak and Daniti stood next to him with wide smiles.

The high priest and priestess came next, moving to the other side.

The crowd fell quiet. Hattu looked at the open doorway.

From the dark inside, Tesha approached the threshold and stepped through. The people's acclamation burst out, growing louder and louder as she turned in each direction to greet them.

Looking at her beauty, Hattu couldn't move. The diagonal pleats of her deep red skirt were edged with golden disks that flowed like a stream with each step. The snug bodice trimmed with gold beading accentuated her full grace. She had chosen to adapt the style of her priestly gowns into a royal one. The result struck Hattu as grand and holy and in every way regal.

The dark silken locks that he longed to bury his face in were bound into intricate braids intertwined with looser tresses tied into swirls that surrounded her face and fell halfway down her back. Her linen veil was so fine that it fluttered translucent like a wisp of fog clearing at dawn, revealing glimpses of the elaborate hair underneath.

Her lips held a calm, secretive smile, as if contemplating some divine wisdom she could share if needed. Her eyes were wide with wonder. He'd seen that look when Tesha felt closest to her goddess. He thanked Ishana for filling Tesha with her divine presence.

The high priest of the Stormgod approached Tesha. In this rite he became as a god, for only the gods granted the right of rule. He held a silver horn to represent the Stormgod's favored form as a mighty bull. This chalice held purest cedar oil for royal anointing.

The high priest faced Tesha. "The Stormgod, the Sungoddess, and your own chosen goddess, Ishana, anoint you Queen Tesha of Alpara and the Upper Lands."

She bowed her head in assent.

The high priest lifted the horn high, and angled sunlight sparked off its brilliant turns. "Ishana, goddess of love and war, mighty Stormgod and all-seeing Sungoddess, you are parents to the queen. Anoint her and exalt her now! You will build her high in reverence and strong in power."

Tesha stepped forward. A priestess held her veil and hair out of the way, and Tesha tipped back her head.

The high priest poured drops of oil onto her forehead. "Let your head be anointed with the divine oil of life and destiny. Behold, this one is queen!"

Tesha straightened. She held the people spellbound in reverential silence. Hattu looked out and saw Tesha's wonder reflected in the faces gathered in the plaza.

The high priest raised the shimmering horn again.

In a voice that rang through the plaza, Tesha recited, "A father I have not, a mother I have not: You, O Gods and Goddesses, are my father and mother. I am your servant. You alone, O Gods, have put the rule of a queen in my hands. To the one who is hungry, I will give bread. To the one who is naked, I will give clothing. If one of my people suffers the heat, I will place him where it is cool. If he suffers the cold, I will place him where it is warm. I am the shepherd of my people and the judge of their deeds."

The high priest placed the curling staff of ivory and gold in Tesha's right hand, the match of Hattu's. She tipped it forward in blessing over her people. A joyous cry broke out from them, rising into a deafening roar.

When finally they quieted, the high priest continued, "May Queen Tesha be dear to the gods. The land belongs to the thousand gods. Heaven and earth and the people belong to them. The gods make the queen their administrator over the land and people of Alpara and the Upper Lands. Whoever assaults the body and territory of the queen, may the gods destroy him."

Another priest stepped forward with Tesha's royal vestment. He laid it across the arms of the high priest. It was a supple leopard skin, its spotted fur gleaming in the golden light of morning, its claws a menacing reminder of Tesha's new power. Hattu's lips turned up at the thought of how much greater her power was than any of his people knew. They would benefit from that. They did not need to understand it.

A priestess lifted the queen's braids and veil, and the high priest draped the leopard skin over her shoulders and down her back. Another priestess stepped in front. She held two golden sun disks joined by a chain. She attached them on either side of the leopard skin, holding in place the giant beast's legs crossed over the queen's chest.

Tesha scanned the people. To Hattu, her expression held both the beauty and the ferocity of a leopard. Her graceful form suggested a leopard's lethal agility, and he knew how truly her mind reflected that dexterity. He saw a drawing back among those standing at the front of the crowd. His heart surged. He was the people's formidable lion in battle, but she could speed to their defense just as surely. A bronze blade was by no means the only weapon, nor war the only strife a kingdom must overcome. He would trust her with his life. He would trust her with his kingdom. He would trust her sorcery. He sent a prayer to Ishana to deepen their bond each day for the rest of their lives.

· · ·

If you enjoyed *Sorcery in Alpara*, the kindest favor a reader can do for an author is to leave a review on Amazon.

Sign up for for Judith Starkston's author newsletter on JudithStarkston.com and get a free short story, book news and giveaways.

Other Titles by Judith Starkston
Priestess of Ishana, Tesha Series Book 1
Hand of Fire, Trojan Threads Series Book 1

AUTHOR NOTES

Sorcery in Alpara is a fantasy novel threaded with accurate history.

For those who ask "How much of this is real?" these author notes offer clarification of the actual history behind the fantasy. The book is written to be enjoyed without this explanation, but for those who enjoy this kind of background information, here you go. These notes contain significant spoilers, so read after you've finished the novel.

The Tesha series, of which *Sorcery in Alpara* is the second book, is set in an imaginary "off-world" empire where magic is real, fantastic beasts participate, the stars glow in a rainbow of colors, and human beings face problems and prejudices remarkably like the ones we all face each day. It is also an empire that purposely echoes an actual time and place in history, the Late Bronze Age in the Hittite Empire. Many of the **places/cultures** and **people** and **events** in this fantasy have specific historical referents. I have purposely made those connections relatively transparent by using some names that echo their originals while adopting fictional names overall so it is clear that this book is written as fantasy, even if there's a big emphasis on accurate history within the fantasy.

Places and Cultures

The **Hitolian Empire** is inspired by the Hittite Empire, dating from the Bronze Age and covering most of Anatolia, i.e. modern Turkey, and eastward into parts of modern Syria and Lebanon. Hittite rule spanned the period roughly from 1650 BCE to 1200 BCE. The **Egaryans** resemble the Egyptians. During the year this novel reflects, 1272 BCE more or less, Ramses II is Pharaoh of the historic Egypt. **Lawaza** is based on Puduhepa's hometown of Lawazantiya, which I've placed at the current archaeological site of Tatarli Höyük in the Adana province of Turkey. There is debate about the actual location of this much-mentioned city, but a strong case has been made to place it at Tatarli Höyük. **Alpara** is modeled after Hakpis, the city Hattusili ruled as his capital/kingdom. I've used the modern city of Amasya on the Green River as the location for Hakpis. Some scholars have identified Amasya as the location of Hakpis, but it's by no means a settled idea. Buried under much later fortresses, there are Bronze Age ruins on top of the mountain there. Amasya is a dramatic location that works well for this story. I've traveled there and know what it looks and feels like. All that led me to choose it as Alpara. The **Upper Lands** is the actual name used by the Hittites for a northern region of the Hittite Empire, but the region Hattusili (Hattu) ruled encompassed other "lands" also. The Upper Lands were only a part and not his central part. I chose to use that single name for clarity and simplicity. Even Hakpis did not lie within what is usually identified by historians as the Upper Lands. The entire northern region of Anatolia, divided into many small "lands," was disputed territory as far as the Kaskan (Paskan) people thought. I've simplified this political and military conflict zone. This region was problematic for the Hittites to the very end. Indeed, although we don't know who destroyed the capital and the empire sometime around 1200 BCE, it appears likely that the Kaskans were at least one key foe who dealt the fatal blow. The land of Amur where Ahmose desperately wants Hattu to go and restore order is modeled off the land of Amurru. Egypt and the Hittites fought over Amurru and passed control back and forth over the years. Both the Hittite and Egyptian rulers viewed Amurru as a land of rebels and pirates. The particulars of the conflict I portray are entirely plausible but not based on any specific event.

People

The source for **Tesha** is Puduhepa, a long-ruling Hittite queen who, in the historical record, we first meet at age 15 as a Priestess of Ishtar in Lawazantia. Tesha is the Hittite word for "dream," an appropriate name for a woman who received visionary dreams from Ishtar throughout her life. The inspiration for **Hattu** is Hattusili, the younger brother of Great King Muwattalli. He ruled as a lesser, vassal king for his brother over the most challenging part of the Hittite Empire. He was perpetually at war with the Kaskans (Paskans). He served as the lead general against Egyptian Pharaoh Ramses II at the Battle of Kadesh in 1274 BCE. Hattu had a son, Nerikkaili, from his first marriage. I've named him **Nerik**. Indications in the historical record hint that at some point Nerik did something to lose parental favor. **Muwatti** is based on Great King Muwattalli who ruled the Hittites from 1295-1272 BCE. He did indeed send his youngest son, Kurunta, whom I've named **Samsi**, to be raised and protected by his brother Hattusili. Both Hattusili and Muwattalli hated and distrusted their stepmother who had married their father late in his life. They both had scribes record this stepmother's scheming, deadly plans. By Hittite law of succession her sons did not have a right to the throne, but all of Muwattalli's sons were by concubines, so she had some grounds to work with. The Hittite noblemen who conspire against Hattu in this novel have historical parallels who caused a revolt when he returned from the Egyptian war and Lawazatiya. As to the troublesome concubines, we know that Hattusili had a number of them and their children at the time he married Puduhepa. I suspect Puduhepa knew about them before her marriage, but it made for a much better story if she didn't, and we don't know one way or the other. Tesha quite famously got along well with all of her husband's children, both hers and the concubines. **Ishana** resembles the Hittite goddess Ishtar, who, like the Babylonian divinity, is goddess of love and war, but who, sadly from a writer's point of view, did not have ritual prostitution or other love-making rites as part of her worship, but in many ways was the same goddess and was borrowed from Mesopotamia, more or less. The Hittites emphasized her role as god of war over god of sexuality. **Pharaoh Gerose** is Pharaoh Ramses II. **Runda** corresponds to Arma-Tarhunda, Hattusili's cousin and the governor of the Upper Lands until Muwattalli replaced him with Hattusili. More on Runda below under events. Other people in this novel are made up characters with names constructed from actual Hittite names, although considerably shortened because fourteen syllable names don't make for good storytelling. We don't, for example, know if Puduhepa (Tesha) had a sister (**Daniti**), or who Hattusili's (Hattu) right hand man was (**Marak**). We know Hattusili acquired some of Pharaoh's slaves after the Battle of Kadesh, but **Kety** is likewise my own creation. He's quite intentionally meant to make us think about immigrants/foreigners and the false assumptions and fears we sometimes attach to them. The stereotypes attached to him are based in historical stereotypes about Egyptians in the Bronze Age. **Henti** and **Ashu, Utar, Ahmose** and the other secondary characters not described above are fictional based on my best understanding of their roles in this culture.

As to **Bolthar** and his two companions, the Hittites depicted various mythical creatures in their artwork, especially griffins, which show up in frescoes, seals and elsewhere. These fantastical creatures seemed to represent the idea of authority and power to the Hittites. There is a long tradition in the ancient Near East and Egypt of depicting such hybrid creatures, as ways to embody their divinities and other aspects of myth and religious beliefs. Why the human imagination adds wings to a lion with an eagle head or puts a jackal head on a human body or any of the other wonderous ancient amalgamations, I'm not sure, but I love the results as characters for fantasy.

Events

The gaps in our knowledge about Bronze Age cultures challenge historians but prove a boon to a fiction writer's imagination. My goal is to tell a good story first and foremost. No matter what, the extremely fragmentary evidence means that I have to make stuff up no matter how close to the historical record I keep my plots. I do my best to be accurate portraying the culture, material world and the outline of events. Incorporating fantastic elements serves to cue the reader to this honest reality—no fiction set in the Bronze Age is purely factual. Fantasy also elevates the themes and intensifies the engagement of the novel.

Here's an outline of the historically documented information that I used as a starting point for the plots of *Priestess of Ishana* and *Sorcery in Alpara*. This information comes from translations of the cuneiform tablets that have been excavated from the Hittite capital of Hattusa and elsewhere. There are a small number of sites that contain tablets. Most do not. Preservation of tablets only happens when the building containing archives is burnt at such a high temperature that it becomes a giant kiln, and the unfired clay is hardened into fired ceramic. This process happened if earthquakes triggered horrific fires or a city was taken in war and then burned. Otherwise, the clay tablets return, dust to dust, and we can't read them.

In this narrative of what we actually know, I use the names I've created for my characters. They are shorter and by now you are familiar with them. The equivalent real people are listed above. Because *Sorcery in Alpara* carries on from the events of *Priestess of Ishana*, I will include those earlier events in this narrative to some extent. It's much clearer that way.

When Hattu's older brother Muwatti first came to the throne upon his father's death, he appointed Hattu as his Chief of Royal Bodyguards and later he made him governor of the northern regions, displacing the existing governor, his cousin Runda (and turning Runda into a lifelong enemy of Hattu). Eventually Muwatti appointed Hattu king, instead of simply calling him governor (I collapsed this all to the "king" stage). Runda brought charges of some sort early on in Hattu's period as governor. We know there was a trial. We know the charges had at least some modicum of merit to them. Hattu got off because, he says, his goddess stood by him. A divination was involved. Nepotism may or may not have been involved. Hattu clearly saw the whole episode as a very close brush with disaster. Hattu spent many years attempting with some success to consolidate his power and put down the Paskan revolts that rocked his kingdom.

By 1274 BCE, when Muwattalli required Hattu to bring his army to fight Pharaoh in what is today Lebanon, Hattu had pacified his kingdom enough that it could withstand his absence for a while, but Hattu must have felt immensely concerned as his absence stretched beyond a year.

At his brother's command, Hattu took his troops from the Upper Lands and provided essential manpower and generalship in the giant showdown between the Hittites and the Egyptians. The Hittites managed to fool Pharaoh into thinking the Hittite forces were a few days away and then they attacked before he had all his troops gathered. At first it looked like a wipeout for the Egyptians, but some of Pharaoh's reinforcements arrived at the right moment, and it looks like Pharaoh did a good job marshalling his chariot troops and driving back the Hittites. The evidence of the aftermath indicates that the Hittites took back lands they had been forced previously to cede to Egypt. That is, they more or less won. Pharaoh had the whole battle portrayed on his temple walls as a rousing victory for him— actually he claimed to have defeated single-handedly the entire Hittite army—but in Pharaoh's defense against excessive propaganda and lies, this sort of portrayal was traditional among his predecessors. Be careful what norms we set for our rulers. This confrontation between Egypt and the Hittites is known as the Battle of Kadesh (or Qadesh). Hattu stayed behind for a year and settled the newly retaken lands as tributary states to the Hittite Empire. He may have been forced to do this because the Great King became sick either during or soon after the war—with what we don't know, perhaps a wound, perhaps a lingering illness.

Thus a year after Kadesh, Hattu set off for his kingdom, where he'd heard news of revolts, both Paskan and among the Hittite nobility. On his way, however, he stopped in Lawaza to make offerings of thanks to Ishana and there me met Tesha.

Either before or during this period, Runda brought more charges, this time of sorcery, against Hattu. Again Hattu was cleared of charges, and, in fact, Runda and his son were charged with sorcery. I include news of Runda's arrest for these charges early in *Sorcery in Alpara*.

When Hattu met the young priestess Tesha as he made his offerings at the temple in Lawaza, it was the beginning of a deep and long-lasting love, blessed by their goddess—so he reports for posterity in his Apology, a sort of autobiography with political purpose. They both said they had dreams from the goddess in which she commanded them to marry. After they were married in Lawaza, they traveled up to Hattu's kingdom—which is the opening point of *Sorcery in Alpara*.

We know that they journeyed together to his capital. We know he had to fight battles with Paskans and put down a dangerous revolt by the nobles who had been Runda's followers. We know that eventually Tesha became queen beside Hattu. We know she would have met Hattu's son by his first marriage and all those concubines. The number of concubines is probably lower in my book than reality, but we don't know the exact number and too many characters clutter up a story. How the concubines reacted—by poisonous treachery or lukewarm courtesy or whatever—we have no word. Paskan kidnappings and magic are extensions of my imagination based on the information we have about their cultural traditions and ongoing conflict with the Hittites. The blinding of prisoners is a well-documented tragedy that both sides engaged in, but I find it mentioned only in the letters from this northern part of the empire, so its origin as a practice may lie with the Paskans as I have portrayed.

The curses I use in the plots of both *Priestess of Ishana* and *Sorcery in Alpara* are founded in the Hittite obsession with curses. I do take the effects of the curses I depict beyond the dangers that the Hittites blamed on curses. Usually things like people's illnesses are attributed to curses. To my knowledge no black cloud consumed soldiers and the centipedes are a creepiness of my own psyche. But the core idea of curses and the "rules" for all the magic in these books starts with Hittite concepts, such as analogical magic and maintenance of harmony between divine and human worlds. For example, the mood-altering invocation Tesha uses is a figment of my imagination, although the Hittite priestesses performed many rites to restore mental harmony and other "psychological" processes in ways we would define as "magic."

In Conclusion

I hope you enjoyed being immersed in a genuine and accurate sense of this little-known period of history while being entertained by fantastical elements that give me as a writer liberating space for exciting, thematically rich plots and characters.

The Hittites are a part of human history that scholars largely ignored—mostly because the empire was literally lost under the ground until the twentieth century. A woman as leader of a world power—and how she got to that position—is a tale worth hearing, especially since Puduhepa/Tesha excelled at aspects of leadership that the world wants and needs. She was renowned for her diplomacy, humane pragmatism, and unswerving dedication to fair justice. I find Tesha particularly compelling for the modern world, including her Bronze Age way of seeing things—magic and all.

For more background history to this series and a bibliography, go to JudithStarkston.com

PEOPLE AND PLACES IN SORCERY IN ALPARA

<u>Places</u>

Hitolian Empire, Tesha's country, one of two most powerful empires at the time

Egarya, the other most powerful empire, ruled by a Pharaoh and based around a big river

The Upper Lands, Hattu's kingdom in the northern part of the Hitolian Empire and bordering on the lands of the Paskans, inveterate enemies and raiders of the Hitolian Empire

Alpara, the capital of Hattu's kingdom, a mountain fortress above the Green River

Lawaza, Tesha's hometown, in the southeast of the Hitolian Empire

Amur, a city-kingdom in the eastern borderlands between the Hitolian and Egaryan empires

<u>People</u>

Major Characters

Tesha, Priestess of Ishana now married to King Hattu

Hattu, the younger brother of the Great King, himself King of the Upper Lands and the best general in the Hitolian Empire

Daniti, Tesha's older sister, who is blind and brave

Marak, Hattu's second in command, a wily fighter with a good sense of humor

World Rulers and Hostile Peoples

Muwatti, the Great King of the Hitolian Empire, Hattu's older brother

Pharaoh Gerose, the leader of Egarya whom Hattu defeated in battle a year before this novel starts, one of Hattu's enemies who holds grudges

Paskans, a tribal, semi-nomadic people who want their ancestral pasturelands back from the Hittites and have been fighting Hattu for years

Other People of Note in Hattu's court or Lawaza

Nerik, Hattu's son by a previous marriage, the Crown Prince of Alpara

Samsi, Great King Muwatti's youngest son whom Hattu is fostering for his protection

Shatim, one of Hattu's most trusted counselors in his court in Alpara

Katte, Shatim's wife

Ahmose, Egaryan ambassador with an urgent mission for Hattu

Utar, physician in Hattu's court. He is fanatically hostile to magic and must hide his origins.

Agat, the oldest and most powerful of Hattu's concubines

Ija, one of Hattu's concubines

Pasul, one of Hattu's concubines

Narizu, Agat's father

Anna, Healer of Ishana, Tesha's mentor priestess at the temple back home in Lawaza

Servants

Kety, Hattu's Egaryan slave who functions as a groom and who can calm any animal or person

Henti, Tesha's maidservant whom she's known all her life

Ashu, Tesha's other maidservant, a recent addition to Tesha's life

Previous Conspirators from Priestess of Ishana

Riam, the conspirator who escaped in *Priestess of Ishana*. Tesha damaged him with a demonic spell and he hates her

Runda, a cousin of Hattu's who became a life-long enemy when Muwatti replaced Runda with Hattu as ruler of the Upper Lands. In *Priestess of Ishana*, Runda conspired against Hattu with accusations of sorcery for which he hoped Hattu would be executed

Kudur, one of the key conspirators with Runda. He pretended to be a blind seer. Kudur learned some Paskan magic and used it against Hattu in *Priestess of Ishana*.

Non-human characters

Kurala, Tesha and Daniti's lap-sized pet with cat body, deer hooves, bat wings and eagle head

Bolthar, Crenon and **Lila**, mythic creatures

ACKNOWLEDGMENTS

It takes an extended community to complete a book, even if a lot of solitary time is spent in the actual writing. I have a number of dedicated, smart, generous friends who conjure up plot ideas, critique rough drafts, and edit more final ones. Diane Benitez graciously helps me through *all* the stages. Writing is way more fun with her in my world. Several writers gave me developmental suggestions that utterly wowed me. This book is far better for their ideas: Anna Castle, Margaret Morse, Michele McGinnis, Margaret Morse, Kristin McQuinn, Margaret Spence, and David Waid. The Tapestry Writers group gave me invaluable critiques during our bi-monthly meetings. Jessica Cale of Historical Editorial did an excellent copyedit. Heather Senter again designed a stellar cover. Trevor Bryce, Professor Emeritus of Hittitology, has answered my history questions and steered me to the right sources. Sevil Çonka, Istanbul-based archaeologist and historian, has been the best of guides for each of my research trips to Turkey. Her familiarity with the large number of active digs that are relevant to my writing has been crucial. Without her, I would never have visited modern Amasya and found the historically correct model for Alpara with its stone fortress atop a steep mountain next to the Green River. I owe many thanks to her depth of knowledge and willingness to explore. Many thanks also to Professor K. Serdar Girginar, Director of the Tatarli Höyük site, for his generous offering of time and expertise. I want to thank my friends in the HFAC forum who give me practical advice with publishing and marketing. I am indebted to the staff at the Poisoned Pen Bookstore, especially Barbara Peters and Patrick King, for their advocacy on my behalf. Deepest thanks go to my husband, Bob Starkston, for being there to cheer me on through the sometimes disheartening process of book writing and production. He also takes charge of the technical jobs that baffle me. I couldn't do it without him. Thank you also to my two adult children for their much-appreciated support and enthusiasm for their mother's writing obsession.

ABOUT THE AUTHOR

Judith Starkston has spent too much time reading about and exploring the remains of the ancient worlds of the Hittites and the Near East. Early on she went so far as to get degrees in Classics from the University of California, Santa Cruz and Cornell. She loves myths and telling stories. This has gotten more and more out of hand. Her solution: to write historical fantasy set in the Bronze Age. *Hand of Fire* was a semi-finalist for the M.M. Bennett's Award for Historical Fiction. *Priestess of Ishana* won the San Diego State University Conference Choice Award.

Judith has two grown children and lives in Arizona with her husband. Judith is represented by Richard Curtis.

Sign up for Judith's newsletter on JudithStarkston.com for a free short story, book news and giveaways.

Made in the USA
Columbia, SC
19 September 2019